Tim Taylor was born and grew up in a poor working-class family in the North East of England, leaving school at sixteen to work in the motor trade and retiring early at sixty-two with the plan to travel as much as possible but then Covid arrived and confinement began. His Plan B was born, always having been an avid reader who believed he could write a book, so this is the first.

To get in touch, Email atimctaylor@gmail.com

For Anne, who I wish I'd met at 27 instead of 57; who knows what we would have achieved?

Disclaimer

This book contains the 3 S's – Sexual content, Strong language and Speaking Dogs

Tim Taylor

TRIGGERS

AUSTIN MACAULEY PUBLISHERS
LONDON * CAMBRIDGE * NEW YORK * SHARJAH

Copyright © Tim Taylor 2025

The right of Tim Taylor to be identified as author of this work has been asserted by the author in accordance with sections 77 and 78 of the Copyright, Designs and Patents Act 1988.

All rights reserved. No part of this publication may be reproduced, stored in a retrieval system, or transmitted in any form or by any means, electronic, mechanical, photocopying, recording, or otherwise, without the prior permission of the publishers.

Any person who commits any unauthorised act in relation to this publication may be liable to criminal prosecution and civil claims for damages.

This is a work of fiction. Names, characters, businesses, places, events, locales, and incidents are either the products of the author's imagination or used in a fictitious manner. Any resemblance to actual persons, living or dead, or actual events is purely coincidental.

A CIP catalogue record for this title is available from the British Library.

ISBN 9781035878970 (Paperback)
ISBN 9781035878987 (ePub e-book)

www.austinmacauley.com

First Published 2025
Austin Macauley Publishers Ltd®
1 Canada Square
Canary Wharf
London
E14 5AA

To Anne for giving me the confidence to follow my dream and to Jarvis Gooden at Austin Macauley Publishers for getting me on the ladder with his wonderful uplifting review of my book.

Foreword

WHAT WOULD PUSH YOU OVER THE EDGE?

For 99% of the population suffering from post-traumatic stress disorder (PTSD) and severe depression, their final push over the edge would be a sudden family death, a life-threatening event or a terminal illness. What happens if you are trained to fear nothing, to never admit to anyone that you have problems to show nothing, to have a pain tolerance off the chart, to be trained to be the ultimate soldier, the highest-ranking martial arts expert in the army, what would happen if that was taken away and you were faced with bringing up your four-year-old daughter in an alien civilian life, what would happen if left untreated and years later, the one thing that has never let you down did. What would happen if you lost control?

One

It was a lovely warm June afternoon as Jo stretched out increasing her pace; at nearly thirteen, she was the fittest pre-teenager in the school. She had also inherited her parents' looks, so she was also the prettiest, but with a dad like Stone, any boyfriend material was ruled out till at least twenty-five. The half marathon course ran through the beautiful countryside following the river in North Yorkshire. Jo had upped her pace to under six-minute miles at the seven-mile target something she had discussed with her dad, and she at once pulled away from the chasing group. Some of the older girls tried keeping up but Jo dug in and hit a five-thirty mile.

Her dad had had her building up her leg strength for the last six weeks, switching between heavy six reps for six sets to fifteen reps for four sets doing variations of different types of squats either rear, front or goblet then leg presses along with a breathing pullover which increased her lung capacity, in the well-equipped home gym and it was his idea to keep banging in the six-minute miles. Jo checked her internal clock having passed the two miles to go marker, legs felt strong, her breathing strong, bit of a chewy stomach, but Jo put that down to the carbing up she had done so there would be plenty of energy in the tank; checking her stopwatch, good she thought around twelve minutes at this pace, running time under eighty minutes which would beat the existing record, just got to keep going.

The one mile to go sign came into view and Jo increased her pace as she still felt good but her stomach was starting to cramp up making her whistle through her teeth with the pain, grit, and determination were now the order of the day plus she couldn't stand the thought of letting down her dad. She existed to make him proud. She was the ultimate daddy's girl having lost her mum when she was four. Cramping and wincing in pain now, Jo entered the school grounds. Several teachers lined the final stretch cheering her on. She grimaced as she ran past Mrs Fothergill who had a worried look on her face as she ran past her. Mrs Fothergill grabbed her phone as Jo ran past, at last Jo saw the finish line and wished her dad could see her. Of course, there were no parents here plus knowing her dad, he'd be running beside her shouting encouragement and not even breathing hard; if his army buddies were there, he'd probably run the last bit backwards. Man, he was a show-off, but he could back it up in spades and she loved him unconditionally.

With a final grimace, she crossed the finish line and ran straight into the outstretched arms of Ms Sanders who quickly covered her in a tin foil blanket. Ms Sanders was her form tutor and took her for history. She was her favourite person in the whole world except her dad and granddad, but her face was what caused Jo to stop and ask what was wrong instead of asking her race time. That and the fact that her car doors were open and the engine running. "Jo, please get straight into the car," said Ms Sanders, her normally beautiful face and perfect make-up giving way to a concerned and worried look. Jo obeyed without question not because she had perfect manners but because the cramp in her stomach made her bend over and cry out in pain. Jo who was nearly as tough as her dad almost started to cry. Ms Sanders gave her a quick hug as she pulled her seat belt over and snapped hers on, slammed the door shut, slammed her little Toyota into first gear and headed towards the town at great knots.

"Jo, listen to me, sweetheart, I'm running you straight to the hospital. Dr Goldberg is waiting in emergency for you and I've called your dad."

Jo thought *why Dad* but just whimpered, "Ok, what's wrong, Ms Saunders?"

"We aren't in school time anymore, Jo, just call me Angie. You're bleeding very heavily, I think you've started your period but because you've been running hard, your heart rate and blood pressure are high; you might be haemorrhaging which can be really serious." Jo just looked up bright red and embarrassed and started to cry quietly, Angie grabbed Jo's hand to give this special girl some comfort and said, "It's ok, Jo, it happens to all girls only most of them aren't out destroying seniors' records while still a junior."

With that statement, Jo stopped her tears and despite the severe pain managed a grimace of a smile and asked, "What was the time?"

Angie smiled, "One hour seventeen minutes and fifty-three seconds knocking over seven minutes of the junior record and crushing the seniors by nearly a minute." Jo had run just over thirteen miles at an average of under six minutes a mile something only her dad thought she was capable of!

Stone was in the gym at the Garrison; he had a couple of hours before his next training session and because he didn't relish being idle and had had his sleep quota, a workout was the next best idea. Teaching hand-to-hand combat kept his skills up; being in the best physical shape possible was ingrained in him. There were maybe fifteen grunts in the well-equipped gym. Stone was in the corner at the power rack doing chins slowly and methodically, headphones on 'Enter Sandman' by Metallica blasting out, eyes closed focused on both the pulls and music, what he didn't see were several of the bulked-up younger guys watching his technique with awe. Stone had started his final set of eight to ten reps and the guy looked like his namesake or possibly granite might have been better, what made the others stare when the two 25kilo weights hanging on a chain from the waist support harness; they were doing the maths in their heads and watching the display, but of course, he was their commanding officer for the precise reason that everything he did demanded attention.

Stone finished the set eyes still closed keeping focus, the sleeves of his gym tops straining to hold the muscles now fully pumped, as Stone readied himself for moving onto dips. Private Jones approached him looking a bit apprehensive but making a beeline straight for him. Jones didn't want to interrupt his commanding officer's workout but the message he had to give him was urgent and he had no choice. Stone stood up and waited, "Could I please have a quiet word, sir?" And turning to talk in his commanding officer's ear so that no one could overhear, "There's been an incident at your daughter's school, sir. She's been taken to hospital by Ms Sanders, her form teacher and she has asked that you get there as quickly as possible. Ms Sanders has said it's not life-threatening but could potentially be very serious, I have Ms Sanders' personal mobile number should you want to contact her."

Stone numbly took the slip of paper from Jones thanked him and headed to the changing rooms his mind in turmoil; he grabbed his phone, put on a hoodie, dashed out to his bike, fired it up and dialled Ms Saunders who answered on the second ring, "Hello, Angie Sanders speaking," looking at the unlisted mobile number.

"Hello, this is Colonel Stone, Jo's father. I've just been passed a message about my daughter needing to be taken to hospital, is she with you, what's happening, is she ok?" Angie had a split second to register two things; one the man was a colonel and panicking and two, he had a voice that made bits of her tingle. *Jesus, Ang get a grip* she thought. She replied trying to keep her voice calm and authoritative even when she knew she was talking to the powerful father of her favourite pupil, "Jo started her period while running the school half marathon, I don't know how she kept on running but she was covered in blood and grimacing in pain as she passed my colleague Mrs Fothergill who phoned me and I drove to the finish line at school. I should have picked her up coming out of the forest but she only had under half a mile left to complete the race and to be honest, the look of determination on your daughter's face stopped me. I'm sorry Colonel Stone, I got her to hospital as quickly as possible. She's with Dr Goldberg now, I rang you straight away I'll be here when you get here, I'm not supposed to have favourites in class, but Jo is my favourite pupil."

Stone's reply caught Angie off guard, "Thanks for letting her finish the race. I take it she won and set a course record at the same time?" Angie thought it was an odd thing to say at the time, but Stone went on to say, "Jo has enormous drive, I'm an army colonel and she has more determination to get the job done than me, I'll be there as quickly as possible, thank you."

Dr Goldberg had Jo lie down and the chaperone nurse was talking gently in Jo's ear trying to ease her fears. Ike Goldberg had been a trauma doctor in the army and at fifty-eight, he had a great sense of humour; his patient care was like talking to a friend so much so that everyone always gave him little thank you cards and gifts, the thank you cards were on display along with twenty-five plus medical honours in his office and around the hospital however the little gifts usually the chocolate variety, where also on display by the girth of his waistline. "Jo, you don't do anything by halves just like your bloody dad, you've lost several pints of blood just to win a race, even Dracula wouldn't have taken as much."

Jo despite the pain relaxed a little. "Right, madam, your heart is very strong, and your blood pressure is almost back to normal, let's get you cleaned up and replace some of your fluids, blood being one of them. I'm going to give you something to stop the cramps being bad it might hurt a lot," and Ike pulled a massive twelve-inch syringe from behind his back.

Jo just looked with no fear at all. "Ok," she said leaving Ike dumbstruck that his joke syringe didn't faze the girl, he just looked Jo in the eye, "Yep, you are definitely J T's daughter," and took the standard syringe out of his pocket and injected her, he then instructed the nurse to set up the blood transfusion and fluid replacement. "Honey, you'll have to stay with us for tonight, but I'll make sure you get an extra helping of ice cream, however, if there's any chocolate on the menu, it is mine. Ms Sanders said your dad's on the way; better have you spick and span for when he gets here that man can spot a speck of dust from one hundred metres."

Stone powered the bike down as he pulled up to the front of the emergency department, took off his helmet put it into the storage box and quickly walked to the entrance where two rent-a-cop guys eyed him with undisguised distaste. The smaller of the two spoke while the bigger hulking one just stood taller, flexed his steroid-bloated body, and scowled trying to intimidate Stone with his mere size and presence, which being Stone he totally ignored, "I'm sorry, sir it's not visiting time and you can't come into the hospital dressed like that." Stone who had grabbed a hoodie as he ran to his bike still had his training shorts on, his thighs and calves looked like corded steel girders his short hair shone with dried sweat and his hoodie now had sweat stains from the where the gym top didn't cover his skin.

Stone in a hurry and under pressure to see his daughter ignored the smaller man and sized up the larger man looked him in the eye and said, "I'll give you £100 for your jacket and trousers I'm going in with or without the costume change." The look in Stone's eye was enough to get the big man to start unbuttoning his jacket, just as Ike came out of the side ward where he'd been treating Jo intending to let Ms Saunders know how she was and to wait for Stone. Angie on hearing someone say her name looked up as Dr Goldberg approached, but her eye caught the most beautiful man she had ever seen, he stood around six feet two or three and looked like he'd just come off the cover of Vogue.

Angie who at thirty-four thought she knew herself had a reaction as she had only read about her pulse raced, her pupils dilated, her body which she knew was well above average decided after so long a drought to respond, and her nipples swelled and my God, she felt her boring cotton panties suddenly become moist; she stood there mouth open, breathing hard taking in this vision, when Dr Goldberg waved at Stone and said to the two rent-a-cops, "It's ok, lads. I'll vouch for this shady character," and walked up to Stone and threw his arms over the huge shoulders and embraced Stone who hugged Ike back. "Long time J T," said Ike. "I see you've been letting yourself go," looking Stone over, who replied, "And you, my friend, still eating the full bars and not just a piece of chocolate."

The two rent-a-cops watching the display of affection from one of the most senior doctors also had their mouths wide open. "Ok, let's go see your daughter," and still with his arm around Stone's shoulder, walked towards the room where

Jo was. Angie just about got her mouth closed as they both approached, "Ms Sanders, this is Colonel Stone, Jo's father."

Stone looked directly at Angie and her pulse double-tapped as she stared at the bluest eyes she had ever seen. Stone held out his hand and gently took Angie's hand in his and then placed his other hand on her hand as well; for such a big man, he had a very tender touch and Angie unable to have any control over her body couldn't help the small gasp that escaped her lips and wondered what the man's hands would feel like on other parts of which of course increased the moistness in her now wet panties. Stone held onto her hand, "Thank you for helping Jo," and kept his gaze on her.

"This way, J T," as he escorted Stone into Jo's room, Stone still holding Angie's hand, "please come with me I'm sure my daughter would want to thank her favourite teacher and she won't like telling her story twice." Anyone else would think this was cute, but Ike knew Stone needed support and it was his way of asking.

All three entered the room; Jo had been set up with her drips and sat quietly watching the nurse check her vitals. Stone walked straight up to his daughter kissed her full on the lips, hugged her gently and whispered in her ear, "Try not to do this ever again, I'm an old man now." Then tenderly he wiped her brow with his bare hand and said, "I love you, Josephine Roseanne Stone," giving Jo her full name, which meant he was really shaken up. Jo had only heard her full name from her father's lips a handful of times. As tears sprang to her eyes, Angie was astonished that this man could display his love for his daughter in such an open manner.

Jo looked back at her dad. "It's ok, Dad, I love you too. I'll try to be a good girl for the next 20 years." But despite or maybe because of the emotional situation Angie's body betrayed her even more at the sight of him bent over in workout, short with those muscles, hubba, hubba. Jo then realised her teacher and her doctor were standing behind her dad. "Thank you for getting me here so quickly, Ms Saunders."

"Jo, it is Angie, we are not at school."

"And Uncle Ike, thank you for putting me back together again."

Ike looked at Jo wise beyond her years. "This man would have cut off my chocolate supply if anything had happened to you," and then whispered to Angie, "He'd have cut off more than my chocolate," and busied himself checking Jo's charts.

Stone grabbed a couple of chairs and he and Angie sat down. He immediately held his daughter's hand and Angie felt the emotion of the situation. Ike happy with the readings kissed Jo on the cheek and pressed his hand on Stone's shoulder, "Don't be a stranger, J T," and left the room. Angie wondered what she was missing there were obviously some things of which she wasn't aware.

"Ok Jo," said Stone. "Tell us what happened?" So, Jo told them about the run and the cramps and the pain, Stone's face showed distress when Jo said about her period, "I'm sorry, Jo, I didn't think."

Angie who was listening said, "Well, it's usually the mam that tells the daughter the birds and bees." Angie thought Stone was showing distress before she looked at the man and he looked empty, emotionless.

"Gemma left us when Jo was four." And at the same time, Jo grabbed her dad's hand so tight that his fingertips went white and both of them looked lost. Angie thought, *yep there's a lot more here than meets the eye here*, but her betraying body wondered how a mother could leave this wonderful child and doting father.

Jo was first to get a grip on her emotions, "I won, Dad, and I beat the school record."

Now Angie smiled at her star pupil. "Both records juniors and seniors."

Just then the nurse barged in, "Visiting time is over, she needs to rest."

Stone stood up, "I'll be staying." The nurse looked at the man overseeing the muscular physique and thought, *I don't need this shit with the shift she was having.*

"Sorry sir, but policy is policy. I'm afraid you can't stay, it's against hospital rules."

Stone picked up his mobile and rang Ike who was still in the building, "Ike, can I stay with Jo?"

Ike who knew how Stone was reacting, "Put the nurse on."

She listened to Dr Goldberg and then just said, "I'll get you a blanket, sir." Angie had watched and had no doubt why this man was a colonel.

"I'd better head off, Jo, I'll let Mr Foster know you'll probably be back at school on Monday and if you're feeling up to it, we'll sort a little trophy presentation out for you."

Stone stood and kissed his daughter's brow, "I'll escort Angie to the door; be back in five minutes." Jo looked at her dad for using Ms Sanders' first name and a small flash of annoyance passed her lips. Stone slipped his hand into

Angie's back and escorted her out of the door, as she took out her keys Stone said, "Thank you, once again, I hope we meet again under better circumstances." Stone held the car door open, and Angie got into her car very aware of his presence and even more so his physique and prayed her betraying body would not let her down. Angie put her little Toyota into gear wondering why she felt so much emotion in one day than she had in the last five years as Stone waved and walked back in to be with his daughter.

The prissy nurse had left him a couple of blankets on the chair next to Jo's bed. He looked at his daughter and as she looked back, Stone could read the emotion there; another benefit of just the two of them spending the last nine years in the big house, he wondered why he didn't downsize and get a smaller house next to the river. "Ok, Jo, I know that look, what's on your mind?"

As he sat on the chair and blankets, "Dad, I know you still think of me as a kid, but in 'here'," and Jo tapped her head, "I'm quite grown up, after all, I'm now officially a woman."

Stone stood and sat on the bed and held his daughter, "I know how grown up you can be, it just seems like only yesterday when you were covered in freckles and had them cute little pigtails in."

"Oh, that wasn't my best look, Dad." Jo was quietly chuckling to herself remembering it was her dad that used to comb her hair when he was on leave and put her pigtails in while Jo talked endlessly about anything and nothing a proper little gob shite. Another memory entered Jo's head and she actually laughed out loud remembering her dad and his magic marker covering her face in additional freckles while she was asleep and her walking up in the morning and going to comb her hair in the bedside mirror and turned deadpan very funny daddy I thought I was the kid in this family.

"Dad, can I ask you to do something for me?"

"Ok," realising this was another big moment brewing, Jo grabbed her dad's hand, "Could you leave Ms Sanders, Angie alone? She's not your type, she's a really nice person, she's super funny and yes, Dad, I know she's gorgeous and sexy and has an amazing body, but I don't think she would want the same things as you, Dad."

Stone looked at his deadly serious daughter, "Why is Angie not my type and I wasn't aware I had a type anyway."

"Dad, I see the way women look at you and despite us not having the talk, I know about sex and stuff, and I've seen all your cool moves." Stone raised his eyebrows intrigued rather than annoyed, Jo dropped her voice, "Hi, I'm Stone," in a passable imitation of her Dad's powerful voice, then she looked directly into his eyes, grabbed his hand and began to stroke the back with her thumb, "Are you looking for someone, can I help you?" Stone laughed yep busted, he wondered how much more she knew of his technique. Jo continued, "Then you do all the gentlemanly things like open the doors, but you always manage to cop a feel."

Stone burst out laughing, "No, I don't."

Jo continued now almost purring, "Can I get you anything? Can I take you anywhere? Have you had dinner or lunch? Depending on what time of day it is, I know this great little restaurant, Dad, you even have Uncle Mario's on speed dial so it obviously works most of the time," Jo was on a roll. "They get their, meal, you get your sweet," and raising her eyebrows just in case he missed her meaning, "you then drop them unless the sex was good then you go back for seconds."

What had started as a plea from Jo had now become an angry confrontation. Stone was about to raise his voice to his daughter something he rarely did when suddenly he realised, she was right in every way. Since Gemma's death, he'd used whatever male talents, he possessed to lure as many women into his bed as he needed; sex had become one meaningless night of lust after another. Stone realised it was his way of not feeling as lonely as he indeed was. He looked at his daughter with newfound respect and wondered how she knew so much at her tender age. "Ok, Jo, if I ask Angie out, I'll take you along as chaperone and I promise to not even kiss her till at least the third date." Stone realised also that he'd shut the rest of his family and friends out of his life especially his dad and Ike who was his father's best friend and also Jo's Godfather. Stone had to learn to live again not just exist and to be there to watch this remarkable person become all she wanted to be. Stone kissed his daughter, he grabbed a blanket getting on top of the bed, "Budge along, let's get some sleep and no farting or snoring." Stone lay there looking at the ceiling trying to decide how he could change.

Two

Angie arrived home still deep in thought, she needed to think, and as she pulled into the drive, a huge head with an enormous tongue appeared dribbling all over her recently cleaned window the eyes twinkled the happiness in his features so easy to see even from this distance. *I'm sure I closed the adjoining door this morning* as she walked up and tapped the window, "Bonzo, how did you get in the living room? You're a bad dog." **Bugger master's home and I shouldn't be in the living room; hope I haven't left hairs on the couch**, and she opened the door. A massive ball of fur and drool put his front paws on her shoulders and began licking her face, over ten stone of bull mastiff showing her how much she was missed. Angie wondered once again why humans were regarded as the most intelligent things on the planet, when you get a dog that loves you unconditionally, never strays, protects you with his life and all he requires from you is food, shelter, a walk or two every day and in the case of her beloved Bonzo, lives only ten to twelve years and devotes his whole life to making her feel loved, fuck, in her eyes humans where well down the list. Bonzo named after the legendary Led Zeppelin drummer, because she was a Zep fanatic, had dropped to the floor waiting for his head stoke, kissing and stroking the top of his head while Bonzo's tongue hung out of his mouth panting with joy **belly rub belly rub then I get a walk.**

Angie thought, *yep you wouldn't get a man doing that* and suddenly the desire was back imagining Stone's tongue and her panting. *Shit, Ang get a grip*, she needed a walk and the dog needed emptying, although he had a two-way dog flap in the back door into the garden, she grabbed some pooh bags, extra-large and extra strong, no more accidents, ugh? Grabbed Bonzo's full harness as he stood still but his whole body moved from side to side with uncontrollable joy at the prospect of squirrel-chasing his favourite pastime after ball chasing and swimming; **Yippee! I get to have a run with the squirrels!**

Angie closed the door and headed towards the woods hoping Bonzo would get there before her next-door neighbour saw them Amy Harris would be out wanting to chat about everything, including the weather and she always had little treats for Bonzo. She knew everything Bonzo had got up to while she'd been teaching. Several of the kids from school were out playing as the evening light began to fade, of course, Bonzo went extra hypo; he loved kids and despite his size, they loved him, and sometimes they had sweets in their pockets and slyly fed him hoping their teacher didn't spot their hand movements. Angie who had been teaching for over seven years had seen all the sleight of hand movements and pretended not to notice but adjusted Bonzo's supper to account for the treats, the same as she did when Amy Harris had fed him treats over their adjoining fence keeping him healthy might put an extra year or two on his life span. She'd got Bonzo three years ago at eight weeks old; it had been his birthday recently and she'd made him a cake by putting three candles on top. She'd taught him to blow out the candles and helped him eat it sugar-free, all healthy and could not imagine life without her best friend.

"Hello, Ms Sanders," said Tommy, Vince, and Adrian as they tried to keep playing keep-up while stroking Bonzo and keeping him away from the ball. There had been an over-enthusiastic moment last week when playing in the woods and Bonzo had joined in putting his powerful front teeth straight through the ball and sitting down feeling the air on his face wondering why the game had to stop, Angie mortified had gone out the next day and bought three new footballs (special offer save the pennies) giving each boy a new football. Bonzo was now considered a great goalie by the boys as long as he didn't have to make any saves. Bonzo still sniffing around the boys for treats was reluctant to leave; he had quite enjoyed the air in his face the previous week, but the scowl from Angie told him his football-playing days were over. Chasing squirrels had become his new favourite pastime and turning and dragging Angie towards the darkening woods. By the little brook, Angie took Bonzo's harness off and he had a quick drink dashing off into the trees in his ever so quiet ten-stone-plus way, Angie shook her head maybe if he decides to take a dump, it'll be in amongst the trees and he'll be back to chasing squirrels by the time she catches up with him. She definitely didn't want another bag-splitting incident **come on out you little grey critters I'm here to chase you down.**

Angie walked on head down trying to think but her thoughts seemed to be all about rampant sex in every position she could think of with the dad of her favourite pupil. Here she was not exactly a virgin, but could still count her bed partners on one hand, promiscuous she certainly wasn't. Her last relationship had ended amicably eighteen months ago. *Jesus*, Angie thought, *I haven't had sex in nearly two years*, so yep, the thought of sex with a handsome, tall, muscular man wasn't a surprise but what was, was just the touch of his hand had set off so many long dormant emotions in her, yes lust was definitely top of the list, but God did he feel good. She continued to walk further into the now darkening woods troubled by a reaction she couldn't understand given the type of person she knew herself to be. Still troubled by her own thoughts, she heard what sounded like twigs snapping and loud male voices, Angie had taken martial arts and had been good at sports especially gymnastics when she was at school, but she didn't know where Bonzo had got to and she didn't want to shout for him and alert whoever it was up ahead, she stood still and looked round to get her bearings.

One voice was raised above the others who appeared to all want to talk at the same time, "Listen, you two motherfuckers, you will do exactly what the fuck I tell you to do when I tell you to do it, otherwise your extra pocket money gets stopped and you both get seriously hurt, get my fucking drift? Now get the fuck out of here and be ready to start Monday who knows maybe you'll make enough to stop your own little sideline." They split up the two who had been getting shouted at headed towards Angie who deftly moved behind the big oak tree out of view her breath caught in her throat and she wondered where Bonzo had run off to; the two boys passed by Angie unaware she had seen them in the fading light, but she recognised the two lads Barry Jackson and Tommy Bowman, both sixteen, she had them in her class on Tuesdays and Thursdays, both smoking she could smell the distinct smell of skunk.

Her breathing and heart rate had returned to almost normal when she heard a loud shriek, "What the fuck was that?" The voice cried out several octaves higher than it had been less than five minutes ago. "There's no fucking bears in these woods; the goon squad would have shot and eaten the fuckers," bursting through the bushes ten feet to her right came two grey squirrels and ten feet behind them tongue lolling out of his mouth eyes sparkling and tail wagging with happiness, came Bonzo oblivious of everything except the chase, 'I'm gaining on you two,' the squirrels jumped onto the huge oak tree next to Angie and stopped around eight feet in the air on one of the larger branches looking down at Bonzo who now sat happily wagging his tail under the tree beneath them. 'I must learn how to climb trees, but great chase, you two, be back tomorrow and we can do it all again.' Angie still a little shaken put Bonzo's harness back on and walked back the way she'd come; she'd go home and stick something in the microwave and feed herself and Bonzo then she'd have to have her Zeppelin fix and a bubble bath.

Stone awoke having slept off and on as the nurse came in to check on his still sleeping daughter, she looked surprised but didn't mention the fact he was in the same bed albeit on top. To Stone, this was normal; Jo had only turned four when Gemma died and he went through a phase of finding his daughter in bed with him (before the one-night stands started), and her bed wet from both tears and urine, he never once scolded Jo just changed the sheets and put back the pictures of the three of them, she kept under the pillow with her torch. His father and Ike had helped her grieve by talking about her mum, just as they'd helped each other over the loss of their wives they'd been friends for over 40 years with weekends now spent fishing or golfing.

He climbed off the bed kissing his daughter on her brow and went off to freshen up and find a decent cup of coffee, reading the wall graffiti he had to laugh in the toilet, £15 million basic building costs for the most up-to-date medically equipped hospital in this part of England and the morons couldn't even spell properly, washing his hands and hoping the few coins he'd found in the pocket would get him a normal coffee not one of those mocha sludge fests, he rounded the corner and spied the all singing all dancing coffee machine, joy gave way to dismay, £3 for a fucking coffee! Settling for a can of diet coke for £1, Stone looked up to see Ike did the man need no sleep he thought, as Ike approached, "I bet you're on the board of governors here, £3 for a lousy coffee no wonder you and dad can afford those green fees and go faster golf carts."

Ike amused by his best friend's son replied, "Your dad's spending your inheritance, when he pops it, you'll be destitute," knowing full well Stone's house was valued at over a million, the army paid great bonuses for risking your life something Stone had done plenty of times up until Gemma's death. "I'll be up to see my goddaughter in about ten minutes," calmly reminding Stone how close he was, "oh and by the way, your dad's coming up on Sunday morning and I thought I'd tag along he tried phoning to let you know but could never get through and you know how much he likes leaving messages," which was another dig at Stone who had avoided his father after his man's death and had continued the pattern when Gemma died

Stone hoped he wouldn't be here much longer, one of the benefits of his current job was that he got every weekend off and thought he'd spend it with Jo, maybe go to the boat and do some fishing. Although Jo made him put everything he caught back. He needed some father/daughter time maybe he could educate his daughter in the riff brilliance of Zeppelin, Sabbath, and Purple, the three staple diets of any proper rock fan, not the second-rate later stuff Jo listened to. Arriving at the ward, Stone saw Ike and Jo in deep conversation which stopped when he walked through the door, "Sorry if you want to talk about me, I'll go back outside for ten minutes."

Ike just looked at him, "Yes, but you have ears like a bat and can lip read from fifty paces," which he actually could. "Besides we were talking about a certain somebody's thirteenth birthday coming up, J T, she wants a puppy or a horse; me, I'd get her a dog, horses bite your arse when you're not looking and they kick you in the nuts."

"See, Ike, that's why I keep you away from us your always teaching my daughter bad language."

"J T, you have lived too sheltered a life; if you think them words are bad, anyhow you can take her home we've had a little chat about what Jo needs to do, just please no heavy lifting and for God's sake don't take her for one of your gentle jogs. Don't forget your dad's arriving Sunday morning. I'll probably tag along maybe take the boat and try a spot of fishing if it's a nice day, which means sitting on deck drinking beer and telling war stories."

Stone knew when he was being backed into a corner the three closest people in his life all had their own way of reaching out to him. Taking his daughter out of the hospital, he slapped his forehead. "Shit, I'm on the bike." He was about to suggest a taxi home when they turned the corner and Jo squealed with glee seeing the powerful gleaming thunderbird and he realised he had a pillion passenger. *Oh well*, he thought, *it's about time someone got on the back of him*. Gemma had loved the bike the speed like a drug to her and he thought look how that turned out. He lifted out Gemma's helmet complete with the midget gem logo, which they both thought was a riot when he'd had the helmet custom painted for her because, of course, Gemma at only five feet was a midget to him, "This was your mams, Jo," as he placed the helmet on her head and fastened the strap, looking at the framed face of his daughter he was blown away by the resemblance to his dead wife. "Jo, when we get on the bike, your feet go there pointing to the foot blocks, grab me round the waist, hold on and when we corner you follow my movements, don't worry, I'll take it easy just keep behind me at all times, you'll be in my slipstream and the wind speed won't be too bad," and put his helmet on.

Jo did what she was told excited to be on the bike at last and the helmet still smelt of her mam's shampoo which gave her great comfort, at the start of the bike, Jo jumped a little surprised by the roar coming from the engine. Stone turned around and pulled down the fixed radio mike having switched the intercom on and spoke normally to Jo, "Right, we're all set, you sure, Jo, we can get a taxi?"

She nodded her head then realised she could speak, "Yes, Dad, I'm fine let's burn some rubber."

Stone chuckled and shook his head, "Ok hang on, here we go," and pulled out of the hospital car park heading for home. Two corners later with his daughter cuddling into his back, Stone who didn't do slow opened the bike for the first time with his daughter behind him. She squealed and shouted into the open mike for all her worth which Stone took to mean she was enjoying the ride and he opened the throttle wider, flying along the A1 and glancing at his police camera monitor (good to have friends in the police force). The motorway was quiet and Stone was an exceptional rider but knew it only took one idiot and although his reactions were quicker than 99% of other human beings and he didn't doubt his ability to avoid an accident, this was the first speed trip of his precious cargo, so at 120mph having almost been deafened by his daughter's screams of delight, he slowly cut the throttle and returned to the posted limit of 70mph and the screams died down a little.

As they slowed even further, he turned into the village and a thought occurred to him, he should have done this before the obvious delight of his daughter; the feel of her hands around his waist was the best cure for depression that Stone now realised he was suffering with. Pulling up onto the enormous drive to the equally enormous four-bedroom house, Stone thought *once again how big is not always better, perhaps a smaller house further into the beautiful Yorkshire countryside or maybe by the river and pondered making the move knowing he would have to get Jo to say yes.* The look of absolute joy on Jo's face as she took off the helmet and the dried snot all over her face would be yet another memory that would stay with Stone. "Ok, let's both get showers." Stone had day-old sweaty gym gear on, and his daughter obviously would be uncomfortable with her newfound woman's problems, poor kid bleeding like a pig every month for the next thirty plus years and hoped she didn't get the personality disorder so associated with monthlies.

After showering, Stone set about grabbing cold-cooked chicken from the fridge and making a salad. Jo grabbed a couple of frozen baked potatoes and popped them in the microwave and poured them both a drink of fresh lemon and lime water, their go-to drink made every night in a two-litre bottle and stored in the fridge they both took their health seriously making sure they were always hydrated. Stone added the freshly crushed spices to the salad; Stone liked cooking he found it very relaxing especially when the Bose system was cranked up. He switched the system to random play, but left it at a sub-teeth-chattering volume Jo knew what was coming next, sure enough as he placed the food on the table, and grabbed the little notebook and pen out of the kitchen drawer, "Right, Jo, ten seconds, name of artist or band, album title and year."

Jo huffed for effect but she loved playing this game with her father, "It's my turn, Dad." Jo liked most of the older stuff her dad listened to, but the newer stuff was more her style and they took turns playing this game.

Stone was a sixty, seventies and eighties rock fanatic. Jo loved the later stuff being only twelve, but he kept trying to educate her in the riff age of his favourite era telling her stuff about each track the whys and wherefore his face taking on an innocence and joy as he told his stories that she treasured. The first track came on as they ate their meal, Tony Iommi's cough left in by the sound engineer gave it away and before the monstrous riff had even kicked in Jo said, "Sweet Leaf, Black Sabbath, Masters of Reality, 1971," gaining the look of approval look her dad and a maximum eight points on the board, chewing his salad head bopping along with Ozzie's vocals and Jo hoped her dad wouldn't start singing along although he had a great voice if the song had a chorus he'd expect Jo to sing that bit with him when she did he'd go full-on rock God and do all the posing grabbing whatever he could to use as a microphone and strut around the house like a peacock which cracked Jo up every time, she'd laughed so hard sometimes she'd have to change her trousers and pants.

Today, however, he was aware of his daughter's predicament and just nodded along to the beat, "How about after lunch we go on the boat?" Jo looked with astonishment at her dad; her granddad and Ike had been the only ones to regularly use the boat since her mum's death; her dad had been on alone a few times but had never asked her to come with him, "Ike said no excitement, thinking what he would say if knew about the bike ride, so we could fish and if we catch anything we'll put them back, alive and unharmed," knowing without those terms he hadn't a chance of getting his daughter's approval for the trip. Jo was so stunned she missed the next intro another easy one 'Brighton Rock, Queen, Sheer Heart Attack, 1973.'

Stone wanted her approval so much, "Yep, another eight points," totally disregarding the twenty-second pause at the start, and they both settled down to listen to Brian May's blistering solo. Jo listened intently to the next track, but she couldn't remember hearing her dad play it before and there were no vocals yet to try and pinpoint any details, her dad being dad had gone to the kitchen cabinet and gave two peeps on the air horn he kept in there, "Time's up, me beauty", making Jo think it was some sort of pirate impression, "this is Speed King by Deep Purple from Deep Purple In Rock 1970," knowing it was a proper curve ball as Ian Gillian's vocals didn't start till two minutes or so in, "Ok, thanks for the info, Dad, I hadn't a clue. Can we go to the boat on the bike?"

Stone knew now he might as well get rid of the discovery in the garage only rain and snow would keep Jo off the bike and even then, she'd probably dig out their old water-proofs. "Ok, grab my backpack out of the bedroom; take what you might need with your condition."

Jo went red, "I'm on my period, Dad," and Stone then went red, they looked at each other with red faces and both started giggling.

"Grab your swimming gear although it might be better to catch some rays so bring some shorts and that peach suntan cream you like, I'll pack water, fruit, and protein bars, and we'll get lunch from Uncle Mario's," and because he knew he could rib his daughter, "and grab them ten-kilo dumbbells out of the corner of the gym might as well get in a light shoulder workout." But Jo headed in the direction of their home gym. So, Stone had to shout that he was only kidding. Stone shook his head thinking how he'd explain to Ike that his goddaughter picked up some weights and haemorrhaged; sometimes he wondered who was the kid. "You'll have to wear the backpack," as he put the bag over her petite shoulders and re-adjusted all the straps, closing the door and setting the alarm they put on their helmets and Stone powered down the drive on the short journey to where the boat was moored.

Three

Angie woke to hot breath on her face and foul-smelling air; when you have a ten-stone-plus dog, you have to accept the flatulence as a sign of being comfortable but on a good day, rotten eggs had nothing on Bonzo; **them minty sticks might work for my teeth, but they do nothing for my arse, master has tears in her eyes**. Escaping to the clean air of the bathroom and thinking Bonzo needed a couple of those breath-cleaning chew sticks the fetid breath needed some work too, minty fresh might do it. While the coffee machine was brewing, proper coffee in the morning was her vice; she filled Bonzo's bowl with his morning dry kibble; she had learnt from her earlier puppy stage mistakes fresh meat in one end didn't mean fresh meat out the other, the garden had been pebble-dashed; luckily, the rain washes it into the grass, so Bonzo's was also a green environment tree hugger. Opening the patio doors while hoping he didn't take a dump in the middle of the lawn, he knew to keep away from the flowers and usually did his business under the apple tree, which then turned to mulch and fed the apples.

No breakfast for her as she usually practised intermittent fasting, only eating twice a day, around one after her fasted morning run with Bonzo; then again around six. Whole food and she tried to avoid sugar; she still had the same figure she had at eighteen; pity there was no one to share it with. Immediately, her betraying body responded with thoughts of I know who I'd like to offer it to visualising those muscles, blue eyes, and perfect rump. She scolded herself for behaving like a teenager as the coffee burnt her lips. Bonzo burst through the patio doors in his usual subdued manner nearly taking one off its hinges; she'd already changed the glass in them for some sort of unbreakable distortion plastic costing her a month's wages but figured Bonzo was worth it. The experience of him seeing himself in a mirror and ten stone of bull mastiff charging at himself had left them both panicking and shaking; luckily, he'd only totalled the wood surrounding the mirror, but even now Bonzo sniffed around any mirrors having learnt his lesson.

Bonzo went to his water bowl and started the messy process of drinking his own body weight in water, or so it seemed. The gallon bucket was on a huge tray and somehow the carpet still got wet. Bonzo stopped his drinking to check his food bowl, bloody kibble, yet again, I need proper food, not those dried rabbit droppings, however, Angie knew once she mixed the kibble in with his real meat then it would disappear at lightning speed. Her second coffee finished, Angie filled the big duffel bag with Bonzo's requirements extra super strength poop bags, a travel bowl, a two-litre bottle of water complete with a cool bag, a huge rubber bone play toy and two massive towels not forgetting to add a small bottle of water, protein bar and packet of gum, for herself. Bonzo looked at the bag, his body shaking, tail wagging his bag being packed meant it was swimming time; mastiffs love the water and once he was in wouldn't come out so she always took his favourite toy even then she could spend half an hour trying to get him out.

Bonzo jumped easily into the remodelled (by him) Toyota, no package tray, eaten not very tasty spat out, back seats permanently down, plastic reclining hinges, no longer MOT standard, plastic, not nice spat out, support spring stretched straight, seats chewed, covered in saliva and hair, the general appearance resembling a bomb site; grunting, he adjusted his weight to his favourite position and looked around to see if he could find the chew bone he'd been eating the last time. Putting the duffle bag on the passenger seat and her belt on, she looked at Bonzo and hoped he behaved himself.

Arriving at the river car park fifteen minutes later, Bonzo had his head up onto the seat, the tail wagging started as she lifted the tailgate putting on his harness aware of the looks of non-dog lovers. Just because he was the size of a small pony didn't mean he was violent which was reserved for humans. Bonzo was just a big bundle of love on four legs that just happened to have very sharp teeth! Sniffing the air, happy to be out of the small tin can, Bonzo walked beside Angie. He was actually very well-trained and super-protective of his owner, walking down to the marina among all the hobnob boats some of which cost more than her house, as she was passing one boat Angie could see the back of a young girl who clearly had an impeccable taste in music as the opening chord of one of the greatest riffs ever started, 'You need cooling, Baby, I'm not fooling, I'm going to send you back to schooling. Way down inside, Honey, you need it, I'm going to give you my love, I'm going to give you, my love.' She thought of just standing still and getting her Zep to fix 'Whole lotta Love' being one of her go-to songs, she got plenty of stares and not all directed at her dog the fact she was wearing a light blue top with the iconic Zofo label on the front covering a pair of full breasts and the even more iconic Zeppelin one front cover album on the back, very short cut-off jeans snugly hugging her backside and showing her tanned legs plus her hair was up a bun showing of her slender shapely neck never entered her head that some stares were at her despite several men walking past more than once.

Earlier, Stone and Jo had stepped onto the 'Gemstone,' and unpacked the backpack. Jo was busy applying suntan cream having changed into her bikini top while keeping her black shorts on when Stone decided to catch some rays and was trying to apply sun lotion to his back without success. "Dad, turn around, I'll get your back." She who was used to seeing her father topless and in just cycle shorts was not phased at all by the physique. however, the same couldn't be said of several boat owners' wives or girlfriends who looked at him with undisguised lust. Going into the cabin, he switched on the sound system aware that some of his boat neighbours might not like classic rock, but basically not giving a fuck, setting the volume to a decent level, he turned to Jo, "Right, I'm going for a swim, no tests today, just enjoy these are all classics and even the young bands you like play them in their sets. Don't take no shit from any of these old fogies it's not too loud and most of them are deaf anyway." With that, he turned, walked up the boat and dived into the cool water below. Jo thought her dad might just be coming out of his funk; she'd get Granddad and Ike to do an assessment on the quiet on Sunday.

Jo was lying in the padded deck chair her foot tapping away to classic Bon Scott-era AC/DC; she loved his voice far better than Brian Johnson something she and Dad agreed on. She loved her dad and knew how much he loved her considering how hard the army had trained him; she knew from her granddad and her Uncle Ike that to be the best of the best going through ridiculous manoeuvres using live bullets, going through sleep deprivation and hunger, trained to show no fear ever, no emotion, the army took the best and made them better, but the top 2% which her dad was one just soaked it up and became super soldiers who did the impossible jobs with impossible odds and kept on doing it. Her dad had been like that, never questioning orders given to him by some fat bureaucrat over a five-course lunch at his privileged country house, until her mum died then he slowly became human again.

Over the last nine years, as she was growing up into a thoughtful, contented, almost teenager, she had seen her dad shake off the army's super solider programming; she would never admit it to anyone, but she knew her mum's death gave her back a father she loved and worshipped who was gradually becoming human again. Although only four when Mum died, she remembered the dad who was there but not there, super observant, hypercritical, like a machine that couldn't switch off. Now having grown up, she could look back at that time and hardly ever remember her dad being there, he was always in some godforsaken hot spot, fighting the fight of politicians interested in having an endless supply of oil. When he was home, he didn't know how to handle his growing daughter; he couldn't communicate with the demanding feed me, clean me, play with me, rock me to sleep, a bundle of pigtails and freckles. Jo who was a happy, content, and perceptive little girl knew her daddy's head was always somewhere else, yes, he gave her plenty of playtime and cuddles, but he didn't know how to communicate what he was feeling and even at four, she knew parts of him she could never reach. Her dad had been programmed to be an unthinking totally focused super solider, the human being part of him had been switched off, but with the death of his equally focused career-driven wife, he made the tough decision for a career army man and asked to step down from his inevitable in Jo's eyes suicide, after all, how many impossible missions could one man accomplish! His army file was classified and restricted, but gradually he'd become human again. After Mum's death, he often talked with her, never going into gory details, but she was now looking at a father she thought she would never have, and she would do anything to keep the man he was becoming and not the machine he was.

Jo wondered at herself knowing most girls her age were focused on make-up, boys, and clothes and here she was thinking how could get her dad to be more dad, deciding to sneak a diet coke while he was swimming, before he went on about all those artificial sweeteners; your body doesn't know what to do with them he'd said, but he'd missed the point it tastes good and an ice-cold drink is what she fancied. As she stood up, she saw the back end of a massive jet-black dog and smiled how something does that big shake all over and continue forward? They'd had a dog when she was a baby an old scruffy mutt that never left her dad's side when he was home even if he'd been away for months the dog returned to his side as if he'd never been away. The only time she'd seen her dad cry was when the dog died; she hadn't seen him cry when Mum died, but he'd been close yesterday with her little drama.

She watched forgetting the coke; there was something about dogs; she'd asked for a dog or horse for her 13th birthday, pretty sure she'd get a dog. Maybe, it's because they don't have jobs, mortgages or commitments she thought watching as the owner turned to take off his harness the dog now shaking even harder slobber and drool covering the ladies' gorgeous legs (Jo knew gorgeous, she'd overseen some of her dads cast-offs leaving their house after their nights or mornings of passion), giving the rest of the woman the once over as woman do, oh yes, definitely a ten good job; Dad's not around he'd be perfecting his pickup lines. Looking past the bare neck, she suddenly realised it was Ms Sanders. Angie having only seen her in her school work clothes or workout gear, never out on a sunny day looking as Dad would say like a ten.

This wasn't sexist but an in-house joke between her and Dad, he'd told her she could only date boys eleven and over, so it had gone back and forward between them. Jo stated she didn't like younger boys, but an older boyfriend was around sixteen her dad said the score count was eleven the mark of perfection, not the age. She was just about to shout when the huge dog took off at a great knot and belly-flopped into the river soaking Ms Sanders who roared with laughter. Ms Sanders, her now soaked to the skin teacher turned around to see Jo waving from the boat playing classic rock and walked over, "Jo, cool music, kid," she said. "What are you doing down here?"

"The music choice is Dad's; I like newer stuff. But Dad's educating me in classic rock, so I have an appreciation of where it came from. Dad is gone off for a swim, you wanna come up and I'll grab you a towel, who's is the dog?"

"That's, Bonzo, he's mine."

"Does he bite? I want a dog for my birthday." And Jo had become a normal motor mouth pre-teenager again, "You want a coke, Ms Sanders?"

"I'll have a coke if you start calling me Angie, it's the weekend no school, Ms Sanders is for school days, ok."

"You wanna coke, Angie?" Angie smiled, yep, definitely my favourite pupil, looking over the boat and checking on the buffoon in the water trying to chase the fish, but being big and bulky he had no chance, but Bonzo always just kept on playing; he'd tire himself out in an hour or so maybe then she could coax him out of the water, she wondered if dogs got wrinkly skin if they were in the water too long.

Jo saw Angie looking at the name of the boat 'Gemstone.' "It was Dad and Mams, he always came alone up until today, this is my first visit. Is your dog, ok?"

"Yep, he's fine. I think he was a mermaid in a previous life." Drinking their cokes and listening to the music, Angie thought great looks, awesome body, own boat, and a rock fan if she had a type, Stone would have ticked all the boxes, wondering if his daughter realised the effect her father had on her. "I take it you're a Zeppelin fan," spying Angie's soaked, but drying in the sun t-shirt, and before she realised what she was going to say, she blurted out, "You and dad will get on like a house on fire[he's three top bands are Zep, Purple and Sabbath; he calls them the three staple diets of any proper rock fan," cursing herself thinking her dad would put the moves on Angie anyway, especially if he saw her looking like she did now, and hoping that when she got breasts, they'd be as good as Angie's who was completely unaware of what the cold water had done to her nipples.

"Great quote from your dad, I like the other two bands, but Zeppelin just does it for me, no matter what sort of shitty day I've had or how much of a wreck of a place Bonzo has left me, I can always find something from their back catalogue to get me out of my funk."

Jo picking up on the dog's name said, "You called your dog after the greatest drummer ever John Henry Bonham?"

Angie was surprised at Jo's knowledge, "Yep, the best."

"Dad watches their concerts on DVD all the time, and we have a game we play; he plays the old stuff; I play the newer and we get to guess track title, artist or group, album title and year. Dad's super brilliant at the old stuff, but not that good at the new; he says unless it's a rehash of old stuff like Greta van Fleet who he calls the diet coke Led Zeppelin, and we sometimes have a sing-along where Dad sings and I do the chorus, but then Dad goes off into rock God mode and starts prancing round the house with a brush for a microphone and I crack up," at which Angie laughed out loud at the image she now had.

Four

Bonzo thought fish were not really into playing games; they swam too fast separating in all directions when he got close and not keen when he tried to paw them on their head with his version of tiggy. Bored with this game, he might climb out of the water and see if he could coax some treats out of his master when he spied something swimming at a decent pace towards him; mastiffs have very little fear and he was sure it wasn't a shark, but a human and thought he'll play my game better than them stupid fish and started paddling towards the man. Stone enjoying the exercise and the feel of water on his skin spied what looked like a huge dog in the distance and thought what the hell is it doing as he watched the dog turn and head straight for him.

Jo and Angie were looking out at the sun hitting the river on a beautiful sunny day when Jo spied the broad shoulders of her dad cutting through the water with ease, "Looks like Dad is on his way back," pointing up the river. Angie caught site of the head and shoulders and her body reacted yet again.

She then saw her big buffoon of a dog paddling towards Stone, "Jo, is your dad frightened of big dogs?"

Jo laughed, "Dad's frightened of nothing and he loves dogs, why?" Angie pointed to Bonzo paddling towards her dad; Jo dashed into the hold and grabbed the camcorder thinking this was going to be good and began filming as the distance between her dad and Bonzo closed.

Stone continued towards the large dog; he knew that soon they would have a dog; it was a foregone conclusion that Jo would get one for her birthday. He had seen the pleading look in his daughter's eyes at the hospital, he was also putty in her hands, and he loved dogs; they were so loyal and giving. The one approaching just wanted to play, Stone could read faces, human or animal, and it had saved the lives of himself and his men more than once. A few feet now from the meeting, Stone started treading water and spoke quietly to the big dog, "Hello, boy, what you're doing out here on your own?" Bonzo recognising the friendly tone chuffed loudly yes play time, and Stone being Stone held out his arms wide and said, "Come on then, let's have a cuddle," and Bonzo all 10 stone plus did his best Free Willy impression and jumped into Stone's awaiting arms who caught and held him easily **wow, this human's super strong.** Jo filming the scene laughed when her dad put out his arms, "I can't wait to show this to Granddad and Ike tomorrow." Angie just looked and wanted ever so much to be in Bonzo's position, her body letting her down yet again.

Stone and Bonzo continued to play in the water, splashing and chuffing each other. Jo filming started laughing at their antics, Bonzo now getting into the game went from chuffing to barking so Stone did the same, **big man's going to be my new friend**. "Jo, Bonzo hardly ever barks."

Jo deadpan, "Well, Dad brings out the best in everything that's why he's a colonel at thirty-eight!" Clearly enjoying each other's company, Stone chucked Bonzo over his back, grabbed his front paws and dived underwater. Bonzo thought **I've died and gone to heaven the man knows how to play mermaid**, Stone moved towards the boat saying, 'Ok, big boy, time to find your owner.'

Stone looked up while treading water and there on the deck with his daughter, stood Angie Sanders not looking anything like the last time he saw her; her hair was up showing her long neck and extenuating her face which was stunning, made even more stunning by the fact that she was laughing at his and the dogs' antics. Stone thought Angie was beautiful, but when she laughed, she was in another class entirely. When he got to her body which had only had a hint of before, the still damp light blue t-shirt with a logo he recognised showed full breasts and erect nipples, his erection straining at the sight of a slim waist, she obviously looked after herself, taking his eye to perfect tanned legs moulded in cut-off jeans making his erection strain even more. He could see Jo with the camcorder filming away so taking a very deep breath to calm himself and not embarrass himself, he continued towards his boat; obviously, the owner of the dog was Angie.

Angie was also aware his daughter was less than two feet away filming, and when Stone stopped and looked up, his muscular torso gleaming, she felt a desire take over her body, and the man was beautiful; he just oozed sex appeal. Bonzo was first out of the water, Jo stopped filming and sat on the floor, Bonzo beside himself now that he had found two new friends today rushed over into the waiting arms of Jo **cuddles I love cuddles**, totally ignoring Angie's call to heel, Jo squealed with delight as the huge mastiff began to lick her face in earnest face tasting and cuddles. Angie mortified by her dog's bad behaviour gave a loud whistle; the dog obeying the command sat next to his tail wagging, her full attention on Bonzo she missed Stone's climb onto the boat his erection receding enough to be just uncomfortable. Putting on Bonzo's harness and saying, "You are to be on your best behaviour, young man, or no more squirrel-chasing. Right introductions; Bonzo, this is Jo," and the dog barked softly nodding his head, which set Jo off laughing again; **young girl tasty face good at cuddling**. Angie turned to Stone and her breath caught in her throat, he had grabbed a towel and was drying his short hair, every muscle in his body was gleaming, his chest muscles jumped from the tension and his six-pack moved in and out with each breath. Angie didn't dare let her eyes drop any further, aware of her hesitation, "And this is Stone who you've already met. This is Bonzo who 99% of the time is a good boy." Master's voice changed mermaid man might become her friend too. Stone couldn't take his eyes off Angie, all his chat up lines no longer important; he had to get to know this woman, aware of Jo's warning, but also of his own feelings totally alien to him over the last nine years, tongue-tied for the first time in his life and aware of her looking straight at him. Jo looked at her dad, at his hesitation unable to believe that he was stuck for words never was her dad struck for words, he'd lead missions, his men loved and respected him and here he was stuck with his mouth open catching flies.

Stone finally spoke, "I think John would have liked you calling your dog by his nickname after all off the drums he was a cattle farmer and bred Hereford cows, and Bonzo's the dog version of a Hereford."

Angie replied, "I'd like to think so, I called him Bonzo as a mark of respect and honour one of the best four rock musicians who have ever lived, he was the pendulum, their music gets me through every type of situation." Angie thought wow that's deep for me, already explaining to Stone a bit more than she should on a first meeting. "So, Zeppelin is your favourite band?"

"Yep, but Purple and Sabbath are well up there too," Jo watched her dad and teacher talking and knew warning her dad off would have no effect she could feel the energy bouncing between them. Bonzo had heard his name mentioned and looked at his master; **her voice is different when she speaks to the mermaid man; softer more emotional; however, I need to**

warm up and proceeded to shake himself dry which stopped any conversation as everyone and everything was sprayed with droplets of water.

Jo decided it was the best possible moment to push her luck, "Daddy" (not dad this time) and Stone knew exactly what she was going to say, "Can I have a dog like Bonzo for my birthday?" And then quickly to deflect a straight yes/no answer from her dad, she turned to Angie. "I'll be thirteen on July sixteenth and Dad said he'd get me a horse or a dog," therefore making it impossible for his dad to impress Angie if he said no. Angie thought, smart girl; she knew exactly how to get her dad to do what she wanted, she wished life was as easy for grown adults. Angie saved Stone from making a commitment he might not want to and also soothe her renegade body by making a little play of her own, "Jo, a dog is a massive responsibility; there are all sorts to consider, have you got time to teach him, have you got space, can you afford the vet fees, the slogan a dog is for life isn't just a slogan it's true, he's a total commitment and requires all your spare time, you won't have time for boyfriends, and if your poorly you still have to look after your dog." Jo was thinking hard about what Angie was saying aware of how big her decision would be, but boyfriend or dog was a no-brainer, she'd wait for a boyfriend, but she'd wanted a dog for years and having met Bonzo, she wanted one even more.

Angie saw the look in Jo's eye as she looked at Bonzo, she would do right by a dog; it would always be first with her she was certain Jo would be a good owner so she added perhaps to get Stone to think also, "When you have a dog that dog never lets you down, gives you total and unconditional love every minute of the day, protects you even if it means his or her death, he/she looks after you when you're ill, knows when you are happy or sad a dog will commit to its owner, will never stray or intentionally hurt you, and the best thing of all is to get all that and more all they ask is for you to love and feed them."

Wow, Angie, way to go she thought, lay your cards on the table and you're not sure the man is even interested in you, but at least my favourite pupil should get her dog. "It's five weeks to your birthday, Jo, how about you spend some time with Bonzo, you can come round after school if your dad agrees and help me walk Bonzo in the woods, get to know what he wants and expects you can even pick up his poop, I've got extra heavy-duty bags." Now she said shuddering with the memory. Angie thought to herself after her little speech, Well, that's my bit said; if Stone was as intelligent as his daughter he now knew where the boundaries lay should the obvious spark between them ignite.

Jo listened to what Angie was saying; she was a responsible person, wasn't fazed by the task that looking after her own dog would demand all her spare time, the poop thing didn't bother her; it would just be part of the care she would have to show her dog, looking into the huge brown eyes of Bonzo who was now sniffing her crotch area; she already loved this huge dog and it wasn't even hers, it was her teachers, who looked at her dad like he walked on water, which she was pretty sure was not something he could do. She'd warned him off making a move, but Angie wasn't like all the other bimbos she was cool and had her own way of doing things, she was a brilliant teacher, history not even Jo's favourite subject took on new meaning when Angie got on a roll in class, she was funny, really funny she was always interested in her pupils' observations which made her in Jo's eyes a great teacher.

Stone stood up from his chair observing his daughter and Angie the ease of friendship and decided to grab a bottle of water to try and get his thoughts in order, "Either of you like a bottle of chilled water " Angie said she'd love one, Jo who'd just had the diet coke said no and Stone disappeared into the hold, giving Angie a chance to talk to Jo. Angie had seen Bonzo sniffing Jo's crotch and realised waste blood of a female would be like a beacon to a male dog and she didn't want to embarrass Jo in front of her father, she leaned down gently and whispered in Jo's ear, "Did you pack any pads with you? That's why Bonzo is sniffing you so much"; then so the girl wouldn't be mortified or embarrassed, "When I'm in the same state, muggins lies with his head in my lap and I have to lock myself in the bathroom to pee for a whole week, when you have your own dog, it's one of the benefits their smell is a thousand times stronger than ours."

Jo reddened but realised the situation could have been a lot worse if Dad had still been there, "Yep, Uncle Ike told me what I have to do." Angie thought it was strange that Jo called Dr Goldberg, uncle, but had seen the camaraderie between Stone and Dr Goldberg so she just thought maybe they'd met a few times. Jo had the backpack open grabbing a fresh pad and underwear to make her fresh again and hid them behind her back as her dad appeared with two frosted bottles of water and she went into the hold leaving Angie, Bonzo and him alone for the first time.

Jo didn't know what to do she wanted a dog, she'd like to know what she was going to get into when she had her own, oh yes, she knew she had got round her dad he had sat there observing her with Bonzo analysing the reactions between her and the dog, after twenty years in the army it was second nature so Jo sat there trying to decide if it was a good idea to spend time with Angie and Bonzo which meant that Angie saw her dad more often which lead to what she thought, then realised they were two adults it was up to them she was still a kid, she didn't really understand nor work out why her dad had to have an endless supply of big breasted bimbo's, looking from Bonzo to Angie. Jo thought she was not a bimbo, and she was not stupid or a slut, although Jo didn't really know what the word meant she had overheard Tracy Wilkinson talking about Emme's mam who she said was putting it about like the slut she was, so the desire to have her own dog outweighed protecting Angie against her dad. Angie could look after herself, plus her dad hadn't made any moves at all yet in fact he'd done that speechless thing earlier maybe he was losing his touch.

Stone handed a bottle to Angie who was really nervous for the first time, and it slipped through her fingers, with his lightning-fast reaction, Stone managed to get his other hand under Angie's and push the bottle back into her palm; the touch of their hands made Angie's body tingle with desire. Angie now flustered went to twist the top of the bottle but her hand was wet, Stone gently took the bottle out of her hand unscrewed the top and placed it back in her hand touching her hand once again in the process, all the time his beautiful blue eyes were on hers and she felt the desire increase once again. Bonzo, on the other hand, decided he'd quite like a bit of cold water and nudged Angie's arm looking at the bottle **you going to share that?**

"Ok, Bonzo, but let me have a drink first and tipped the bottle into her mouth a little bit running down her chin," Stone's body reacted instantly to Angie's long neck, her mouth on the bottle and the water dribbling down her chin, this was the most erotic vision he'd ever seen his erection was so hard he had to quickly sit down and cross his legs. Angie turned; Bonzo tilted his head up and began lapping loudly as she slowly poured water into his mouth his tongue going fifty to the dozen. Angie aware that Jo would come back any minute said, "I'm sorry if you hadn't wanted to get Jo a dog for her birthday, I went on my little rant; I detest animal cruelty, what humans do to each other defies belief, but to an animal it makes me boil up."

Stone couldn't help himself; he took Angie's hand he needed her touch, "I've seen the worst the human race can do to each other, I've been there got the t-shirt, or in the army's case the medal, sometimes the only way to avoid a bad situation is to take decisive action, but animals, yep, I get exactly what you mean," and quickly released her hand as Jo re-appeared. Angie was lost in thought his touch had made her tingle all over, he seemed sincere in what he was saying, but she knew from Jo it may just be one of her father's moves, however she didn't care, if he could make her feel like this with just the touch of his hand then what if she offered much more, would it hurt to be used and discarded and how would that affect Jo who she'd see much more often than just at school when her father says she has to learn how to look after a dog.

Angie didn't doubt Jo would get her dog, having observed them together a few times, she knew the man would do anything for his daughter's happiness. She'd also like a bit of happiness herself even if it ended as quickly as it had started, she told herself she could handle it. Jo had seen her Dad's hand in her teacher's; maybe the moves were coming back she thought, but then she looked at them both, Angie was blushing slightly, and her dad couldn't keep his eyes off her, Jo didn't know what to think. Bonzo thought bored now needed sleep looked at where the young girl had been lying and decided **yep, that's a good spot catch me some afternoon rays** and claimed the spot rolling and shuffling on his back putting on his own scent, smacked his lips together a few times and gave a huge sigh closed his eyes content in the sun and the comfy bed.

Stone turned to his daughter, "You're going to have to get a deck chair out," secretly pleased that he had this beautiful woman with him for a bit longer. Stone's original intention today was to spend time with his daughter, maybe a bit of fishing, get lunch from Luconi's it was Jo's favourite restaurant, a few extra carbs wouldn't make a difference if he got his protein quota from the chicken. There was no reason to change plans just get extra helping; after all the swimming he was hungry now anyway. Stone turned to Angie, "Me and Jo are getting our lunch from Luconi's now that Bonzo settled in for a kip you're very welcome to join us. I'll ring Mario with the order and go collect it on the bike, give you a chance to discuss the finer points of being a dog owner with my daughter."

Stone thought see I can also play this manipulations game. Angie looking at her sleeping dog knew she wasn't going anywhere soon, Bonzo would sleep a couple of hours wake refreshed and then it would be squirrel-chasing time again. She loved Luconi's food; she also liked being where she was rather more than she should have scolding herself, "Great food, I'll go half's with you."

"Nonsense, I have a special deal with Mario and Gabrielle and food's part of it."

"Ok, I'll have the chicken with Luconi's special pasta and sauce."

Stone looked at Angie, "You've been before I take it?"

Having the exact choice himself, "Dad, can we get some of those fresh little wholemeal bread rolls too?" Thinking she might as well keep pushing her luck, as her dad grabbed his phone and started to dial Mario's number.

Five

"Is that Mario, the fat Italian stud muffin? I'd like to place an order and I'll collect it if you can tear yourself away from the delectable Gabby."

"It's ok, Stone, knowing exactly who was on the phone, I gave her good loving less than an hour ago, she'll be good for another hour yet." Angie looked up surprised and even more so when he said, "Yep, Jo's here," and put the phone in his daughter's outstretched hand.

"Hi, Uncle Mario, yes it's on the sixteenth of next month, yes, I know what I'm getting, I'm gonna get, hang on," and put the phone to her bicep, "Angie what sort of dog is Bonzo?"

"He's a bull mastiff," replied Angie now listening to the conversation. Stone's eyes just popped' not only had he agreed to get his daughter a dog now it was one that would probably outeat him. Jo returned to the phone, "A bull mastiff, Uncle Mario; no, I haven't picked one yet, I'm not sure where to get one from but as long as it's around my birthday I can wait," giving her dad the look, "I'll put Dad back on."

Mario was chuckling, "You've been played and outsmarted, my friend. You want your usual?"

"Don't I know it? Yep, but double the order and can you put in a dozen of those small soft wholemeal bread rolls?"

"Jesus, Stone she must have worn you out, you want carbs too, must be a two-star if still there maybe finally got a three-star pretty gymnast to do anything in bed. You want me to put in some watermelon to replace the essential fluid you left behind in some warm dark moist crevices."

Stone was now scarlet, his daughter laughing but Angie was just smiling. *Jesus*, he thought, *why the fuck didn't I go into the cabin to make the call.* "No, Mario, it's not like that. Jo's teacher owns a bull mastiff; the dog is now asleep on my boat and Angie agreed to stay for lunch."

Mario whistled. "Don't tell me you got Angie Sanders on your boat, she way out of your league, she definitely not bimbo, she most beautiful girl in the village; your super cool moves won't work with her, she too smart, solider." Mario unaware that Angie could hear the conversation continued, "Angie Sanders, eh Stone, well, well, well, your standard of bimbo yes one, two maybe a three-star. Angie Sanders; she a ten, beauty and total class." Stone, his ego now destroyed by his friend informed Mario that Angie was sitting right next to him and had heard every word!

"Sorry, Stone," said Mario and called out, "Hi Angie, sorry you overheard."

"It's ok, Mario, it's nice to know you rate me as a ten." And looking Stone straight in the eye, said, "I'll have some watermelon," and raised her eyebrows.

Hearing this, Jo totally cracked up, "You've been busted big time, Dad."

"Mario, you better add watermelon to the order, I'll be down in ten minutes," and put his phone down on the table and without looking round at either his laughing daughter or the smiling Angie, he walked into the cabin to change. Angie and Jo looked at each other and roared with laughter; even Bonzo opened an eye at his owner's laughter.

Stone emerged from the hold wearing cut-off jeans and an iconic 2112 Rush t-shirt, and Ray-Bans the man oozed sex appeal without even trying, although the ego had taken a giant hit thanks to Mario. Picking up the phone and bike keys, "I'll be back in around an hour." Knowing that Mario being Italian would talk and prepare the food fresh, and to be honest, Stone wanted a bit of time to himself. Angie's presence had knocked him for six and Mario had knocked him off his pedestal. He'd do something he would never do in combat turn and run.

Angie just couldn't help herself enjoying Stone's discomfort, "Great t-shirt another legendary drummer sadly lost, don't forget the watermelon," and smiled. Stone knew that he'd finally met his match.

Jo just getting over laughing kinked over again, "Dad, if you and Angie were playing for points, you've just lost in the first round." Stone muttering under his breath jumped off the boat and onto his bike to get away from the hiding he was taking. Angie watched him leave, her body shuddering with desire, her eyes following Stone and forgetting his daughter's presence hoped she could remember every detail because the rampant rabbit on the top of the wardrobe might get dusted down and get some use later. Unaware that Jo had been observing her, she sighed loudly, "Yes, my dad has that effect on most women and some men."

Angie decided the truth was the best option, "Your dad is the most attractive man I've ever met; he has everything; looks, muscular body, deep voice; he's the total package and I'd have to be in my eighties to not be affected, plus he's a rocker. Bonzo likes him and I'm not going to lie, you're his daughter who I also like very much; I can't pretend otherwise." Bonzo on hearing his name had woken, stood up, stretched, and produced the loudest fart, ninety decibels on the Richter scale but what followed was the stench that could peel paint, and had both running into the cabin closing the door tightly behind them and knocking over a couple of pictures in their haste. Bonzo turned sniffed the air, not bad and plonked back down to continue his dream. "That's a prime example of what you must learn to put up with when you get your dog, if they eat something they shouldn't you either get world-class farting or pebble dash diarrhoea. I have a face mask at home for when it's bad, but he's a good boy when he sees the mask he goes and lies in the kitchen."

"Dad will think that's a good thing, keep any boyfriends away, not that I want a boyfriend. What about if you have a boyfriend over, Angie?"

"Ha, that's easy: any boyfriend material has to pass the Bonzo test, and nobody has," although Angie knew Stone had passed with top marks from Bonzo.

Angie bent down to pick the fallen pictures off the floor seeing a small petite blonde holding a gorgeous little girl around two years old with pigtails and freckles. "That's me and Mum," a catch in Jo's voice, as she looked at the photo she hadn't seen in years. Angie watched as the young girl gently caressed her mother's face obviously deeply affected by the image. The other photo in Angie's hand was of a uniformed Stone with his arm around Jo's petite mother looking straight at the camera, not smiling just looking on guard a bit like a bodyguard does when on protection duty, handing this photo over, Jo just looked, "Oh, Dad" and began to cry.

Angie's instinct took over pulling the young girl into her arms and gently stroking her hair while Jo began to cry in earnest, "Let's sit down," leading Jo to the big double love seat where Jo folded herself into her teacher's arms and allowed comfort from someone other than family to take over for the first time in nine long years. Angie just held the girl allowing her time to get herself together, "I'm sorry I didn't know dad still had that photo; it's the last one taken before mum killed herself two weeks later, by accident we think but who knows? I was only four and Dad was away being a super soldier in some godforsaken shit hole protecting some future terrorist arsehole."

Angie heard the bitterness in Jo's voice, "Mum was training to be a doctor, always pushing herself hard to try and get through the exams; she had no family or close friends, and I was only little, wanting attention all the time and Dad wasn't home; she started taking pills to get her through the day, and pills to get her to sleep. I was being clingy when Dad was home; he was this machine that never switched off, he didn't know how to handle me, all I wanted was a cuddle." And Jo's crying renewed, "Maybe a bedtime story and tucking in, but although Dad did all the things, he was supposed to with me; he was hyper; he never let his guard down, never just my dad. Mum hid the tablets from Dad when he was home; they didn't really talk anymore; they both had their careers; the doctor who was prescribing the pills started asking Mum too many questions and the tests were getting harder and more complex, and I wanted more of Mum's time.

"She went out one night, left me with a neighbour and got some black-market pills to keep her awake. Mum started taking a couple every couple of hours to try and get through the test; she was very unhappy. She and Dad weren't talking; she had a baby she didn't want, and on her last night, I had a really bad ear infection and she hadn't been able to get some sleep so on top of the tablets she was taking, she took more than a handful of sleeping pills and I found her in the morning and she was cold and she wouldn't wake up. The coroner said they were laced with strychnine." Jo went back to being a four-year-old and reliving the moment oblivious of Angie being there. "Mum, Mum, Mummy, please wake up. Mummy, please wake up," and really started sobbing.

"Oh my," Angie said and cuddled her in tighter and rocked this precious beautiful girl.

Jo had never sat and told anyone outside of the family the circumstances of her mum's death; she pulled herself together and continued talking, "After trying to wake Mum, I went to Mrs Davidson next door, then Uncle Ike came and gave me some pills and the army got hold of my dad; he came home and we buried Mum, then Dad was home all the time and I got my dad back eventually." Angie could now understand the bond Jo had with her dad, forged from guilt and circumstance, no wonder the two of them were so close, Jo continued, "I was lucky I was only four, Ike and Granddad used to spend hours with me talking about Mum. I know now it was to get me to grieve but Dad refused all help and blamed himself, I've never seen Dad cry over Mum and no matter how hard I try, I can't get him to open up and talk about Mum, he talks, but I know, he won't or can't tell me everything, but now I have my dad, a proper Dad who has feelings, who's funny and who loves me."

"He was a super soldier doing impossible missions taking more and more risks so some politician friend could become a foe and a future terrorist to then plant a bomb and kill more innocent people; my dad is still one of the most highly trained and decorated men in the army, but he's my dad and he's not ever going to be a super soldier anymore; he's gonna stay at home and watch me grow up." Angie sat and rocked this wonderful girl; if she got to know Stone at some point, she was going to have to tell him what his daughter was truly afraid of she could not allow him to go back into the field under any circumstances it would destroy Jo, and even with the feelings she had for Stone, because she knew they were there despite all the denials her own body told her, she would not allow him to leave his daughter under any circumstances.

Angie waited until Jo had regained her composure, "You know when I'm sad, I try and think of the good things we take for granted. I mean look at that face," and pointed at Bonzo lifting his head and catching the rays of sun on his chest, hot, hot lifting one paw off the ground and then the other **maybe I should go into the shade but I'm a tan all over dog**. Angie placed the photos back onto the hooks and looked at Jo's bloodshot eyes, "Let's get cleaned up and I'll start on the dog owner lessons before your dad comes back with lunch."

"Thanks, Angie, can we keep this between us? I don't want Dad to worry."

Angie kissed Jo on the forehead; it just felt like the natural thing to do, and she wasn't even her child, "We are just two girls having a chat, men, especially dads, don't need to know what about, we should do it whenever we feel the need."

Traffic was quiet for a Saturday afternoon. Stone parking easily outside Luconi's restaurant, half-full mainly locals who knew how good the food was. Gabrielle, Mario's wife of over thirty years was handling the patrons with ease the two of them worked side by side with never a wrong word. Mario loved his wife as much as he loved his food, twenty-plus years of pasta had given them both a thickening waistline. To the surprise of both of them, their relationship had deepened when their two boys went to college; now they worked ten till five and took Sundays and Mondays off; they had enough put by after their boys' college tuition fees to even think about retiring but Mario would still cook, it was part of his Italian heritage but neither of the boys wanted to be a restaurateur, so maybe the answer was to sell the company but stay on as chef.

Stone opened the door and Gabrielle seeing who it was shrieked loudly and began speaking in super-fast Italian making a beeline through the staring patrons. Stone waited for the inevitable as Gabrielle grabbed him by the sides of his head and kissed his face, a bit like Bonzo would do, speaking Italian so fast he couldn't understand hugging her back she began to calm down as Mario appeared at the kitchen door, "Put the man down, woman, you get all my loving day and night and you still on the lookout for a replacement."

A laughing Gabrielle responded, "Man comes with muscles and a six-pack and just needs a few minutes to get it on**,**" ribbing Mario as she did every time Stone was here, she even went through the same ritual when he brought his dates/conquests. "Give the woman a kiss, Stone, it might satisfy the hussy in her then maybe you can come on back and we'll get your food sorted."

Stone gave Gabrielle a huge big kiss on the lips and she waved her hand in front of her face and cried out, "Oh my, oh my," like some badly acted porn film she even added much to the amusement of the watching patrons, anyone got a cigarette, Mario never the one to miss a line. "Honey, you don't need any more you've had five today already," and swung his hips and grabbed his crotch.

Stone got in on the action, "Well, first thing, Mario, you wash your hands," he gave Gabrielle a final kiss on each cheek Italian style and strode over to Mario and into the kitchen.

Mario was a little more sedate with his greeting merely kissing Stone hard on each cheek and grabbing him in a bear hug; even with the extra centre baggage, Mario was a formidable man and still as strong as an ox. He owed the man in front of him his life and would not accept any money for any food from Stone; he never would every time Stone had offered Mario money, Mario had just looked at him and said, "Without you, I no children, without you would not have come back home to my Gabrielle, do not insult me, my friend, you are family, family's eat for free for life." Mario had been knocked unconscious by a hidden landmine; lucky, it had been badly made and planted in haste otherwise there would have been nothing to carry. Stone had field-dressed the wound and slung him over his shoulder oblivious to his own weakened state due to shrapnel stuck in his thigh, carrying Mario from enemy ground for over twenty-four hours with no food and very little water. Mario had recovered in the field hospital with no problems except for the time it took to recover. Gabrielle used to say his memory wasn't what it was, but that was just to playfully rib her husband. Stone had taken longer to recover after contracting septicaemia and the shrapnel had to be very carefully removed as it was millimetres from the femoral artery, but as Mario used to point out it was a good way to get his kit off in front of the ladies.

"I'm sorry, Stone, I didn't know you should have used a code word or something letting me run off in the mouth like that and Angie Sanders, of all people," Mario looked closely at Stone, he said and pulling open the kitchen door, "you got a sec, Gabby."

"Yeah sure, just don't keep me too long, I don't want anyone sneaking off without paying." Stone looked puzzled as both came into the kitchen and Mario quickly explained the phone call order and who was on the boat while Gabrielle kept her eyes concentrated on Stone, then clapped her hands with joy, "Yes, Mario, you are 100% correct."

Stone was now completely stumped, "What the hell are you two on about?"

"Well, my friend, I'm not going to spoil your surprise," and Stone wondered if perhaps his friend had received more damage than shrapnel. Changing the subject, Mario asked about Jo, and Stone filled him in about Bonzo and Mario very quietly said, "Getting Jo her own dog would give her something else to love as well because she watched after her dad far too closely." Stone thought this had been one strange day, he hugged Mario, grabbed up the food, including the huge watermelon, kissed Gabrielle on the way out, who gently held both his hands and said, "You are the finest man I know, Justin Travis Stone, you deserve happy ever after, after everything you have done for your country and your friends, whatever happens just let it," and Stone thought the day just got even stranger; it was like getting your future read only by a couple of ageing Italians instead of the show ground fortune tellers.

Bonzo saw his master and the girl appear from the galley doorway with his harness and realised it was walk time, **oh great, not the usual area so there'd be new smells to investigate maybe he could have another swim with the big strong man then it would be time for some food and as he wasn't at home so it wouldn't be kibble maybe he'd get a treat some of that human food meat in a bun as long his master takes that awful green thing out, he didn't mind the red stuff covering the meat but the green thing would be spat out and buried.**

Putting on his harness while telling Jo, "This is quite important; when you get your pup one of the first things you will have to do is get him or her used to a full harness; when he grows up, he/she will be super strong and easily capable of pulling you off your feet, most dogs hate being covered up especially anything touching their backs so from the day you get your dog you have to put his/her harness on, when your dogs a pup he/she is like a baby and this is the time you must teach him or her, they learn very quickly so you also have to teach them who's the master," eyeing Bonzo. "I don't think that lesson worked with this huge beast it's still a work in progress and he's three." Bonzo harness sat on Angie's left side tail wagging and body shaking ready, "He's actually being quite good today; he's probably realised it's the weekend and he gets extra time with me instead of being stuck in the house and garden with his toys and having to amuse himself while I'm at school. That's the other thing that's very important, Jo, dogs are pack animals, they don't like being alone for any length of time; you must get them used to you not being there all the time from the puppy stage. When you get your dog, you're going to want to be with it 24/7, but you can't; that bit is very hard on you and your dog, but you must do it.

"Most dogs that chew are basically fretting because all of a sudden they are on their own and they start to panic. You start by leaving your dog on its own for a short time, stay out of sight in the same house and listen; if you have enough toys for your dog to play with, and bedding with both your scents on, some background music so it's never completely quiet, fresh water and dried food plus a way for your dog to get in and out then your dog has sufficient input from all these things to be able to be left alone. Also, you must tell your dog they are getting left, when they understand the command that they are being left they don't tend to fret then you gradually increase the time apart. Jo, it's very hard to do, but you must get it right, imagine if your dad just left you, no warning just wasn't there, now we as humans can communicate, you'd just phone and say where you at, a dog cannot do that they totally rely on their master, you have to learn to be a good responsible master at the same time your teaching your dog."

Jo was thinking over what Angie had said, "It's a pity, us humans don't have the same classes then maybe some kids wouldn't feel abandoned." Angie was stuck once again by how perceptive Jo was. Bonzo was itching to get moving but hadn't received instruction from his master so he rocked backwards and forwards on the spot which when thick set and over ten stone looked like a wobbling jelly. Jo looked down at Bonzo, who looked at her then at Angie. "See, he's impatient but he's not pulling on his lead just doing his. I'm in the starting blocks move waiting for me to say, 'Come on, Bonzo'," and he stood to heal now doing his shaky side to side standing on the same spot move. Jo made sure everything was off and grabbed her phone and sent her dad a text 'Have gone out for a walk with Bonzo and Angie text when you're on your way back and we'll meet you back at the boat xx.'

"I've let Dad know we're out walking cos sometimes when he gets with Uncle Mario, they're like two old clucking hens."

"Is Mario your uncle?"

Thinking that's where Stone might have got his dark complexion from, "No, he's just a very close ex-army buddy, he says dad carried him for over 24 hours through enemy territory with shrapnel in his leg. I asked Dad he just said, 'You never leave a man behind,' and showed me his scar which is here." Jo touched the very top of her front leg. "You can't really see it anymore cos of all the muscle you have to get very close." Angie's rebelling body let her know what it thought of this information. The three of them arrived at the big green a couple of minutes walk from the boat where a few people were walking a few smaller dogs without leads, Angie looked to Jo, "Bonzo's been asleep for a couple of hours, what do you think he'll need to do?" And deftly produced the poop bags.

Jo groaned, "If you're a lucky girl and your dog has eaten well, you're going to get a nice big pile that you can hold your breath and pick up and drop in one of those dog litter bins you see dotting about, but if your dog has been sneaking treats from school children in your street," Bonzo looked up having heard his name mentioned, "yes, I'm talking about you, big boy," looking at Bonzo who knew by the tone of voice she was telling the girl about something naughty he'd done, "then food that he shouldn't have had does wonders to a dog's stomach and you'll get a splattering to pick up. They are definitely not fun and you'll need to learn to hold your breath for quite a long time, what you must always do is clean up after your dog even if it's a right mess; just do the best you can." Angie removed Bonzo's harness and bolted off towards the trees, Angie handed the bags to Jo, "Do you want to do the honours?" with a twinkle in her eye and off they went after Bonzo, Jo silently praying Bonzo hadn't had any extra treats.

Stone's phone buzzed as he was about to set off and he read his daughter's message; seeing the two kisses, and hoping she would always send kisses after her texts, still pondering what the hell Mario and Gabrielle had been on about, he set off trying to keep his mind on the road and not Angie Sanders. Texting his daughter that he was back, he began shuffling the food onto the boat, his mouth salivating at the smell of food, having a wry smile as he picked up the huge watermelon. Jo looked down at her phone pleased to have got rid of the smelly offering from Bonzo, 'Food's here,' as Angie put Bonzo's harness back on, felt the excitement of seeing Stone stirring inside her plus fine food and this wonderful girl made her feel happier than she had for a long time. Jo texted, 'Back two minutes, Dad xx.'

Stone began laying out the food already neatly packed into plastic picnic containers, which he would return to Mario on his next visit, remembering Angie's touch as he got three bottles of frosted water out of the fridge and ran some fresh water into Bonzo's bowl. Stone saw them coming back, the big black dog happily shuffling along beside Angie, with her arm around his daughter happily talking away unaware of being watched; he took a moment to put this image into his memory bank, his daughter didn't do touchy-feely with anyone but family; the fact that she allowed Angie to put her arm around her meant that she was completely comfortable with that person; the fact that she was the first female since Gemma died was not lost on Stone, then he looked at Angie and couldn't take his eyes off her; in fact, she was a stunning looking woman, but laughing and carefree, she was just a different class, it finally hit him what Mario and Gabrielle had been twittering about. As he took in the sight of Angie, he realised he wanted her to be in his life; he couldn't and wouldn't go back to the Stone of old; his true feelings no longer dormant couldn't be held back even if he had wanted to try.

Six

Bonzo was the first to lift his head and sniff **oh, something smells really yummy** as they approached the boat, his keen sense of smell telling him something good awaited and the dreaded kibble was just going to sit in his bowl at home. **How can I get some of that maybe he could persuade the big man with his paw begging trick that nearly always worked on master.** Jo still deep in conversation with Angie laughed at something Angie said as she climbed up first into the boat. Angie ruffled Jo's hair as she climbed up followed by Bonzo, Stone saw the connection between his daughter and Angie had become more than friendly and hoped that his connection to Angie would do the same; it was a wonderful sight to behold; the obvious affection between his daughter and his what he thought, what do I want her to mean for me, and then Angie looked up into Stone's eyes and he knew it was everything.

    Jo kissed her dad on the lips, "Dad, there are some not-so-cool parts to having a dog," and went off to wash her hands. Angie watching the kiss knew for Stone and Jo that it was completely normal and having had the chat with Jo, she totally understood. It might be frowned upon when Jo got a bit older, but for now,, it was a reminder to them both to never take each other for granted; how Angie ached to be part of this family. It never entered her head that Stone would be feeling the same. She had no ego, most days she took what life threw at her and accepted her fate but looking into Stone's eyes, she realised it wasn't enough anymore. Bonzo was looking from Angie to Stone to the food on the table and back again. "I think the big guy is hungry, Ang," shortening her name, something so simple yet it made such a difference to her.

"Well, if I let him, he would clean the table, but he's been a good boy and he doesn't really care for kibble; it is only chicken so maybe if we have enough and you have an old dish, we can let him have a treat."

I think I'm in here and pulled his face into his most impressive I'm a good boy who deserves feeding look, **nailed it.** Angie handed the harness to Jo saying, "Whatever you do, do not let him anywhere near the table, I'm going to wash my hands" and walked into the galley with Stone's eyes firmly planted on her sublime rear. Jo a few hours ago would have berated her dad; instead, she just held onto Bonzo. Stone passed Angie the old bowl he'd found and she took Bonzo's harness off pointing to the bowl, "Young man, this is going to be full of chicken scraps; all you have to do is be a good boy," instructing Bonzo to 'lie down' and taking her seat next to Jo. Bonzo did a super-fast calculation in his head **be good equals a bowl of food easy-peasy** and lay down awaiting his feast as the humans tucked into Luconi's prepared meal. Jo thought she was on a roll now.

"Dad, don't forget to eat your watermelon."

"Josephine Roseanne Stone, you think you're such a funny girl," and winked at Angie.

The music stopped so Stone walked into the galley and stuck on Pink Floyd turning the volume down a little so it could be heard but they could talk, taking his seat to the opening bars of the classic homage to Syd Barrett, 'Shine on You Crazy Diamond.' Angie smiled at Stone, "Total class," she said.

"I have 'Pulse' on Blue Ray at home, they don't move about much, but the effects and the music are brilliant," Stone said.

"I've got Gilmour at Gdansk the version of 'comfortably numb' and 'echoes' are mind-blowing especially very loud and on a big screen plus Richard Wright's last performance before he died."

Jo piped in, "Dad's got this TV and sound system that cost more than a new jaguar and these huge comfy chairs, he used to have a popcorn machine in the corner, but then he hit thirty-five and couldn't maintain 8% body fat easily," gently ribbing her dad.

Stone looked at his daughter, "It wasn't me who ate all the popcorn, the little fatty over there used to guzzle two or three boxes every time she watched one of her chick flicks and for your information, Josephine Roseanne Stone, my body fat is 8% year round and when I was fighting in competitions, it was around 4% but I don't have to do that anymore."

"You don't compete anymore, Justin Travis Stone, because there's nobody left to beat, you've either beat or scared them away and as you reminded me, Daddy, you're not a young man anymore."

Angie just looked at Stone, "Your parents named you Justin Travis, no wonder you learnt to fight and everyone calls you Stone or J T and Roseanne is a lovely middle name, it was my mam's?"

"Was," said Stone, "yes, mam died six years ago from lung cancer; it was long and painful and a blessing when she went. I try to not get bitter and twisted but mam was a good person, why would an all-loving God put someone through that." Stone and Jo didn't have an answer and then Stone suddenly realised why Angie had talked so openly about her mam. Jo must have talked to Angie about Gemma, so she was letting his daughter know in her own way that losing someone was just a part of life and then realised that the song playing held a special meaning for Angie as David Gilmour sang 'Remember When You Were Young, You Shone Like the Sun'.

Clearing away, they all pulled what was left of the chicken into the bowl for Bonzo, who realising it was time for his feed started huffing and puffing **feed me feed me** as he stood and watched next to Angie, "Just put a little bit of pasta in with it, Jo, please and no sauces remember I told you what would happen."

"Yes, we don't want that happening, do we?"

"Another lesson for you, Jo, proper dog feeding is important, you have to get a very excited and hungry dog to wait patiently and then not bolt his food down because if he does, chances are it will come right back up again. As your dog gets older, he gets used to your commands when it's just a pup you have to watch closely, now Bonzo here will demonstrate perfectly."

"Ok boy, food time," and Bonzo moved back and sat to create space tail wagging **yes, it's all mine** and began to stroke his head gently watching the dog intently, **yes, yes come to Papa, delicious, yummy, yummy**. Angie turned to Jo and passed her the bowl, "You can feed him, all you do is put the bowl in front of him, take a step back and issue the command," and turned to whisper in Jo's ear, "Eat," then while he is eating, stroke the top of his head keeping the touch gentle and loving, he doesn't want to think you are going to take his food off him; he just wants to know you're there.

"Sometimes especially, a young pup, they eat too fast and choke on their food. Bonzo hasn't done that for a while but a young pup will, I'll show you what to do when that occasion arises, when he starts to eat his food if you think he's going too fast just issue, the command," turning to Jo and whispering, "slow down, but you do it with a firm voice and when he's finished eating, you just tell him good boy and point him to his water bowl, then 30 minutes later, you need to walk him. With puppies, you're going to have lots of little accidents until you both get the timing right. Are you ready?"

Jo nodded and placed the bowl on the floor, stepped back looked at Bonzo, "Eat" and began to stroke his head gently watching the dog intently, "Yes, yes come to Papa, delicious yummy yummy." What she missed was her father take Angie's hand and caressing it with so much feeling it was impossible to miss the meaning. Angie returned the touch in spades by gently stroking Stone's hand with her thumb. Bonzo had finished his food been told good boy and was now bathing his face in the water much to the delight of Jo who turned round to pass comment only to see her dad and teacher holding hands and gazing at each other.

Stone reluctantly let go of Angie's hand, displaying affection was not something he was used to showing other than with his daughter and his very close friends, yes, it came naturally with Jo now but it had taken the death of his wife, a step down from combat and several years of gentle prodding from his daughter, dad, and Ike. With Angie Sanders, it had taken hours, even with Gemma, it had taken months to feel this comfortable. If he were being totally truthful with himself, he hadn't felt anything at all the last three years of his marriage, everyone blamed always having to be combat-ready but once Jo was born, they both changed; he'd felt his marriage was over there was no longer a spark. Stone had wanted combat because basically, he didn't want to be home. With Angie Sanders, he felt complete, he needed to be in soldier mode, analyse the situation, and control his spiralling emotions he must try and get the one thing back that he'd never lost before, control.

Jo grabbed a towel for Bonzo's face and gently removed the excess water thinking about her dad and teacher; he didn't just want sex, even at nearly thirteen, Jo knew how his dad treated his conquests and she had never seen him like this; she looked up at Angie, her teacher smiling. Jo wondered what she could do; she wanted her dad to be happy. Angie tingled all over from Stone's touch; it didn't feel like a game to get her into bed; it certainly wasn't on her part. She didn't have very much sexual experience; she liked sex and didn't just lie there, but got involved; however, there were lots of things she didn't dare try. There were a lot of things she'd asked herself about previous relationships, she'd never tried or been given oral sex always wanting to try, but never felt comfortable enough to give or receive.

Had she ever been truly in love and willing to give herself completely? No, she thought, did she know what an orgasm felt like, she thought of the five men she had slept with in her lifetime; shit Ang you're thirty-four, there are sixteen-year-olds with more notches on the bedpost, three had lasted less than a month and were grope, fumble and get the condom on wham thank you, was it good for you? Shit, the other two were longer term but both inexperienced lovers leaving her disappointed, but Justin Travis Stone, he would get everything, there was no way on earth she was going to tell Stone what she was feeling; she'd wait for him to make a move, then what Angie thought, and then she'd give him anything he wanted, the thought shocked her to her core she wasn't like this as a person but here she was she glanced over at Stone as she stood to put Bonzo's harness on and she knew how she felt when he looked back and smiled.

Needing to get a grip on herself, Angie said to Jo, "You want to walk him, your dog will be a lot smaller but will grow to Bonzo's size if you get a boy and girls are not much smaller, and I'd like some girl time with my favourite pupil." Angie needed time away from Stone to give her a chance to get herself together; she also needed to speak to Jo privately. It was only mid-afternoon "I'm going to clean up and get one of Dad's fishing rods out sit on the deck and do some fishing, and yes, Jo, I'll put anything I catch back in alive with no damage I promise," and crossed his heart.

Jo walked up to and kissed him on the lips, "I love you, Dad."

"I love you too, sweetheart," and gave Jo a hug, "Take your phone and take all the time you need, make sure a dog is really what you want it's a big decision even for a super intelligent beautiful almost teenager," and Stone put his fingers in her hair and kissed the top of her head. Angie had been getting Bonzo ready making sure she had poop bags and little doggies' treats and didn't want to intrude on father/daughter time. "Ang, you got a minute before you go," Angie passed the lead to a perplexed Jo.

"Just keep a hold of him a minute Jo as long as he knows he's going for a walk, he'll be ok," Jo beamed and took Bonzo off the boat to wait for Angie.

Stone unsure what he was going to say but needing to say something looked at Angie with his piercing beautiful blue eyes then he spoke quietly so his daughter would not overhear, "Ang, I would really like to get to know you better, I know my reputation precedes me, I'm not the person people assume, I want you to know…" Stopping he took hold of both of Angie's hands, aware his daughter and Bonzo were waiting, he continued, "This" and he looked at their intertwined hands, "this," he said again, "this is what I want," and he gently kissed her on the lips; their first kiss was devastating in its effect on both of them; for Angie, no man had ever had such a profound effect on her, and for Stone, contentment now he had said what he wanted out loud.

Angie walked down the steps; Jo looked at her, "We really need to talk."

"Yes, yes, we do" and they turned and waved goodbye. Bonzo now the centre of attention felt he should always be walking with his pack mates; **I wonder what time the squirrels in this area started moving hoping they liked a chase as much as he did.** Angie found a quiet park bench with a lovely view of the river and Bonzo took off after some squirrels giving them a fair head start. Angie took Jo's hand and looked at her directly "I said I would never lie to you; I know you saw me and your dad. I know you love your dad and want what's best for him, I don't want to get between you and I don't know what the future holds but I am absolutely certain that I want to be part of his life and yours very much yours too, Jo."

"My dad is not a normal dad, he's seen and done things few people have, when Mum died, his priorities changed, he had me to bring up; there's only been him and me in our house for nine years. Ike says I need a dog for myself to love, I'm way too intense, always watching my dad too closely to see if he slips back into super soldier mode, he said if I share my love between Dad and my dog, it would allow my dad to have space and perhaps build a life that involved more than just me. I want my own dog and I want Dad to be really happy instead of pretending, he doesn't fool me by saying things are ok, we do the quizzes, and he does his rock god thing, I know he loves me, and I love him, but he needs someone to love him as an adult and my dad really likes you, and you really like him, I saw you kissing. You had your eyes closed, it looked different to when Dad kisses me. What was it like?"

"It was wonderful," and she kissed Jo on her brow, "and so are you."

Bonzo had found some new friends to chase **huh they don't quite understand the game they bolt as soon as they hear me approach, and he was sure he was being his normal stealthy self** but these squirrels just sniffed the change of air and took off he had no chance of catching up with them they even separated and ran up different trees they were no fun! So, he trotted back to his owner and the young girl. He'd sniffed out the treats in his master's pocket, he'd last eaten over two hours ago, **maybe if I do the one-leg begging thing along with the cute eyes, she might give me some treats.** Bonzo sat directly in front of Angie and did his academy act, Angie looked down at him turned to Jo and said, "See, this is what you have to get used to the standard of begging gets better as they get older," and Bonzo thought **I'm in here** and did a final extra cute side to side face moves with the eye roll, **and the Oscar goes to**, as Angie took out a handful of chocolate doggie chocks his favourite treat, treats scoffed he sat down between Angie's feet content might have a little snooze he thought and closed his eyes with a big sigh.

Angie said, "Right, young lady, you've seen how Bonzo behaves, decision time, are you really positively certain you want to take on a dog?"

Without any hesitation, Jo answered, "YES."

"The next big question, boy or girl puppy, boys are bigger, but more of a handful, girls are more loyal, but you have to be super cautious twice a year when they come into heat plus it can get really messy, buggers can't put pads on!"

"I want a boy then. Bonzo can teach him his cool tricks and my dog can learn to be a good boy like him." Bonzo who had been drifting off to sleep on hearing his name looked up at Angie and Jo thinking **they were talking about me**, did a quick eye roll that he knew was cute and returned to his nap. "Boy, it is and I just happen to know where there are some six-week-old puppies and in two weeks they will be looking for someone to love them and take them home, you know anyone that fits that description?"

Jo thought she'd burst with excitement, "Yes me, me, and me."

"Do you think your dad will let you have your present a bit early," already knowing the answer, Stone would do anything for his daughter the intensity of their love went both ways. "Could you make yourself available tomorrow around lunchtime?" And Jo nodded her head, "Right, tomorrow stick on some old clothes and we'll go and pick out your dog," and Jo launched herself into Angie's arms, "Thank you, thank you, thank you," and Angie sat with Jo in her arms and

Bonzo sleeping under her feet and felt a contentment with life she knew where she belonged. All she had to do now was ring the Stephenson and tell them she wanted a male pup from the litter produced by the big beast at her feet as her payment for stud fees.

Jo was buzzing with excitement, as they returned to the boat. Stone had the fishing rod over the side but was lying on the deck chair wearing just his cut-offs and Ray-Bans soaking up the rays, hands behind his head tapping his feet along to whatever rock classic came on his MP3 shuffle, Jo thought Dad looks relaxed, Angie looking down at his chiselled physique Stone lifted his glasses and winked at Angie, "Come on, tell me when, where and what he or she is going to cost me," not even trying to negotiate he'd seen the look in his daughters face it didn't matter about cost he just wanted the look to continue for at least another thirty years.

"Well, I want a boy dog and Angie is going to take me tomorrow to choose him, she knows where there are some puppies waiting for homes, but they're going to their new homes in less than two weeks, so I'd like my present early please, Dad."

Angie explained to Stone about the agreement she had with the Stephenson's.

Angie bent down to put on Bonzo's harness acutely aware that she didn't want to go home, but he wanted his tea, and she wanted a nice long bubble bath. "Jo, give me your number and I'll ring you when I'm on my way to pick you up," Jo walked over and gave Bonzo a hug and then she turned into Angie's arms, "Thank you," Angie kissed her on her head saying, "you are very welcome, my angel," turning to Stone, "are you going to put a shirt on and walk me to my car?"

Stone went into the cabin returning wearing a new crisp white t-shirt that clung to his muscular frame, and turned to his daughter. "I won't be long," walked off towards the car, as they reached her little Toyota Angie opened the tailgate Stone looked at the mess, thinking 'Jesus what's Jo's dog going to do to my Discovery' as Bonzo jumped in and made himself comfortable having a sneaky look for that mislaid chew stick, Angie opened her door, saying you have my number ring me.

Stone couldn't just let her go and took her in his arms not concerned one iota that it was broad daylight and they were in a public place and kissed her properly for the first time, no hesitation from either of them mouths open tongues meshing together, somebody walking past shouted 'get a room' but they just remained locked together. When the kiss ended, they both just looked at each other, well, you sure know how to kiss thought Angie, feeling every nerve of her body on fire and got in the car. Stone closed her door giving her a gentle kiss on the lips and watched her drive away. As he returned to the boat, seeing his face his daughter said, "Don't worry, Dad you'll see her at lunchtime tomorrow," then her face full of mischief said, "And if you can't wait till tomorrow, you can always ring her tonight."

Angie couldn't concentrate on driving home and pulled into the first lay-by to clear her head, Jesus, she thought she'd kissed really kissed a man she hardly knew not only that but if his daughter hadn't been on the boat she'd have gone back to the boat and let him fuck her till she screamed, her panties were wet and her nipples were rock-hard, her lips where he'd kissed her ached, her breathing was still too fast even Bonzo had his head up checking if she was ok, she pulled out her phone and rang Stone, "Ang, what's up? You ok?" He answered on the first ring, "I'm sorry, I had to ring, I've pulled over I don't care if you think I'm easy I've never been kissed like that in my life, I still haven't got my breath back, I don't care how sudden it is, I just had to let you know what effect you've had on me."

Stone chuckled "Ang darling, if that's what one kiss will do, imagine what I'll do when I get you alone."

Stone meant it to sound blasé but he hadn't pulled it off his voice had cracked with emotion which Angie had heard, "What are we doing, Stone?"

"I have no idea, Ang, but there's nothing either of us can do about it. Ang, drive safe I'll ring you later." Angie started the car, checked her mirrors, and pulled into the traffic.

Stone locked up the boat and with Jo riding pillion he drove carefully back home, "What ya fancy for tea, young lady?"

As he walked into the kitchen, "Those fresh steaks and low-fat oven chips sound good, Dad." After their evening meal, they decided to check out Netflix in the cinema room, "Your choice tonight, what's your fancy?"

"I don't know, Dad, I'll have a scroll down the list one thing I do know is it won't be a rom-com!"

Seven

Back home, Angie opened the back door just in case Bonzo needed out and went into the kitchen to prepare his meat and kibble; she wasn't that hungry and couldn't be bothered to cook anything extravagant so she settled for a mozzarella cheese omelette with added chia seeds, turmeric, and black pepper. She'd eaten four bread buns at lunch as they were freshly made and still warm and were delicious so she'd do without the carbs tonight. She was careful what she ate, thinking while eating her omelette that it was a good choice, *after all, I must look my best now, I may be getting naked with a man soon* and blushed to herself.

Picking up her phone, she rang the Stephenson. Mark and his wife Lynn had been breeding mastiffs for the last five or six years; they'd had many litters and currently had three breeding bitches; surprisingly they struggled to get the male stud dogs they needed from within the local area. Angie or more rightly Bonzo had been a godsend, his pedigree was impeccable; each pup could fetch up to £2500 and the average litter produced eight pups, and sometimes up to sixteen. Angie didn't want to be there to watch the lining, absolutely no way, so she'd taken Bonzo and told him he was going to have a very special treat and would collect him in three days.

Angie's recollection of collecting Bonzo was reminiscent of a teenage boy losing his virginity; he'd strutted around the house for days; she was so pleased dogs couldn't speak. The conversation with Mark traumatised Angie enough, 'we introduced young Bonzo here tapping him on the head to Suzie, she had one litter last year that gave us nine pups six bitches and three dogs so we knew she was OK with doing the deed, they had a bit sniff of each other no signs of aggression from either dog.' Bonzo rose to the occasion magnificently and rather swiftly they coupled within thirty minutes of the meeting, the donation that Bonzo gave rather happily was received successfully by Suzie, the second day and the third day were both resounding success if the matting was a success, we should see signs of pregnancy from Suzie in around thirty days and she should produce her litter between fifty-six and sixty-six days from conceiving. Angie could not look at Bonzo when he came back from his stud weekend now strutting around the house like the dog version of a gigolo.

"Hi, Mark, it is Angie Sanders; how are those beautiful puppies?"

"All fit and well, bit of a handful for Mum being eleven of them, we're having to keep an eye that they all get some food but they're six weeks now so we're starting the bigger ones on puppy food, Mum's getting really tired, poor girl, you coming down to choose your pup then?"

"I am; I have a very special girl who wants a boy dog. I personally vouch for her. She's Colonel Stone's daughter Jo and she wants a dog for her thirteenth birthday on 16 July but we can take the dog at eight weeks, no problem, I'm going to school her with Bonzo and I'll be taking her for obedience classes and I'll be hands-on with her dog," knowing Mark and Lynn would need to know about any new owner.

"When do you want to come down, Angie?"

"I've arranged to pick Jo up tomorrow around noon so I'll be there around one."

"No problem, Bonzo's next stud session should be at the end of August with Grace. I'll buzz you when she starts her season and given the last successful coupling, you should get another pick of the litter, either way, you'll have a happy dog in Bonzo. I'll see you around one tomorrow." Angie looked at Bonzo pleased that he couldn't understand the conversation but mentally preparing herself for another week of strutting in late September or early October should super stud do the business again.

Bonzo stood shaking from side to side while Angie put on his harness ready for his evening walk, checking for treats and poop bags. "Ok, big guy, no stealing treats if the boys are out playing and please if you're going to crap wait until we reach the forest." They reached a few minutes later, taking his harness off and telling him to be good he took off to find his little friends, **they knew how to play the game he thought.**

Angie deep in thought decided not to overthink, just go with it, lie back, and enjoy it having a small chuckle to herself at the great play on words.

Up ahead, she could hear a conversation getting louder the closer she got. It was still relatively light and she knew a lot of the older kids came to the forest to smoke dope, meet their friends or try and catch a feel of their latest girl/boyfriend so she wasn't unduly concerned until she overheard the same aggressive voice from last night. "Listen, you fucking dumb little bastard, you will do what the fuck you are told," and she heard a loud slap and a cry of pain, "I told your ball-less friends the same fucking thing one hundred pills each £5 a pop and you walk away with £100; do the maths, you dumb cunt, £100 easy and you have over five hundred potential customers. We've added a little extra; makes them more addictive, so you see numb nuts, potential to make more than pocket money."

Angie was frightened she had overheard the thug and didn't know whether to shout for Bonzo or try and hide when a voice behind said, "Well, look see what we have here, nice legs and that arse mm like to get my head into those sweet cheeks then fuck you."

"BONZO," as loud as she could. Bonzo who had never heard his master's voice as frightened did what he had originally been bred for and went into protection mode bounding out of the tree's hackles raised to protect master from harm **nobody hurts her while I'm here**, teeth barred, ten-stone-plus of pure fighting fury, "Fuck me" the voice said and ran in the opposite direction. The voice she'd heard the previous night then said, "It's a big fucking dog, you moron, it's not a fucking bear, it's a fucking dog and it's pissed off, let's get the fuck out of here," and the woods went quiet.

Angie gently stroked Bonzo who gradually calmed down from attack mode and shaking badly they walked out of the woods towards home, what the fuck was happening in the quiet little village. None of the usual kids were out, just as well as she was really shaken up, trying hard to calm herself so that Bonzo would calm down, she knew he could sense her fear and until she got it under control he would remain on high alert. Having originally been bred as an attack dog but never having seen him in that mode, she was very aware she had to calm down otherwise her wonderful happy boy might regress to his original programming.

There was only one person she could ring; the fact that it was a man she had known less than twenty-four hours was not lost on her. Ringing Stone and stroking Bonzo and she told him what had happened in the woods over the last two days; he went very quiet when she told him what the thug behind her said, "Give me ten minutes, I have a good friend in the police, I'll ring you back." He would ring Detective Inspector Mike Bishop on his personal mobile, they'd become good friends after Stone had set up self-defence classes for the Yorkshire police force. The army lent out their best hand-to-hand combat fighters and the police let the army collect their younger members after too much to drink rather than lock them in with the normal civilians. It was a rule that off barracks they carry their warrant card and if a drunk and disorderly arrest was made, the barracks were called, possibly saving their careers.

Dialling Mike Bishop's number, who answered after a few rings, "Stone, nice to hear from you, been a while, your lot have been on their best behaviour, could be cos you scare the fuckers."

"Not me personally, Bish," resorting to the man's nickname, "army just come up with a new fine scheme, drunk and disorderly costs a month's wages, no excuses."

Bishop replied, "Yep, I can see how that would work, all those go faster cars sat on drives cos they can't afford to put fuel in them. What's up? You wouldn't ring my mobile on a Saturday evening just to set up some more of your dance classes."

"No, I need you to take a statement from someone on the quiet if you can, Bish, as a favour to me and then put the feelers out, there's been no offence committed except threatening behaviour, but she's pretty shaken up."

Bish knew the man never asked for favours so he knew this was important to him but couldn't resist a dig, "This one must be pretty special, do you get laid if you get help?"

"No Bish, this lady is very special."

"Ok, Stone, not a problem, Brenda's watching some shit on TV anyway; give me the address."

Stone realised he didn't know Angie's address, "I'll ring you back in five," and killed the connection.

Angie picked up on the first ring. "Give me your address."

"Why?"

"I've rang that friend in the police; he's going to come out now and take your statement, its unofficial nothing on record because nothing happened, but I'm not taking any chances."

"Ah, it's 23 Bellevue."

"I'll ring him; he'll be with you in 20 minutes. I'll grab Jo and we'll see you soon."

"You don't have to come over. I'm a big girl you've done enough listening and getting someone to take my statement."

"Ang, I need to see you in the flesh; I want to make sure you ok." Angie didn't know what to say, he obviously cared for her it wasn't an act and she wanted, no needed him to hold her, too fast thought Angie but said OK anyway.

Returning to the cinema room, Jo saw her dad's face filled with tension, "What's up Dad?"

"I must see Angie there's been an incident in the woods, she's OK just she and Bonzo are both shaken up, I've rang Bish he's going to meet us there."

"I'll get our jackets."

"Thanks, sweetheart," and rang Bishop with Angie's address.

Stone and Jo arrived before Bishop. Angie saw the bike pull on her drive and told Bonzo to sit and that the people who were coming to the house were friends. Angie opened the door and was immediately encircled in Stone's arms which were exactly what she wanted and needed. Jo was the first to speak, "Are you and Bonzo ok?" Totally OK seeing her teacher in her dad's arms. Bonzo seeing his two new friends waged his tail but with more restraint than normal, and Jo sat down next to him talking gently, "Thanks, Jo, that's exactly what he needs."

"Stone, you want coffee? Jo, you want a diet coke?"

"Yes," in unison. Angie's living room was all modern furniture, a nice snug, warm room with a 42" TV and a very expensive B and O sound system but what made the room special where the walls, everyone full of Led Zeppelin artwork and in pride of place was a huge framed print of their 1975 Earl's Court stage show, signed by all the members of the band, "Wow," said Stone.

"My dad originally got me into them and I inherited a lot of this stuff when he died, less than a year after mam, doctors couldn't tell what had killed him, but I know after spending nearly forty years with mam the way she went just destroyed him," Angie thoughtfully caressed the picture, and walked into the kitchen to get the drinks.

Bonzo barked at the knock on the door. Stone said, "That'll be Bish; I'll get the front door."

Angie said "Jo, think you can look after Bonzo for me? I'll put the patio lights on; his toys are out there, he's very protective of me right now and I don't want to upset him anymore, he needs distracting by a pretty girl." Outside Bonzo thought **Great, master seems calmer now mermaid man is here, and I get extra play and with young girl**. Angie pulled the patio door stroking Jo's hair as she passed. Angie could hear a voice deeper than Stone's talking and after some back-slapping, the men walked through into her living room both built like tanks; the new arrival was taller than Stone by a couple of inches, wider and thicker set, with kind eyes and he was jet-black. "Thanks for doing this, Bish, this is Angie Sanders, Ang, Detective Inspector Mike Bishop, Bish to everyone who knows him."

Bish stuck out his hand and Angie's looked tiny in his massive paw, "Pleased to meet you, Angie." Bish looked at the walls studying the artwork, "Great taste in music, Angie, you've got some rare stuff on those walls."

"I was telling Stone that Dad was the original fanatic, I inherited all of his collection though I've added a few pieces of my own." Bonzo had been happily playing with Jo when he looked up to see his master, new friend and another huge man, **wow he's the same colour as me, I need an introduction** putting his head against the plastic and drooling down the window. Angie seeing Bonzo and Jo turned to Bish. "My dog is fascinated by you, are you OK with dogs?" Bishop nodded, "Big dogs don't frighten me only Stone does that," looking round at the huge dog and a girl standing next to him, "Stone that's never Jo."

"Yep, it is." As soon as the doors were open, Jo squealed and jumped into Bishop's arms, who swept her up with one arm while the other stroked Bonzo on the head. "Been a long time, little girl, who's not so little anymore, you have been drinking your dad's protein powder?" Putting Jo down, he turned to give Bonzo his full attention who started licking his face, **could be paint I'll keep licking and see if he changes colour.**

"This is Bonzo I'm so pleased he was with me tonight." Introductions done, Angie asked the detective if he wanted coffee, and he said yes, and she went off to get them all a coffee. "Jo, you want a diet coke?"

"Yes please, Angie." Bonzo still licking decided **the colour is real, must be purebred, I'm doing really well with new friends at the moment.**

Angie returned with three coffees in pint mugs and a diet coke which Stone raised an eyebrow at Jo, "Told you, Dad, it tastes nice, its calorie-free, and yep, it is full of artificial sweeteners."

Angie smiled, "Not this one, it has natural stevia instead, bit more expensive though."

"We'll have to get some. Dad, make a change from the lemon and lime."

Stone pulled the tab took a slurp, "You may be right, it is quite good," and handed Jo the can.

"Jo, can you take Bonzo back outside while I talk to the Detective Inspector and your dad? I don't want him upset anymore tonight, there's a water bowl and water hose in the shed he'll be thirsty with all the excitement, thank you."

Stone passed around the coffee, "Good, proper coffee I like mine black like myself, see Stone no added sugar, only took me three months to kick the habit." Both men appreciated the flavour. "Brenda has me on yet another diet, you need to come to the house."

"Bish, lift some iron." Bish took out his pen and notebook and asked Angie to tell him what had happened in the woods and she recalled the events of the last two nights. Bish was gentle with his questions, "You recognised the two lads that went passed you on Friday night?"

"Yes, Barry Jackson and Tommy Bowman both 16, I take them in my class on Tuesdays and Thursdays."

"You didn't see any of the others, especially the one who was doing the talking?"

"No."

"What about tonight?"

"No, I was still too far away, but I'd recognise the voices if I heard them again, especially the bastard that sneaked behind me." Stone sitting next to Angie stroked her hand at that statement; Bishop raised his eyebrows and looked at Stone gazing at Angie, and looked at the hardest man he knew who was looking at this woman like she was the love of his life, not that Bishop would say anything to Stone but the person who had threatened his woman better have found a rock to crawl under, Stone was a great friend but as an enemy well there was only one outcome. "Do you think they can recognise you, Angie?"

"No, Barry Jackson and Tommy Bowman didn't see me. They may have seen Bonzo' I know the one doing the talking and the one behind me did."

"Um, so if they have a few brain cells they may canvas the area looking for Bonzo and in turn you. Sounds like they're getting ready to flood the area with drugs since we got the last lot from Liverpool. Thanks to Stone, some army lads and our lads undercover, there's been nothing major. There's a bit of dope and pills getting dealt maybe it's some new team with a new setup, I'll put the feelers out."

"Thanks, Bish," said Stone and added, "but the bastard behind Angie, he needs finding."

Oh boy thought Bishop *I can't wait to tell Brenda Stone's finally become human*. "Angie, do you have another route that you can take Bonzo avoiding the woods?"

"I can put him in the car; the river's only ten minutes' drive, or I can walk him around the old industrial estate."

"Good and carry your mobile with you at all times, if you see anything, give me a call on my personal mobile. You could get lost in the system going through the switchboard," and looking at Stone, "You are obviously very important to my friend." *No denial from Stone* thought Bish and Angie programmed Bishop's number into her phone. "Stone, we'll get some undercover lads to check out the woods; however, if they feel threatened, they'll hold their meetings somewhere else. Anything else you can think of Angie?"

"No, I can't think of anything."

"If you remember anything else, call me direct." Bishop stood to open the patio door, "I'm going to have a chat with Jo since she's grown a foot since I last saw her," and left Stone still holding Angie's hand.

"How are you doing, Jo?"

"I'm good, Bish, Angie's taking me tomorrow to pick a puppy, Dad's getting me a dog for my birthday, and I can have him early, I'll get him in two weeks."

"Jo, you always knew how to get what you want out of your dad," all the time Bishop and Jo were talking Bonzo had been licking Bishop's arms, *yep, he thought same colour as me*, not paint "Do you know what dog you're getting?"

Patting Bonzo, "I'm getting a bull mastiff like Bonzo."

"You sure, Jo, he's a big dog."

"Angie's going to teach me how to look after and train him. She's my favourite teacher at school and she's my friend also."

Bishop thought he would have a little prod with Stone's daughter, "She's helping you a lot, isn't she? Is she your dad's friend as well?"

"Yeah, they only met yesterday, but they really like each other. Dad is different around Angie and Ike said I should allow Dad to find someone and be happy. I like Angie; she's not like his bimbos, she's funny has her own ways and isn't afraid of Dad and I'll have my dog soon so Dad will need someone to keep an eye on him."

Angie and Stone sat holding hands, "I wasn't sure I wanted you here tonight, I was wrong I needed that cuddle and this, looking at their hands, I was really frightened if Bonzo hadn't been there I don't know if I would have frozen or fought."

"A lot depends on your training, Ang; some personal trainers forget about the fear factor in women and don't teach them properly."

"Would you teach me?"

"No, I won't, but I have a female colleague who's world-class and one of my closest friends." Angie looked a little surprised, but Stone continued, "I couldn't; it would mean getting rough, grabbing you when you didn't expect it, you would have to learn to fight me off it would be hands-on and very physical and I'm barely able to hold your hand without wanting more," and kissed her gently on the lips and she knew what he meant.

Jo, Bonzo and Bish came back into the room all three aware of the atmosphere, Bonzo sat at Angie's feet still being protective. Bish shook Angie's hand, kissed Jo on her forehead and turned to Stone, "I'll do what I can, I'll keep you both informed of any developments," and the two men hugged goodbye. "Angie, when we go lock your doors, anything strange you ring me, if you need to talk, ring me, I'd better get Jo home and bed she's going to be hyper till she sees those puppies then she'll be even worse for the next two weeks."

Jo knew her dad would want to say more to Angie, so she patted Bonzo. "Angie, I'll see you tomorrow; Dad, I'll be by the bike," walking out the front door leaving them alone.

Stone turned quickly to Angie kissing her so hard it took both their breaths away, Angie's body practically vibrated where his erection pressed into her. "God, Ang," breaking off the kiss, both breathing hard, "I have to walk outside, Jo will be focused looking for signs and let's be honest here," and pointed to his erection the signs are fairly clear.

"Yes, I'd say that's a fairly large sign."

"I have to go, let's both try and get some sleep, see each other tomorrow, see how we feel and take it from there." Stone gave Angie a gentle kiss and said to Bonzo, "Look after your master she's very precious." Jo was waiting patiently next to the bike, "Everything ok, Dad?"

"I honestly don't know, darling, let's go."

Stone and Jo sat with a cup of low-fat sugar-free drinking chocolate each wound up in their own way, "Dad, you really like Angie, don't you?"

"Yes, Jo, I really like Angie."

"That's good, I really like her as well, goodnight, Dad, and I love you."

"I love you too," giving his daughter a kiss, "try and get some sleep big day tomorrow." Stone his thoughts on Angie turned out the downstairs lights and headed to bed, the longing almost crushing him, clothes off, into bed hands above his head trying to shut his mind down ready for sleep, his phone rang, "I wanted to hear your voice before I try and sleep, whatever this is between us let's not analyse it or fight it, I'm missing you, how is that even possible I don't even know you."

"This is new to me too, Ang, but I wanted to see you and it was very hard to leave you, I like you, Ang, I like you very much, get some sleep because Jo will be a handful tomorrow."

"I'll try, Stone, night see you tomorrow."

Stone had been trained to sleep when needed, even in the theatre of war so he had managed to calm his heart rate and relax with his breathing techniques but his first thought when waking at his usual 6.00 a.m. was of Angela Sanders. Going through his morning ritual of a glass of lemon water, stretching and martial arts of which he was a black belt at the highest level in jiu-jitsu, karate, judo, and Taekwondo and even the rarer foreign versions in the British army. In a ring he was virtually unbeatable, what made him world-class was his total mind control doing everything so much faster than normally possible. However, he was a man and he couldn't fight what he couldn't control which were his emotions rather than continue with martial arts or weight training, he'd go for a run today; pounding the streets always soothed him and he could work through his emotions, putting on running shoes and leaving. he left Jo a note; he quietly closed the door.

Eight

Angie had a lousy night's sleep, and the rampant rabbit was still collecting dust on top of the wardrobe, admitting to herself she wanted the real thing not some pathetic piece of rubber. Bonzo, who usually slept in the kitchen where it was cool, had stayed in protection mode all night consequently, he was lying on the bed twitching in a light sleep. Setting the coffee machine going and putting fresh water and the dreaded kibble out for Bonzo, she opened the patio doors, and he took off down the garden towards the apple tree; *good* she thought *no cleaning up.*

Deciding to walk Bonzo a different route, as Bish had suggested, this morning they walked in the opposite direction and onto a bit of old development land with boarded-up factories. Angie did not see Tony Greaves, career criminal and leader of the 'woods' gang looking out but he'd spotted the huge dog, "Well, well, well, look what we have here, Jeff, Rich over here now." Both lads obeyed instantly. Tony Greaves took no shit from anyone. "Isn't that the dog we saw in the woods with the woman that Ronnie was gonna fuck?"

"Looks like it, boss," said Jeff. "Ok, job for you both find out who she is, where she lives and don't let that fucking dog see you or smell you."

Stone nicely warmed up and began to increase his pace onto the old industrial estate; in the distance saw a big black dog being walked by a lady and the only person around the area who had a dog that big was Angie. Stone increased his pace. Angie totally unaware she was being followed was enjoying the morning. Stone could see it was indeed Angie and Bonzo; he could also see that 20 yards behind and obviously tailing her were two youths around 20-21. Stone did the calculations Angie was heading home, the two tails were hoping to find out where she lived. Stone took his phone placing it in its plastic jacket on his arm; it looked like an app tracking his run and set it to record and kept running hoping to get the tails on camera, he pulled onto the road turning to say 'morning' as he ran past the two lads managing to capture their faces on video. The two lads looked at Stone's physique and just as politely muttered 'morning' not wanting any confrontation just for him to fuck off so they could follow the big dog and woman.

Stone ran past and continued towards Angie; on hearing pounding footsteps, Angie looked round and her heart accelerated and then her body reacted, Bonzo chuffed and wiggled, stopping next to Angie, "Whatever you do, do not look behind me look straight at me." Angie did as he asked. "There are two lads following you, they either recognise you or Bonzo so we keep walking and chatting like friends but you don't go anywhere near home in fact head away from your house, ok."

Stone phoned Bish, "Morning, Stone, what's up?" Stone filled him in, "I may have got their faces on my phone, but if you can send an unmarked with a camera, yeah, she's cool behaving like a pro."

The two lads looked on in dismay as the big guy stopped his run to talk to the lady with the big dog, "Fuck it, Rich, what do we do now?"

"We keep following; maybe he's a neighbour and she's still going home."

Bishop shouted of Ted Barnett. "Yeah, boss."

"Grab a camera for the unmarked and get to the disused industrial estate, you'll see Colonel Stone with a pretty girl; her name's Angie Sanders, and she has a huge black bull mastiff with her behind them are two men, they're following Angie, Stone's leading them away from her house. I want you to get some decent photos of the two."

Bish rang Stone back, "Ted Barnett is going to be along any minute in the unmarked, hopefully, get some decent photos, yours will be a bit jumpy."

"Thanks, Bish. You are doing great, Ang, just keep walking." Ten minutes later, the unmarked police car came past them.

"Which way have you walked this morning?"

Angie told him the route she'd taken from her house. Ringing Bish again, he said, "They're holed up in one of the warehouses on the old industrial estate they must've spotted her or more probably Bonzo from above, yeah, I know wild goose chase, no I don't want Ang re-tracing her steps they may send reinforcements to push the situation. I think the two following us will just keep at it, if we go for breakfast, they'll think we're mates, hang around and probably phone their boss and wait or return to their base, whatever happens, Ang is with me."

"Did you say 'breakfast'?"

"Yep, Mario the old goat is dying to meet you and Gabrielle will spoil you rotten, Bonzo?"

"He'll get a treat with an early breakfast too," at which Bonzo's ears pricked, **proper food, kibble can wait.** Punching buttons on his phone, "Is that the fat Italian stud muffin?"

"What's up, Stone? You need some actual chat up lines that work, cos there's no way you've got to even first base with Angie Sanders."

"Actually, Mario, I'm on my way to you for breakfast with said person and a rather large attack dog trained to bite annoying Italian restaurant owners, you know any Mario, maybe one that keeps putting his size thirteen in it?" Stone gave Mario a quick run-through of the situation. "We're about ten minutes away, we'll come inside with Bonzo, he's house-trained, has huge teeth and only bites on command, you might want to let the locals know and tell Gabrielle to speak slower, yeah she still gets her grope, with you soon."

Jeff Marshall rang Greavsie and told him what happened. "Just keep following and don't fuck up, you dumb fucks, see if you can get the man's picture, but don't get caught, physique like that he doesn't eat fucking doughnuts and maybe he's a bit handy." Entering Luconi's, Stone saw the two followers sit on the wall opposite, Gabrielle approached them cautiously eyeing up Bonzo who's nose was twitching; **the food smells wonderful; I'm going to be a good dog he thought good equals rewards no kibble diet bring it on.**

Mario said, "He trained to bite on command if I try for some good loving."

Stone and Angie both laughed and Stone gave Gabrielle a huge hug and kissed both her cheeks. "No, he only bites males, the fat boy in the kitchen Gabby."

"Yeah mumbling to himself think he's getting forgetful talks to himself all day gives me no loving." Gabrielle touched Angie's hand as Stone headed for the kitchen out of earshot, "That man best deserves happiness; long time lonely man you make him happy you eat here free for life, ok, we find you and doggy seat in the corner," and escorted Angie and Bonzo past the gawping patrons.

Mario and Stone were deep in conversation, "What you think going on, Stone?"

"Well, I've been talking with Bish, and he thinks it's some mob taking up the drug slack after that lot from Liverpool got pulled, we just wait for a break, in the meantime we eat."

The food was placed on the table and Mario looked at Bonzo, "I have a special treat for the big dog, but I check with the boss first, I have cooked bones for soup stock is the dog allowed to eat bones?"

"I sometimes get him a marrowbone for his teeth and the calcium is good for his joints."

"I bring him bone you get your breakfast in peace."

"Bonzo won't greed at the table. I give him the command and he knows he gets fed when I'm finished, if you bring him a bone give it to him then that way he knows it's a treat from you, and you'll have a hairy friend for life."

"You have a very well-trained dog, you going to try and train Big Hunk also."

"He's already trained just hasn't realised it yet," winking at Mario. Mario brought a huge bone and Bonzo thought **I hope that's for me** putting on his best good boy look. "Bonzo want bone," **silly question, of course, I want the bone; hurry up before she changes her mind**. Mario placed the bone on a large tablecloth next to Bonzo's feet, big doggie for you eat up.

Jeff phoned Greavsie again, "There in Luconi's having breakfast even the dog."

"Just keep watching. You got any pictures yet?"

"Yes, boss, we took quite a few."

"Well, just sit tight then till they move."

"We're hungry, boss, we ain't had breakfast."

"Dumb fucks should have had ya porridge this morning then, keep an eye, if they move, ring me, I'll get Neil and Terry to take over at lunch time, can't have you fuckers get too scrawny, can we?" And put the phone down.

Stone's phone rang it was Bish, "Ted's done the drive-by, we're going through the books trying to identify them, I'll let you know what we turn up, what's happening at your end?"

"The two are just sitting on the wall opposite they must have been told to stay on us, might be a good idea to get eyes on them they may pull a swap."

Stone picked up his phone and rang Jo, "Morning, sleepy head."

"Morning, Dad, you don't sound out of breath," and he filled in his daughter on the morning's events.

"I'll bring Angie and Bonzo to the house. Are Granddad and Ike there yet?"

"No, well, they usually arrive early so text me when they arrive sweetheart, yeah she's here you want a word OK I'll pass you over, Ang, Jo wants a word."

"Morning, Jo, no we're fine, your dad's got the situation under control, yes he's with me, Mario gave him a huge bone big guy in his element. Shit, I hadn't thought of that, no I can't go back to my house, I'll have a word with your dad, OK Jo, I'll see you in a bit." And handed the phone to Stone, "No, Jo, we've had a cooked breakfast, but I'm missing my coffee, ok, Jo, be back soon, love you."

"Stone, I can't get my car and I've got to be at the Stephenson's for one o'clock."

"I'll take you and Jo, Ike and Dad can look after Bonzo for a couple of hours, probably even teach him some new tricks."

"Stone, I need to talk to you if we're going to see each other, it's something Jo said, and I need to make sure you know something that your daughter will not have told you, but you cannot under any circumstances let Jo know we've had this discussion. I'm very close to Jo, she trusts me and tells me what she's thinking and feeling I don't want to hurt her in any way." And Angie sat and told him about his daughter's fears. Stone listened intently never interrupting; the man's a good listener, another box ticked, when she was finished Stone was quiet for a while.

"I can understand why she thinks that, but she has the reasons wrong, I'll never go back to what I was I'm too old for the front line now, but I wouldn't go back because of Jo, and I wouldn't go back under any circumstances now I've met you, now I'm going to tell you why Jo's wrong and you must never repeat what I tell you." Stone then told Angie how unhappy his marriage had actually been, why they didn't love each other, the reason he'd never cried and why he couldn't tell Ike.

"Dad and Ike will be turning up any minute and along with Jo they think they can fix me; the trouble is as you now know, there's nothing to fix regarding my marriage."

Bish rang Stone, "I've got eyes on those two."

"I'm going to make a move and I'll keep Angie with me, anything breaks just ring me." "No problem, Stone speak to you later."

Mario appeared from the kitchen with a bag for Bonzo's now half-eaten bone, "All checked, Stone, no one watching, out the back go down the alley right turn back into traffic and don't scratch the car. I've taken out the shelf-folded seats; put cushions and old sheets in the back."

"I'll get Dad and Ike to bring your car back this afternoon."

"Tell George and Isaac to make it after 3.00. We'll close the shop early break out the war stories and discuss love lives, lots of new stuff to share, giving Angie a warm smile, keep an eye on him pointing at Bonzo. Don't let him chew anything." Stone said goodbye to Gabrielle and much hugging later they jumped into the top-of-the-range Mercedes, "Nice wheels," said Angie.

"Yep, they make a good living, but they put the hours in, so they deserve the perks."

Arriving at Stone's home, Angie looked out at the magnificent house and gardens, "Jesus, Stone how could you afford this?"

"Well, when I was a super solider as Jo calls me, the government used to send me on life-threatening missions, when I returned, they paid me untraceable amounts of money for my services and I put the money into this house to stop Gemma getting her hands on anything she could sell, I own it outright there's no mortgage but I hate the house, but Jo's lived here all her life."

Spying the Jaguar in the drive, "My dad and Ike are here, and I apologise in advance, they love me but they're like two nosey neighbours wanting to know the back end of a fart and they're both ex-army."

"Gosh, you make them sound like ogres."

"No, Dad is great, just doesn't do bullshit and he can smell it a mile away."

"Hello, anyone home?" Stone shouted.

"We are all in the cinema room son watching your latest Oscar-winning performance." Stone, Angie and Bonzo headed to the room, to find them watching Stone and Bonzo's swimming antics. George Stone looked at his son's face on the huge screen, and a gruff voice from the front said, "Justin, you lead over fifty missions look at that face son and tell me what you see, and son it may begin with an L but it certainly ain't lust. No secrets there, Ike."

"George, Angela Sanders isn't your normal girl next door, she's beautiful and funny and once you meet her you won't forget her."

"Well, I never saw him look at Gemma like that, not once."

"Dad, shut up," said Stone and walked into the room. General George Stone retired stood and at sixty-one, he looked like he could still fight he was in supreme shape; he wrapped his arms around his only son and said, "Justin, your eyes always gave you away, to those that love you, you got good at hiding your emotions, but a blind man can see by the look on your face that."

"Dad, please stop, she's here with me." Jo turned in her seat saw Bonzo and ran to greet him and Angie. George turned to look at the doorway and at the beautiful woman who had her hand round his granddaughter chatting away like they were best friends, walking up to greet her, "Hello, Angie, I'm George, Justin's last to know anything father."

"Dad, be good, we're in my home not the army interrogation room, no waterboarding or pulling out her fingernails."

"I'm pleased to meet you, sir."

"Ang, don't call him sir, he'll think we're hiding something."

"Son, looking at those pictures, you and the lovely Ms Sanders ain't hiding jack shit. Ike, I can die a happy man now."

Ike stood. "You're getting soft, George, now you turned sixty, I thought you'd interrogate these two for at least a couple of hours."

"What's to interrogate, Ike? Look at them, ain't no secret to tell, it's all out in the open, no sport here Ike." Ike who knew George Stone better than any man alive knew the man had just approved Stone's choice of girlfriend with flying colours.

Stone hugged Ike standing behind his dad, "Ike, you know Angie."

"Not as well as you do, J T, but a man can always dream."

"Ike, be good, the man's already whipped."

"Yeah, George, but I have to get my licks in while I still can." With one on either side of Angie, the three of them set off to follow Jo and Bonzo, while Stone trailed behind, "I need coffee, this is going to be worse than I thought." They sat discussing the current state of rock music and the loss of many of its greatest pioneers Chris Cornell, Lemmy and Neil Peart when Jo said, "I think a ten stone mastiff needs a good name, I'm going to call him Lemmy, Granddad what you think?"

"I think it's an inspired choice young Josephine; I think Mr Ian Fraser Kilmister would have liked to be considered a bull mastiff he was a genuinely sweet man even after a couple of bottles of Jack Daniels," and George Stone went on to talk about who he'd met, who he still knew and sadly who had died.

Stone's phone buzzed, it was Bish. "We've identified them two lads and it's not good, Jeff and Richard Marshall are small-time led be-the-nose types, trouble is they've always worked for Tony Greaves whose real bad ass news and will deal with anything. We can't prove it but last year in Blackpool his E tablets laced with rat poison caused eight deaths and fifty plus blue light stomach pump jobs. He has some nasty pieces of shit on his payroll if he's behind it this is going to be a shit storm, if he can get people addicted, he'll add anything to make more money, the man has no scruples and if he's sussed Angie then you got to be careful. The school kids angle means he's going to flood the schools with drugs probably tablets cos there easy to conceal and sell. Angie overheard him say £5 a tablet one hundred tablets he makes £400 pays the kid £100 costs pennies to make once you source the right raw materials, probably has plenty of kids on his books pushing them Barry Jackson and Tommy Bowman will just be two that we know of. We need eyes in the school."

Stone's mind went into overdrive, "I'll run a plan past Brigadier Marshall first thing Monday, see if we can produce a co-ordinated effort same as when the Liverpool lot turned up. Good live hands-on training for the lads is better than imaginary drills. What about the industrial estate and woods?"

"We'll send a couple of teams, the woods get the ramblers association and bird fanciers, and the industrial estate get council types with boards looking at rejuvenation. Plain clothes are having a pub crawl, see if they can spot anything iffy, maybe your Brig can get some army lads in teams of two, no red flags cos it's an army base anyway so it's good cover."

"Will see what I can do, I'll get Chris and Tony with me plus Mach and the lads, and Hardcase to cover the school. Thanks, Bish, stay connected and watch your back."

"You too, Stone."

"Ang, can I have a word, please?" All serious as they walked out into the garden closing the door and letting the others know this was serious. "This is what we know," and relayed what Bish had said. "I'm not taking any risks with your safety; I know you won't like it and it's not a good way for us to start seeing each other but you're too important to me. Monday I'm bringing my team into school, I'll be the new gym teacher, and I'll set up some self-defence classes. Bobby Newton will 'take some personal time' and he'll get a monetary incentive to step aside, Bish will speak to the school directors. Chris Stewart and Tony Fielding will come in as supply teachers; they're my colleges and best friends. Ang, you can't go home. Once Jo has picked her pup, we'll go to yours and you pack what you need and you stay here, with me and Jo, we have spare rooms, I do the school run, and we're all going anyway. Ang, I need you safe, I can't get this guy and his team if I'm worrying about you, he's a monster he added rat poison to make extra profit causing eight deaths and fifty-plus stomach pumps."

Angie accepted the information, but she was far from happy, "I want you to do your job; I'm a realist, Stone, you and Bish do what's needed. I'll be ok; besides, I get to spend more time with Jo, George, Ike, and you of course."

"Ang, one more thing," pulling her into his arms and kissed her. George Stone looking out into the garden watched and felt a calm he hadn't felt since his son was born, finally God willing, his amazing son who had done so much for others now had someone who would love him as he deserved.

Unbeknown to Stone, George knew the history between him and Gemma. Returning inside, Stone told them what they knew, but George and Ike knew it wasn't everything but accepted Stone's version. "Jo, its puppy picking time," said Stone, "and Bonzo what should we do with you while we look at your sons?"

"Can we see any old men that need to walk off a bit of paunch'," as Ike stood up.

"Looks like Mr Golden Cup just took temporary control of you, Bonzo."

"Under no circumstances do you give him any chocolate it can kill dogs, I'll leave him some treats on the kitchen table," said Angie. "But if you take him for the w word, take some poop bags and keep him on his harness, he's a good boy but he doesn't know you or George very well yet."

"So, Dad, been a while since you been on bodyguard duty and coming into school as relief gym teacher should be an interesting next few days. Can you see the school newspaper history teacher and new gym teacher caught groping behind the bike shed?"

"Jo! Your dad does not grope me." Thirty minutes later, with Planet Rock filling the car and all three had been involved in a music discussion, they arrived at the Stephenson's kennels.

"Jo, you can only choose ONE, you have first choice from six pups, but they will all go to new homes only you will know which one is the right one or the dog might even pick you."

Mark appeared, "I've pre-done all the verification paperwork, Angie, hello, Colonel Stone, Jo," offering his hand. "Jo, when you walk in, don't make any sudden movements or loud noise, eleven pups are a lot and mam is really tired and grumpy." Jo sat on a stool in the pen with the dog puppies, mum and the girl puppies watching from the adjoining pen, so they didn't get distressed. Five of the pups came trotting over and Jo studied them looking at number six by far the biggest he sat head moving side to side, curious without being obvious.

Jo walked up to him, "Hello, Lemmy, you are coming home with me soon," and went to stroke him and he lifted his head so she could stroke his chin.

Mark said, "That went well, you chose each other, I'll get you some booklets to prepare you, Jo, and as he's the biggest of the litter and the most demanding on Suzie; you can take Lemmy home next Saturday, the others are a little underweight so will stay a bit longer. Angie tells me she's helping you in the first few weeks and Bonzo will teach by example. Any questions, Jo?"

"No, but I wish I could take him home now." Still stroking Lemmy under the chin.

Driving home, Angie asked, "Why him, Jo?"

"He sat and took everything in, reminded me of Dad, cool under pressure," causing all three to laugh.

Nine

When he realised that the woman, man, and dog were no longer in the restaurant, Jeff Marshall phoned Greavsie. "You simple little fucks, a simple fucking job what the fuck am I paying you for, bring your fucking phones with the fucking photos and then keep the fuck out of my sight. I'll phone you when or if I need you again."

Rich turned to his brother, "Well, that went better than I thought." Tony Greaves booted the metal bin so hard that it hit the wall next to Terry Wheeler who just kept his head down and said nothing; they all knew to let Greavsie calm down, the metal truncheon in his drawer had seen all their blood. "Neil, those two dumb fucks are bringing their phones with the photos. Terry, find out who the fuck they are, the woman heard mine and Ronnie's voices, possibly saw me talking to Jackson and Bowman and she may know them."

"Yes, boss."

"And Terry, Neil, on the fucking quiet, got a feeling that bloke is a bit capable might have to call in some of the goon squad put him out of the picture," and Neil shivered.

Stone went to see his dad. "I'm taking Angie to pack a suitcase then I'm going out again. Dad, the mob leader is Tony Greaves, a nasty piece of work."

"You're going to push this, aren't you son? It's what you would have done before I got you pulled from active duty."

"WHAT DID YOU SAY?"

"You heard me. Justin, who the fuck do you think had enough clout to pull one of the most decorated soldiers in the army out of that fucking suicide mission you were on."

"What fucking suicide mission?" Both raised their voices, unaware that Ike and Angie could hear, fortunately, Jo was in the garden telling Bonzo about getting one of his boys. "What fucking suicide mission, Dad?"

"Son, you think I didn't know, didn't see the miserable cunt you were, the shitty way that fucking bitch of a wife treated you, you were, still are a fucking outstanding soldier, I was the proudest fucking father in the army, you are the best fucking thing I ever did, but that cunt you married was a conniving cheating junkie slag and you were hell-bent on destruction, you think I don't know my own fucking son? You'd rather take on impossible missions than be at home. Justin, you would have been killed it was only a matter of time, I love you, son, but just in case you haven't been paying attention, I'm not the only one, Jo is petrified you return to super solider.

"Son, remember changing the fucking sheets, remember your wonderful daughter crying every time you left the room because she thought you were leaving her, and now Angie Sanders looks at you like you fucking walk on water, she's beautiful, funny and she fucking loves you, Justin, and you're willing to risk that to what, prove you've still got big balls. You're thirty-eight Justin, yes, your hand-to-hand is extraordinary, but you've been out of the war zone for nine fucking long years. Justin, it's not your fucking fight, the drug scum are not your fucking enemy they're everybody's and you are just a cog in the wheel of justice. Think about it, how are you going to explain to Angie if you go on the attack, what if your skills scare her away, we both know what you can do with your bare hands, what the fuck do you think the woman who loves you is going to think of that Justin if she sees you go super fucking soldier close up, you think Angie's going to want their hands on her?

"I waited your whole fucking life for you to find someone who would love you for the fucking extraordinary human being you are, and she's here, in your fucking mausoleum of a house where your fucking slapper of a wife got fucked in every hole in her body so she could get a bit more junk in her arm. You gave her, a beautiful home, a daughter who is extraordinary in every fucking way and she sucked cock to get her next fix, so when she overdosed on whatever she stuck in her arm. I begged the brass to remove you from the theatre. YES, SON, I GOT YOU OUT OF YOUR SUICIDE MISSION."

Both father and son were breathing hard. "All this time you knew."

"Yes, son, I did, I even considered overdosing the fucking bitch myself, and all I ever wanted was for my only son to be happy, fuck even your own thirteen-year-old daughter knows you were depressed. All that meaningless sex just made you even lonelier, you need to become a cog."

With a huge sigh, Stone looked at his father, "You're absolutely right, Dad, I'm sorry, I love you," and "I love you, son."

Jo was in the garden with Bonzo, "I think Lemmy might grow up to be even bigger than you," she said as Angie came out to make sure Stone's daughter had not heard the meltdown between her dad and granddad.

"How are you doing, Jo?"

"I'm better now that I know I'm getting Lemmy next Saturday, but I have to leave him on Monday and I don't think it's enough time to train him to be left on his own."

"Well, I may have an idea, leave it with me."

Ike looked at his best friend, "I lost it Ike."

"I know, George, Angie and I heard the full riot act, she's gone to check on Jo, who's outside with Bonzo. That boy's as bull-headed as you, you kept too much to yourself for too long, it was all bound to come out one day, and speaking as an ex-trauma specialist today was the trigger, the boy left you no choice, you had to get through to him and you did George, unorthodox method but effective. You'll have to talk to Angie though I don't think she minded the swearing, but she might have wanted to tell JT she loved him before his father blurted it out."

George went looking for Angie seeing her in the garden with Jo and Bonzo was again struck by how close they were, the huge dog getting attention from both of them, "Hi, Granddad, I get Lemmy next Saturday he might even grow bigger than Bonzo, Mr Stephenson said I could take him early cos he's so big and drinks all his mams milk and the others need extra feeds, Angie's going to teach me and Lemmy so that we are as good together as her and Bonzo."

"Well, darling, I think you will make a wonderful master and I'm sure Angie will teach you well. I need to borrow Angie, Jo, will you be OK out here for ten minutes, its boring adult stuff," and George hugged his granddaughter.

Angie followed George into the cinema room closing the door behind her, "Well, first, I'm very sorry you had to hear what went on between me and Justin. I've tried to stay behind the scenes, tried to help out where I could, but I couldn't allow him to do what he intended, I had to get through to him. Ike says I'd kept too much to myself, today was the trigger especially as you would have been in the middle of any confrontation and I'm sorry you had to find out all our dirty secrets in such a way. I thank you for checking on Jo; some of what I said would have upset her, but she was only four, so her memory is only short, thank God. I apologise for the crudeness and language, that woman was a complete bitch, and she knew how to manipulate Justin, and finally, I'm sorry for letting my son know what you think of him it wasn't my place."

"George, you didn't lie, and I'd be rather petty if I said it was my place to tell him, you did everything you could to prevent your son from making a huge mistake."

George and Angie hugged for a long time. "I and Jo need a favour from you, George, Lemmy arrives next Saturday and we are both at school Monday to Friday, I'd like you to watch Lemmy as well as Bonzo until this thing is over if your circumstances allow"

"Angie, I'm retired. I live next to all the other old farts at the top of the village, I'll talk to Justin now we've finally cleared the air, and I'll stay here, spend time building bridges with my son, get to know my son's girlfriend and watch my granddaughter's dog."

Stone knew deep down his dad was right, everything he said about Gemma was true; no matter what he'd tried to do it was never enough. He'd fucked up his home life and he'd continued fucking it up, pushing his dad away and not talking to Ike. He sat drinking his coffee contemplating his life, really thinking about his choices. Ike walked into the kitchen and grabbed a coffee, "Ok, JT, do you feel like talking? We both know you're a stubborn son of a bitch like your dad, but now is the time, no more putting off, let's get the fucking gloves off this thing. Your dad may not have used the best tactics, but you're sitting here feeling sorry for yourself, I love you both but you both need to learn to accept that you're going to make mistakes and to talk things out rather than bottle things up.

"George held everything inside until today, put yourself in his shoes and imagine Jo was you, you were your dad, the man is a fucking living legend, the army still regards him with huge respect yet he couldn't talk to the person he loves most, couldn't tell him he was fucking his life up, and then we have you, an incredibly gifted solider who forgot how to be a human being. JT, you need to allow yourself to feel it's not a fucking weakness to feel love for another person. Gemma was a massive mistake but not all women are like her, your daughter loves you for what you mean to her, for what you are, not because of your skills, your father, daughter, me and yes maybe Angie all love the man you are now. You're human, JT, and you have to learn that making bad choices is part of that, look at where you are now, what you've achieved in the last nine years, and your extraordinary relationship with your daughter nobody sat you down and said, 'this is what you do,' you did it, JT. You have a relationship with your daughter a closeness that most fathers never get, you did that with no book, no military plan, you yourself, you are not what you were, nor that you think you are, you are much better, so ask yourself why you think you are so much of a fuck up."

Stone started talking, "All my life, the one thing that has never let me down was my ability to have control over every situation, I don't know how to get a handle on what I feel for Angela Sanders."

"Why do you need to get a handle on me?" Angie said as she walked into the kitchen.

"Sorry to interrupt, Ike."

"No, Angie, come sit down, we all know that you're the main trigger for JT's meltdown. His father, my best friend, would have taken what he said to his grave; his daughter would have continued to keep a close eye on her dad, thank fuck she was outside when he decided to get into a shouting match with the man who kept him alive."

Angie took hold of Stone's hand and repeated her question, "Why do you think you need to get a handle on me?"

"Go on, JT, tell the lady; it ain't no big secret, your father got it inside ten seconds, who do you think you're fooling, nobody, just admit it, it scares the shit out of you. In case you hadn't noticed she feels the same way, and the most gifted hand-to-hand soldier this army has ever produced is scared of losing control. Look at what you have holding your hand; now stop being such a fucking baby and man up. Now, I'm going to find your father, daughter and Bonzo and take Mario his top-of-the-range all bells and whistles Mercedes back and sit around and talk shit." Ike stood up and kissed Angie on her cheek, "The groundwork's all done, Angie, it's up to you and JT to build the house," and left them sitting holding hands.

Stone looked at the woman he loved unconditionally, "Ang, I'm scared."

"Of what?"

"This, us, what I feel, I can't control it."

"And you think I can, Stone, I went from lusting after you to you meaning everything within twenty-four hours, I can't switch it off. Do you want to switch it off, Stone?"

"No, Ang, I want to be able to control it."

"You can't, Stone, neither can I."

"What do we do, Ang?"

"Stone, I don't know all the answers, the first time you kissed me, you know what I felt, I felt complete, the second time I knew."

"You knew what, Ang?"

"I'll tell you later then I'll show you, and we build the house."

"Now, I think we should get my stuff and get back here while we have the house to ourselves, we'll go on your bike, you like bikes?" Angie nodded. "It'll be a lot quicker," and pulling her into his arms kissed her with no holding back, saying, "I need to tell you something later," as he released her. In the living room, Stone hugged his dad hard, "Thank you," while Ike turned to Angie, "Your house building ahead of schedule," and winked.

"Dad, we're going for Angie's stuff while you take Mario's car back, he's closing at three so don't be too late, Jo has school tomorrow."

George turned and winked at Angie, "You two be alright on your own for a few hours?" Stone was on alert as they pulled Angie's drive, she had on Stone's old bike jacket with the sleeves rolled up and spare helmet, but he was taking no chances and they left them on till they were in the house. Angie went to pack her personal and school things and told Stone to grab any music or DVDs that took his fancy. "Ang darling, the only thing that takes my fancy is you and I won't be grabbing," right on cue, she thought as she opened her underwear draw digging at the back for the long-forgotten pink thong, matching front fastening bra, pink hold-ups and a sheer pink baby-doll nightie all unopened, on-line clearance sale purchases made years ago when Angie thought if I find the right man someday, I might fancy playing dress up like a slut, never really believing she would ever wear them for any man, smiling imagining Stone's face then added the more sensible stuff along with her clothes and toiletries including her new unopened perfume that she'd got on a spending splurge, well it was in the half-price sale.

In the living room, Stone had picked some DVDs that he didn't have, bagged and ready to go, grabbing a bag of the dreaded kibble and some toys for Bonzo, helmets and jackets on Angie followed Stone out of her home knowing her life was about to change forever.

"Well, look at this, we've got this big house all to ourselves," trying for bravado, but being so nervous, Angie just walked up to him and kissed him like she'd never kissed any man. "I want to make love with you," she said. Stone's reaction time was still superb; only this time it was all physical, the kiss intensified, Angie moaned into Stone's mouth and his hand cupped her firm buttocks and he lifted her easily and gently so she could feel his firm erection pressed against her inner thighs only material between them. Stone moaned, all his conquests became irrelevant, he loved her, he couldn't stop himself anymore and for the first time in his life, he said the three words and meant it, "I love you," looking straight into her eyes.

"I don't know how in such a short time, but I know I love you, I want to make love to you so much, I want to kiss every inch of you, I want to be with you for the rest of my life, I'm really nervous and I'm so excited, I want so much for this to be right but I'm on a hair trigger, Ang, if I touch you, I'll explode."

Angie already knew how much she loved him; the depth of just how much increased with his admission, here he was a very experienced man telling her how much she affected him and she looked into his beautiful blue eyes and for the first time, not to her parents or her dog, but to a man said, "I love you and I'm not nervous I'm going to make love with the man I love for the first time, we have our whole lives ahead of us, the first time doesn't need to be all singing all dancing; we'll make love thousands of times, Justin, make love to me."

Stone took a huge breath to try and calm himself and took off his shirt and trousers, standing there in his boxer shorts; his painful erection struggling to stay in, Angie looked at Stone's incredible body with his firm erection and her breathing and desire went into overdrive; she was so excited she tingled and her stomach muscles contracted and he hadn't even touched her, "I can't take off your clothes, Ang, I mean I can, but not the first time." Angie obliged and stood there in her white cotton bra and panties, trying to hold it together but her body was betraying her; she wanted this man her panties were moist, her nipples erect, her heart rate off the chart, and her need was building inside her and still Stone just stood there looking at her taking all in, "You want to take my bra and panties off, Justin?"

"No, Ang, I'm too close," removing them herself she stood naked in front of the man she loved for the first time. Stone's voice cracked, "God, you're so beautiful," and dropped his boxers kissing, lifting and entering her in one swift move, Angie unprepared bit her lip and cried out. Stone said, "I'm sorry," and went to pull out of her. "No, stay where you are, don't move, let me get used to how you feel," staying still, he was painfully hard inside her but he stayed still which only increased how much Angie was feeling, he laid her gently on the bed taking his weight on his elbows. "Ang, I have to move," and he began to move inside her pulling nearly all the way out and pushing back as slowly as he could, gritting his teeth trying to control his movements. Angie felt her whole body go hot and her heart rate tripled there was a warmness starting in her stomach moving down into her uterus, she started to moan as the waves got stronger and stronger then she held her breath as the most wonderful feeling she'd ever experienced took over. Stone was fighting not to come, the man who'd done this act a thousand times couldn't control himself, as Angie's soft moaning got louder he gritted his teeth harder and then he felt her beginning to shudder her moaning louder still until she pulled herself against him and with her head next to his ear and screamed as she came, as soon as he heard her scream, he released his seed with so much force that he stopped breathing. Angie had never experienced anything like that telling him over and over again, "I love you; I love you," as she looked him in the eye and he gently moved her hair off her face. "I love you, Ang, I do I really love you," and pulled her close kissing her and felt the most content and complete he had ever felt in his life.

Angie had just made love with the man she loved, it was perfect, well actually, it wasn't, Justin was so close, his self-control didn't exist, but she managed to have her first orgasm with a man she practically buzzed a man who had control over everything he did couldn't control his own body when he was with her because he loved her, Justin loves me, he loves me and she started to cry, it was all too much it was to perfect he was everything she had ever wanted in a man and he loved her, at thirty-four, she now knew what an orgasm was now and how unbelievable it had felt, she could feel Justin's sperm trickling out of her still warm it felt wonderful, her vagina muscles where throbbing she felt totally sedated and she wanted to feel like this lots more. She would learn, Justin would let her know what he liked, and she would reciprocate, but right here right now she just wanted to be held naked in his arms. "Ang darling, why are you crying?"

"I'm crying, Justin, because I've never been anywhere close to being as happy as I am right now, I'm crying because we both feel the same way about each other, I'm crying because it isn't a dream it's a reality, I'm lying naked with you I can feel your heart beating, I can feel where you've been, oh my can I feel you; I finally had my first ever orgasm and boy was it worth waiting for, I can feel. Oh shit! Justin, we didn't use a condom."

"Well, darling, Ike is going to be back in around an hour; you can ask him about the morning-after pill and see what contraception he thinks you should have then we can do this all the time."

"Ike is your father's best friend so they both going to know what we've been up to."

"Ang, take a look at your face in the mirror," and Ang naked, but comfortable he was the man she loved after all, climbed out of the bed to look in the mirror, she looked radiant her eyes shone, Stone climbed out also naked, put his arm around her and looked in the mirror to see twins as his eyes also shone and he couldn't stop smiling. "My dad saw what I felt from a camera, my daughter saw us kiss and knew, we had no chance of hiding this, as he pointed at their eyes, and I don't want to I want everyone to know I love you." "I think they already know," and reached up and kissed him. "I love you," and the kiss turned deeper, Angie felt his erection pressing into her stomach and the need took over again, taking hold of his erection for the first time, feeling it pulse and get even firmer, she moved her hand slowly up and down the shaft, hearing Stone take a huge breath, amazed that she could bring this reaction from him with just a simple touch, make love to me again, and he lay down pulling Angie on top of him pushing himself into her; this time moist and ready but they both still took deep breaths and moaned. Stone held her lovingly kissing her softly feeling her breath and her heart rate accelerate, felt her need building, "Show me, Ang, show me what you feel," releasing his grip and she sat straight up taking his full length, arching her back, head back eyes tightly closed as her orgasm built, "Justin, I'm gonna explode," she cried as the waves kept building and building and all she could feel was him inside her going slow and hitting all her nerve endings as he pushed; she couldn't get enough air and began to moan loudly, the waves got stronger and she began to rock faster as her need for release continued to grow resting her hands on Stone's waist, her shaking and moaning became louder.

"Justin, I love you but my heart's going to explode if you keep going slow." She put her hands on his stomach and felt his amazing muscles contracting harder and harder and she sat up straighter getting every little bit of him inside her and then she screamed as she began to come wave upon wave right from her toes to the top of her head the waves powerful and breathtaking then she heard Justin's orgasm building felt his magnificent body shake uncontrollably as his orgasm started and heard him roar as his hot seed shot into her; her own orgasm became a tsunami when she felt him and shuddered with her own release and collapsed onto his chest her breathing was so fast it thundered in her ears and she felt the sticky wetness still warm slowly dripping out of her body onto Justin's thighs, as he held her there and she continued leaking their love making efforts from her body onto his.

Stone stroked Angie's hair getting his breath back, it had been the most intense orgasm of his life, "Ang,, please don't ever change the way you make love to me you gave me your body, soul and your heart. I love you, Angela Sanders, I will remember this forever," taking her face in his hands kissing her as his tears fell.

Angie looked at Justin crying, "I know, Ang, it's catching up with me, I am so in love with you," and held her still trying to get his emotions under control. "Ang I can cope with seeing you naked, I've fired all my bullets for the time being, now shower and try not to look as if we've spent the afternoon making love." The shower was a long walk and Stone looking at her breasts took the soap and gently massaged her, she still hummed from the orgasm but she loved his touch and pushed back into him, "Ang, good job, I've no bullets left."

"There's always later, I've always wanted to make love in a shower wanted to try lots of things, I want to try everything with you, Justin."

Ten

Sitting at the kitchen table holding hands, "You got any watermelon left, Justin?"

"I love that you call me Justin, only my dad calls me that and only when he's trying to make a point."

"It would be rude to call you anything else. I like calling you by your given name, and I love that you shortened mine to Ang. I could call you 'stud' or 'sex god' if you like?"

"Ha, it will be bad enough you are calling me Justin if front of everyone, like a beacon flashing 'those two just had sex'."

"Justin, we didn't have sex; we made love, there's a big difference."

"Oh, I'm still throbbing but I'm not complaining."

"If you're throbbing, how do you think I feel, my very first orgasm followed by a second that was even more intense, I never knew I could scream that loud."

"We'll get some throat spray and some soothing Sudocrem, or I could just kiss you better and see if you cum louder and harder on your own. Do you realise how beautiful you are, and you just gave me everything?"

"I can't do anything else when I'm with you."

Arriving home, Jo took Bonzo into the garden to do his business while George went straight to the kitchen, looking at his son and then Angie then back to his son, "I'll say one thing for you, son, you know how to complete a task."

"Dad, it was no task."

"Well, it was hard at times," said Angie, "but we managed to get through it together," her meaning clear.

"Bugger, you two are no fun anymore," but his smiling face told them how happy he was. Ike had followed the sound of voices and kissing Angie's cheek whispered, "Way to go, Angie Sanders, the house is flying up." Bonzo now spied his master and came charging through the doorway in his unique style, "Hello, big boy, have you been good?" Bonzo sniffed and looked at his master **smelled** different, looked very happy mermaid man must be doing her good, Angie cuddled Bonzo and whispered, "I love him, Bonzo," letting her dog know the reason for her change in smell and her happiness. **I made puppies when I felt like that.**

Jo took Bonzo out into the garden and Angie stood, "Ike, can I have a private word?" She said and blushed. Stone smiled like the cat that got the cream. "JT, it takes two you want to join the conversation."

"Er no, it's ok, Ike. Ang can explain."

George listening and grinning said, "Boy, this gets better, you two behaved like teenagers, what's the worst that could happen?"

"You get another grandchild," and Angie walked off with Ike leaving George speechless. Angie kept on blushing all the way through the conversation, as Ike outlined her options. "Think about it, do you want children while reminding her of her age, anyway in the short term, come to the hospital in the morning and I'll get you the morning-after pill and I'll give you information on long-term options."

"Dad, can you make supper while we take Bonzo for his evening walk?"

"It's ok, Angie, I've made Justin's supper many times, Greek yoghurt, cottage cheese, scoop of vanilla protein powder, a banana, and some berries, ultra-healthy but it's delicious, full of texture and flavour, me, and Jo, both eat it. We keep trying to get Ike to join us instead of his chocolate biscuits and tea, man's been a doctor thirty-five years we keep telling him the crap will catch up and he wouldn't pass the army physical now."

"George, enough, how about a compromise? I'll drink some sludge if I can add chocolate sprinkles."

"Done deal," said George, knowing there were no sprinkles!

Bonzo, harness on and ready to go realised things were different, his master was different, **her voice was slightly lower especially when she talked to mermaid man the area was different which meant new smells and squirrels to chase, hoping these ones knew how to play the game.** Stone checked that Angie and Jo had their mobiles with Bish's number in, and a whistle each, "If anything happens, you leave me."

They both said, "No," in unison.

"Yes, you do, Jo, you know what I can do, Ang, I take no risks with you, one of you phones Bish, this lot is looking for Bonzo, they've seen me and you Ang,

I don't think it's dangerous, yet, but it will get worse before we sort it. Ok, let's get walking. Ang, you got plenty of bags."

"Yes, Justin."

"Oh my," screamed Jo, "it must be love; you just called Dad by his first name."

Angie put her arm around Jo, "I did, and it is," she said.

The two girls chatted away. "Angie, you love my dad?"

"I do, Jo. I knew I was in trouble when I saw him at the hospital."

"I kind of guessed. I spied you two kissing and Dad has never done that anywhere near me, I mean all his conquests never meant anything, my dad loves you, I mean he's so different around you, he's definitely not super cool and the way he looks at you."

"Well, Jo, it is mutual."

Stone was walking a few paces behind scanning the area. "There's a nice bit of dirt track a couple of hundred yards further on, it's open with a few trees and the track goes right the way round he said. This is where I usually start my morning run then off into the fields and down by the river, but we just need to be able to let Bonzo off his lead to do his business and then we can get back for supper." Bonzo took off sniffing, darted into the trees and dropped his back legs, "Good boy, see, Jo, environmentally friendly," and the two of them started giggling. Stone loved the sound but remained vigilant, **a bit of a let-down no squirrels nothing to chase** Bonzo thought and trotted back to his master, his two new friends and home. **Hope there's no kibble and I can finish the bone that nice funny talking man gave me**. George and Ike looked at Stone, the question unasked, but Stone said, "All quiet tonight but like I told the girls it will escalate, especially when they start pushing tablets at the school and realise both Ang and I work there. Ang can recognise two of their voices, so we take every precaution."

"There's a big bowl of protein and fruit yoghurt on the table and some dishes, help yourselves, even Ike's going to try some with chocolate sprinkles."

"We don't have sprinkles, Uncle Ike."

"No worries, I'll leave it all for you, I'm going to shoot off anyway. I'll come over about 7.30 tomorrow night, sort out some fishing and golf days, see you all," and Ike left.

"We are never going to get that old bugger off chocolate, he'll go home and have a cup of tea and a packet of biscuits, bloody doctors," said George. "Angie, do you feed Bonzo at this time of night?"

"No, he just gets a couple of chew sticks for his teeth makes him minty fresh and when he licks you his breath doesn't knock you over, there's a reason it's called dog breath," looking at Bonzo who thought **no kibble but not getting the bone either.**

Stone outlined the plan of action. "Drive you both to school, you wear your whistles and always have your phones on you, anything looks iffy, phone me or Bish. I'm going to see Brigadier Marshall in the morning to draw up a plan like what we did with the Liverpool mob. The headmaster will know all this by ten am, Bobby Newton will take some personal time and I'll replace him on a temporary basis starting Tuesday this is so the kids bringing the drugs into school aren't suspicious.

"Jo, it's ten o'clock, bedtime, and all your homework better be done."

"Angie, where does Bonzo sleep when he's at home with you?"

"Usually in the kitchen, he has a large basket with his toys and the internal doors are left open, when I had my scare, he slept on top of my bed but that's because he was being extra protective."

Jo, listening said, "I want Lemmy to sleep in my bedroom."

Angie replied, "Lemmy will sleep where you teach him too, the drawback to having a dog in the same room is if they start farting, you remember Bonzo on your dad's boat."

Jo giggled, "Yeah, he stunk worse than dad and granddad combined."

Angie continued, "Lemmy will settle better if he's with his master, but young pups get really messy and always wear slippers," and Jo giggled again. The two elder Stone's where watching the conversation both struck by the bond between Angie and Jo, both keenly aware of what Jo had been missing in the last nine years.

Jo thought hard. "Angie, do you think Bonzo would like to sleep in my bedroom? It's nice and cool my windows are on vent, there's plenty of room and I can leave my door open so he can wander and if he farts, I'll hold my nose," giggling again.

"I'll get his bed and toys and if Bonzo settles, we'll leave him with you." The girls went upstairs George turned to his son. "I know, Dad, they've really got close quickly; Ang was Jo's favourite teacher and Ang used to call Jo her favourite pupil, I went to get food coming back to see Ang stroking Jo's hair completely unaware I was there, so it wasn't for effect. I think Jo had talked about her childhood; her eyes where puffy as if she'd had a cry." George went on to explain about Lemmy and being asked to look after him, "Dad, you have your own room here and I want you to stay, if I'm gonna fuck up, I want someone to tell me."

"You'll not fuck up, son, she's too important."

Bonzo settled in Jo's bedroom doors open so he could have a wander, Jo was reading *The Bon Scott Years* and Angie picked the book up. "Great read this book, Jo, I prefer Bon to Brian, but Brian is a very cool man, Geordie were a great Northeast band."

"My dad was a Zeppelin fanatic and I inherited his excellent taste in music and his collection when he passed but I've been adding to it over the years. I'll be able to concentrate on Lemmy now you and Dad are living together." Angie was going to say it was only temporary till the threat was over but she looked at Jo.

"I'm exactly where I want to be, Jo."

"Good," said Jo and their conversation continued effortlessly for the next twenty minutes neither of them being in a rush to leave the other. "Well, he seems to have settled quite well," Angie pointed to Bonzo snoring softly at the bottom of Jo's bed. "I'll leave him on your bed but he shouldn't get used to being on it."

"It is ok, I'll wash the cover if he gets it dirty. I do all the washing and ironing in the house anyway, I don't think Dad knows how to work the washing machine." It felt natural to kiss Jo on the lips and say goodnight and Angie had tears in her eyes as she returned to the living room.

George looked at the time past eleven o'clock, "I'll leave you two lovebirds," and kissed Angie on both cheeks. "Thank you, Angela, for being you and Justin, no secrets ever."

"Yes, Dad," and they hugged, George Stone going to his bedroom in his son's house for the first time in over a month. Stone sat with Angie.

"That went well, Dad and Jo accept things."

"Or maybe it's because they can see their son and father happy," said Angie.

"Yes, I am very happy, I'll be happier when Tony Greaves is locked up, but I'll be a cog. Choice of four bedrooms, Ang, where would you like to sleep?"

"There's only one place I want to sleep, in your arms, Justin."

"Excellent choice, would you like me to put the Sudocrem on for you or do you want me to kiss you all better?"

Angie grinned, "I've already applied Sudocrem, but tomorrow I may make a different choice."

"Angie, I'm up at six; I do an hour of martial arts or weight training every morning, at thirty-eight, I have to stay supple. I'll re-set the next alarm for seven that's when Jo gets up or should get up sometimes, she's a bit of a sleepy head, but I've found an ice cube usually gets her up."

Wrapping arms around each other, Angie said, "Let's always end our day in each other's arms," and looking into his amazing blue eyes, "I love you, Justin, I'm not scared by how much, it just is I couldn't fight what I feel, and you know how easy I am sleeping with you inside the first week."

"Well I must love you, Ang, you are still here so in my eyes you're an eleven."

Stone's alarm went off at 6.00 the next morning; he woke with pins and needles in his left hand and a beautiful woman asleep in his arms. He couldn't draw his eyes away from her face; she was stunning, his self-discipline, which he prided himself on, made him get out of bed, put his keikogi on and go into his gym, full of weight training gear, climbing racks, boxing bags, you name it he had it. He put on his boxing gloves and did a light, for him, speed bag workout, then worked on the bars, one-handed press ups, chins with static holds, core work dips with twists, hanging pelvic knee raises, then onto the padded floor where he did more stretching still able to do the splits with ease. Stone started his balance work working each arm and leg separately, now his body was ready for the martial arts moves he needed to work on, starting slow he did a whole series of moves, blocks and throws gradually speeding up until his hand and leg speed was where he wanted them.

Totally at one with himself and completely focused, he didn't see Angie by the door wearing his dressing gown watching astonished that a human being could move that fast and with that much precision, the total focus showing on his face, the way his beautiful body flowed with movement was like watching a world-class gymnast and ballet dancer in one person. George tapped Angie on the shoulder, "Impressive, isn't he?"

"I've never seen anyone move so fast and with so much grace," and they continued watching.

"I used to watch him all the time, once he's on that mat he is totally at one with his body, all these years and I still find it amazing the mental discipline needed is astonishing." Stone's movements which had been a blur began to slow and he began his Tai Chi movements, precise and unhurried, finally, he stopped and did some breathing exercises and now covered in a sheen of sweat grabbed a towel. "I don't know whether to bow or clap, you do this every other morning."

"Yes, Ang, I alternate between martial arts and weight training; morning, Dad, you spot anything."

"Yeah, son, your balance is a little off with your left arm."

"I know, I've had a gorgeous woman in my arms all night," and kissed Angie lightly on the lips and went off for a shower.

"I'm going to get Bonzo," said Angie.

"Do me a favour, Ang, nudge my daughter."

"Justin, don't forget I have to call in and see Ike at the hospital before school."

"What for?"

"Oh shit, yes we'd better make sure of that."

George looked at Angie, "Well, something he's not well disciplined in," and Angie blushed bright red, and went to get Bonzo, who was lying on his back listening to the birds quite content on seeing his master approach he stood stretched, farted loudly, and had a good shake. Jo woke up, "Oh bloody hell," jumped out of bed and opened the two windows wide, "Jesus, I'd rather have my father shouting Josephine every thirty seconds than wake up to that." Bonzo just wagged his tail, **yes, it was me** he thought **good brew this morning**, he thought then he ran to the girl for a morning cuddle **me too me too**. "You're a big smelly dog, Bonzo," said Jo, "and I'd better get him emptied otherwise he'll be farting round the breakfast table and curdle the milk, come on Bonzo, I'll tell your dad you're up Jo," as Jo disappeared into the adjoining bathroom, "nice dressing gown, Dad has one just the same."

Opening the French windows, Bonzo took off like a bullet to the trees at the bottom of the huge, enclosed garden, 'good dog' she thought, and felt big strong arms wrap around her, followed by an erection pushing into her bottom. "Justin, we really have to do something about your hard edges," turning and wrapping her arms around him pressing her body into his and making no effort to get away from his bulge, she kissed him. "Oh please, no," Jo said as she came out of the bathroom. "It's too early in the morning and I haven't had any breakfast, my dad and my teacher necking in my bedroom, I could be permanently scarred for life." Bonzo came running back in looking at his master in the big man's arms curious he thought then he ran to the girl for a morning cuddle me too me too.

George had ground the beans the coffee peculator bubbling away was sat at the table with his first coffee of the day, "Superb coffee, Justin, might just get addicted to it," smacking his lips as he took another taste.

"Angie, you want to try this coffee, said George, it's that good you might never want to go home." Angie thought to herself, I don't want to go home amazed that she'd give up her independence so easily. Breakfast over George said, "Put everything in the sink I'll do the dishes, you have to get to the hospital before school."

"Hospital?" Stone looked at his dad. "Nothing to worry about, Jo, just a quick two-minute visit."

Angie handed George some paper, "I've written some notes, when and what to feed him, what commands he answers to when you take him for a W, don't let him off his harness till he follows your commands."

"Angie, I'm looking forward to getting to know Bonzo, I have a feeling he'll soon be part of the family."

Stone with Angie in the front and Jo happily relegated to the back seat of the Discovery set off for the hospital where at the reception desk, Angie asked for Dr Goldberg who appeared like magic and gave her hug to the amazement of the reception staff. Follow me, Angie, in his office, he handed the contraception pill, the morning-after pill and a plastic cup of water, "The pills will work within eight hours or so. Angie, no more sex till you get home tonight," and Angie blushed, "and don't forget when its babies time, see me, you may retain a little extra water on the pill, but if it doesn't suit, you could always have the implant, but if you both want kids then it may stop you getting pregnant for a while OK I'll see you tonight around 7.30."

Two minutes later, Angie was in the Discovery heading for school. "This is going to be fun," Jo said as they pulled into the yard where lots of eyes popped at the top-of-the-range Discovery and saw Angie Sanders in the passenger seat sitting next to a very handsome man with Jo Stone sitting in the back. The teacher's common room overlooked the yard and several teachers put their books and papers down to see what was going on. "Don't look now, Angie, but several of your colleagues are watching and my friends are gathered over there," and Jo waved, "be an even better show tomorrow when Dad goes into the school, I suppose I'll have to remember to call you Ms Sanders."

"And I'll have to remember that I can't do this," turning to Jo and kissing her lightly on the lips, might as well give them a show she thought, but in reality, she loved the girl and she wanted to show it. Jo got out of the car and walking to her dad's side kissed him on his lips, "Yes, I know, Dad, be careful," and went off to join her friends.

Angie said, "Are they all still watching?"

Stone moved just his eyes, "Yes, two practically hanging out the window."

Angie leaned over into Stone and kissed him like she loved him which she did, Stone responded in kind, "I love you," said Angie, "and I love you too. Did the Sudocrem work?"

"Yes, I won't get sore."

"Good, did Ike get you sorted?"

"Yes."

"Then how about the bicycle shed at dinner time for a knee-trembling quickie?" Laughing Angie kissed him, and said, "I know, Justin, I'll be careful," and got out of the discovery and headed for the teacher's common room ready for the twenty questions. Stone looked around blew Angie a kiss and drove off to camp.

Anita Fothergill caught Angie as she entered the building, "I've come out to warn you the knives are out in there, and we thought some of our girls were bitches."

Angie walked into the teacher's common room Sophie Preston was bitch one, "Wasn't that Colonel Stone with his tongue down your throat I'd have thought you would have had more sense than to get involved with his type."

"And what types that, Sophie?"

"He's a user, Angie, he'll take what he wants and then discard, move on to the next one."

"You speak from experience, Sophie."

"No not me personally, but the man is gorgeous and that body, but he never sticks with anyone for more than a day or two at the most."

"You think, Sophie, anyone else wants to discuss my love life or are you going to wait until I'm not in the room? Or do you want to ask the man himself tomorrow he's the new temporary PE teacher, and yes, I am sleeping with him and yes, he is gorgeous, but he's not permanent staff so really, it's none of your business."

Barbara Robinson decided to be bitch two. "Didn't I see you being inappropriate with Colonel Stone's daughter, Josephine?"

"If by inappropriate you mean I gave her a kiss and a cuddle, yes she's a pupil at this school, she's also my boyfriend's daughter, at school, she will call me Ms Sanders at home she calls me Angie."

Sophie chipped in, "You're setting yourself up for a huge fall, Angie, a leopard never changes its spots."

"What are you both trying to say that I'd let a known womaniser with a reputation of being a one-night stand merchant have sex with me, several times in fact, over the course of the weekend and then dump me after he brings me to school with his daughter, doesn't quite look that way does it girls, but you can ask Justin any further questions tomorrow," and pouring a coffee Angie set off to see Mike Foster the headmaster.

Anita Fothergill had hidden around the corner, "Well, Angie, how did it go?"

"Sophie and Barbara have me down as a slag and Justin as a womaniser."

"Stupid bloody women," said Anita. "But guess what, because of something he and the police are working on he starts here tomorrow as our new temporary PE teacher, and he's extremely protective of me so it should be interesting," and Angie knocked on Mike Foster's door. Mike was Angie's secret weapon at school always putting the interests of teachers and pupils first, he was a great headmaster and after seven years a good friend.

"I saw Colonel Stone drop you and Jo off, did you kiss him like that to piss off those two idiots?"

"No, Mike, I kissed him like that because I'm in love with him, and to piss them off."

"Jesus, Angie, no man for what eighteen months then you fall in love over a weekend, and you bag the number one stud in the village."

Mike as well as her friend was gay, "So you going to spill the beans, is he as hot as he looks."

"Mike, he's so much hotter, plus in about thirty minutes, you're going to get a call, I'm here to let you know what is going to happen and filled him in about the drug gang."

Stone arrived at the barracks and said hello to some of the guys on his way up to Brigadier Marshall's Office. Susan his long-time clerk, told him to go straight in he's expecting you. Standing to attention and saluting, "Good morning, sir."

"At ease, Stone. Formalities out the way. How's your father, Justin?"

"He's great, sir, playing golf and fishing, he's back at my house babysitting my girlfriend's bull mastiff and watching DVDs, happily retired."

"Hard shoes to fill your fathers."

"I hear from Bish that we have a real big problem brewing and they've officially asked for our help, no point telling you, Justin, we can't allow drugs anywhere near the army the penny pinchers at central funding would cut our budget even further, the best army in the world controlled by jackasses. What's your take, Justin?"

"Sir, the mob leader is a Tony Greaves, a nasty piece of scum, his men are loyal, some very deep in the background, we have solid information that they're going to target the schools as well as pubs and clubs. Greavsie will cut the tablets with something addictive, he used rat poison last time, eight deaths, and fifty-plus near misses, and the man has no scruples. We think he'll have around ten kids pedalling tablets into our school, five hundred plus kids plenty of money to be made and that's all he cares about, getting them addicted. I'd like to go into the school under the guise of a PT instructor and team to do a martial arts and self-defence demonstration followed by a two-week teaching programme, the police under the command of Detective Inspector Mike Bishop along with our lads in teams of two are covering the pubs and clubs. Army area, good cover, and good exercise for the troops. I have a very personal stake in this, sir, my girlfriend is a history teacher at the school and my daughter goes there, I was thinking of Chris Stewart and Tony Fielding.

"Chris and Tony are cool under pressure, plus Mack and the lads and Hardcase to do the actual course, hell, if we get good feedback we could roll out the programme for other schools it'll do wonders for the shy kid's confidence, I can head up liaison with Bish and the local police lads, Sir this lot need stopping fast. Greaves has supply in place, is efficient, tactically if he gets a hold, we'll have serious problems."

"You want to head our side up, Justin?"

"Sir, yes if I can, I know Bish really well and most of the police force I've trained at some point in hand-to-hand."

"When do you want to start, Justin?"

"Immediately, sir."

"Get Stewart and Fielding on board, liaise with Bish. I'll have a look at the rota to see who's available for pub duty. Sort out a workable plan and get back to me by the end of today, and Justin, this is a police operation Bish will have the final say, we're support when needed only, no going gun-ho."

"Yes, sir, already had that speech from dad."

"Aha, so George finally told you, bugger was getting ulcers trying to protect you from yourself, and this girlfriend, Justin, not a one-night stand I take it."

"No, sir, definitely not."

"A man needs to have roots. Get back to me by 15.00 hours and give your father my regards."

"Will do, sir," and saluting left the office.

"Susan, do me a favour."

"Any time, Colonel Stone, anything for you, anytime you want it, ooh wow the rumours are true, you didn't even bat an eyelid."

"What rumours, Susan?"

"The grapevine has it that you and a certain very pretty history teacher have spent the weekend shacked up at your mansion on the hill."

"You see, Susan; this is why there are no spies in the army anyone can keep a secret."

"Is that a confirmation or a denial?"

"If I tell you, there would be no fun, Susan, let's just let you find out."

"Oh, I'll find out, the lonely women of the village will be devastated if there's no hunk available to service them."

"Can you tannoy Chris Stewart and Tony Fielding to my office please, please?"

Stone sat in his office, coffee percolating in the corner, if he had a vice it would be the Italian beans that Mario brought from his homeland and still got sent regularly, he was sitting with coffee in hand when Chris Stewart and Tony Fielding walked in, "Morning, boss, love visiting you to get our coffee fix."

"Help yourself, lads, then take a seat."

"Either of you heard of Tony Greaves?" Both shook their heads. "Well, he's a drug dealer based out of Manchester and his current plan is to move his band of merry men into Yorkshire and infiltrate the pubs, clubs, and schools with his product, but this bastard has a sick little twist and adds addictive substances to his product; last year, he added rat poison to his Es resulting in eight deaths and fifty plus near misses. We are going into our school, and you two as Ofsted observers, basically sit in a classroom and watch, I'm going in as relief PE teacher, I've run it all past the Brigadier.

"Our job is to help Bish, and the lads gather evidence so we can get this shit and his gang convicted, we just need to keep our eyes open, we see anything we report to Bish; he's point on this. My girlfriend is the history teacher, and we go in tomorrow. This afternoon, we see Bish get updated, you both OK with that."

"Boss, back up a bit, girlfriend you don't do girlfriends," Chris said, "thought you were strictly wham bam thank you, ma'am."

"Hang on, Chris," he said, "'the history teacher' and that's Angela Sanders, wow, you're dating Angie Sanders, you lucky dog."

Stone had caught up on his paperwork, got Alan Schofield to take his martial arts classes, looked at the time and rang Angie, "What colour panties are you wearing?"

"Nothing exciting, plain white sensible cotton and at the moment they are quite dry."

"The Brigadier is on board and I'm going with two of my finest to see Bish this afternoon, he's running the show."

"Everything is OK here and I've got your daughter in my next class."

"Bet she slips up and calls you Angie, I love you; speak to you in a bit."

"I love you too, Justin."

Stone arrived at the police station for his meeting with Bishop, "Got some decent coffee since you were last here, Stone, budget stretched to this, and Bishop pointed to the percolator in the corner, even got some beans from Mario, so pull up a chair grab a brew and let's kick up some ideas. Right, we think Greavsie crew is around thirty, these are the photos of who we know." Stone studied the photos of Tony Greaves, Jeff and Richard Marshall, Neil and Terry Wheeler, Ronnie, and Chris Taylor, Stone memorised their faces taking particular interest in Greavsie and Ronnie Taylor, "Their files with their previous, he likes to use brothers anything goes wrong he sets one against the other, you can take those files. Results from our search of the woods where Angie said they just had the usual fag ends and roaches, a couple of biscuit wrappers and we found four buildings on the old industrial estate with signs of use, we could have done fingerprints, but it would cost a small fortune and we already know the main players.

"We've told our lads to be more vigilant, especially with strangers, the pubs and clubs have all had visits some will do the decent thing if they see anything. What have you got sorted, Stone?"

"Well, pending my next chat with Brigadier Marshall, Chris, Tony, and I are going into our school tomorrow morning, we keep our eyes open, we should also get a few two-man teams going round the pubs."

Eleven

Tony Greaves sat at his desk tapping his fingers; today it starts, lunch time at the schools his under-eighteen's start pushing the pills, and tonight the older team get down to business in the pubs then Thursday onwards into the night clubs. His team of chemists had assured him the pills were as addictive as fuck and adding the extra ingredient made them dearer to produce but swings and roundabouts once addicted he could cut the active ingredient and up the addictive after all they wouldn't fucking know or care by then. Terry Wheeler knocked on his boss's door, "Yes, Terry, what have you found out for me?"

"The woman's Angela Sanders; she's the history teacher at the local school, she's had the bull mastiff called Bonzo for three years; she lives at 23, Bellevue but she isn't there, I've got eyes on the house should she turn up. Boss, you're not going to like the next bit, the bloke is Colonel Justin Travis Stone, this fucker is the real deal, martial arts expert, fucking big scary dude if he's got something to do with the woman he'd have to be taken out, he trains the plod in martial arts and the black cunt is one of his best friends."

"Good info, Terry, well done, leave the file with me, you and Neil are on watch duty hang round the school check on the teacher to see where the colonel fits, if necessary, I'll bring in the goons," and Terry shivered.

Lunch time at school, lots of little groups of kids scattered round the large fields, Barry Jackson stood with his friends from the class took out the silver foil and the rolling kit, "Got some grade A here, lads," and started to make the joint mixing the skunk and tobacco. Jackson lit up took a huge draw held it then breathed out slowly coughing a little, "Mighty smooth, who wants a hit?" And all the hands went up, all taking their turns. "Right, who wants some it's £40 a quarter, week tick payable next Monday, no excuses?" Jackson took the orders, "Also, got my hands on some nice pills, £5 a pop extra strength Es, four-hour high minimum drop one after your tea sorted, I get £100 for every five hundred I shift, I can get any amount but to look like the dogs bollocks I need to shift lots, so I'm going to give you all ten each to start with, you bring me £50 and I'll give you a tenner, but lads this goes through me only," and Jackson handed out the small bags with ten pills in each. "Go forth and multiply," he said, thinking if I can do a thousand a week, I might be able to sort out a cheaper price. Over on another part of the school field, Tommy Bowman went through the exact same pitch with several other kids all doing the same.

Back at the barracks, Stone collected Chris Stewart and Tony Fielding and all three went to see Brigadier Marshall. "Twice in one, day Colonel Stone," said Susan, "he's expecting you all to go straight in." Stone relayed what Bish had told him and showed them the photos. Brigadier Marshall wasted no time. "You all go to school tomorrow. Stone collects the radios and the earwigs on the way; they're good for half a mile; just look like a button on your shirt and the earpieces are flesh-coloured so unless you're close, they can't be seen. I've got four teams of two doing the pub circuit, they'll report to me direct. Bish has his whole team aware of Greaves and his cronies, the plan is to catch them distributing, bring them in and move on up the drug food chain. Greaves is layered so it'll be hard to get him, but his underlings if we get them on possession or distributing and we get enough of them, he will go to ground."

"Unless we find a way to entice him out of his hole," said Stone.

"Maybe," said the Brigadier, "but that's up to Bishop, we're just back up, remember that!"

Stone swore under his breath, "What's your bug, Colonel Stone?" Brigadier Marshall said.

"It was my girlfriend that brought this to Detective Inspector Mike Bishop, I asked Bish as a friend, Angie was threatened twice, if it weren't for her bull mastiff it could have been really serious. The key players know what she looks like and the dog's distinctive, so it's personal, sir."

"Stewart, Fielding, start tomorrow, you both can go. Stone, stay." When they were alone, the Brigadier said, "Your dad is still one of my best friends, I've had a phone call this morning, young Angie Sanders made quite an impression on your father, however, she's made an even bigger impression on his son. He also said you've cleared the air at last, life should be all about family Justin, I'm sure you'll keep doing the right thing. Do your job, Justin, and protect your lady. I'll see your father next week; we've got a round of golf booked."

"Yes, sir, thank you."

Stone, Chris, and Tony spent a few minutes getting their comms working and checking signals. Stone said, "We know there are at least ten kids pushing Greavsie pills; we need to pull them in, put the frighteners on them, Barry Jackson and Tommy Bowman, we know from Angie, that they carry skunk, on a random pull, we search them in the headmaster's presence and video record the interviews, they might just be stupid enough to have the pills on them."

Chris said, "You know, the more we shake, the more dangerous the situation for Angie."

"I'll talk to her tonight, and you'll be with her at all times observing her class. I can't see them doing anything inside the school, too high profile. I think they'll mount an attack when she's out with Bonzo and I'm with her then."

"Yeah, but you're only one man, boss and as far as we know, you can't stop bullets, this punk likes to get close up and intimidate his prey."

"She has a fucking huge dog bred to rip people to bits plus I've got Dad staying with us even at sixty-one he's still a tough son of a bitch, I'll be walking point, he's still got good instincts and he's quite fond of Ang so he's with her." Chris and Tony had worked with Stone for nearly seven years they knew what he could do but they'd never seen him this way, so Tony said, "Angela Sanders is more than just a girlfriend isn't she?"

"Yes, Tony she is."

"If we push this, she's going to be in a very risky place."

"Yes, she is, that's why I have my two best men with me."

Stone arrived at school a little early, classes were still in session, several heads turned teachers and pupils alike, at six feet two inches and two hundred and twenty-five pounds of solid muscle with around 8% body fat got out of the Discovery, Stone was a presence but in his colonel uniform that presence was magnified. Sophie Preston and Barbara Robinson were in the staff common room supposedly marking papers, but having a general chit-chat, and now they were both staring out the window at Stone, Sophie said, "Wow, that man is sex on a stick, look at those bulges, and little miss prim and proper is supposedly getting shagged by it."

Barbara chipped in, "It'll not last, that man can't be tamed by just one woman, I'd let him fuck me up the arse if he wanted, he'll frighten Angie Sanders away I bet she's never swallowed in her life," and they continued to stare till he went through the school's automatic doors.

Stone walked up to reception, "Colonel Stone to see Mike Foster, he's expecting me."

Anne buzzed Mr Foster, "Yes, sir, go straight ahead first door you come to," and watched Stone walk away, yummy, and yummy she thought. Stone knocked Mike Foster stood up to great his visitor and thought wow, way to go, Angie, the man had it whatever it was, Angie was right up close the man was hot, hot, hot, be still my beating heart Mike thought.

"Colonel Stone, welcome to our school offering his hand which was taken in a grip like steel. Angie's on her way she's just finished classes for the day, while we wait would you like tea, coffee, or water Colonel Stone?"

"It's Justin or Stone whichever you prefer, I'll have a bottle of water please."

There was a small knock on the door and in walked Angie, Stone stood immediately and kissed her gently, taking both Angie and Mike by surprise. "Wow," said Mike.

"Sorry, Mike, never been in love before just winging it for now."

Angie then kissed Stone full-on in front of Mike, "And neither have I, Justin. Angie's let me know what she could tell me, do you have further details?" So, Stone let Mike know the plans Mike sat thinking for a while, "The law is specific on under-18s, and I'll get Anne in with me when you do your interviews, so we have another staff member plus video evidence."

"Bring them in one at a time and we'll shake the tree, Mike, the person leading this gang is ruthless so the situation will get worse before it gets better. I don't think they'll try anything inside the school, but I won't take any chances. Angie will have a bodyguard with her at all times, we have a radio set up between the three of us and my two lads are good at what they do."

Stone finished the briefing and left Mike's office hand in hand with Angie, "Justin, dress uniform is not exactly low profile."

"That's the point, Ang, if Greaves has eyes on the school I've been noticed, any idea where Jo will be?"

"Yes, down the hall to the right," and Stone took off still holding her hand intent on finding his daughter. Angie was aware of the stares, but she would not let go of Stone's hand.

Jo and her friends came through the door, "Jo there's your dad with Ms Sanders," said her best friend, Ella.

"Hi darling, good day," kissing her on the lips in front of her friends.

"Dad you really have to get a handle on this love thing," and she took his hand they walked down the corridor to the astonishment of her friends. Jo turned to Angie, "I only slipped up twice today calling you Angie."

"You did great Jo, I'd give you a B, and however your dad gets an F." Stone whispered in Angie's ear, "I hope the F stands for what I think it does" and they left the school.

Bonzo was contemplating, **his master was very happy, she spent a lot of time with the big mermaid man he liked the young girl she gave him lots of cuddles, he liked cuddles and gave him extra treats when his master wasn't about, he liked the different house more rooms bigger garden and last night he stayed in the girl's room, lots of animal noises better than traffic. Today was different again his master had left him with the old man he knew she'd return to walk and feed him, so he wasn't stressed he had the boom-boom music and his toys. He'd tried his little repertoire to avoid the dreaded kibble, didn't work, but managed to get a couple of chew sticks, give me a week, and maybe not even that.**

George Stone loved dogs thinking they were more loyal than a hell of a lot of people, Bonzo was a big happy beast, and Angie had done a good job. "Right, Bonzo, time for some exercise," putting Bonzo's harness on much to Bonzo's delight, **a walk is a walk** he thought. George followed the same route as Angie and his son had taken to get Bonzo used to the area, letting him off Bonzo took for the trees and George thought great one less mess to clean up. Nice day thought George so rather than turn back kept walking. A little scroat skiving off school, named Peter Jones, saw him walking with the big dog that the brothers were looking for. Thinking he could make a few quid, he rang Neil Wheeler, "What you after, Jonesy, you skiving off again."

"Yes, but I have some info, worth a few quid, that big dog you are looking for, well it's in front of me with some old bloke I've taken some photos, what's it worth."

"Jonesy, I'll sort you £20 but if you follow them get the address ring me and I'll up it to £50." Jonesy had nothing else to do and £50 would get him some prime weed.

Bonzo was in the garden catching some afternoon rays with his eyes closed, hearing the Discovery looked up to see his master, mermaid man and the girl, galloping over to greet them with slobber. Going inside, Angie thanked George for looking after him, "He looks happy and contented."

"No problem, we've had a good time, me, and the big mutt for a long walk, I've sampled some different coffees, watched The Bon Scott Years on DVD," and Bonzo followed Angie and Jo out of the room.

When they were out of earshot, "Justin, there was a young kid taking pictures of me and Bonzo, who followed us home, so Greavsie knows where you live."

"Thanks, Dad."

"Remember son, you're a cog." Angie and Jo came out of their rooms looking like sisters, both wearing jeans and t-shirts bearing the Motorhead first album cover. Stone just looked at Angie, well her breasts. "I'm up here, Justin," and George roared with laughter at his son's red face. "I'm going to make tea," George said, "I've defrosted four T-bones, them with baked spuds and salsa salad, OK for everybody?" Jo went off into the garden with Bonzo to do her homework, and Stone told him, and Angie were going to chill and watch the David Gilmour Live at Gdansk DVD unless his dad needed a hand. "Justin, I've cooked steaks for forty years, go and spend time with Angie." The second the cinema room door closed, and the lock button clicked, Stone took Angie in his arms, kissed her and running his hands down her back cupped her bottom pulling her tightly into him. "Justin, you're going to have to learn restraint," grabbing his bulging erection, continuing to squeeze, "See, Justin restraint, now I'm sure I can find a safe place to store this," and gave his penis a final squeeze, "but we'd better put the DVD on first to drown out all the screaming."

Stone sorted the DVD, set the volume loud and turned to find Angie minus jeans and panties. "Off with your trousers and boxers." And pointed to the love seat, Stone did what he was told Angie sashayed over purposely wiggling her hips, 'not quite ready' eyeing Stone's bulging erection, so kneeling down, took a man in her mouth for the very first time sucking gently. Stone took a huge breath and went stiff, Angie took her mouth off him and said saucily, "I could be wrong, but he appears to be crying."

Stone looked at her, "Ang, get up here now."

Angie smiled, "Oh, you are ready now, dear."

"Ang enough, please, now," and Angie climbed onto his lap crying out as he thrust into her, mouths finding each other they orgasmed together within two minutes groaning loudly into each other mouths. "Ang, I want to make love to you next time, not someone you think I need. I love you; I don't need the come-on signs and my dick in your mouth. I love you for you, yes, I know you haven't got much experience, I might have done this act more times than you, but I want to make love to the person I love, not what she thinks she should be."

"Justin, I'm very sorry, I just want to be everything you want."

"You are Ang, you are; now let's get cleaned up, where are the tissues and watch the DVD."

Angie could still feel Stone, "Justin, can we make love again later."

"You don't have to ask, Ang," and as she started to cry.

Justin lifted her into his lap, "Why are you crying, Ang?"

"I've upset you because I don't know how to do things; because I want to do things with you that I've never done before; because you might think I'm lousy in bed."

"Ang, you're being silly."

"I'm so in love with you, Justin."

"Then just be yourself, Ang, because it's you I love, just be you, don't try and be something you're not, because the person you are is the person I want to make love to."

Twelve

Tony Greaves sat in the disused warehouse; he now knew where Stone lived and that his father took the huge dog walking; thanks to Jonesy, a punk kid that Neil paid off, good information to have. Reports on the first day of pills in the schools were ok, Greavsie expected a slow first week, but once addiction took hold, it would be like printing money. Pubs where different, yes, the pills would do their job, but Greavsie could get anything, and he needed people to know that 'ten grams of coke.' Give me an hour; that was the beauty of his organisation everything was available at a price and if he stepped on someone else's patch, well that was what he paid the goon squad for.

"Tea's ready," shouted George, Jo and Bonzo came in; Bonzo thought **I'll try my pleading eye thing** but just when he thought **yes**, Angie and the mermaid man walked in, "Busted, Bonzo," said Angie, "sit" and reluctantly Bonzo obeyed. "See, Jo, notice the pleading eyes when you get Lemmy. You must not give in, well not very often."

"Dad, have you seen Gilmour in Gdansk? Ang was right; comfortably numb is mind-blowing."

"I might watch it with Bonzo tomorrow," and everyone tucked into their steaks, Bonzo's eyes following all the eating. Once everyone finished, "Jo sweetheart, can you get Bonzo's bowl," whose ears pricked **I'm in here** and did his waggy tail and chuffed, **feed me some of that** he thought right Jo we'll put all the steak bones with half his wet food and just a handful of kibble, now you know his commands and what to do, and Jo carried out the commands.

Stone went through his day for the benefit of Jo and Ike, who'd arrived just after seven. "The situation now is Greavsie and his gang can identify me, Ang, Bonzo and now dad and they know where we live. The cameras are on 24/7 they don't know about Ike, but have probably found out about Jo. This man and his accomplices are dangerous. Ang, you've heard his voice, and he may think you saw him, thanks to these photos we now know who these people are, and we now need to get photos of more of his crew for Bish. Tonight, Jo stops with Ike, me, Dad, and Ang walk Bonzo, and I get some pictures of anyone lurking around."

Angie and George had Bonzo out for his night-time walk walking the same path that George had earlier. Father and son had comms on, "Dad, there's a couple with eyes on you to your left; show nothing, don't alert Bonzo; go round a couple of more bends then let him off his lead as normal." Stone stood behind the two men, took pictures, and moved away still able to move with stealth. "Come back around the way you came when Bonzo's had a run."

George walking with Angie said, "It isn't in Justin's nature to be a cog, to sit back and wait, he's a born leader, he'll do the right thing now because of you, you're his controlling trigger, me and Jo love him but only you can keep him safe from himself, you're his focus, it's a lot on your shoulders if you notice his behaviour change tell me, he can't be allowed to return to what he was, he has too much to lose now."

Returning to the house, everyone got together in the kitchen, Stone rang Bish, "They know who we are and where we live; I'm sending you some pictures of the two watching us. Brig is on board, and Chris, Tony and I are going in tomorrow; the plan is to pull in Jackson and Bowman on a random search we know they carry and supply skunk. Mike Foster, the head, and his secretary Anne will attend and video the interview. Anything happening on your end?"

"Nothing so far." said Bish, "but tomorrow things will change if the drugs are tainted then we're gonna have signs. I'll send Ted Barnett down to school he can do the formal interviews, what time are you dragging them in? We'll get them at morning break 10.30; that way, they may have stuff on them, they're in Angie's class, we get them coming out Chris is on Jackson, Tony on Bowman. We watch, we wait, catch them in possession with a bit of luck, the head has master key for lockers. The Brig is sending Mach and the lads for the school demonstration."

"When's Jo getting her dog?"

"Saturday, buggers going to be bigger than Bonzo and she's going to call him Lemmy."

"Good kid, good choice, I'll get over at the weekend sometime got to get my caffeine fix and you got to show me some ab stuff, getting a bit of a paunch missuses isn't happy, Bish, you can't spot reduce; you need to lose body fat all over your stomach will be the last bit to go, come and train with me and the lads, how's your romance going."

"Angie's staying with us; now they know where she lives."

"I got the impression that Angela Sanders meant a lot to you, Stone, I'm pleased for you, really pleased, a man needs someone to come home to."

Stone looked over at Angie. "Yeah, Bish feels like home."

Angie and Jo had spent time chatting, George and Ike had sorted out some fishing trip on the boat and their golf itinerary, doors locked, alarms on everybody settled for the night. Stone with Angie in his arms kissing each other when his erection pressed into Angie's stomach, their kissing intensified. Angie's right hand gripped his stiffness and squeezed, loving the feel of him in her hand and began to slowly move her hand up and down taking mental notes where and how he liked to be touched, Stone's left hand stroked the top of her thigh moving towards her vagina stroking her short hairs before slipping a finger into her moist sex, "Justin, make love to me," and she opened her legs wide, causing Stone to moan out loud; not breaking the kiss, Stone entered her causing them both to breath in, wanting to go slow but unable to stop himself Stone thrust and within seconds, he felt his unstoppable orgasm building having already been in Angie's warm hand he couldn't hold back and moaned loudly and spurted his seed into her. "I'm sorry, I didn't give you a chance to even get going."

"It's ok, it was lovely, all thirty seconds of it," and giggled, Stone loved that giggle.

"I love you, Ang, I'm sure I'll be able to make it up to you."

"I love you too, Justin, but swap sides, you can have the wet patch seen as how it's mostly yours," and giggled again.

"You want some tissues to clean up?"

"No, Justin, I like feeling where you've been," smiled and cuddled in his arms closing her eyes content, not in the slightest frustrated.

For the second day, Stone woke up with Angie in his arms trying to slip out of her arms; she woke kissed him and said, "Can I come with you?" And started to giggle realising what she'd said, "I meant to train," so dressed in workout gear they went and did a full body weight training workout, Stone used the reverse pyramid system, heaviest weight first then dropped the weight by 10% for three sets aiming of ten reps each set, Metallica's Master of Puppets, classic album followed by AC/CD's Highway to Hell, the last Bon Scott masterpiece, played while they trained both pushing each other. Stone was exceptionally strong, but time was moving, and recovery was an issue, so the two-hour workouts were now sixty to seventy minutes. Angie had listened to Stone's instructions getting a much better workout than if she'd done on her own. With only core left to do, Angie swung round the bars, a bit of a gymnast at school and still flexible, "Very impressive, Ms Sanders," and Stone took the skipping rope and started skipping; then onto one leg then jumping on the spot getting faster and faster until the rope was a blur. Angie removed her gym top and sports bra and pulling down her jogging bottoms revealed thin blue panties, "Ang, that's cheating," as he tripped up and dropped the rope.

Angie giggled and stood with her hands on her hips smiling, "I said, I'd make up for last night's sub-par performance, what did you call it, oh yes, 'a wonderful thirty seconds'." Angie giggled again.

"I love your giggle," looking directly into her eyes, "and I love you, I'll show you how much locking the gym door and placing a towel on the workout bench, lie down."

"But Justin, I'm all sweaty."

"Ang, please, cos I need my breakfast," and kissed her mouth moving from her face to neck and onto her breasts. Angie's breathing accelerated as he lightly kissed her stomach feeling her muscles contracting with excitement, and then he kissed from the top of her inner thighs to her knees and back, noticing how wet her panties he kissed her very lightly through them. Angie groaned loudly and pushed toward his face, but Stone moved away so that the contact was still light, putting his hands on her stomach he felt her muscles shuddering and putting his whole mouth on her soaking panties over her clitoris feeling the bud harden. Angie's stomach muscles spammed, "Justin, please," as Angie again tried to push her sex into his mouth, he pulled off her wet panties and kissed her stomach, the short hairs and both her inner thighs again.

Angie's legs where shaking her need growing, Stone placed her legs over his shoulders, cupped her bottom and gently put his mouth on her clitoris feeling the stiff nub pulsing, flicking the edge of his tongue over her clitoris Angie moaned loudly, the waves building inside her the warmness turning liquid, Stone excited, but intending this to be just for Angie, forced himself to lick gently and slowly knowing that her orgasm was given but wanting to drag out the intensity and pleasure. Angie began to moan and her legs began to shake, Stone stopped licking and opened his mouth gently sucking her bud using his bottom lip so all the nerve endings got touched, Angie's orgasm took hold, "Justin, I'm going to cum," her voice deepened, stomach muscles locked hard and the contractions impossible to describe began, and Angie roared as the orgasm took over as he held her in his mouth feeling the bud pound with its contraction and felt the warm liquid gush from her body.

The ecstasy lasted for over a minute, but the contractions stayed with Angie for several minutes, as her breathing slowed a little, she found she could breathe again, it was the most intense sexual experience she had ever had and she had finally discovered the joy of oral sex. Stone gave some final licks, and she wiggled in his hands, "Stop, stop, stop, Justin, it tickles." Stone sucked her clitoris and looked up smacking his lips. "Beats a bowl of porridge, I'll be able to taste you all day. You'll be wanting breakfast now you've burnt off several hundred calories," regaining her breath and having a beautiful throbbing post-orgasm clitoris, "you can do that to me anytime again, Mr Stone, it was wonderful," and Angie laughed, "Justin, I'm throbbing, I have to walk into school and all I can feel is where your mouth has been, Justin, I'd like to return the favour."

"Well, Angie, if you're sure and when you feel you want to I'm not going to stop you, just not now, we're late for breakfast already."

When Stone and Angie entered the kitchen, Jo, George and Bonzo were already there. "Cutting it fine, Dad, you two been kissing again?"

Stone looked at Angie, "Yes, Jo, we've been kissing." Ang smiled and giggled and began to say good morning to Bonzo whose sense of smell revealed **she's been doing more than kissing mermaid man this is the happiest I've ever seen her so the big mermaid man must be doing it right.**

"Morning, son, sleep well." said George with a twinkle in his eye, "better get some extra nutrition after the morning workout to replace all those calories," winking at Angie who blushed bright red. Both opted for salted caramel protein shakes with oats and fruit followed by mushroom, bacon, onion, and tomato omelette, made by George and two cups of coffee. "Bloody hell, Angie, you can eat," said Jo.

"Yes, Jo, I guess your father's eating habits are agreeing with me," and Stone's coffee spurted over the kitchen table!

"Dad, take your iPhone with you when you walk Bonzo today, if you spot anyone watching see if you can get snap them. Do the same route, at a different time and see if they always have eyes on us, the home system showed movement last night but nothing on video. Right, we need to go, I need to introduce Chris and Tony to Mike who'll introduce us to the staff. Jo, be extra careful they probably think you're my weak spot, they've no idea you have a black belt, but only use your skills as a last resort."

"I didn't know Jo was trained."

"Dad taught me, I got my first belt at seven and my black at eleven, I'm also learning judo with Dad, he's taught me some cool stuff that's not on any course. Dad says sometimes it's the fear that makes you freeze and that's what he can't teach me, so I must go to judo classes as well that way I learn to fight against people other than dad."

"Jo's very supple and super fit with all the training and running we do; in fact, she's good at anything she sets her mind on, which is why she gets Lemmy. Right, ladies, let's go meet and greet."

At school, "Jo, you want to hang with us, see Chris and Tony before we go into the meeting."

"I don't think Tony will speak to me, my judo coach said I should get used to tackling a larger opponent and Tony got dragged out. I threw him within ten seconds." Chris and Tony were waiting in reception and both stood up when Stone, Angie and Jo walked through the door, "Morning, boss," said Chris while Tony who was two inches taller than Stone and thirty pounds heavier and only twenty-four lifted Jo off the ground, "How you doing, young ninja, beating anyone up lately apart from me, of course, I could use the excuse that you're my bosses daughter and I was taking it easy but that third put down wasn't good for my ego, I didn't know that move existed."

Jo laughed. "It doesn't, it was one of Dad's specials."

Stone said, "Angela Sanders, meet Chris Stewart and Tony Fielding, my two most trusted colleagues and good friends," who politely shook hands with her. Chris, at twenty-seven and six foot was considered a good-looking guy with a dark Mediterranean tinge from all the water sports he competed in and was always surrounded by beautiful women, was astounded by her beauty, and could understand his boss losing his head. Looking at Jo said, "Look how much you've grown this last year and filling out, boss got you training with weights as well?"

"Yeah, I've just destroyed the school half marathon record for juniors and seniors."

"Wow way to go, Jo."

"Chris, Tony, the line is you're OFSTED observers so it's not obvious that you're keeping an eye on anyone. Chris, you're with Ang."

Chris spoke to Angie, "Mine and Tony's kids go to the junior school, I don't think this mob will be targeting them yet, but the boss reckons you could become a target, so I'll shadow you till the boss says I don't anymore. Tony, you wander the building, you have permission to sit in on any class, use your skill for sussing things out of place."

Mike Foster and his secretary Anne came out of his office and more introductions where made and headed to the teacher's common room which fell silent as soon as Mike walked in. Mike addressed the twelve assembled staff, (two were on holiday and Booby Newton was taking personal time). "We have a situation in school that requires these three gentlemen to be here," all the teachers looked the three men over, Barbara Robinson stared at Stone trying seductively bending forward and showing plenty of cleavage; Stone didn't even glance. "This is Colonel Stone and he's going to tell you why." Stone stood in the middle of the room checking that everyone was paying attention, Angie hadn't seen this, the working side of him before and she was impressed, he filled the room with his presence, Angie smiled to herself she could still feel his lips on her and she wondered as he began to speak if he could still taste her.

"Good morning, everyone, please call me Stone it's what these two reprobates call me or boss, the dark handsome one on my right is Chris to my left is a gentle giant called Tony. We are here because drugs are being brought into school, we are working with the police, Detective Inspector Mike Bishop is leading the investigation, and our job is to watch for any signs of drug use. The leader of this drug team is extremely dangerous, the pills coming into school are laced to be as addictive as possible, bottom line, he doesn't care, and he wants to make as much money as quickly as possible and human lives do not matter to him in the slightest. We will do our best not to get in your way, but we want the situation sorted fast. Any questions."

Darren Smyth raised his hand, "Is there anything we as teachers can do?"

"Yes, watch for signs of drug use, dilated pupils, odd or threatening behaviour, excessive aggressiveness, mood swings, some of these drugs are like a switch one second normal the next paranoid, do not try and sort them out yourself it could be dangerous let one of us three know. Our main concern is the protection of Angie; she initially brought this to our attention having overheard this gang, but she has been seen and threatened by them, this gang know who she is and where she works. It is very unlikely that anything will happen in school, but we are taking no chances," and any doubts anyone had about Stone's relationship with Angie were put to rest as he gently placed his hand on hers.

"Please go about your jobs as usual, there may be as many as twenty kids pushing these pills, do not say anything to the pupils if anyone asks these two are OFSTED observers and I'm temporary cover for Bobby Newton, any pupil who asks too many questions let one of us know. It's my intention to keep you all in the loop; I'll give you all a briefing in the staff room at 08.30 every morning. Thank you for your time."

Stone, Chris, and Tony checked their comms and Angie led the way to her first class, two long corridors later, Stone kissed her 'bye' ignoring the stares and murmurs of the pupils. "Chris, you're with Angie, I'm going to PE and Tony's going to check Jackson and Bowman's lockers with Mike. Ang, we'll be back around 10.30, see you then," and squeezing her hand they walked off.

Angie said to Chris, "Whatever you do, don't show this lot," pointing at the class, "any fear," walking into the classroom. Angie addressed her class, "Happy Tuesday morning you lot, I want you on your best behaviour for the rest of the week, this is Mr Stewart, he's going to observe the class."

"Is that other man your boyfriend, miss?" Rebecca said.

"Yes, Rebecca he is."

"He's very handsome, miss."

"Yes, he is, Rebecca. I'm very lucky."

Stone and Tony went to Mike Foster's office; Anne said, "Just go through, you two ready for coffee yet?"

"No thanks, Anne we'll hang on till ten thirty."

Leaving the office, Mike said, "I've the keys and locker numbers 105 and 117 for the two lads. Shall we go there first after taking Stone to his gym class?" And to Stone, "We've amalgamated four classes, so you've got one hundred plus pupils, they don't know why or for what. The PA system and head mic are live so you can speak and move around the room at the same time." Stone had given this talk many times usually to army or police recruits and it was always a success, but he'd never talked to under eighteens, but self-defence worked at any age. Mike continued, "You have two teachers with you, they will have all the students' details," and walked into the auditorium. "Colonel Stone this is Ms Sophie Preston and Ms Barbara Robinson."

"Pleased to meet you ladies," Barbara bent forward cleavage on display. "What do we call you, Stone sounds so formal."

"Stone's fine, almost everybody calls me Stone, Chris, and Tony call me boss to my face, probably some other things behind my back, ok, ladies," and nodding to Mike, they walked into the centre of the hall.

"Morning, students," said Mike, "today and for the next two weeks our regular PE classes have been suspended, Mr Newton has been called away urgently, in his place we have the honour of having one of our army's most decorated soldiers with us. Colonel Stone, who held up his hand in acknowledgement, who will explain what is going to happen, Colonel Stone, the class is all yours, and left the room to do the locker search with Tony."

"Good morning, young ladies and gentlemen, I teach self-defence to the army and police forces, Mr Foster thought it would be a good idea in Mr Newton's absence to give you a talk about self-protection and to demonstrate some basic moves, Ms Preston and Ms Robinson will take your names should you wish to participate in part two of this course. I'm not allowed to demonstrate any moves with you personally; however, if you would like to take my basic course then see the teachers and get a parent to sign a disclaimer form, as with any contact sport, you may get injured and we don't want any of you suing the army, to be honest, the most that you'll get hurt is probably a sprain from falling wrong. The course begins next Monday; just see the two teachers at the end of the demonstration should you wish to get involved, I will tell you all that it will do wonders for your self-confidence. All your training will be done on mats with a few bruises at worst, honestly, would I lie to you?" getting a small laugh from his audience.

"Today we will give a demonstration and here are five of my army buddies who will be teaching the course, we will also have a female instructor later, can I introduce you to Mach, Steve, Trevor, Andy, and John," all standing and taking a bow as their names where mentioned; they all looked apprehensive but glad of the break from mooning around the barracks, Mach whispered to Stone, and Stone removed the headset. "Boss, it's really good to get out of the barracks but if I'd known you were going to beat us up I'd have gone on leave."

"Relax, Mach, it's only a demo and you get school meals again for three weeks and maybe you need a new girlfriend look at those two over there," looking over at Sophie and Barbara, "they're both available big strapping hunk of men like you, maybe get some three in a bed action."

Stone put the head set back on and said to the pupils, "In a street fight, there are no rules, so to demonstrate these five will attack me at the same time, I'm going to get Ms Preston to count to five."

Sophie started, "One, two." Stone moved on one, "Three, four," and by the time she said, "Five," all army recruits were on the mats unhurt, Stone helped his now even more sheepish recruits up, winking at Mach, "Remember I said there were no rules." Stone said addressing the pupils. "Next, Mach, Steve grab those baseball bats, we're on as soon as you pick them up." Mach went left, Stone allowed the bat to come down and with astonishing speed, he flipped back out of the way and flicking his right foot kicked the bat out of Mach's hand, chopped with his left hand winding him and put him on the mat with his left foot. The arc of the bat from Steve was heading right for Stone's head, a quick sideways move, up with his right leg straight into Steve's groin and he was down, total time of three seconds.

Stone addressed the class, "Hand-to-hand combat is about speed and being aware, the second bat coming down towards my head if I wasn't focused it would have crushed my skull and remember in a street fight you don't hold back punches. The winding chop to Mach, in a street fight would have been a neck chop and the knee in Steve's groin would have ended his chances of having kids, the point I'm making is films and TV glorify fighting, all the moves are carefully choreographed, in the real world this fight would be over and these two would be in hospital. You will know from having seen fights here at school that the reality is much different. I'll demonstrate with Mach."

"Not again, boss," was heard over the headset and the pupils laughed. "A fight usually starts with a disagreement that cannot be verbally solved, then you get into an argument that goes backwards and forwards that usually ends with one person losing his cool completely and throwing a punch, now because that punch is thrown in temper, the heart rate is up, the fight or flight response controlling adrenaline is off the chart, the punch when thrown has no direction, no thought and no concentration behind it, for a trained martial arts fighter it would be no contest.

"Mach has just got his 3rd Dan in Jiu-Jitsu so compared to 99% of the population he is a supreme fighter, I'm the only 9th Degree Red Belt in the army, now I'm not bragging I just would like you to see the difference, so we compare. Mach will now do a series of moves watch his movements closely."

Mach did his demonstration. "Now I'll do exactly the same moves." Stone's speed was astonishing; it made Mach's look like he'd been standing still. Mach had a huge grin on his face as did the other four army sergeants, Stone slapped Mach on his back, "Now the reason for the demonstration, why am I so much faster than Mach? Because of this." Stone tapped the side of his head, "My thought process is faster than Mach's because I've spent years, up to twelve hours a day, doing martial arts. Even now every other day, I train at six a.m. for an hour and I haven't seen active duty for nine years; basically, my mind tells my body what and when to do it in milliseconds, the only difference between Mach and me is years of practice. The course Mach and the others teach is a very basic defence-orientated one, how to avoid getting hit in the first place, using your mind to avoid confrontation, you will be taught to use your mind and allow your body to follow. Like Mach and I demonstrated, once you learn it just becomes practice and more practice. I was very lucky I had a natural aptitude and some very good teachers, I was in the army going up against better opponents and I had the drive, determination, and desire to get there, yes natural ability, flexibility and basic strength all count, but this tapping the side of his head, this is the key."

Stone looked around the pupils, "Somewhere amongst you is someone who has the potential to be world-class, all it takes is the ability to use your mind before your body and then practice, but the knock-on effect helps you in all areas of your lives, your grades should improve, and your relationships should improve, and hopefully you will be better young ladies and gentlemen. Thank you." Stone got a huge round of applause, took off the microphone, and switched off the PA.

Mach came up to him grinning, "Boss, you talk some shit."

"Mach, I'm doing you a favour, got you five out of barracks for weeks training school kids, plus you get to eat here much better grub."

"Yeah, I suppose there's that."

"You lads aren't back on till 14.00, and then we'll see how many have shown an interest in signing up."

"Boss, you doing the same demo again?"

"Why, you think I should change anything?"

"Yes, boss, don't pick me and Steve again, I know you pulled your throws, but Steve's nuts and my stomach's sore and your hands are like steel, and what was that shit about practice, 'You do six maybe eight hours a week'."

"I do twenty still no contest. Must be my natural ability, Mach."

"No, boss, it is cos you're Superman without the cape."

Mike Foster had crept in and stood at the back of the hall watching the pupils file out, many of them were signing up for part two of the course. Stone joined him, "I might tweak this afternoon's demo."

"Why, you got your points across? There was plenty of the 'ooh' 'aargh' factor with the demo and you didn't glorify fighting."

"I missed a couple of things; on reflection, notice it's all boys wanting to sign up, girls need to learn more than boys they're the bigger risk in today's society, I'm going to get our lady instructor here for the afternoon demo she's just over five feet, very pretty, soft-spoken but incredible in hand-to-hand, get her to do a demo let the girls see it can be done then see how many sign up and she also has a super fit body which could persuade some of the unsure boys to sign up."

They went over to the teacher's table, "Ladies, how did it go?"

Barbara said, "Forty-three out of one hundred and fifteen only six girls though."

Sophie looked at Stone, "Might get more girls if you do the demo topless," clearly flirting.

"Good idea Sophie, I think Jane would have to wear a sports bra though." Stone rang Jane, who answered immediately seeing who it was, listened intently and said, "Yes, Stone, I'll be at the school at fourteen hundred this afternoon, but only if you wine and dine me after."

"Jane, I can pay for dinner, but I can't take you, sorry babe."

"So, the army grapevine got it right, the army's most eligible bachelor has finally been smitten by a woman. Do I get to meet her maybe beat her up a little?"

"Yes, she'll be here."

"Bugger, Stone, you not even trying to deny it, it must be love."

"Yes, Jane."

"Shit, what's her name?"

"Her name's Angela Sanders."

"Does she feel the same way?"

"Yes, Jane."

"How long have you known her?"

"Three days?"

"Stone, you're kidding."

"No, Jane."

"So, I won't be getting sweaty with you."

"Jane, you never got sweaty, see you at fourteen hundred." Stone turned to see the conversation had been overheard by Mike, Barbara, and Sophie, "Jane's coming for the afternoon lecture, now I'm off to see Tony and check in with Ang and Chris." Mike went off to prepare the interview office and check if Ted Barnett had arrived.

Leaving Sophie and Barbara on their own, the latter said, "Fuck, Sophie, little miss goodie two shoes must be a hell of a fuck."

"Maybe he loves her, Barbara."

"What, in three days, well, he didn't respond to your drooling, or even my cleavage, and this Jane has the hots for him, should be an interesting afternoon."

Thirteen

"Tony, where you at?" Stone said.

"I'm outside Angie's class, your woman has had Chris dressed as a Viking, a knight and now a World War I soldier."

"Chris will be in his element."

"Yep, he looks like he's having a ball, all we need now is the ninja turtle."

"Justin, you got a sec?"

"Yeah, Mike."

"We've got a couple of lads in Darren's class showing symptoms of drug intake."

"Tony, we may have a problem bring your medic-kit, I need your eyes for a second opinion."

"What class number, Mike?"

"225 second floor."

"Room 225, Tony." Up in room 225, Neil Todd and Shaun Stevens sat totally unaware of where they were, both sweating and shaking, eyes like pinpricks, the other pupils eyeing them up. Stone and Mike arrived and seconds later Tony from the opposite direction. "I'll go in," Mike said, "then it doesn't look odd," even without Darren Smyth pointing the two out it was fairly obvious. Mike went in and had what looked like a normal conversation with Darren, "They're getting worse, Mike."

"Right, end the class," and Mike went out.

Darren addressed the class "I need to see Mr Foster now, you can all have an extra ten-minute break time," and the pupils packed their bags and began leaving the room, the two lads were so far out of it they hadn't moved, the rest had left the room.

"Chris, don't react," Stone said speaking into the mic. "Don't let Angie finish the class, me and Tony are tied up, got two lads in trouble." Chris had a quiet word with Angie, who announced to the class that it would run till eleven instead of ten forty-five and they would take second break rather than first. Chris had some more costume changes, and most of the class was so engrossed in the history lesson that they didn't care.

"Neil, how you doing, son?" Tony said as Shaun tried to stand Stone gently pushed him back down. "Boss, his heart rates of the chart," and Shaun began to struggle. Tony had a quick look, "Amphetamine-based."

"GET THE FUCK OFF ME," shouted Shaun trying to get out of the hold Stone had on him. "I agree, Tony, pass me some ties," and Stone gently placed Shaun's hands behind him and locked his arms together over his wrists but on his shirt so as not to be too tight. Tony had his Med-kit open taking out two naltrexone and a small bottle of water, "Boss, hold his head," and Tony gently pushed on the sides of his jaw, put the two tablets in his mouth and massaged his throat to make sure he swallowed the tablets while Stone moved Shaun's head back. Neil had remained out of it. While Tony phoned for an ambulance, Stone phoned Mike's office, Anne answered, "Yes, Stone, I'll put you through."

"Mike, get back to room 225 and bring the video camera if Ted has arrived bring him and quickly." Tony was checking the vitals of the two lads, blood pressure was far too high, Neil's 145/90 pulse 140, but Shaun's at 170/100 pulse 195 was cause for concern. Mike and Ted arrived, and Stone ran through what had happened so far. "Now Ted and I are going to search both lads, Mike, can you video?" Searching Shaun first as he was the most agitated, going through his pockets and finding a small, wrapped silver foil package in his right pocket then removing his shoes finding a small plastic bag with eight white tablets in his right shoe, "Mike, get a close-up."

Neil had nine white pills in his left pocket but nothing in his shoes. Two paramedics ran into the room and quickly took over as Tony gave them his report. Ted took out a couple of evidence bags and wrote the find details on each bag ready to take to Bish after the interviews. One of the paramedics arrived back with a wheelchair and Stone gently took off the restraints making sure the paramedic observed there were no restraint marks. "Mike, can you finish up here we need to get to Angie's class. Chris, we are on our way."

On the way, Stone asked, "Tony, what's in lockers 105 and 117?"

Tony showed the photos he'd taken, everything had been put back in the exact same place, saying, "They both have skunk wrapped in silver foil in a padded envelope and white tablets in clear bags; look to be around sixty to seventy in both lockers so we have them for dealing providing they go to their lockers."

Stone pulled out his phone, "Mike, I need the master locker key again."

"Ok, Justin."

"Shaun and Neil are with the paramedics, oh and can you bring the video camera, this is urgent, Mike, right now, please!" Mike arrived in two minutes and Tony set about taking a lock out an empty locker opposite and setting the video camera to record activity at lockers 105 and 117. "I'll follow Bowman instead of you; Chris has Jackson. Mike, can you let Ted Barnett know what's happening and both of you go to your office this is going to come to a head soon?"

Stone looked in Angie's classroom in time to see Chris dressed as a ninja turtle, aping it up in front of a laughing audience; *shit* thought Stone *should have had an extra video camera* and took out his iPhone and shot the scene paybacks a bitch, and speaking into the com mic, "Nice outfit, Chris, you love being in limelight; we can always hire yourself out for parties."

Chris grimaced, "You can't tell the lads, boss."

"Oh, I think I can do better than that, Christopher," and waved his phone through the window, "now can you do that dance again I think I missed the beginning?" Angie called the class to quiet and thanked Mr Fielding for his participation and the class applauded. Giving Chris time to get back into his work clothes, she completed the lesson formalities and then dismissed the class and they started to leave in small groups. Chris followed Jackson nodding at Stone as he passed. Bowman was starting to stand up as Stone went into the room, quickly and quietly telling Angie, "I'm following Bowman. Their lockers are full. Got to go, love you."

Stone spoke into the comms, "Looks like my boy is heading for the locker. Chris, how about you?"

"Jackson is standing talking to four other lads, OK there moving."

"Tony, how are you doing?"

"Video is in place should pick up six lockers with 105 and 117 near the centre."

Stone took out his phone, "Mach, I need you and the lads hanging around by the lockers. Mach, lunch can wait, I'll make sure you all get lunch, there's two dinner times in schools you numpty."

Stone called up Chris and Tony, "Mach and the lads are going to the locker area."

"Good, Jackson still has his four mates with him and at his locker." Tony, with his back to Jackson, had his phone on video who was well into his sales pitch. "I'll give you all ten each," and opened the locker.

"Chris, Tony, Mach, the lads should be around; we don't pull till we see what Bowman's going to do. There's still plenty of cover with all the kids about."

"Ok, boss, we're on it, capture on your word," and on queue, Bowman opened locker 117, took out the bags of skunk and the pills, as he'd pocketed the pills, Stone stepped up and put a hand on his shoulder, "Just a sec, lad," and took the pills and dope out of his pocket in full view of hopefully the video camera. "Chris, now," and Chris, Mach and the others stopped all five lads. Chris takes them to the headmaster's office and Tony brings the camera.

In the headmaster's office, Stone turned to Ted Barnett, "How do you want to do this? We have six to interview instead of two, do you want the four minor players first, they're lined up outside with a couple of members of staff, me and Chris will sit in Anne's office with the two main culprits. Tony has the video camera so he's in with you, Anne, and Mike."

In Anne's office, Stone said, "Mach, Trevor, Andy, John, Steve, go get your lunch, be back to the gym at 14.00. Mach and Steve eat as much as you want, you other three light meals only gentlemen, don't want no puking." Mach and Steve high-fived each other. "I have some great footage of young Christopher here."

"No, boss, please," winding Chris up.

Tommy Bowman spoke, "Those pills and skunk are mine for my use only."

"Son you're in a heap of trouble, but your mate there, he's going to get done for dealing, so I suggest you both shut up and wait for your interviews."

Everything was ready and Ted called the first boy in and started the interview, "Give me your name and address, Mr Foster can you verify these details? How do you know Barry Jackson?"

"I get the odd joint off him it helps concentrate on exams." Ted continued, "And the pills. We knew nothing; he was going to try and give us all ten each to sell on if we sold ten, we'd get £10 plus he'd do our dope cheaper, thought we'd get some dope then just give him the pills back next week." One by one, the next three all gave a similar story.

Ted then brought them all in together telling them. "Legally, you haven't committed a crime, just being stupid doesn't count the skunk we take off you, your parents will be informed and you will get randomly searched by Mr Foster or one of his staff, from now on any further drugs found on any of you will have dire consequences," and turning to Mike asked, "Mr Foster, what would you like to do with these four?"

"I'll ring the parents and tell them what has taken place and follow up with a formal letter, so we have something on file. You four can go to lunch after which you report back to my office, and we'll sort some detention," and turned to Anne, "Can you ask Colonel Stone to send Tommy Bowman in?"

Two minutes later, a defiant Bowman sat across from Ted Barnett, "That stuff is mine; I want it back you can't keep it; I wasn't selling, it was for my own use," video running and Anne taking notes, Mike sat in the corner watching proceedings.

Ted was aware of the video, "You have over a quarter of skunk, that's too much for personal use in one day unless you have a very bad habit, but I can order a blood test which would tell me how much cannabis is in your system, either way, you don't get the dope back. Now our main interest, the pills, we know this was a packet of 100," showing Bowman the confiscated pills, "There are 49 left, we know you got these pills Monday today is Tuesday, 51 tablets gone, I need to know who has them and who gave you them to sell?"

Bowman turned white and clammy, "No way I'm telling you who gave me them, I'll tell which five lads got ten each, I tried one myself last night, but I'm not telling where I got them."

"Give Mr Foster the five names, Tommy, then I'm going to take you down to the police station once I've interviewed Barry Jackson. My boss will want to talk with you, and he will want the name or names of those who supplied you, this is a very serious matter, maybe he can offer you a deal, go back and wait in the secretary's office and have a think about what you've done and got yourself involved in."

Barry Jackson knew enough to know he'd been caught red-handed and was in trouble but when Ted started the formal interview things got worse. "Barry, you are in serious trouble, lad. Neil Todd and Shaun Stevens are both on the way to hospital having taken one or two of those tablets you supplied to them." Barry Jackson just sat, "Barry, you will be taken to the station and charged with possession with intent to sell, selling a class three drug, and depending on what happens to the two lads, there may be more charges. You will not get just a slap on the wrist. You will go to court, and you will go to juvenile prison."

Still, Barry just sat. "Do you want to say anything before we see my boss? He will want the name or names of who supplied you. I already have five names from Tommy do you want to add any more? Nothing to say. Right, go and wait in the other office until your lift to the station arrives."

Ted rang Bish and relayed the interview details, requesting transport to the station. Bish asked him, "Do you think they'll give up Greaves' crew?"

"They're only sixteen, sir, the thought of going to juvie prison turned them both white, but Greaves gets by on fear and intimidation so they might be more frightened of him than us. I need a squad car with two uniforms for Jackson, I'll bring Bowman in myself, I'll need a uniform to accompany me, he was the more shocked maybe if I tell him stories about juvie, he might be cracking by the time you see him."

"Good idea, Ted, see you in a bit." Ted went into Anne's office asking Stone to step outside and filled him in on how the interviews had gone. "I'm going to take Bowman to the station myself, he's already jumpy, thought I'd tell him some stories about juvenile detention, worry him up, then Bish might get him to name and shame. Jackson is tougher and won't crack even now that the pills have two lads in the hospital. It's up to Bish; it's his case, if we get the names, we get closer to Greavsie." The whole school watched as the squad car left with Jackson, and Ted taking Bowman.

Stone went to see Mike, "Did you get everything written down and recorded?"

"Yes, and Sergeant Barnett has the original statements, videotape of the lockers and the interview videotape."

"Now it's up to Detective Inspector Bishop, and lunchtime for us," and Chris and Tony went off to the school canteen.

"Bloody hell, school meals have changed since I was a lad," said Stone tucking into chicken breasts with a huge salad. "I think you got four kids portions, boss; the dinner lady has the hots for you and you didn't even notice. All that grub you'll be the one puking this afternoon," said Tony.

"Oh, I'm not fighting this afternoon lads. Hardcase is coming down."

"You are shitting me," said Chris, "boss, that's not one of your best ideas you realise how she feels about you she's like a puppy around you and you are bringing her to school, what if she meets Angie."

"She's specifically asked to meet her."

"Fuck, boss and you're OK with that?"

"Yeah," Jane said, "she'd only break her bones if she hurt me. Chris, you don't know Jane like I do; I need to make sure she's OK with me and Ang. Tony, did you know about Chris's costume changes?"

"No, boss, please," said Chris. "Tony, I have a video I'll get you a copy it'll look good on the camp's big screen. It's great getting my own back," as they both looked at Chris's aghast face.

"Well you did video, the boss singing and strutting in the shower," Tony said.

"Yeah, but I blanked out below the waist."

"Yeah, but a colonel doing I want to break free with no clothes on, I think you deserve your comeuppance."

Angie spying Stone grabbed her lunch and sat next to him across from Chris and Tony, turning she put her tray down and kissed Stone, "HI, honey, how your day has been?"

"It's been action-packed, and I hear you have a video star in class," taking out his phone to show her the video of Chris the green ninja, "it'll look good on the barracks' big screen." Chris looked at his best friend and boss and saw a side of him he'd never seen before, the man was so in love he just didn't care who knew, and Angie was breathtaking when she smiled, you could feel the atmosphere between them.

"Oh, Justin, I think green goes with Chris's eyes."

Another revelation, he thought, *she calls him by his first name*! Barbara Robinson and Sophie Preston sat at the table opposite watching, "Jesus, they should get a room," said Sophie.

"Well, it looks like it's a mutual thing to me, Sophie," said Barbara, "let's see what happens when the army girl turns up."

From where Jo was sitting with her friends, she could see her dad, Chris and Tony and saw Angie get her food, join her dad, and kiss him, "Wow, Jo, Ms Sanders just kissed your dad."

"Yeah, she's his girlfriend. Oh shit, Dad's coming over with Angie and they're holding hands."

"Hardcase is going to do this afternoon's demo; only got six girls signed up, Jo."

"Dad, does Jane know about Angie?"

"Jane is the army's top women's martial arts trainer, she's small, very pretty and deadly in hand-to-hand, she has also had the biggest crush on me for years. I love her but not in that way, she heard on the grapevine about us, and she wants to meet you. We've a few minutes before dinner times up, you want to tell me about your morning or kiss me some more," and Stone practically dragged her into the empty corridor.

"I'll fill you in on events tonight," taking her in his arms and kissing her so hard it took her breath away.

"Wow, Justin you sure know how to kiss," and kissed him back with equal frenzy as the dining room doors opened and out poured pupils and teachers. Jo, being the first to spot them. "Way to go, Dad, low profile again."

Stone caught up with Chris and Tony, "Chris, you're back to dressing up, Tony with me, we'll do this lecture, then I'll ring Bish to find out what's next." While they waited at the school entrance for Hardcase to arrive, Tony said, "Boss, this woman scares me, you look at her you think pretty, short, soft-spoken spoken and then she goes hulk in the ring."

"Jane had a lot to deal with growing up, she's as good as me with her mind to muscle coordination, just I'm one hundred plus pounds more muscle, you think she'll like Angie."

"I think she'll be pissed; it isn't her."

"It never was going to be. I look at Jane like a close sister."

"I know how you look at Angie, seen it close up, me and Chris might have well not been there."

"Tony, what you and Chris have to remember is, this is new to me, all my life has been about control, and with Ang, I have none."

The bright red Firebird came roaring into the school grounds; the rider lifted the bike onto its back wheel and wheeled onto the drive, Hardcase had arrived, "Boss, she's a female version of you, likes an entrance." Jane Casey stowed her bike helmet grabbed her kit bag, ran, and jumped into Stone's arms kissing him on his lips to no response.

"Jesus, Stone it's like hugging a steel girder, you look and smell good too."

"Hi, Tony, congrats on the 3rd Dan, it's all practice and speed from now on, boring, breaking heads is much more fun, your woman here then, Stone."

"Jane, you promised to be good."

"Oh, Stone, I promised I wouldn't break any of her bones, the love of my life loves another, I need to be beating someone up."

"Jane, you know I love you only like a sister, shit, Jane, I didn't exactly plan this."

"Yep, but Stone, that's not how I love you, let's go and beat some people up, it always makes me feel better then you can introduce me to your woman."

"Jane, her name is Angie."

"Lead the way, I need my fighting fix."

Tony whispered into Stone's ear, "Oh boy, this is going to be a fun afternoon." Tony remained at the front of the school and as Stone and Jane moved towards the gym, said, "Boss, you sure I'm not needed," looking over at Jane.

"Thanks, but I have to sort this myself." Tony knew to say no more.

Stone knew Jane was pissed off, but she knew their relationship was what it was, like everyone else who knew Stone well they didn't think he would ever do serious. Jane could tell just by the way he said Angie's name that he'd never felt that way towards her, the hope she'd carried when he was doing one-night stands had gone. She had to meet Angie, put her mind at rest and get over the loss and accept she had his friendship and love but not in the way she wanted.

Entering the gym hall once again, Mike Foster did the introduction and Stone took the floor. "While I'm quite pleased with how many signed up for part two of the course, nearly all boys, the facts in our country are that the most vulnerable people are young girls, either from rape, assault, abused or groomed in the big cities, all are far too common. It is our belief turning, and showing his team, that even basic self-defence will help in a situation where men prey on the supposed weak. Statistics show that at least one in four females will at some time face some form of physical or sexual abuse. If you want to sign up for part two, where you will learn practical moves to help you, should a bad situation happen, Ms Robinson and Ms Preston will take names at the end. My team this afternoon are Mach, Steve, Trevor, Andy, and John these five young upstarts will be your team on part two plus I'd like to introduce you to Jane, the lady who will be taking the girls," and Jane Casey stepped forward a pretty, petite and dressed in a red sports bra and tight cycling shorts, every young boy's fantasy, "on the barracks her nickname is Hardcase, and you are about to see why."

"You five big five men now get to have a little fun with this short defenceless woman."

Mach's "Oh shit" was loud enough to be picked up on Stone's mic, "Jane is out for a nice walk, and these five men see a pretty little thing and decide to have some fun, go," said Stone. All five men dropped the mat within seconds, Jane's hand and feet speed was amazing to see, five men down and she wasn't even breathing hard which you could see by the way her body moved. Stone spent a few seconds looking at Jane wondering at the nature of this strange world, she was very attractive, on par with his physique and attracted to him, why did he not feel the same way and why had Angie had such an effect on him?

Fourteen

Angie and her class, including Jo and Chris who sat next to her, were watching the demonstration, Stone smiling when spotting them in the crowd, Jane noticed and following his eyes saw Jo and a very beautiful woman next to her and knew just by the way she looked back that she was Angie. "Something's, off, Angie."

"Jom the lads are hurt, it's only supposed to be a demo," and Chris stood up. Stone waved him back down, shit, what Chris, me and Tony warned him. Stone looked over at the team and a clearly shook-up Mach, who did his eye roll which indicated something was very wrong with the situation. Stone also knew that Jane in this frame of mind was dangerous, her childhood had included indifferent parents who didn't know how to show love and fighting off several of her mother's lovers who fancied a threesome, and in her eyes, Stone had now fallen for someone else and rejected her, she was hurting, she had to vent and Stone was the only person who had a hope of controlling her. "Too easy, Stone, you should fight me," which was picked up on the mic. Angie and Jo watching looked at each other. "Oh, fuck not here," and Chris stood again, Stone held up his hand and he sat, shit fuck.

"Angie, something isn't right, look at Dad's stance, and Mach and the lads got taken down far too hard, Jane looks like she wants to hurt Dad."

Jane stood defiantly, "Come on, Stone; let us see if I'm better than you."

"You're not," and Stone removed the head mic, handed it to Mach, "Switch this off."

"Boss, not here."

"It's ok, Mach," and Mach looked at Chris letting him know all was far from ok. "Jane, you didn't pull your punches, you hurt your friends and you need to dial it down, now. This is an exhibition only; the lads have done nothing to warrant your piss poor attitude and I've done fuck all wrong." Only rarely did the lads hear their boss swear and the fact that he dressed Jane down in front of them, they realised the situation was getting out of control. "This is a demonstration only, whatever frustration you feel is with me not the lads and if you think that means you can take me on, well come and try."

Oh shit, Mach could tell by the boss's attitude that Jane had taken a step too far and he was just as pissed off as she was, looking to where Angie and Jo were seated trying to make them aware of the rapidly unravelling situation, up now you two said Chris this is going wrong too fast. Mach saw Chris stand with Jo and Angie her eyes showing concern; Mach shook his head letting them know the boss was trying to defuse the situation and he looked back to the two people he respected most, touching Stone on the shoulder, "Boss, maybe not here."

"Mach, I'm sorry nobody assaults my friends and my team."

Stone stood over Jane clearly angry and very quietly said, "Yes, I love someone else. It was never going to be you. I never led you on, you're like a baby sister to me, get over it, and it has happened, it is beyond your control or mine. The problem with you, Hardcase, is you are overconfident, there's always someone better, you need to lose the attitude or one day you will get really hurt, you understand?" Oh fuck, not here oh fuck, thought Mach as he watched his friend go to a place he hadn't been to for many years, he looked up at Chris conveying his thoughts with his facial expression, move now girls Chris said. Stone looked over at Jane, "You're sure you want to do this?"

"Yes," practically spitting the words out. Stone looked to where Angie, Jo and Chris stood and mouthed 'I'm sorry.'

"Oh fuck no, no, no Dad," whispered Jo and grabbed Angie's hand, "we have to stop this somehow." Angie already realised the seriousness of what was taking place and the fact that this was the first time she'd ever heard Jo swear, but it was a long way and shouting wouldn't work as it was very noisy with the hum of something going to happen that wasn't on the script so she grabbed Jo's hand and began to move through the throng of school kids hoping they'd be in time, Chris ordered the kids out of the way as most where now standing.

Meanwhile, Stone took off his shirt and looked at Mach and the other four none of you get in the way as your commanding officer this is a direct order. Mach had one more attempt, "Boss, please not here," but Stone just looked, and they all stood back he'd gone super solider.

"Daddy, no," and Jo started to cry, Jane sneered, "You might still have the physique but you are older, slower and not in combat anymore, I am."

"Jane, there is always someone better, it's just not you."

"Well, we'll see." Stone could tell by the way Jane moved that she wasn't messing about, he allowed her to get a few punches in might calm her down, "Fuck it, Stone, you're not trying," she knew he'd allowed the punches through, Stone thought enough was enough as Jane moved forward but Stone moved quicker picked her up and flung her on the mat pinning her down and whispered, "Jane, I have no control who I fall in love with." Jane pulled out of his grip trying for a scissor kick, again Stone was just too quick, beckoning her to try again he stood, she couldn't miss but she did, Stone moved faster than the naked eye picked her up and once more slammed her into the mat, "Jane, I'm not your parents, I'm not abandoning you, you are one of my closest friends."

"But I wasn't close enough for you to love, was I?"

"No, Daddy, please stop," Jo shouted.

"Justin, stop this please." Mach put his arms out telling Chris it was a direct command to keep out of it. "Angie, only you and Jo can stop this, we'd get court marshalled."

What followed was a series of kicks and punches that were truly world-class, they were going at it full force, connecting arms, shoulders, thighs, and shins, and both were going to have serious bruises. Angie and Jo had both started shouting stop, but the school kids were in a frenzy now realising what was happening wasn't right, but still too far away to do anything about it. Mach with the four stepped forward saying, "Enough, both of you, enough, boss, Jane."

Stone looked, but was too far gone now, "You all keep the fuck out of the way, I've done fuck all wrong and SHE needs teaching a fucking lesson," and the look on Stone's face frightened them enough that they stepped back. Mach shouted at Angie and Jo, "Hurry up," at the top of his voice, but Stone didn't even acknowledge the shout, "Come on, Hardcase, you think you're the real deal, come on what you are waiting for, come on hit me." Jane tried every move she knew, and Stone avoided every move, "Not so good now are we, let me have a go," and with astonishing speed, he lifted Jane up above his head intent on throwing her onto the mat and doing some real damage.

"NO, JUSTIN" shouted Angie running towards them with Jo immediately behind her. Stone finally seeing the two people he loved most in the world realised he was out of control, and he still had Jane above his head and put her gently back down on the ground and gave her a huge cuddle, "I'm sorry, Jane." Jane had realised her mistake when she had tried hitting him and missing that he'd gone to another level, even goading her and when Mach and the lads had tried to break it up the look in his eyes scared her, but then when he'd picked her up with ease she knew his breakdown was even more apparent than hers. "Stone, we are a right couple of fuck ups."

As Mike quickly called an end to proceedings and Mach moved forward, Stone turned and hugged his daughter and Angie as tears ran down their faces. "I'm sorry, so sorry, so very sorry," Angie picked up and handed him his shirt still crying it was impossible to miss how much she loved him, Jo held onto her father for dear life, "Dad, DAD, DADDY please come back to us, please daddy," and shook with her pleading and force of her tears, he looked at his daughter and the woman he loved. "I'm ok, really, I'm truly sorry," he said, "but it was the only way I could think of to get through to Jane, I tried talking to her but she wasn't listening and wasn't going to back down, then I got angry and I lost control. Can you take me home, Ang please, and Josephine Roseanne, I'm sorry."

Jane watched, she knew how much the man who loved her as a friend had tried to get her to listen, she now knew his trigger was the loss of control, that loving Angie, who she could see with her own eyes he did, was a loss of control and her goading him was too much adding to his being in love and having no control over his feelings. She walked over to Stone and her tears fell, "I didn't know, I didn't realise, I was bloody stupid pushing you like that, I should've known you would never abandon me, I hope you can forgive me, Angie, I'm sorry I caused this."

"You didn't, Jane, this was always going to happen at some stage, don't blame yourself; you were the only one trigger there were others, hopefully, Justin will pull himself back to the present."

"You really do love him, don't you, Angie?"

"Yes, Jane, I do; now I'm taking him and Jo home."

"Mach, can you get Chris and Tony and the rest of the lads, then please give us an hour and come to the house, he needs his friends around him and that includes you, Jane," looking directly at the woman for the first time, "we all need to talk."

Angie drove the discovery home, Stone sat very subdued in the passenger seat with Jo leaning forward and her arms wrapped around him still crying. Arriving earlier than expected, George looked with raised eyebrows and Bonzo came to a bounding stop sensing the change in atmosphere wagged his tail unsure, Angie stroked him as she passed him as he followed, he could sense they were all upset. "Come on, Dad, sit down," George looked at Angie as she began to cry trying to explain between tears what had happened in the school gym. George immediately rang Ike and told him that Justin needed him, and Ike arrived within fifteen minutes. Ike spent some time with Stone alone talking quietly gauging Stone's answers and then told George, Angie, and Jo. "It isn't a full breakdown just a meltdown. Jane was just the final trigger he didn't need after falling so deeply in love with you, Angie, he did what he just did to convince Jane she wasn't being abandoned, he loves her, but like a sister and she will have seen the change in him when they were fighting, she needs to talk to him."

Angie asked, "What can we do? I've already asked his friends including Jane to come to the house."

"He needs reassurance, mostly that your feelings have not changed, let him hear your voices and he will come out of it. George and I have been dreading this day but look we are nine years further on, his bond with Jo is incredibly strong and he loves you, Angie, you and Jo will bring him back. Go; be with him," a very confused Bonzo sat at his feet **wondering why mermaid man was sad and his master was the most upset he'd ever seen her even the young girl and the old man where upset**. "You think we need diazepam or something similar Ike, slow his brain waves down."

"No, George, I think he talks it out now and we listen, your lad has had so much bottled up it's a wonder he's been able to function, it might not seem so at the moment but this is the best time this could have happened, love can cure any sickness it is different between father and son and father and daughter, Angie will stop him regressing, he loves her."

Tony and Chris were first to arrive, Tony as a trained medic said, "Fuck, George, it was just his way to get through to Hardcase, she thinks he was abandoning her, fuck it he risked his own mental health to save her I fucking hope she knows what she's done," as Jane came through the door.

"I'm so sorry, George."

"Don't fucking tell me, Jane, go, and tell my fucking son."

Ike stepped forward and put a hand on his shoulder, "George, Jane was just the trigger." Jane burst into tears and Ike pulled her into the kitchen, "Jane, you can't blame yourself, you didn't know what would trigger his relapse, hopefully, it is only temporary but me, George and Jo have lived like this for nine years, that woman, pointing at Angie, has had three days, she needs our support, for whatever reason he loves her not you, be his friend, Jane."

Mach and the other four lads arrived Bonzo eyed them all but felt no hostility, **something had happened with the mermaid man,** Stone could feel his daughter and Angie next to him, he knew he was loved, he knew where he wanted to be and with a huge mental effort, forced himself back into the present, "I'm ok, Ang, I'll be ok, Jo, stop crying I'm here, I'm not going anywhere, I love you both."

George approached with Ike, "How you're doing, son?"

"I'll be fine, Dad."

"You want to talk about it, JT," said Ike, "maybe, later when it's not so crowded just the family. Is Jane ok, we had quite a set too before I lost it, she's a tough son of a bitch, I didn't hurt her did I, I couldn't get through to her, is she here, can you find her dad," and George went to seek out Jane who was crying in the kitchen.

"Pull yourself together, Jane, my son wants to see you." Jane got a grip on her emotions and went through to Stone. Angie stood, giving up her place next to the man she loved; this simple gesture was enough to crack Hardcase wide open.

Ike moved close, aware of the emotional cost to Angie as Stone hugged Jane saying, "Let's not fight ever again"

"Stone, I'm so sorry, I was stupid, I pushed you; I caused this."

Ike stepped in, "You didn't cause it, Jane, you were just the final straw, the main trigger is standing next to you," looking at Angie and smiling, "for J T to do the job, he was doing in the past, he had to become completely unemotional about every situation, he had to become as near to a machine as possible. Gemma dying was the first trigger, bringing up and learning how to be a father to Jo was the second trigger, the third and final trigger was falling in love, not a long drawn out like each other get to know each other, no this was as close to love at first sight as possible, thank God you feel the same way.

"For a man who can shut his emotions off, J T finally on the third trigger lost what he always took for granted, his control, me and his dad knew what this would do. George has already had a very heated argument about J T just being a cog, it's not in his nature, strike one, your own emotional state Jane strike two, and the loss of control fighting with you, strike three, so Jane you can't blame yourself, the same as George couldn't blame himself, nobody including J T knew what would set him off, you walked into that gym and asked him to fight, it was enough. What we must do as people who love him, is make sure now we know his triggers that they cannot harm him anymore. I'm going to see Mike Foster and see if we can spin this a little there's over a hundred kids gone home tonight that won't understand," said Ike.

Stone stood up, "I want to address the school assembly tomorrow morning."

"J T, that's not a good idea, make yourself even more emotional and maybe cause a true breakdown, you talking to kids, who have no concept of who you are or what you've done for your country and been through, and quite frankly don't care, you can't control every situation."

Angie spoke, "I think Justin should do the assembly; he needs to explain himself even if it is just to get his own thoughts out. Ike, I think you should talk about PTSD then Justin should talk."

"I agree," said Ike looking at Angie with a newfound respect, "the genie is out of the bottle and it's never going back, we don't and won't let Justin bottle this back up." Jane sitting next to Stone was totally blown away by how much Angela Sanders loved him, how in three days she had worked out how his extremely complex mind worked, she also knew she couldn't love him in the same way as Angie and was determined to become her friend. "George, what do you think?" Ike said.

"I agree, let the kids see a human being, not a machine, Justin gets stuff off his chest in a controlled environment, maybe the kids don't care, but they deserve an explanation and the only person that can do that is my son. Long term it could make the triggers further apart, it was nine years, Ike, maybe he'll never have another one."

"George, J T won't ever go into combat again, so maybe the human side gets old, fat, and happy."

"Ike, I'm never getting fat, but I'll settle for old and happy," stretching out his hand to Angie.

Ike addressed his friends, "Thank you, his friends, for coming to support JT, we hope this is just a blip and ask everyone to continue to treat J T as they did before this incident, if any of you would like to attend the school assembly tomorrow you are very welcome. Tony, Chris, would you let Bish know what went down this morning and afternoon, now J T needs a night's rest."

Tony was the first to stand, "Ready, Chris, we'll go and catch Bish and Ted at the station, night boss" and the others followed suit.

Ike said, "Jane, we need to schedule a sit-down, you need to talk this out."

"I know, fit me in as soon as possible."

"No better time than the present, if you don't mind, George," who nodded his agreement. "I'll use the gym and off he went with Jane."

George turned to Jo, "How about we take this big fella for a walk?" And Jo knowing Angie and her dad needed to talk agreed and went for his harness. Bonzo never a dog to not see a silver lining chuffed and wagged his tail at his master *is it all right to go*, "Yes, Bonzo, I'm fine you go for your walk," satisfied with the tone of the answer Bonzo chuffed even more.

"I'll keep an eye out, I've got my phone we'll be about a half hour," said George.

"Thanks, Dad."

"I'm so sorry, Ang, I've really fucked up."

"Justin, sorry for what, being human, not being Superman, having a hidden illness, or a past that catches up? You recognised you were in the wrong when you saw me, and Jo and you put it right. You are not a weaker in person in my eyes, you are mentally affected by your past, and you cannot always control every situation. Justin, you went nine years without a triggering incident, you may not have another, or this drug thing may push you into one tomorrow. I love you as much and exactly the same way as I did before, you are not diminished in my eyes, you are the person I fell in love with, still love with all my heart."

"But."

"No buts, Justin, now take me to bed, make love to me, show me what you are capable of feeling," and leading Angie to his bedroom closing the door removed his clothes then removed Angie's and laid her gently onto the bed holding her close and made love gently kissing her lips, he looked at the woman he loved, her eyes closed, and breathing getting faster, mouth slightly open gently nibbling her own bottom lip, as they approached their orgasms Angie opened her beautiful eyes and looked directly into his as their orgasm built they continued to lock eyes not even closing them at the moment of orgasm. Angie felt his warm seed splash within her as she felt her own spasm within her; finally she closed her eyes enjoying the sensation of him in her body, the feel of his sperm inside her feeling a love she knew she could not live without. Kissing him passionately, "I love you, Justin; I always will; I want to be here with you for the rest of my life." Angie felt tears on her face; Justin didn't need to say any words; he just cried quietly knowing she would not think any less of him for at last being able to show emotion.

Fifteen

George, Jo and Bonzo returned; Jo at almost thirteen didn't question why her dad and Angie were not about and helped her granddad set about making tea. Ike appeared with a tearful Jane having discussed her childhood abandonment, feelings for Stone, misplaced aggression and admiration for Angie, the last thing Jane had said to Ike was it was obvious how they felt about each other you could feel it when you were near them and, yes, Angela Sanders was the best choice, and she hoped one day that they could be friends, really good friends. "Ike, Jane, you are staying for tea," said George leaving no doubt that a no was not going to be accepted. George knew that having his son's trigger in the house and his most trusted friend and doctor may help him come to terms with his episode, but he also knew that by the none appearance of him and Angie that Angie was aware of what his son needed most of all.

Jo stood, "Granddad, I'll sort Bonzo's food out give me practice for when I have Lemmy." Bonzo **heard the F word, apart from the W word it was his favourite and one followed another, hoping the pretty girl would forget the kibble and master and mermaid man had sorted things out I may be a dog, but I can feel the distress but unlike humans, it won't ruin my appetite, I might get the leftovers they smell yummy.**

When George was stressed, he loved to cook and having a son and granddaughter into health and nutrition, he'd learnt all about keeping the most nutrition in food even when he was at home on his own, so a huge healthy fry up, all the meats first cooked in the oven and then browned off in the grill. "Jane, you're not one of them feminist vegans, are you?"

"No, I like meat, didn't get much as a kid now I make up for it."

"Ike, if you eat your meat and veg, Justin might not twist at your triple chocolate cake with full-fat cream."

"Granddad, if I eat my meat and veg, can I have some cake?" George's cake-making was legendary; you put on three pounds just looking at it.

"Jo, sweetheart, I don't think your dad will mind tonight."

"Mind what?" Stone said, appearing and looking more relaxed; still wet from the partial shower he had taken with Angie. "I've taken a chocolate cake I made out of the freezer, son."

"What one of your 500 calories per slice ones."

"Sounds lovely, can I have a piece after tea then, George?" Angie said as she came in wearing a short black skirt and one of Stone's white shirts tied just above her waist showing off her waistline. Stone just looked, she had put her hair up and put a tiny bit of make-up on; she took his breath away with her beauty.

"Wow, Angie," said Ike, "you clean up well." Jane looked appreciating another woman's beauty and curves in all the right places, in decent proportions, she felt plain in comparison, she also couldn't fail to miss George squeezing Angie's hand warmly as she walked past to sit down.

"I invited Jane and Ike to tea, and me, Ike, and Jo will take Bonzo for his evening walk, I'll set the comms up just in case we get company. J T, you'll need some fresh air too. Jane wants to get to know you, Angie," said Ike knowing that Jane would not ask but knew how important it was to Jane, and if Angie knew Jane, it would help her with J T doctor physiology still working.

"Well, Dad, I think after the day I've had, I'll treat myself to a small piece of your cake and come for a walk to burn some of the calories off knowing that Angie wasn't threatened by Jane in the slightest."

Alone in the house, Angie and Jane finally had a chance to talk, "Ok, Jane, talk, I won't repeat anything you tell me even to Justin."

"I wanted to hate you, but the exact opposite happened, I've been in love with Stone for five long years ever since I arrived at camp to start teaching. I knew a little about Gemma. I knew he never got attached to any of his, let's call them, and dates so I was safe with my man crush. Stone treated me like one of the boys; it's only ever been friendship he wanted from me. Having Stone as a friend is something hard for me to describe; my father and mother made sure to tell me I was a mistake, when my father died my mother went completely off the rails she started drinking, bringing men back to the house, when I was thirteen and starting to develop some of the men started to take a little too much interest in me. Mother would pass out with the booze and then these men would take a serious interest in trying to remove my clothes, I started to carry a knife around with me, I practised shifting it from one hand to the other and throwing it when I was in the woods, to my surprise I had a natural talent.

"I was good at PE, and I joined the local judo class to get out of the house a couple of nights a week I was above average, I learnt to protect myself and the men who tried to rape me never succeeded. At sixteen, I joined the army, they trained me, I got better and better and got offered this post and my nickname became Hardcase, not because of my fighting ability but because I didn't have anything to do with men ever, I figured I could do without sex having witnessed my mother's parade of losers. Then I met Stone who was my commanding officer but he just had this way with him; he made you feel special; he lifted you up; he made you feel you could achieve anything; he was a superb leader; he treated the people who are under his command with so much respect and it was so easy to think I'd fallen in love with him.

"I was wrong, Angie, I had no idea what love was till I saw you two together. I felt rejected yet again when he told me about you and I put Stone into a position he couldn't get out of, for that I will be sorry till the day I die. I'm even more sorry about the position I put you in, I've hurt you more than I hurt Stone, the time you've known each other is irrelevant, you love him so deeply and completely. I could never love him like you do, your understanding of him is amazing in so short a time I honestly don't know how you know what he needs without him saying, he is different around you; there are no hard edges he's so in love with you, you've made him human I love him, but I know I'm not in love with him like you are. I only let men I trust completely touch me he's the closest of my male friends and his friendship is all I want. Do you think it's broken?"

"No, Jane, Justin's had a few adjustments to make they've thrown him, but he's strong and he knows he has plenty of people who love him, all in different ways, he'll be ok. This drug thing might set him back, but he has too much to lose now, I know he loves you; he risked himself for you as only a true friend would do, and you haven't lost a friend Jane. Justin's friends are carefully chosen and extremely important to him; he keeps his friends for life," and Angie reached out to Jane who said in a very quiet voice, "Can I be your friend, Angie?"

"You already are, Jane; all of Justin's friends are my friends too."

Bonzo had run off squirrel-chasing, Jo held her father's hand something she didn't do as often as she used to, George and Ike where further back checking about and jabbering about golf handicaps and great golfers in rock. "Dad, are you really ok?"

"Jo, I'll be fine honest."

"Do you think you'll marry Angie, Dad?"

"Yes, darling, I do."

"Whoopee, Dad that makes her my mam, do you think I should call her Angie or mam?"

"Well, when it happens, you will know."

"Dad?"

"Yes, Jo?"

"I love Angie too."

"And she loves you, Jo."

"Dad, do you think that Lemmy and Bonzo will get on, after all Lemmy is Bonzo's son."

"I'm sure they'll be fine together Bonzo can teach Lemmy all his neat little tricks."

"Dad, when you and Angie get married, can we get another house?"

"I thought you liked our house it's the only home you've ever known."

"I don't it's too big, we don't need as much space."

"Well, Jo, where would you like to live then?"

"I'd like a house by the river, you and Bonzo can swim do the mermaid, Bonzo can teach Lemmy, while me and Angie sunbathe, you can give your boat to Granddad and Uncle Ike. If we get a house with an annexe, Granddad can live with us, he doesn't like where he lives says it's full of knobs and snobs."

"Josephine Rosanna Stone, you've been doing an awful lot of thinking, how about I call the estate agents and see if we can find our new house?"

"Great, Dad, can I tell Granddad and Angie."

"I don't see why not, I've wanted to sell our house for a while and I like the idea of living by the river."

"Do you think Angie will want to sell her house?"

"I hadn't really thought about it I like her being with us, I don't want her to go home."

"Neither do I, Dad, it feels like family with her, Bonzo and Granddad, although you haven't shown them your rock god yet, maybe stick some Zeppelin on and Angie can join in." Stone held his daughter's hand as they continued to walk thinking how strange and unpredictable life was, a major meltdown followed by thoughts of a new home and a wife, it was one of the easiest decisions Stone would ever make, he loved this woman, yes, wanted her with him forever, did he care enough to want her to be his wife, hell yes, now he just had to wait a respectable time.

The phone in Stone's pocket buzzed on the way back to the house, "HI, Bish."

"Stone, are you ok?"

"Yes, I am. Ike thinks it was just a blip I've had some major changes and Jane was just in the wrong place at the wrong time. We're cool; she's up at the house with Ang."

"Chris and Tony have run through the day's events I'll not burden you tonight, but we need to have a one-to-one tomorrow morning."

"I've got to do school assembly first, apologise and try and explain my actions, Ike's coming with me plus some of the lads will be there to offer support, Ang says I will feel better if I explain myself even if no one listens."

"You've got a great lady there, Stone; you've left her with Jane, too very brave."

"Ang is not threatened by Jane; she needs to know Jane so she can help me."

"Stone, as your friend, a bit of advice, she's a keeper, she has you sussed out in three days imagine what she could do in a lifetime."

"I'll see you tomorrow morning, bye, Bish."

Stone walked into his house, "Honey, I'm home," and Bonzo followed Stone, Bonzo darting off to check on his master found her sat with the short pretty lady.

Angie stuck out her hand and stroked his head, "I'm ok, big guy," still being protective Bonzo sat between Angie's feet, Jane said, "He's very sensitive for such a big dog."

"Yes, he can sense moods, especially mine, he recently saved me from a very awkward situation," and went on to tell Jane about the woods.

"No wonder Stone was ready to relapse, he wouldn't have known how to protect you and he'll be worried sick this Greavsie escalates the situation, and he won't trust anyone else to protect you. Angie, would you like me to shadow you, this Greavsie has seen Stone, George, and Jo, and I could just be a friend it will also free Chris up."

"Justin, we're in here," Stone entered the room and kissed Angie gently on the lips.

"Justin, Jane has an idea that may reduce your stress, I think it's a great idea, basically, she takes over from Chris," and repeated what Jane had suggested.

"Good idea, honey, I'm getting a coffee. Anyone want one?"

Jane stood, "No, thanks, I'm going to head off, Angie, I'll meet you at school at 8.30, Stone, you and me are OK now, aren't we?"

"Yes, Jane", picking her up in a huge hug, "soak your bruises girl, you got me with some great shots, Hardcase, you certainly don't hit like a girl."

"Jo, George, it was nice to see you both again despite the circumstances. George, say thanks to Ike for me, straightening my head yet again, I'll see you tomorrow, Angie."

George raised his eyebrow but said nothing. "How are you, Justin?"

"I'm feeling much better now, Ang, I know why I had my meltdown and Ike clarified it for me, I don't think it will ever happen again, I have something to ask you when we're alone but this blip and your reaction to it just confirmed what I already knew. I've also had a very interesting conversation with my daughter; seems she doesn't like this house much, and Dad's never liked it since Gemma made me buy it. I've always wanted somewhere near the river with four or maybe five bedrooms somewhere that feels instantly like home, I'm not putting anything on hold anymore. Ang, follow me," and Stone shouted, "Jo, Dad, family conference in the kitchen right now, everyone, grab a coffee, Jo, diet coke the brand with stevia that Ang had."

"Oh, thanks, Dad"

"This is what I'm going to do, this house goes on the market and tomorrow I go to the estate agents and see if there's anything suitable with a bit of land near the river."

"Justin, this is your decision, I have my own house."

"Ang, I want you to think about where you want to live, where you want to be," and Stone squeezed her hand, "right next topic, tomorrow's school assembly, I probably scared a lot of kids and some teachers, so I'm dropping myself out of part two. Mach and the lads will do the course give them a bit more experience. Jane will take over from Chris which frees him up to tag along with me and Tony. Ike will do the introduction talk about PTSD, a lot of kids suffer in silence, the suicide rate is sky high in teens maybe I can get through to some of them, if I, a trained solider can still be suffering then maybe the kids suffering in silence might find the courage to come forward and ask for help. Dad, Jo what do you think? Angie says she doesn't see me as a weaker person because I'm mentally affected by my past." George placed his hand on Angie's thinking what a perfect answer.

"Right, I'm going to watch the world's greatest ever drummer throw his sticks away and play with his hands, for three points, Jo, name the song and the drummer."

"Dad, you're not even trying."

"What, you don't know, bet Dad and Angie do."

"Of course, I do. Dad, can we have it on loud?"

"Jo, Mr Bonham would expect nothing less, grab the popcorn, Ang, bring Bonzo I want to see a ten-stone-plus bull mastiff head bang, and bring that broom I feel the rock god might make an appearance," and as Stone walked towards the cinema room, Stone in his best Percy impression sang, "you need cooling, baby I'm not fooling, I'm going to send you, back to schooling." Two hours of singing later that no one could hear because it was that loud. "Angie's right, best band ever," said George, "maybe we can change the quiz have girls versus boys," said Jo, "that way I won't get beat by such a wide margin, throw in some Zeppelin questions we might win for once."

"Jo, let Bonzo the headbanger out before he settles down for the night," said Angie, "next time we do that, it'll not have to be as loud Lemmy's ears will adjust, but not straight away maybe six or seven before we hit eleven."

"You can't name a dog Lemmy and him not be a headbanger besides, he'll copy his dad." Everyone stopped at Jo's bedroom, Bonzo got on the bed, and Angie just smiled, night, "Dad, love you," and kissed her father on his lips, "Night, Granddad, love you," and gave him a hug, "Night, Angie, love you," and kissed Angie on her lips bringing tears to Angie's eyes.

"I love you too Jo," clearly taken aback and emotional.

Leaving Jo and Bonzo and walking back towards the other bedrooms, Stone said, "Ang, you are now part of this family, Jo never kissed her mam on the lips, it's only ever been me," the emotion was too much for Angie and she began to cry.

George cuddled Angie "And I love you too, night, son, see you both in the morning." Angie couldn't ever remember being as emotional as this, Stone walked her into his, no their bedroom and undressing her laid her on the bed quickly got undressed himself and then held her close while she cried, "I love this family, Justin, I love your dad he's so much like you and Jo I love like she was my own daughter. How is all this possible and you, you are my whole life; I can't believe how much I feel." Then finally getting a grip on her emotions, "You wanted to ask me something, Justin?"

"Ang, it'll keep till the morning you're far too emotional at the moment, let's just get some sleep, I love you."

"I love you too."

Sixteen

Stone woke as usual before his 6 o'clock alarm, stretching his arm to switch the alarm to silent. Angie was asleep with her head on his chest, he could feel her gentle breath moving the small hairs, his only thought being *this is how I want to wake up with the woman I love in my arms*, having absolutely no doubt about what he was about to ask after only four days. He didn't care, it wasn't an impulse she made him whole, and he couldn't imagine his life without her so why wait. Because protocol says you must know someone for a certain length of time before you make such decisions, most people overthink things, he'd had to make decisions that involved life and death in milliseconds, of all the decisions in his life marrying Angela Sanders was the easiest to make. He didn't care a fuck what people thought it was not their relationship. Dad and Jo had both told her they loved her, and they wouldn't say it for effect, they meant it, seeing the bond build between his wonderful daughter and his future wife was one of the greatest pleasures of his life.

He hadn't realised how much Jo had missed a significant mother figure in her life, obviously, she'd developed a deep friendship turning to a love for Angie simply because it was reciprocated. Jo had found someone who treated her like an equal with respect but most of all loved her, that's what had been missing from Jo's life, he loved his daughter, worshipped her in fact but it wasn't the same way a mother would and he had no doubt that Angie would make a wonderful mother, did the future hold children, who knew at thirty-four, Angie was still young enough as was he, thirty-eight was not old to be a dad again, who knew what would happen. If anything was certain after yesterday it was that you only have one go some decisions are simple marrying Angela Sanders was easy, spending the rest of his life with her was easy, so it was just four days, some eyebrows would be raised, the people in his core, Jo, Dad all love her, waiting was just stupid when he knew days, weeks or years would make no difference.

Angie stirred, knew Stone was awake and would want to get up and go training with him, but she lay with her head on his chest, and Justin didn't get out of bed. "Ang," and she looked up into his beautiful blue eyes, "that question, babe, left over from last night."

"Yes, what did you want to ask me?"

"Will you marry me?"

"What, what, Justin?"

"Marry me, and get our house by the river now not in six months but now, marry me, Angela Sanders."

"Yes, Justin Travis Stone, yes, yes, I'll marry you."

Stone and Angie walked into the kitchen, George drinking coffee said, "I wasn't sure about breakfast this morning, I thought I'd wait till everyone is up." Stone looked at Angie who was overcome with emotion and cried into his arms.

"I'm so happy, Justin," she whispered.

Stone held her while she pulled herself together, "You sit with Dad, I'll get your lazy dog and my lazy daughter."

George looked at Angie, "I don't know what you did, but he's back to his normal self this morning," and Angie blushed again, "Jesus, it's like talking to Justin, what a pair, you can't hide anything."

Jo was up, and in the shower and Bonzo seeing the mermaid man approach thought **I'm in trouble** as he had snuck onto the still-warm bed, caught red-handed, and mermaid man didn't tell me off, "It is ok, big lad," and opened Jo's French doors and Bonzo took off to the trees down the bottom of the garden. "Jo, you are gonna miss breakfast."

"I'm out, Dad, just getting dry, two minutes, hmm," said Jo as she walked back into the bedroom dressed in her school uniform and towelling her wet hair. "Royal treatment my own dad comes to get me up."

Stone just smiled, "Oh boy, Dad you've asked her, haven't you?"

"Yep," and Stone's smile got bigger and his eyes shone with happiness. "Wow, I get a dog, a new home, and a mum, oh boy oh boy, does Granddad know yet, I think he will. Angie practically glows when she's anywhere near you. Dad, you'll have to make it official; Angie's birthday is on 7 September; you need to buy a sapphire engagement ring. Can I come with you please, Dad? I kind of know what she likes, in a history class on royals through the ages, she really liked a sapphire ring like the one that Queen Elizabeth I wore. I can get a picture, the originals are over five hundred years old and valued at over five million but I'm sure Samuels could make or get you something similar and you're not stingy so what's a few thousand, after all, Lemmy should have cost you around £2000."

"You are not surprised at all, are you Josephine Roseanne?"

"No, Dad, I had you down for under a week so four days I beat granddad he said within a month."

"You are alright with this, aren't you, Josephine Roseanne?"

"Dad, I know that by calling me by my full name how important this is to you, I told Angie yesterday I loved her, she loves me, she'll be my mam she won't ever hurt us, you're the happiest I've ever seen you despite yesterday's blip, despite the drug gang, so f…frig what anybody thinks. I'll get the library book and print some copies of the ring; we'll go Thursday night they're open till eight then once you have the ring you can make it official with an engagement party at Mario's."

"Jo, you really do think ahead."

"Yes, Dad, us girls do now can we get breakfast all this planning has left me hungry."

George sat with Angie who was still blushing, "You always this emotional, Angie or is there a special reason?" Watching Angie blush again, "Bugger, I lost the bet."

"What bet?"

"The bet that said my son would ask you to marry him within a month, Jo said a week," and Angie blushed yet again and began to cry, George stood and cuddled in Angie who continued to cry. Stone, Jo and Bonzo came into the kitchen, Bonzo saw his master in old man's arms **happy tears,** so he sat next to her waiting, **I want a cuddle too**. "Justin, can you fix breakfast?" And continued to hold Angie as her tears kept falling.

Ike arrived just in time for breakfast, "Morning, Uncle Ike" said Jo, "I won the bet," as he saw George cuddling Angie.

"Ok, George, my turn," and cuddled Angie, "So you love this man more than I love chocolate, I take it" and Angie started to cry again.

"Take no notice of the tears, Ike, it's like her blushing she just can't help it."

"It's mid-thirties hormones, George, doesn't just affect women though," and they turned to see Stone wipe away a tear as he made the omelettes.

Ike said, "J T you're sure you want to do this today; it's been highly emotional already."

"Ike, I love her, I don't want to be without her ever, I'm selling this house and we're all moving to a house by the river, when we find one, Dad can sell his house, and you and he can have the boat and get the name changed."

"You want me to live in your house, son?"

"Yes, Dad, you'll have two dogs to look after, I know you hate it where you are, and Dad without you, I wouldn't have any of this so it's not a sacrifice, we spent far too long walking on eggshells because of my past I want you here with us, besides you're my partner in the rock god game."

Ike said, "Right, J T, let's go we'll follow behind."

"We?"

"Yes," said George, "just because you're my son doesn't mean I can't be there to support you and I'll have Bonzo with me."

"Dad, what are you going to say?"

"I don't know something will come to me."

"I don't think anybody will care, but it will make your dad feel better about himself," said Angie.

Arriving at school, George waited outside with Bonzo while Stone, Angie, Ike, and Jo went straight to Mike Foster's office. "Morning, Anne, he's expecting us."

"Just go through." Mike looked harassed.

"Are you sure you want to do this, Justin?"

"Ike, can you get Dad? Yes, Mike, I need and want to."

"Ok, these are the statistics you asked me for, handing over the papers and some parents have arrived, plus the press are sniffing around."

"Let them in, Mike, and let's go." Stone held his daughter's hand in one hand and his future wife in the other Mike walked slightly ahead, into the assembly hall where all five hundred plus pupils and their parents and the press waited. On stage sat his dad, Bonzo, Ike, his friends, and Brigadier Marshall. Stone saluted and introduced Angie and Jo, saying, "He's my boss and had final say in what I do."

Stone looked around the stage, Jane next to Chris and Tony, said in unison, "Morning boss, nice day to finally unburden yourself, morning, Angie, Jo," and at the very end sat Mike Bishop. Going over to him and still holding hands with the two women in his life, "Why are you here, Bish?"

"You need to ask, I'm your friend, you wanted all your friends here besides I'm here to speak to the organ grinder and not his monkeys," causing Chris and Tony to smile.

"Bish, you sure have a way with words."

"Been lots of developments, Stone, get this done and we speak," knowing Stone needed to get this out of his system once and for all.

Ike stood and walked to the podium and called for quiet in the hall, "Boys and girls, teachers, parents and members of the press, and friends and family. For those that don't know me, I am Dr Isaac Goldberg, currently a doctor at our hospital but for over thirty years, I was the army trauma doctor. I specialise in post-traumatic stress disorder or PTSD which a lot of you will have heard of from the many war films on TV etc., but you probably don't understand what it is or means. This illness is very deliberating and extremely stressful, especially to the family and friends of the person suffering it. What happened yesterday will be addressed directly by Colonel Stone, but we, his friends and family have waited nine very long years for Colonel Stone to be in a position enabling him to talk and unburden himself, as you can see, we are still 100% behind this most remarkable man. You are all wondering why it is important enough for us to address the full school, well, yesterday some of the pupils witnessed first-hand the effects of PTSD and this will have been quite frightening for them, so we are here today to explain."

Grabbing the figures from Mike Foster, he continued, "There are around five hundred of you here; fifty of you will commit suicide fact! You may not have a father who loves you as much as former Brigadier Stone loves his son. You may be able to hide your true feelings from even your closest friends; fifty of you will die because you can't cope with life, fact! The best quote I can give you is from Colonel Stone's partner. 'I do not see you as a weaker person because you were mentally affected by your past.' What I would like everybody here to do including the parents is to listen to the people that follow me and remember what Angela Sanders said. If any of you need to talk, there will be phone numbers on every school notice board, everyone no matter who they are, what position they are in life, will at some time in their lives feel that they can't cope, and they'd be much better not being here. Do not be afraid to ask for help. You are going to hear from the most remarkable human being I have the pleasure of knowing and calling a friend, please listen, if he can ask for help, once you know what he has been through, so can you. Colonel Stone's commanding officer Brigadier Alan Marshall will speak next."

Brigadier Alan Marshall, "Ladies and gentlemen of the press, please be aware that what I tell you involves the Official Secrets Act, should not be printed and should you try and get more information than I am willing to disclose we have measures in place to identify you and you will be prosecuted. Colonel Stone is one of the army's secret heroes; he led over fifty successful missions and never had a failure. WE, the army failed, we taught and turned this most remarkable human being into as near as possible a machine. Hand-to-hand combat, he is the best there is, his mind was trained to withstand anything waterboarding, food and sleep deprivation, mental and physical torture. We sent him on missions where the success rate was very low, he became our secret weapon, a super solider, his wife committed suicide leaving him to raise his four-year-old daughter Jo," and he pointed to Jo sat holding Angie's hand, "and still we wanted more.

"His father, one of my best friends, begged for him to be pulled from active duty. This man was my rank, loved and feared by his men, but he begged the top brass, 'Please let my son live and bring his daughter up.' That was nine very long years ago. We, George, Jo, Ike and his close army family and friends have spent the last nine years waiting for a triggering event, that event which happened yesterday, and I quote Angela, 'We do not see you as a weaker person because you were mentally affected by your past.' Colonel Stone did not fail, we, the army did. Fifty of you will not have the courage to ask for help, are you listening out there you fifty, Colonel Stone is a hero in every sense, we the army failed this man, the signs are there in every one of you, find the courage to ask for help, this man has. Colonel Stone."

Stone walked up to his Commander, "Thank you, sir," and stood ready to address everyone. "Yesterday, I finally asked for help," pausing, "I'm sorry I upset some of you." Pausing again, to get his thoughts together, he continued, "I spent a great deal of my life training either my mind or body to react without thought. I was given many missions that where considered suicide missions, I was regarded as expendable as long as I achieved my objective first, to withstand anything the enemy could throw at me. I out trained everyone, even now nine years later I still can, some of you saw that yesterday. What no one can see is the cost to my mental well-being, I had, as my daughter has reminded me, become a machine, and over the last nine years, I have had to overcome my training to learn how to feel emotion, compassion and love. So, why yesterday, after nine very hard years, as my daughter, father and my doctor and friend had watched me gradually become human again.

"I cannot express how much I love my father; he saved my life; I would have eventually been killed. I treated him very badly for many years, but he stood by me and when a situation occurred recently, he told me the truth. I hadn't known my father has used all his persuasive powers to get me pulled me from live duty. I wanted to react to this new situation, but he told me I had too much to lose, and he saved my life again. I regret that only now I can tell him how proud I am that he is my father; without him I would not be here. Kids, ask for help, get someone to listen and TALK.

"When my wife committed suicide and my father pulled me out from active duty, I had to bring my daughter Jo up. I was trained to show nothing. I had to learn from scratch how to be a human being, Jo was only four years old, but she was a very remarkable little girl. I HAD to change, start to feel and get involved and eventually, my feelings returned. I can say now that there are two ladies in my life that I love with everything I have, Josephine Roseanne saved my life by being a wonderful, funny, caring, loving daughter, I love and thank her for all her well-thought-out ways of helping me become a better person. My dad was my first trigger in saving my life; my daughter was my second trigger in that I had to become more human. My third trigger was loss of control which had never let me down before. How did I lose control, I fell in love, big deal you might say, yes for me a very big deal, I had no control, I couldn't, can't control how I feel. I was trained to feel nothing then I met this lady on Friday.

"Within four days, I felt everything, just a few pushes needed to get me to crack. Angie was threatened on Friday and again even more on Saturday, the big lovable dog here pointing to Bonzo saved her. I now have a situation where someone I love is threatened physically. The next little push was arguing with my dad about this situation him knowing what I am still capable of. I lead, I do not follow. I make things happen. I do not sit back and wait. I am a leader. Until my dad pointed out I'm not anymore, I'm just a cog, loss of control yet again. The final push, the one some of you witnessed happened yesterday and involved Jane Casey known lovingly as Hardcase.

"Jane is one of my very best friends, and she won't mind me telling you that she had abandonment issues in her childhood, Jane thought she loved me, she felt safe with her man crush because in the past nine years, I had never been capable of forming an emotional attachment to any lady, until Angie. Remember

I told you that everyone has triggers, family, and friends, you must look for them otherwise we lose fifty of you. Jane heard I'd met someone on Friday and was in love by Sunday, Jane's trigger is abandonment, and I knew that. She used unnecessary force in fighting our five friends in the demonstration and then wanted a fight with me.

"We now had a situation where Jane was out of control, my closest friends knew, but they weren't trained to her standard. I am, I thought I could calm her down; she pushed because she wrongly felt I was abandoning her. I knew her trigger but I didn't know mine, so I knew I had to fight so I allowed her to hit me a few times but Jane was highly skilled and knew I was holding back, I whispered that I had no control over who I fall in love with, my trigger, as I now know was the loss of control and being in love for the first time, my control had gone and my fighting instincts that had been dormant for over nine years returned. The situation was you have two world-class martial arts specialists fighting for real, my friends knew, but they couldn't stop me, but more importantly for me was that my daughter and Angie knew, THEY stopped me, THEIR love for me, grounded me making me realise I HAD LOST CONTROL.

"This has a happy ending; it made me look very hard at my life this morning I asked Angela Sanders to marry me she said, 'Yes.' If any of you feel the need to talk, please reach out, anyone can get PTSD it sits dormant until you have a triggering incident, find someone you trust and talk to them don't be a statistic sometimes the life you want is closer than you think. I thank you for your patience; I had a lot to say, and thank you to Mike Foster for allowing me to do this. Thank you to all my wonderful friends for sticking by me. Thank you to my dad and my wonderful daughter for saving my life and thank you to Angela Sanders for saying yes and making me whole." Angie was in tears yet again as Stone walked over to them and they group hugged, "Did I miss anything?"

"No, son, it came from your heart."

"How do you feel now, Justin?" Angie asked.

"I'm pleased that I had the opportunity to speak. I hope some of the kids in mental disarray listened and perhaps I did some good."

"Jo, you think anyone listened?"

"Yes, Dad, your talk might save someone." As Stone walked towards his friends, hand in hand with Angie and Jo, Ike, George and Bonzo just behind, Chris was the first to speak, "Well, well, well, so you are human, boss."

"And Angie is your red kryptonite," said Tony.

Stone looked at his friends "Thank you all for being here today; it means a lot to me, I promise, you can stop looking for any more cracks."

Jane hugged first Stone and then Angie whispering, "I hope if I ever fall in love for real it makes me glow like you."

George joined them saying, "They're like peas in a pod, very supportive of each other, extremely well-tuned, she's also very strong, very good with him, but she's very emotional at the moment but so is Justin. Ike's saying we just have to keep the stress from building, keep hammering home the point that he's only a cog."

Stone reverted to work mode saying, "Let's get this drug lot sorted as quickly as possible and reduce the stress even more. Hardcase you are going to shadow Angie, me, Chris, and Tony are going to get updated by Bish and see how we can assist. Mach, you, and the guys are going to do part two of the course for the school kids who signed up, along with Jane if she's not looking after Angie or we may bring in another female teacher or two for the girls."

Bish hugged Angie, "Honey, you're just what he needs in his life, now we just have to sort this drug mob out and keep you safe."

"Stone, we all gather in Mike Foster's office in fifteen minutes, and I'll run through where we are at present." Bonzo had sat patiently throughout and now his one thought was **hurry up, I need grass under my feet, or this room will be cleared in ten seconds.**

Stone and Angie grabbed a few minutes in her classroom, "I hear you're going somewhere tomorrow night with Jo, she won't tell me where, our daughter's got something up her sleeve." Stone wasn't surprised in the least that you had become our, but didn't show any outward surprise and said, "I'm surprised she hasn't blabbed; she doesn't keep anything from you."

"It must be really important then, kiss me and go be a cog, Justin," and Stone kissed her with so much passion and feeling, "Kiss me like that again Justin and you'll not get to your meeting."

"God, you make me so horny, woman, I don't want to leave."

"Tell you what, Justin, I have some new underwear back at your house how about tonight you try taking it off using just your teeth."

"Ang, that's not fair, look," pointing at his erection I have to go into a meeting with a raging stiffy, "Ang, what colour?"

"Pink, Justin, see-through lace, G-string, front fastening bra; hold-ups," gently squeezing his erection lead built back up in the pencil nicely.

Angie giggled loving how easy he was to wind up, "I love you," said Stone,

"Well, I know it is not just the mind-blowing sex, Justin," giggling again, "I love you too, now Jane's waiting and you'll be late for your meeting, ring me when you get a chance and Justin no risks."

Stone was unsurprised that everyone was already in Mike Foster's office waiting, "It is ok, Stone," said Bish. "We were just wondering how late you would be."

"And how dishevelled," added Chris.

"Doesn't look too bad," said Tony, "trousers are on the right way and his shirts still tucked in, but look at them swollen lips must have been some serious kissing action going on."

"Enough, Chris, remember your little video appearance that may get leaked and Tony, I can always arrange for you to fight Hardase if you don't pack in trying to wind me up."

"What do you mean boss, trying," said Chris with a huge grin, does red kryptonite realise what she's said yes to yet.

Bish cut in, "While it's been fun winding you up and Chris needs to stop now before he gets on a roll, we need to get rid of this drug gang."

Brigadier Alan Marshall, Stone's boss stood, "Bish, you know where I am should you need me. Colonel Stone now has command of the army's side of this operation. I'm off to visit George and Ike been far too long and we have much to talk about."

Bish opened the briefing, "Right, gentlemen, Greavsie little operation, first off, the little bastards' chemists have added methamphetamine, highly addictive to the ecstasy tablets so you have MDMA a stimulant, causes dehydration, overheating, a thirst which water only just touches, then an addictive in the same tablet. He's knocking them out for £5 instead of the usual £8-10 plus he has his own personal goon squad made up of the usual pikie leg breakers and bare-knuckle fighters, all brawn no brains, in case he steps on anyone else's territory. There's been a few broken bones, but Greavsie is slick, he has the final say, but he never gets involved in the doing. We have thirteen kids in hospital suffering from withdrawal, plus the two you found in room 225 and Tony treated on the spot, thanks, Tony, the paramedic said administering naltrexone to Shaun Stevens probably staved off a heart attack, both are recovering.

"Neil Todd admitted he got ten ecstasy tablets from Barry Jackson, he's a nasty little shit, we have the five names to whom he gave the ten tablets. Mike

Foster has written formal letters to the parents but luckily, they hadn't made any headway in selling any of the tablets, so they just get a slap round the wrist. Jackson refuses to identify who he got the tablets off or where he picked them up from, he's been charged, he's scared and he hasn't turned up for school today, neither has Tommy Bowman. I sent a car to his house, no answer but the neighbours say he's left on his own a lot, has lots of friend's round and spends the weekend high as a kite playing loud music till the middle of the night. He has no dad, and his mam takes on low paid cleaning work whenever she can get it, she isn't surprised he's off the rails because she has to leave him on his own most days to try and make some money. The house is a pigsty with half-eaten takeaways and stinks of dope. He'll turn up eventually, when whatever he's on has left his system and he's hungry, only way he'll ever turn his life around is if he joins one of the forces and gets some discipline."

"Barry Jackson is the more career criminal of the two, won't name anyone, won't admit anything, we charged him sent him home with eyes on him, we watch and wait he'll contact someone from Greavsie lot. We've put a little dent in Greavsie school programme, but we've had more success with the adult market, twenty-one arrested for possession some of whom your lads caught red-handed, they'll get fined, but the word is out to Greavsie that we are not just sitting back, so the pressure to do something stupid will increase. The big mistake Greavsie made was talking direct to Bowman and Jackson, if we get one of them to admit that he supplied them we have him, but Angie can identify Greavsie, Bowman and Jackson so we need to be careful."

"Bish," said Stone, "the only thing that will bring Greavsie out into the open is direct competition. He can get any number of school kids to peddle his tablets and there are plenty of low lives willing to push drugs in pubs and clubs but what if a new gang appeared, even more aggressive and cheaper, Greavsie would either bugger off back to Manchester or call in his goon squad. Apply more pressure and something breaks, you have the drugs in lock up from the Liverpool mob, we make ourselves the dealer and the taker, make sure his boys see the deals being done, we watch, we move when they do. The Brigadier would give us more people he doesn't want drugs anywhere near any army base bad for moral plus the government arseholes can cut even more funding."

Bish thought it over. "I don't know if it escalating the situation, Stone, we've taken some wind out of his sails already, and maybe we wait a couple more days to see if we get any further results."

"Where do you want us?" Stone asked.

"I think he'll try and move more tablets into school so maybe hang around the school grounds watch for any meetings especially with anyone who isn't a school kid, I'll keep a watch on Bowman and Jackson."

"I liked your plan, boss," said Chris once they were back outside. "We're sitting with our fingers up our arses at the moment, we need to get some of his crew, not the kids or the riff-raff, he'll just go out and get more of them, we're not exactly going after him are we."

"No, Chris, we're not, we are being good cogs, which is what we are."

Seventeen

Greavsie sat in his office listening to Neil; the proceedings had gone to shit. "Terry, get Jonesy and some of his lot to find some more kids, we've taken a hit there. Ronnie, Chris, find that little shit Bowman and scare the little fucker, leave young Jackson he'll come to us when he's ready. Jeff, Richard, keep an eye out for that fucking dog, the bitch teacher, the ninja squaddie, and his dad. I've had our chemist's tweak, our next supply of tablets and get the kids to keep selling them for £5 each but up their profit margin the more they sell. We've upped the addiction level, extra rapid heart rate but more of a buzz, clubs open tomorrow night so we should see big business."

"Boss," said Chris, "Bish is wrong, walking around the school boundary looking for strange groups waiting for some kid to die, will do fuck all."

"I understand, Chris, all three of us aren't used to doing nothing. We'll shake things up if and where we can. We see drugs getting pushed we go in hard no finesse knock a few heads about, no being soft with I suspect you're doing this and that, or we'll run you down to the police station. We go in hard, break some bones they go back to Greavsie he then sends his goon squad, chop them down, he sends more we chop and keep chopping them down until he crawls out of the woodwork, and we get him. Yes, I know he may go after Angie, Jo, or dad, but there's only so much being a cog I can do, I know you both feel the same way. If Bish asks they retaliated hard, so we went in harder."

"Yes, boss," said Chris, "and Tony, the gloves were off."

Terry Wheeler easily found Jonesy, hanging around the allotments smoking dope waiting for an opportunity to nick some tools to make a bit of ready cash and get some more green, sell a bit keep a bit. "Hello, Jonesy, want to make some easy money, son?"

"Always, Terry, what you want?"

"I want you to hang around the school with some of your acquaintances, find some kids willing to sell pills, set them up one hundred tablets £5 a pop they're ecstasy tabs should be £8-10 each. They sell a one hundred give you £400 keep a £100 for themselves, for everyone hundred you give out I'll give you £50 for doing fuck all. You find ten mugs willing to deal and you make £500 your acquaintances don't know your deal with me so it's up to you to give them as much or as little as you think you can get away with or maybe you keep all the cash sort them out some crappy dope, you in."

"Yep, Terry, I'm your boy."

"Make sure the kids know who the gaffer is, and everyone plays fair, the goon squad don't care whose legs they break as long as they get to do it on a regular basis. Ok, jump in the car and we'll get you sorted."

Jonesy stocked up, and with two of his mates who'd opted for dope as payment, were hanging around the bottom school gate hoping to catch some of the little scroat's going home or out for lunch. As Jonesy went to this school, occasionally, he didn't look out of place, the two others were older. Stone, Chris, and Tony all had their comms switched on, Tony spoke, "Got a little action at the bottom gate, little shit nickname Jonesy with two older kids hanging around."

Stone replied, "We're on our way, get your phone on video ready till they're trying to deal then we step in." Jonesy spotted some likely-looking punters going into his sales pitch, the other two giving the same spiel to another two groups, Tony could only film one and as he disliked Jonesy who was making the mistake of showing the product, issuing the terms and conditions without lowering his voice, all of which he caught nicely on tape, "We're good, boss," and all three moved in unison, all three culprits were slammed hard into the grass, the school kids took off, the drugs were all on Jonesy, ten packets of one hundred tablets.

Stone and Chris grabbed the other two up off the floor, Stone saying, "Three seconds you tell us what you're up to after three we break some part of your body, one, and two."

"Ok," said one and pointing at Jonesy continued, "If we shift some pills, he gets us some weed for free."

"And you," Chris said to the other.

"Same, man, same, we just wanted a bit of weed."

Stone said, "We are going to let you go, but and remember this, if you or any of your pals come within a mile of this or any other school, there WILL be no three seconds, there WILL be broken bones and you WILL walk with a limp for the rest of your lives, NOW FUCK OFF OUT OF MY SIGHT."

Tony had Jonesy in a painful arm lock who shrieked out in pain, "Jonesy, if I continue to twist like this your rotor cuff will snap very painfully needing surgery plus months of rehabilitation, so on the count of three you tell me who supplied you and what was your deal, one, and two."

"Don't stop."

"What, Jonesy, no, you won't tell or stop."

"Stop, it won't do you any good knowing his name, the fucker, he works for is a psycho and he'll just set his goon squad on you three," and Tony squeezed a little harder, "name."

"Terry Wheeler and he works for Tony Greaves."

"How's Wheeler get hold of you when he needs an errand boy," said Stone and Jonesy looked at his right pocket, Chris moved in and removed the mobile, "Nice iPhone new model too, OK contacts list, Terry W."

"Right, Jonesy, you're going to ring Mr Wheeler."

"No fucking way," and the arm was back in rotor cuff damage territory, "once again on the count of three."

"Ok," said Jonesy, "you ring you pass the phone to my partner."

Terry answered, "What you want Jonesy, I'm fucking busy here," and Jonesy handed the phone to Stone, "Aha, Mr Terence Wheeler, brother of Neil and employed by Tony Greaves."

"Who the fuck is this?"

"Language, Mr Wheeler and me a churchgoer, who I am is unimportant what I have may be. I have Peter Jones on video being caught red-handed with intent to supply your bosses ecstasy plus tablets. We now have one thousand of these little beauties. We have your name and contact number and we know your boss is from Manchester trying to pedal his little drug empire in our schools, pubs and clubs and goes by the name of dumb fuck no that's not right, Greavsie was a great footballer in his time nothing like your fucked up dumb fuck physco boss. We would like to request politely that you all FUCK OFF back to Manchester, or the next dealer we catch gets his legs broken then you could give him a cool nickname limpy or gimpy, what you think, Terence?"

Terry's blood pressure was off the scale. "Listen, you fuck, I don't know who you are but you and your family are going to get fucked."

"Oh, Terence, I never fuck on a first date, I'm too much of a gentleman," and Stone disconnected the phone and handed it to Tony, "do your stuff with that," and rang Bish on his mobile and explained what had gone down, "Bish I didn't know you could swear like that does your Brenda know? Anyway, send a car for this shit, we'll continue our rounds and be down in a bit to give you a written statement, Bish, I love you too see you in a while. Car will be along in five minutes, until then should we feed little Jonesy here some of these wonderful little pills take bets how many before he passes out."

Jonesy eyes popped, "Keep that big fucker away from me, PLEASE."

Ted Barnett picked up Jonesy and laughing said, "You three are on Bishop's shit list."

Chris said, "Well, that went well, boss, apart from pissing Bish off, we just need a few more days like today. Greavsie will escalate the situation, we know he's all about ego and intimidation. We must tell Jane and Angie what's gone on and get someone watching Jo and your dad."

"Beats sitting with our fingers up our arses, doesn't it Chris? Now we're on a roll lets sort some more shit out," and taking out his phone, "Hi, Dad, get ready to take Bonzo for a walk, we're driving over now. If Bish is already fucked off, let's get this done," and they jumped into Chris's car.

George stood with Bonzo, "Son, tell me this wasn't your idea."

"Morning again, sir," said Stone to Brigadier Marshall. "I think we'll have a coffee; it was Chris's idea so he can explain what we've already done," and George and Alan listened to Chris's explanation.

"You've just made the situation more dangerous for us, Angie and Jo, but because it wasn't my son's idea I like it."

"What!" said Stone.

"Son, I said YOU should be a cog, Chris, and Tony they're just grunts on the ground, that right, Alan. So, the plan is intimidating the fuckers till they do something stupid just keep picking at the spot till it bursts, works for me."

"And for me," said Alan. "As your commanding officer, I'll take the flak from Detective Inspector Bishop, not you, Colonel Stone, if Bish asks this was my plan not yours, we don't want him thinking you three have gone rogue. I'm going to walk Bonzo with George, you three do your thing then I'll ring Bish before I return to barracks. George, this coffee is wonderful."

"Yes, it is but the supply is dwindling, son, you'll have to ring Mario."

"I'll do it now, Dad."

"Hello, is that the fat Italian stud muffin," and Mario laughed. "Mr, you're in trouble, my friend, news on the grapevine is that you and the delectable Ms Sanders are a bit more than good friends. Where was my phone call, if I weren't having to service my wife every couple of hours because now there's no young stud anymore, I'd be really hurt?"

"Mario, your feelings were blown away with the shrapnel."

"Stone, I'd put Gabby on, but she's so excited you wouldn't understand what she was saying anyway, so let's get this timeline straight, clearly enjoying himself, I tell you Ms Sanders is a ten you listened to me, first time for everything, then you realise she's a keeper and propose before she can get used to your strange ways and I find out on the army grapevine not a phone call from my best friend, hell I could be hurt. Mario, I would have rung, but as you know, we have a drug gang trying to pedal in the area, basically, it's how I met Angie and why we had to borrow your car after she was threatened, but she only said yes three hours ago, I have Hardcase babysitting and we're currently trying to make some moves."

"You and Jane cool now after your slapping contest."

"Yes, Mario, it was the only way I could get through to her."

"Justin, we all know how far you would go for your friends. I not seen Jane for ages nice to catch up, you bring everyone Friday after three we close restaurant have engagement party, inform Angie of all your faults, my Gabrielle can have a big cry, we talk wedding cakes."

"She knows about the rock gods, Stone?"

"No, Mario, maybe give her big surprise get rid of all the stress building up, I'm sure the lads will be up for it. Yes, Mario, rocking out might be just what I need. Dad's pointed out that my coffee supply is getting low now there's Ang, Ike, Chris and Tony all drinking it, Dad's up to six cups a day so can you triple my usual order next time you ring home."

"No problem, my friend."

"And, Mario, she was my trigger." Mario completely understood Stone.

"All is finally good, my friend, I am very so happy for you, I see you Friday."

George just leaving with Alan said, "You should have found time to ring him, son, he'll be hurt that he didn't hear the news from you."

"Dad, it is ok, he's not surprised, he and Gabby knew on Saturday how I felt before I did I made a joke about them being Italian fortune tellers they just said they saw something in my eyes when I talked about her."

Bonzo was thinking, **master was different is cuddlier, his days were filled with affection from old man, mermaid man, the girl and even from mermaid sidekicks. Old man even gives him treats** today it was cooked bacon bits yummy, yummy, and he gets extra unscheduled walks, his harness on ready wondering because they'd also put a funny head harness on, but a walk is a walk and I'm a happy dog. George, Alan and Bonzo led the way, Stone, Chris, and Tony spread out in front and behind, "Let's flush out the riff-raff," Stone said into his headset. The two watching the old man and the large dog didn't have a clue until they both hit the ground hard, "Afternoon gentlemen," said Stone, "my two associates are going to place your knees in a very vulnerable position and I'm going to ask you some polite questions, you answer you don't hobble for the rest of your lives. Just so the lads know how much pressure to exert a little practice is needed," and Chris and Tony applied a little torque, both men screamed in pain and began sweating, "Good, now question one, who do you work for?"

The smaller of the two tried bullshitting and Tony torqued the pressure on his left knee feeling the tear beginning and then backing off, "That's going to be painful, but in a week you'll be able to walk normally," the second one decided to talk, "we work for Jeff and Richard Marshall, but you already knew that plus I guess you know why we're watching seen as how you're the ninja squaddie."

Stone wasn't surprised Greavsie would keep an eye on Angie and anyone looking after Bonzo. Stone phoned, "Bish, hi dear, how are doing this fine day?"

"Stone, what now?"

"Could you please send a van, we have two low lives caught in possession," looking at Chris and Tony who knew the score, and Stone gave directions, "Ten minutes. When are you coming in?"

"We'll be there in around an hour," and as Chris and Tony searched the two, Stone gave their names to Bish. Tony opened the phones under contacts Jeff M, saying, "Chris, you like this part, your turn," and rang the mobile. "Hello Darren," said Jeff Marshall.

"Sorry this is Darren's phone, but Darren is currently on the ground with a very swollen painful left knee. I'd like to request that Greavsie ups his game. Its amateur hour out here, your two goons have been arrested, caught in possession of hundreds of ecstasy tablets with the intent to supply. If you send any more goons, can we have the A team please," and switched the phone off passing it to Tony, "More work for you, sunshine." The van arrived and the two goons got put in the back.

"Right, lads, home for some lunch and more of my very precious coffee supply, then we'll see grumpy."

"How'd it go, son?" Stone told his dad and the Brigadier.

"George, I'm going to swing by and see Detective Inspector Bishop before these three stooges turn up," pointing at Stone, Chris, and Tony.

"Dad, can you knock up some omelettes? I'm going to make some calls," and as Stone walked away Chris shouted, "Love you, honey."

"Christopher, big screen green ninja, Dad hasn't seen it yet," said Stone.

"Tony, see what you can get out of those phones, please."

"Yes, sir, boss sir, love you big time." Stone was laughing as he went to the bedroom. "Hi, I thought I'd try some hot phone sex, guess what I'm holding in my hand that's firm and throbbing."

"Justin I'm in the middle of class."

"What colour are your panties?"

"Hmm, Justin you're on speaker."

"Oh fuck, Ang."

"Only kidding," and giggling, "they're boring white cotton school pants, but they can become moist if I just slip my finger ooh, feels nice and wet and warm, ooh Justin if it was only longer and thicker and belonged to you."

"Ang, stop please."

"Oh, honey, only five days and already you're asking me to stop," and giggled again. "I need a firm hand, Justin, maybe a spanking and then you can kiss me all better."

"Angela, can you be serious a moment?"

"I am serious, Justin, I've never been spanked, I love that you are so easy to wind up."

"Ang, can you listen for a couple of minutes?" And told her what had gone down, "Ang, be careful, is Jane about?"

"Yes, she's in the corridor, she heard the phone sex part and discreetly left the room, it's hard for her, Justin."

"Well, I agree on the hard part, Ang, I love you please be extra careful. Bish isn't happy but the Brigadier has gone down to the station to smooth things out."

"I love you, Justin, please no hero stuff; I need a husband with all his bits and pieces in full working order."

"Do you want to come with me to the estate agents this afternoon?"

"Justin, I always want to come with you."

"You love winding me up, don't you, Ang?"

"No, Justin, I love you; winding you up is just extra."

Stone then phoned Jane, "Hi, Hardcase, some developments, Chris didn't want to sit with his fingers up his arse and told her what had happened, not my plan I'm a cog. But they may move on Angie if they get desperate, she can identify Greavsie, Jackson and Bowman. The Brigadier has put Julie Maddock on Jo she's young enough to pass as a new pupil even though she's 22."

"Ok, Stone, I'm on my A game."

Going back into class as the kids came out, she found Angie quietly crying, "Angie, what's wrong?"

"Nothing, Jane, nothing I can do anything about, my emotions are getting the better of me yet again. I've been speaking with Justin, I love him so much I nearly always cry after speaking to him, I've already cried three maybe four times today, I keep thinking it will calm down and not be so intense. Before Justin, I'd only slept with five men, had sex maybe fifteen times in my life none any good, at thirty-four, I've got no experience, in how or what to do, it was always wham bam thank you, mam. I've never been in love, never had an orgasm before Justin everything he does makes me so happy I'm practically bursting, I think this feeling will settle but every time I speak to him, I get like this. He kisses me and I melt, anything he asked I'd do, all I want is to be with him, he's my air, we've known each other a week and I know I want to live my life by his side. I'll love him for the rest of my life, God I agreed to marry him, and it was the easiest decision I've ever made, I'm so in love with him."

Jane looked at Angie Sanders, "Wow, Angie, I don't think I'm capable of committing to love one person so completely for the rest of my life and Angie, I do understand even if Stone loved me, I couldn't love him like you do. You have no off switch, he walks into the room, and you glow, I've never seen two people more in love, more in tune with each other whether it be a week or a year. I thought I'd be jealous having had a five-year crush on your man, but that's what he is, Angie, yours, I've known him five years he's never looked at anyone the way he looks at you. Angie, can I tell you my biggest secret?"

"You can tell me anything, Jane, we're friends, and I trust you with my life."

"Angie, I'm twenty-six and still a virgin, never had sex, I'm not gay I like men I just find 99% immature. I hope if I fall in love, it's as deeply and completely as you. Now enough, I have an image to maintain." Angie really liked

Jane she was extremely vulnerable if you got beneath the hard exterior, she hoped she wouldn't be alone forever.

Stone rang his daughter's phone, "Hi, Dad what's up?" And he told her the morning's events, "If you look around your class, you'll see a new starter, short has mousey hair, pretty dressed like you, her name is Julie Maddock, go and make friends with her. She only looks 13, she's 22, self-defence and martial arts trained, and she is your bodyguard. We are going to keep hitting the hornets' nest, it is Chris's plan, not mine, Greavsie will retaliate at some point probably against Angie or me, but it could be you or Dad, so I'm taking no chances."

"Ok, Dad, I understand. Dad, I've got some pictures of the ring Angie liked; it is very pretty."

"Jo, I'm picking up Angie after school and going to the estate agents, you want to tag along?"

"Thanks for asking, Dad, but I think you and Angie should choose where you live, me I'll be happy with any place by the river, but Angie will have ideas of what she wants and it'll be nice for it to be a joint decision."

"Josephine Roseanne, you really are far to wise for your age, I love you be extra careful ok."

"I love you too, Dad; I'll see you at home later."

Stone returned to the kitchen to his omelette and coffee, "Dad, Ang and I are going to the estate agents after school, Jo will be brought home by Julie Maddock; she's babysitting, just in case, Dad always keep Bonzo with you they know you. I don't think Greavsie will do anything yet, but he'll be shaken up, maybe when we get some of his gang he'll make a move probably with his goon squad. me, Chris, Tony, we take them out extra hard no fucking about, they'll be able to fight so we take them out quick, Greavsie gets desperate calls in his best team etc. Now do you think the Brig's had enough time with Bish, tell you what, we'll have another cup of coffee then we'll set off.

"Dad, take Bonzo out this afternoon as usual for his walk, Ang has given you his attack commands, I'd prefer not to have to use Bonzo cos he's a sweet-natured lump but they may send out a couple of handy goons and you're not young or fast anymore."

"Maybe, son, but I still have some moves left."

Eighteen

Greavsie sat at his desk with all his top crew, no one made eye contact they all waited for him to speak. "Let me get my fucking head round this, what a set of fuck up morons you are. Terry, get Jonesy plus two of his dope friends, Jonesy is now at the police station after being caught fucking red-handed giving out my tablets. Some bastard rings you and through you calls me a 'dumb fuck and to go home or the next one gets his legs broken,' is that correct, Terry?"

Greavsie opened the drawer withdrawing the bloody baseball bat, "Yes, boss, but I was only following your instructions so you can't blame me for Jonesy being caught," and the bat crashed into the table, "which is why I'm hitting the fucking table and not you." Turning to Jeff, "You might not be as lucky, your two arseholes were watching Stone's old man and that fucking dog, and Darren gets his knee twisted so we can assume the ninja squaddie or one of his mates is involved, BUT Darren and Stokes's are both in the fucking nick with my fucking pills planted on them charged with intent to deal," and the bat came thundering down on the table again, "I'm out on the profit on those pills which," and he hit the table again. "I'm taking out of your fucking wages."

"But, boss," and the bat bounced off the table, "Jeff, shut the fuck up. I speak you listen, or this bat goes into your thick fucking skull. A different voice now tells me through you, 'I'm a fucking amateur and requests the A team' like I'm fucking playing some sort of game. I've now lost three people and pills, and the one little success we could have had Ronnie fucked up. Ronnie, here, now," pointing to a spot next to where he was standing tapping the bat on his hand, "my specific instructions here that you find Bowman and scare him."

"Yes." Everyone knew what was going to happen next, the bat coming down quick and hard across Ronnie's shoulder breaking the collar bone with an audible snap. "Terry, smelling salts, right-hand drawer," and Terry leapt into action putting them on the table next to Greavsie who stuck them under Ronnie's nose causing him to gasp awake, "as I was saying, you at six feet four inches two hundred and fifty pounds of muscle hit little Tommy and a bit too hard, hand out Ronnie I don't care if it's your right or left." Ronnie in severe pain stuck out his left hand as he was right-handed, the bat came thundering down breaking several fingers and causing Ronnie to scream in pain and pass out yet again. "Chris, down here," Chris looked at his elder brother passed out on the floor, "I take it you still can't control your older brother's urges."

Chris looked down at the floor, "No, boss, he goes off on one more often than he used to especially when he stops taking his tablets."

"Take your brother away, get him seen somewhere, and tell him he's out as of now. When Bowman's slut of a mother sees her son, she's going to call the cops and little Tommy will be having a short stay in hospital. If the little fucker talks he can identify all of us, so see this bat, Chris, it will be the last thing you feel if that should happen, go, and see young Bowman making sure you're not seen, give him this, handing over a £1000 roll and tell him you're sorry for your fuck up of a brother, the money is to keep his mouth shut. It's Ronnie's and your wages. Chris, your next job is to find and bring Barry Jackson to me, if he finds out what your brother did to young Tommy then he may go to the cops, and Chris, he isn't to be harmed in any way till he gets in front of me."

"There's plenty of contact numbers on those phones boss, nothing incriminating though," said Tony.

"Give them to Bish when we get there," Stone was driving the Discovery, a bigger and more secure vehicle than Chris's Subaru. Arriving at the station, Stone, Chris and Tony were ushered directly into Bishop's office, where Tony handed the confiscated phones over, "Gentlemen, I've been speaking with your boss, who's been speaking to my boss, it seems that some people think I should have been more proactive. Young Jonesy insists he was set up by you three, swears he didn't have any drugs on him. Darren Toulmin's left knee is rather black and blue, he's claiming police brutality, but you three aren't police so we're not going to get sued. Ronnie Taylor, one of Greavsie more violent thugs is in hospital; his brother Chris brought him in and reckons he fell badly, Ike looked at him for me, broken collar bone caused by a bat and three broken fingers on his left hand, Ronnie's hardcore won't grass.

"Part of the Greavsie intimidation regime is the use of a baseball bat if someone does or gets something wrong that he hasn't agreed to, plus, thirty minutes ago Tommy Bowman was brought into hospital by his lovely drugged or pissed mother, coughing up blood and in lots of pain. Ike looked him over, a fist mark about the size of a big man's hand into the kidneys, two and two making five, Ronnie's overdone the tap, but neither is talking. We are trying to locate Barry Jackson, but he hasn't been seen in his usual haunts, every copper has a photo and he's on our stop and apprehend list."

"So," said Chris, "the fucker has lost tablets and three of his noncritical team. Bowman's had a beating and Jackson's in the wind, so are we to sit with our finger up our arses again or are we gonna break some heads."

"You see, Chris, that's why you're not a policeman. Now, Mr Greaves is aware we have eyes on him, he'll blend into the background even more; there'll be layers of goons before we get the main man."

Stone said, "Then we take out his goons hard, with your permission of course and the Brig's, clubs open Thursday, we sell top class gear undercut Greavsie, have plenty of your and our lads, comes down to a fight, I have twelve men plus Jane and Julie all highly trained in hand-to-hand against some boxing and wrestling wannabes."

"Greavsie won't fight fair, you called him an amateur, he's anything, but and his goon squad is legendary."

"So, more arse-fingering then, Bish," said Chris.

"Let us be clear, gentlemen, Greavsie is a physco, but a super cool intelligent one, he's never been caught, he knows we're watching him, Stone, he knows this was you're doing and he's going to come after you if you keep pressing."

"Tell me, Bish, what's your master plan?"

"Well Stone, if I was you, unofficially, I'd just keep doing what you're doing, officially, Chris change your finger," and Bish winked at them. On the way back to Stone's, "Bish was a bit cryptic you think, boss," said Tony.

"No, he's got his bosses watching him and his force, but there's no one watching us three, so we keep on shaking the tree. I'm off to pick up Ang and visit the estate agents, you two can call it a day if you like, or you're welcome to some more of my coffee and help walk Bonzo, maybe fuck wit has sent another team."

Stone sent Angie a text 'on way xxx.' Chris and Tony appreciated the early finish offer, but were going to hang with George and Bonzo, if anything happened and they could have prevented it they'd feel guilty. Stone waited in school reception for Angie who walked round the corner followed by Jane, he looked at his fiancée, she was stunningly beautiful, full figured, but what really made her stand out where her eyes, she saw him and smiled, and he was in awe of how much he loved her. Angie had no off button when it came to controlling how she felt and simply jumped into his arms, kissing him hard on the lips not a care that the lobby was full of teachers and school kids, pulling his future wife in and stroking her hair he looked into her eyes, the power of his feelings caught his breath and unable to help himself he said, "I love you," and he kissed her.

"Jesus, you two," said Jane, "don't draw attention to yourselves, please." Unbeknown to anyone, Chris Taylor was watching the lobby thinking that maybe Barry Jackson would turn up, and seeing Stone and Angie realised the ninja squaddie had an Achilles heel that maybe Greavsie could use at some point.

"Sorry, Hardcase, I can't seem to dial it down, even in public, it's a big moment we're going to look for our own house."

"Are we waiting for Jo?" Angie asked.

"No, she told me that me and you should choose where we want to live, she's happy as long as it's by the river, and you will have ideas of where and what you want."

"Stone, you're sure your daughter is only thirteen, she's far too mature and wise."

"Jane, she has spent the last nine years having to watch me far too closely, now because of Ang, she can relax a little. I'm going to train later, you want to spa with me up at the house or maybe do a session on the weights, stay for tea after. Ang, you and Jo can talk decorating crap." Angie's estimation of Stone went up yet another notch; he was not allowing her to feel abandoned.

"I'd like that, Stone, haven't done any lifting for a while, I don't want to fight you anymore not even in practice, might trigger your memory, we could do some drills together." Angie realised that both were aware of the other issues; they were very good friends in tune with each other.

On the way to the estate agents, "You are a good man, Justin, you look after your friends."

"They were all I had apart from Dad and Jo and Ike till I met you, I was a walking time bomb. Meeting you and losing control was the best thing from their point of view that could have happened to me, they just see a normal guy madly in love with the woman of his dreams."

"Darling, there is nothing normal about you." Parking up, "Justin, can we sit a few minutes till I pull myself together, it's not easing off, still full-on with no brakes. Everything is overpowering, you said, 'Marry me?' Yes, let's get a house.

Yes, not once did I think it's only been a week, the only thing I've thought about is you."

Stone grinned, "So you love me then, Ang?" and leaned over to wipe away her tears.

"Oh yeah, boy, do I love you, Justin, I tingle all over every time I look at you."

"Ang, before we go in, I think we should put both houses on the market, pay off your mortgage, mine is mortgage-free and worth 1.2 million, I'll take a million for a quick sale and purchase our new house and use what's left from the sale for any alterations we should do, should be able to complete a sale within a month with no mortgage. I want you to be my wife before the end of the year, not just live together, but to have my name and introduce you to everyone as my wife Angela Stone."

"Shit, Justin," and started to cry again, "just as I thought I was beginning to pull myself together."

"If anyone asks you've got hay fever, bad."

Stone introduced himself and Angie telling the young girl what they had and to sell and what they were looking for and they would like it all completed as fast as possible, aware of a large transaction she disappeared into the Managers office. Robert Charlton, the manager introduced himself and invited them into his office, "Colonel Stone, Ms Sanders, I understand you're looking for a house by the river, and you both have a house to sell."

"Please, its Justin and Angie, my fiancée. Angie's house is to be sold independently of mine."

"Right, Justin and took some details, hmm your house is valued at 1.35 million on today's market, what value are you looking to purchase at?"

"The same or less, its mortgage fee, ideally chain free and a cash transaction." Robert Charlton's mind worked quickly selling and buying fees would lift the profits nicely for the quarter. "Justin, Angie we have three really good properties, one only put on the market yesterday, bringing them up on the computer, and they all have virtual tours." After doing the virtual tours, Justin said, "Which one, Ang?"

"First one, the Old Mill House, its old but beautifully built with nice thick walls, two great garden areas and the back one practically in the river, and it will catch the sun in almost every room. It will need a quite a bit of renovation because it's been left in disarray too long, it'll not be structural as it was built to last, it also has a large barn and a smaller house as an annex with an interior walkway, of the others two one has no character and the other is too new and expensive for what it is."

"Very good choice, it was originally built as the Manor House for the Mill Owner and is about 150 years old," said Robert, "the rooms are all very large, some could be split if you require more than bedrooms, the annexe is self-contained. It is old-fashioned; the late owner was very elderly and hadn't lived in the main house for several years using the annexe instead. It only went on the market yesterday and the family wanting a reasonable price quick sale to keep Death Duties down. I have the keys if you would like to view?"

"Yes, we would," said Justin and Angie together.

"Which one would you have picked, Justin?"

"I'd have gone number three, expensive, but all ready to move in."

"But, Justin darling, it was overpriced by 250,000 and a new build with no character, thin walls, and small rooms, two bedrooms you'd struggle to get a bed in."

"What can I say? I'm just a man, you're the homemaker of our family," and Angie started to cry again. "Shit, Justin bloody tears again, how am I going to look getting married my make-up will be all over the place."

"Ang, you are beautiful; you don't need make-up."

Getting out of the discovery, Angie said, "This is the one, listen to the river and the birds singing, oh look at the fruit trees, and large gardens all fenced in, Bonzo will love it," and chased after Robert Charlton eager to see the main house cobwebs and all. Angie was beside herself when she saw the potential for the master bedroom and when they went round the back of the house and saw the river less than twenty feet away, how she would make a walkway from the garden to the river and be able to sit in the sun with her children, wow Angie thought where did that come from. "This is the house we want, Robert can you contact the seller?"

"If you'll excuse me a moment," said Robert Charlton taking out his phone, eager to make the best commission he'd ever received, "I'll call the seller." Speaking with Bobby Elliott, discussing the asking price and making it known it was cash, Bobby said, "Give me five minutes," and rang his sister, three minutes later, Bobby rang back. Robert Charlton returned to Stone and Angie, "Good news, the Elliotts will accept £750,000 providing the sale is concluded within the month."

"Robert, you now need to get my house sold as soon as possible."

"Justin, your house will go in a matter of days, we have people waiting for a property like yours. I'll put it on-line in the morning and probably have several firm offers by close of day. We have in-house solicitors and can get this done within a week."

"Even better," said Stone, "I can call into the office tomorrow and get the wheels in motion."

Robert said to Angie, "Give me your details and address, any idea on asking price?"

"Robert, I'll leave that to you, just get a quick sale for a reasonable price, we could send one of our staff to video your house and garden or you could do it, Justin it may help to sell yours if we have video back it up nicely, Robert I'll do the houses save time, great."

"Thank you, Justin, Angie," and shaking hands said, "Shall we say ten am?" And left Stone and Angie to take in what they had just bought.

"Justin, we can store all our stuff in the barn and live in the annex during the day while we renovate the house, just make a couple of bedrooms habitable in the main house it shouldn't take that long, you can turn the barn into a huge gym. The annex is ideal for Dad with us, but has his own space and come and go whenever he wants." Angie was totally unaware that she hadn't called George, George but dad another slip up. Stone smiled but didn't say anything yet again knowing the tears would return, hoping he would be there when she did, it would really settle Dad knowing that Angie thought of him that way and he wasn't in any way in the way and he was part of her life as much as Stone was. They spent another half hour viewing and making plans before Stone said, "Shall we go back and tell everyone?"

The lane back to the main road was very quiet, as it only served two properties the Mill House and an old rundown cottage about a mile and a half in the opposite direction, "Justin, stop the car, make love to me here now," and Angie was out and lifting her skirt, walking round to the passenger side he removed his trousers and sat on the passenger seat pulling his boxers over his very erect penis as Angie climbed onto him and moving her wet panties to the side felt his penis glide effortlessly into her warm body. Kissing him hard, and saying I love you, repeatedly until her breathing was so fast, she could no longer speak, and her body began to orgasm and feeling the pulsating he had the same effect, and his hot seed sprayed the inside of her moist body. Angie sat holding

Stone both getting their breath back, the physical act over but the desire for each other still red hot they held each other and kissed and kissed. "I love the feeling of you inside me and you cum at the same, I have to, Ang you are not exactly quiet and reserved when you make love, it's wonderful and once I hear you well it is game over. Ang, I know I've said this before but don't ever change, you are just about perfect."

"Ha Justin, we don't really know each other yet, I may have some strange quirks, didn't stop me from falling in love with you or asking you to marry me or us getting a house together within a week."

"I love that we just bought our house, I love you, Justin."

"Ang, don't cry, you'll set me off and that would really tarnish my image."

"Not to me, it won't, I've already seen you cry."

"Ang, the top of my legs are rather damp and you'll have a damp patch on your seat."

"It's mostly in my panties I'll probably squelch when I walk," and Angie giggled. "Justin, you could always be a gentleman and let me drive; after all, you are the main cause of the dampness."

"Ang, it was you who wanted to stop and make love, remember."

"I remember a member that hadn't objected, Mr Stone."

"What can I say, we all have a weakness."

"Justin, my panties are wet."

"Hmm seems to be a rather permanent fixture for you of late, Ang," and retrieving an old newspaper from the boot placed it on the passenger seat and climbed in pulling his trousers up to his knees and hoping the dampness didn't seep into his boxers. "Oh, you are a gentleman."

"You think so," and fondled her breasts. "I hope I'm not distracting you."

"Justin, I can't drive with your hands on my boobs."

"They are not," and he deftly unfastened her bra and slid his right hand inside cupping her, "now they are."

"Don't you think my panties are wet enough already?" And he flicked his thumb over her nipple which responded immediately.

"Let me drive us home, then after your workout, you can have another workout now are you going to fasten me back in," but he merely bent over pulled out her shirt and sucked gently on her left then right nipple, Angie groaned pulling his head onto her breasts, lifting his head he put her breasts back and fastened her up never taking his eyes off hers, "I love you, Ang," and once more they were in an intense and passionate embrace struggling to get their breath. "It's not easing off, is it, Ang?"

"No, Justin, it certainly isn't," as she drove slowly up the lane, out of breath, panties soaked, and nipples still tingling from his mouth.

"I never liked this house, the gym and cinema room I could do anywhere, the actual house design is not my taste. What makes a house a home is the little touches so gym, cinema room, coffee machine, and nice, equipped kitchen that's about it."

"You can convert the barn into a huge gym and martial arts studio, replace some of the free weights, and get some press machines for legs, calves, chest, a power rack, landmine and cable systems, dumbbells and some 2-inch Olympic bars and more plates."

"Ang, you've been giving this a bit of thought."

"Yes, Justin, I daydream too I just never thought it would come true." Bonzo chuffed as Stone and Angie walked in, George, Chris and Tony where sat in the kitchen drinking Stone's dwindling coffee supply, Jo was in her bedroom doing her homework having been dropped off by Julie, "I'm going to see Jo, leave you gents alone," said Angie having first stroked Bonzo and gave him a fuss, Bonzo thought **master smells a bit different then remembered the smell from his own encounters, ah ha, he thought wonder how many puppies she'll have, I wonder if mermaid man can do who's the daddy and strut like me, she must be OK with it though cos she's really happy again, might try my eye thing on her at tea time maybe get some bacon bits or even some meaty bones** Bonzo followed Angie to Jo's bedroom. "Jo, put that boy down," knocking and knocking and opening the door.

"Mam, you know I don't have a boyfriend, Dad would have a fit and the boy would have no nuts," and Angie burst into tears yet again, kissing her daughter on the lips and holding her tightly.

"You cry all the time and Granddad makes you blush."

"I can't control myself, one week with your dad and I'm mush."

"I think Dad's mushy too, so tell me about where am I going to live," and Angie told Jo all about the Old Mill House with Bonzo looking on.

"Chris and Tony didn't spot anyone goons when I took Bonzo for his walk," said George, "which either means they've vastly improved the lookers or Greavsie going to come directly after you, Angie, or Jo at some point."

"Probably going to be me," said Stone, "the knee damage and the threats would give me away, but we need to hit his leadership team before he comes after me. Dad, about the house," and he told them about the Old Mill House and the attached annexe. "Dad, I want you to have the annexe, you'll be close to us, but have your independence should you ever get involved with a woman."

"I'm not likely to find another like Chrissy, but thanks, son, it is a nice thought. I'll sell my house on the ant hill, and I'll put the money into the annexe."

"Dad, there will be plenty of money left from the sale of this house, but I'll make a deal with you, I'll pay half the costs of the annex renovation. There's a huge barn in decent shape where we can store everything till, we get all the rooms sorted, and we can live in the annex, be a bit cramped, but it won't be for very long. It's a great place dad, it's quite peaceful with the river less than twenty feet away and probably loaded with fish," and going over to the kitchen drawer took out some keys, throwing them to his dad, "the boat is yours and Ike's and change the fucking name, please."

"I can't accept your boat, son."

"Dad, I don't use it, need it, or want it you and Ike can fish to your heart's content. I'll even put a jetty at the bottom of the garden. I made a big saving paying cash for the house plus the surplus from selling this and Angie's house we won't struggle and Dad, I owe you so just take this fucking boat and give it a new name, a whole new fresh start, it works wonders, Dad."

"Ok, son," knowing how much this gesture meant to his son.

Angie, Jo and Bonzo walked into the kitchen just as Chris and Tony were leaving, "You two not want to stick around, Hardcase will be here soon we're going to have a weights session."

"Thanks, but no, boss, she makes me feel weak and deadlifts more than I can, yeah she's only just over five feet and using a sumo stance but the bar still has to come off the floor," said Chris, "you're not fighting, are you, boss?"

Tony asked a bit concerned, "No, Jane's already told me no, we might do some drills together."

"If you going to be deadlifting, boss, you might want to invest in some of those fake plates that look really macho."

"Chris, sunshine, the last time I deadlifted, 700lb came off the floor six times I believe that's quite good three times bodyweight."

"What can I say, boss, just make sure red kryptonite doesn't sap all your energy before you start lifting," and Angie burst out laughing, "Justin, for the wedding, I think I'll dye my hair red just for Chris," and laughed even harder. Stone looked at Angie laughing and thought it was the most beautiful thing he'd ever seen, "Can I have my own nickname like Hardcase, mine could be energy sapper," and giggled.

"Dad?"

"Yes, Jo?"

"Is mam talking about sex?"

"No, Jo, your mam doesn't have sex she makes love."

"Dad, mental image overload and I haven't had my tea."

No comment was made by anyone about Jo calling Angie, mam, Stone, and George were aware of the significance; George had to turn away his own emotions getting the better of him. Angie's eyes filled and she took some deep breaths to calm herself not wanting to spoil the moment. Still laughing, "Boss, she's something else," said Chris as him and Tony left, just as Jane Casey pulled up and got off the red Firebird. Chris couldn't resist, "Hardcase, get energy sapper on the job before the gym session," and he and Tony high-fived and drove off.

"Hi, Hardcase, meet energy sapper," said Jo, "do you want a cup of Dad's special coffee, while red kryptonite works her magic?"

"Jo, at some point in your life, you are going to be hopelessly in love and Daddy is going to remember these times and payback in kind."

"Justin, how about a quick bodyweight session and rename me knee trembler," Angie giggled.

Stone loved her giggle, "You are going to be a bad influence on our daughter," which stopped the giggle cold and she burst into tears again.

"Dad, mams crying again," which set off Angie crying harder and then Jo started to cry.

"Jesus, the hormones in this room," Jane said looking across at Stone who stood there with tears in his eyes, "my god, it's the whole lot of you."

"Jane, we just bought a house together, so we're all very emotional, well, Ang is all the time I'm just coming out in sympathy because Jo is finally going to have a mam who loves her and treat her as the special girl she is," as tears fell down his cheeks.

"Stone, you're going soft."

"No, Jane, Justin is never soft," and the giggle replaced the tears, "me and Jane are going to get extra ripped."

Nineteen

"Sorry about all the emotion, we keep thinking it will settle down but even Jo's picked up on it, Angie will be a great mum, you can see how well they get on and Jo needs to call Angie mum."

"I saw Angie's face it lit up like a Christmas tree it means a great deal to her, I forecast tears for a few days till they adjust to their new titles and if you think that's emotional wait till George calls Angie, daughter or Angie calls Dad, Dad, cos it's happened only they didn't twig, you're not the only one who loves your woman, Stone."

"Angie is always going to be emotional; it's part of who she is."

"She has a wicked sense of humour; energy sapper or knee trembler and she came out with a great one liner at school. We overheard those two witches Sophie Preston and Barbara Robinson discussing why you're with Angie, they were being disgusting."

Angie walked into the room ladies she said, "If you must know why, it's because I'm multi-orgasmic," and Stone roared with laughter he had to put his hands on his knees.

"Tony says you like the challenge of deadlifting, I've only got one Olympic bar now that carries decent poundage, and so we'll have to alternate. We'll start with some band work, just follow me," giving her a green tension band to his blue and did a ten-minute rotor cuff warm up. Moving to the bar and putting one 25kg plate on each side, including the bar total 70kg/154lb, "Ladies first" and taking it, in turn, did six reps, Jane opted to add two 10kg plates 198lb already over twice her body weight, Stone did his set then removed the two 10kg and replaced them with two 25kg 264lb Jane just looked at three times her bodyweight on the bar saying, "Bst I've ever done is three reps."

"Well, you are well warmed up, ok, wrap your knees, put your belt on but stick a towel on your stomach before you tighten your belt it helps you brace, change your gloves wear these heavy-duty gloves and use a multi-grip Jane it's safer now, get that breath into your stomach and think about pushing your feet through the floor, do one rep then re-set position, deep breath and go again yes it's harder cos you have no bounce but it's much safer, take a couple of deep breaths once you hit three then brace and lift come on Jane you can do this."

Jane followed the instructions, straps stopping the wobble and got to four, but Stone knew she had more, "Huge breaths, Jane, push down hard get in past your knees lock the fucker out with your hips and arse," and she got rep five, "Come on, Jane, one more," the wobble started the minute the weight lifted off the floor, and with Stone shouting, "Come on, Jane, you can lift the motherfucker," and pulling every ounce of strength, she had locked the weight, "just drop it, Jane," and she dropped the weight onto the mat and hugged Stone.

"Very impressive," said George who was watching from the door. Stone did three 25kg plates each side with ease still 374lb, then four plates 484lb then five plates 594lb. "Jane, this is why you never compete with this man."

"You going for it, son?"

"Yep, Dad, feeling strong," and loaded another two plates plus an additional two 5kg 726lb a 20lb increase on his best six rep total, George grabbed a towel and Stone fastened the belt around the towel and his stomach, Jane looked curious as he'd done the same thing with her, "This is why most powerlifters have big stomachs more internal air pressure the added towel gives you core something to push against keep you more stable," Stone started the lift series got to four and the internal struggle began, "Come on, son, two more, two deep breaths and up and lock for number five. Next one is the one for a new record, two huge breaths, absolute concentration," and on form, the weight came off the floor and locked. Stone's musculature across his shoulders and arms was unbelievable and he dropped the weight to the floor, "Never in doubt, son, now you can both do lighter stuff, and I'll go and help the girls get the tea ready."

"Ok, Jane, we'll have taxed our central nervous systems, so ask yourself where you need to improve."

"Leg strength for my kicks," and Stone picked up a 25k fixed dumbbell. "Ok this is called a goblet squat," demonstrating holding the weight at his chest and squatting down really low and back up, "works the same muscles as your sumo deadlift but really gets the legs if you do it time volume, do ten reps, stop thirty seconds, count in your head, another set rest thirty seconds again repeating always stick at ten reps, rest time can go up to forty-five seconds but you must get ten good reps, and Jane, this really burns when you can't get ten reps you stop, you need to be able to use your legs on your bike to get home then get a hot bath. If you want to improve your core simply hold the weight away from your chest, flexibility you reduce the rep speed and hold at the bottom, once you tired you'll need all your focus on just getting up and down, do it right Jane you'll have DOMS, delayed onset of muscle soreness just means your legs will be like jelly for a couple of days but it's a nice ache means you've done the job properly."

"I'm going to do some time volume shoulder press using the landmine set up puts my shoulders in a neutral plain no rotor stress. You know what you're doing."

"Yes, Stone."

"Good, cos I'm putting some workout music on, loud, you'll find you can get a few more reps, and rock music is meant to be played loud," and the first few bars of the greatest riff ever, Back in Black pounded out, rock music was still one of the greatest pleasures in his life and he smiled rock gods on Friday he'd really surprise Ang.

Rock music was nearly always on in the house, yes films were watched in the cinema room, but TV was rarely watched, music was Stone's passion being brought up listening to the start of rock in the sixties by his mam and dad. Angie was cooking, George was laughing at Bonzo head banging to the music and went for the video camera he had to catch Bonzo in the act, Jo, Lemmy will copy Bonzo, but we'll have to watch the volume. He came back just as Bonzo's and Angie's favourite track came on, Angie was checking the food with her back to George and went full-on rock chick singing at the top of her voice, 'Hey, hey mama said the way you move, Gon' make you sweat, gon' make you groove, Ah ah child way ya shake that thing, Gon' make you burn, gon' make you sting, Hey, hey baby when you walk that way, Watch your honey drip, I can't keep away.'

George just aimed the video and Angie having picked up wooden spoons and was doing her best John Henry Bonham impression on the table top, Jo joined in on the harmony and their 'gig' moment was captured by a grinning George, all four minutes and fifty-seven seconds of it. Angie hadn't realised she was being filmed; she was just back in her own kitchen doing what she loved, but as soon as the next track came on with the long intro, she started to cry knowing the words by heart, 'If the sun refused to shine I would still be loving you, when mountains crumble to the sea, there will still be you and me the opening lines to Thank You,' she looked round at George, "I always cry when I hear this so this is me being normal, not emotional, it's the best love song ever written by the best band ever. I want this for my wedding song I'll cry all the way through, but I want my first dance with my husband to be this."

Their workout done, Stone went off to shower and change, while Jane grabbed her bag and headed to the guest bedroom. 'Achilles Last Stand,' was playing the volume adjusted so that conversation was possible, when they entered the kitchen, Stone was struck by just how good John Paul Jones' bass playing was. "I'm going to get Angie a set of Ludwig drums as a wedding present, Justin."

"What, why, Dad?"

"We'll have a family moment in the cinema room later, this you have to see, you thought your rock god was impressive, just wait."

Angie whirled around, "What you were filming me?"

"Yes, Angela, my dear right from, 'hey, hey mama'."

"Oh shit, please tell me you didn't get the spoons."

"Well, yep, that's why I want to get you some drums, looks to me like you could do that for real on a proper kit."

"You stopped before the meltdown?"

"Got that too and the reason behind it, no secrets in this house."

"I just did the chops, Angie ably assisted by young Josephine did the rest, Bonzo, you get the bones as a treat," Bonzo decided **I like old man nearly as much as mermaid man**. "Justin, you and Jane will have to have a whey isolate shake as you tried to outdo each other."

"I'd like to get seven fifty before I'm forty dad before my rotors get too stiff."

"Ok we'll schedule some 5×5 workouts but stay away from energy sapper the night before," causing Angie to blush, "maybe get Angie to start working out, lots of pelvic thrusts," and she blushed yet again.

Jane was tucking in, "These are the best vegetables I've ever tasted."

"It's all down to the seasoning and roasting keeps all their flavour, I enjoy cooking and I had time on my hands."

"You'll have to teach me some tricks I try and eat healthy but it's usually quite bland," said Jane.

"I'll strike a deal, I teach you to cook, and you teach me some self-defence," and they hi fived.

Ike arrived, late, "Sit down, I saved you a plate, my daughter did the veg so please let her know what you think." George wasn't aware of what he'd said, Jo looked at her dad, "I'll get the tissues, Dad." Angie was standing by the sink putting the pots in to steep, "Here, dry your hands and wipe your tears," and Stone handed her the tissues and kissed her gently.

George said to Ike "Hormones, Ike, nothing like them," unaware that he'd caused the latest cascade of tears.

Stone's mobile went off, unusual to get a call in the evening and it was a mobile number he didn't recognise, "Stone," he said answering the call. "Well, well, if it isn't the fucking ninja squaddie."

"Who's this? Don't tell me, let me guess, it's dumb fuck, isn't it? Are you moving back to Manchester, Greavsie?"

"You think you are fucking smart don't you, Colonel Stone, you like breaking legs so how about I get some of my lads and they break your girlfriends or your daughters." Stone had switched his phone onto speaker and George switched the music off, everyone was listening, "Maybe have some fun with Ms Sanders first, see if she likes it up her arse and, in her mouth."

Stone went rigid, "Not going to happen, dumb fuck, your goon squad are just wannabes. I and my friends are the real deal you're just drug-dealing amateur, anyone touches any of my family I'll break most of the 206 bones in your body and leave you paralysed. I'm a man of my word; check out my army history I never fail."

"If my goon squad gang rape your fiancée history teacher then we take away what you love, your life is over. You'll never get to me, I'm telling you to back the fuck off, the little, short piece you've got watching her won't be able to stop my men."

Stone looked at Jane, "Hey dumb fuck, come and have a go, and WHEN ALL your men are wearing plaster casts and walking with limps for the rest of their lives, that only leaves you and your 206 bones, which I WILL break one by one and use your smelling salts to keep bringing you back. Greavsie, you won't walk away from this; you picked the wrong person's family to threaten. Get Neil or Terry to check my history and find a hole to crawl into. It has been nice having chatted maybe next time we can do it in person you and your 206 bones," and he disconnected.

Stone rang Chris, "Yes, boss."

"We are good to go, Chris, gloves off, war setting, ring Tony let him know tomorrow we go in hard."

"Great, about time, you going to ring Bish?"

"No, just keep it us three." Putting his arms around Ang, "Him or his men won't touch you, but we've obviously damaged his ego."

"Jane, war front?"

"Yes, boss," knowing he had just instructed her to use deadly force should the situation arise.

"Justin, I'm not worried about me, I'm worried about but you, as will be Jo and Dad, your love for us all might make you take too many risks and trigger another episode."

"Ang, these people might think they're tough and capable, but they're amateurs compared to combat, now I'm going to have a cup of coffee, if there's any left, and walk Bonzo." Chris and Tony said their goodbyes, Stone caught up with them before they drove off, "Lads, tell Mach to get two more watching both Angie and Jo, but not to be seen, and they're also on war front, if anything happens to them Greavsie was right it would finish me."

Stone returned to the kitchen, "Ike, does anyone visit Ronnie Taylor or Tommy Bowman?"

"Chris, his brother brought him in says he fell down the stairs, but he hasn't been back in. Bowman's a loner; his mam might visit if she's sober enough or not working. I'll ask security at the hospital to keep a lookout and I'll ring you if anything occurs."

"Time for Bonzo's walk, Jane, you go with Ang, Dad will you do the perimeter? Jo, you stay here watch the cameras." Stone and George had headsets on to communicate, "Justin, to your right."

"I see them, Dad. Ang, Jane, you walk on, don't look back just continue on as normal, I'll pretend I'm waiting for Dad to catch up, there's only two so far, but he may have more further on. If you feel threatened, Jane will step in; Ang, you keep Bonzo cool use his attack words only as a last resort we don't want to spoil his wonderful happy nature for those scroats, me and Dad will have sorted these two by then, so you'll only be alone a few seconds. I won't let them hurt you; neither will Jane," kissed her and waited for his Dad.

"Dad, they'll move after Angie."

"I know, son, you leave these two to me you go watch Angie." The two men moved towards the girls, George followed them, Stone took off into the woods, and he could see Angie and Jane and heard the deep throaty growl as Bonzo head came up looking at the four men surrounding them and Bonzo.

One of them had a stun gun, "Keep that fucking mutt on his lead and tie him around that tree, then you girls and me and the boys get to have some fun, if you don't, I'll prod him with this, waving the stun gun, probably fry its heart," and Bonzo's growl deepened and his fangs came out.

Stone stepped out of the forest, "Ang, set your phone on video, get behind me and try calming Bonzo, poor boy looks like he's getting upset, Jane, its OK hun, you probably still a little tight in the hips and legs from the deadlifts and squats, me I'm good I've got this."

"Ok, boss," and stroked Bonzo. Angie had never heard this tone of voice from Stone, "Now, gentlemen, who wants to go to the hospital first?" Angie had begun filming but Bonzo heard the voice of mermaid man, and the subtle change in tone **he has gone into attack mode, and he's so strong** so he sat down next to Angie and stopped growling the alpha male of the pack was about to do his thing.

"You may be a ninja squaddie, but there are six of us."

"Wrong, sunshine, there's only four; the other two are a bit tied up, so come on, let's see what you set of wannabes have, oh and I'd put that on the floor, we don't want any accidents and a stun gun rammed up the arse is usually fatal to us humans." Stone's mind had assessed the situation doing calculations, from their posture, he knew how they would attack, four men nothing special, but for the sake of Angie and Bonzo, he wanted the situation neutralised. Jane just smiled she knew what was coming he stepped in the first got a throat punch, fell cold where he stood not even time to cough. Next the one with the stun gun and the arm holding it broken followed by a complete tear of the left knee. The third tried to charge Stone and was hit with a right kick just under his jaw creating an audible snap. Stone moved like lightening as the fourth went for a roundhouse punch and delivered a hammer punch to the lower ribs snapping the breastbone.

"Amateurs, like I said, we might have the A team next visit, but I'll have Chris and Tony with me from now on. Ang, don't worry, this is good we can now get him for assault when these goons speak although that one might not for a while," pointing to throat punch.

"Dad" said Stone into his comms, "you ok?"

"Yeah, son, just a little workout."

"OK, I'll phone Bish for a riot van. Hi, honey. got a pickup for you," and told Bish where they were, "cars are no good, need a van there are six goons. No

Bish, Dad got two, my four-need hospital. Dad's, I don't know, he's getting old taps like a girl."

"I heard that, you cheeky upstart."

"Ok, Bish, I'll message Ike, he can do the paperwork that way we have names. I'll get Tony to send the video Angie shot to Greavsie Facebook page then I'll ring Greavsie. Speak to you later, Bish."

Stone rang Tony, "Been some action, Tony, I'm sending you a video from Angie's phone, can you send it to Greavsie Facebook page and text me when it's done? Cheers," then Stone rang Jo, "Everything ok, sweetheart?"

"Yes, Dad, all quiet nothing on the cameras, how about you, mam, Bonzo and Granddad."

"A little action, we'll be about fifteen minutes, just waiting for the police van."

Next, he rang Chris and told him what happened, "Boss, you get all the fun."

"Some, yeah, but the A team will be next. Angie got the whole thing on video I'll let you see it."

"Boss, I've seen you work, it ain't pretty." It was like a work of art Chris, is that you Hardcase, yep I got guard duty with the big furry one the boss got all the fun, it's still great to see him work, then you can give him marks out of ten for style and flair. "Boss, you're having far too much fun. Stone, you are always a ten."

Tony, text done, so Stone rang Greavsie, "Hi, dumb fuck, have you watched the little video on your Facebook page? Tut, tut, Greavsie, five fucks in one sentence, oh I know about your baseball bat maybe I can use that to break 196 of your bones, leave you ten intact for when I tie you to a tree and let Bonzo at you. Do you know a properly trained mastiff can tear a human head from the shoulders? You ain't walking away, threatening me is water off a ducks back, and I shit bigger than you but threatening Angie and my daughter, welllet's just say you'll probably be butt fucked every day in jail cos cripples can't run. No, dumb fuck, it was four of your chosen men in under ten seconds hardly time to get warmed up, my old man took out the other two amateurs just a few bruises but my four nice clean bone breaks and painful, all on their way to the hospital now, just in case I moved too fast for you to catch the action first has torn vocal cords who'll croak for the rest of his life, Disney might sign him up when he gets out of the nick, second nasty break to arm probably not regain full use it's his left so he can still wank, third broken jaw, that's soup through a straw for twelve weeks and the fourth arsehole broken breastbone, the most painful bone to break and takes longest to heal, three inches higher and he'd be dead but I hit where I aim.

"When the finger-pointing starts and aimed at you, we may even find out how much you're paying them to do your dirty work, but feel free to come and have a go yourself with your goonie squad pussy's sorry possie or are you just a dumb cunt coward and Greavsie I hope the next lot is a better standard I might even break into a tepid sweat. No, fuck face, I KNOW I'm that good check my records. You ain't fuck all, you're just drug-dealing scum, send as many as you like you're not even as troublesome as a boil on the arse and the hospital isn't full. So, how about you fuck off back to where you came from and take your drug empire with you? No, well you mention her name again and I'm going to pull your tongue out with pliers, don't think I won't, I've done it before you lose a lot of blood then maybe I'll feed it to Bonzo give him a little snack before the main meal. You know where I live, come and go if you think your hard enough, bring the goonies I'll bring crisps and popcorn; no, I've told you I KNOW how hard I am I've got twenty-six combat medals to prove it, you're just a piss-ant. Tony, this is getting boring and I'm missing Coronation Street, I need my daily fix, fix ha sometimes I even surprise myself bye, bye, you low-life pond scum."

Twenty

"Well, son, I'd say from what I heard that we'll be having visitors, the bastard might shoot you or get one of his goons to do it."

"Dad, it's not in his profile, he'll not get anywhere if he tries anything here, the army paid top money for the security fence, all of them hidden booby traps, the camera feeds are all underground plus there's not an approach that we won't see on camera first." Angie was sitting in the living room with Jo and Bonzo, Stone went and sat with them, "Are you OK with what you saw, Ang?"

"Justin, I know what you were trained to do, did you see what my big dog did, he shut down from attack mode because he knew there was a more lethal alpha male present and Jane just smiled and stroked Bonzo she wasn't worried in the slightest. Justin you're just doing what you must, Jo and I are both fine, you said you would protect us and you're a man of your word."

"Dad, we're good, honestly, don't worry about us."

"What were you girls talking about anyway?"

"Mam was telling me about the house, and her plans, we're just bouncing ideas about." Getting called mam was almost as good as being told she was loved by Justin. "I love you, Jo."

"And I love having a mam." Angie leaned over and kissed her daughter on her lips and gave her a hug, "Right, I'm going to find a pen and paper get some of these ideas down. Jane's stopping tonight; Justin, her legs are tight and she's going to have a long soak in the bath, the spare room next to Dad is made up ready for her," and off Jane went but she touched Angie's shoulder as she went past, thank you she said quietly.

"She is my mam, Dad."

"Yes, I know, Jo, I see she kisses you the same way as I do."

"Dad she started doing that because she understands why you do it even before I started calling her mam. Dad, do you think she'll get her emotions sorted?"

"No, Jo, I don't, I think what you see is what you get I think we just accept that it's part of who she is."

"It's really funny when Granddad embarrasses her, she goes bright red. Dad, are you two planning on giving me a little brother or sister?"

"I've no idea, Jo, I don't know I haven't even thought about it, Ang hasn't mentioned it I know she loves being your mam she lights up like a Christmas tree when you call her mam, and she treats you like a daughter. I don't think if Ang had a child she would want to work, she'd want to be there, and I don't know if she would want to give up her teaching cos, she really enjoys it. Jo, I love her beyond all reason, but I don't know her that well yet, she seems to have worked me out a lot quicker."

"But, Dad, you're an open book to people that love you, you haven't learnt to hide anything, which is a good thing most people are capable of hiding things even from those they love because of who you were, Dad, you can't and to me that's wonderful I've got a Dad I can really talk to and that I know will always be truthful and honest. How do you think I knew you loved mam, you're going to have to think about kids' cos mam will be watching for your reaction and it will be a massive life-changing moment?"

"You are right, Jo, I'll give it some thought, but it's always been me and you."

"Dad, not anymore, I'm growing up; I might want a little brother or sister."

"Do you, Jo?"

"Classic example, Dad, you don't know because I can hide my feelings on the subject, however you can't so when the subject gets brought up and it will as mam is thirty-five next birthday, mam will have your answer before you open your mouth. I know your answer now and I'm only your daughter."

"How can you know my answer when I don't know myself?"

"Dad, you do, you just haven't said it out loud to anyone yet, but the decision will be yours and mams, the same as where we live was yours and mams."

Ang came back into the room, "You are keeping secrets already, Justin."

"Ha, well according to our daughter, I haven't got that ability."

Ike looked through the door. "JT, you got a sec, come into the kitchen when you're finished chatting with your ladies." Stone looked at the two loves of his life, "Yes, I do Josephine Roseanne, but I'd like to have maybe a couple of years of practice first," and Stone kissed her on the lips and went to see what Ike wanted.

"Wow, Justin, being cryptic, you going to tell me what he meant."

"No, mam, not this time, this time it's definitely up to Dad."

"What's up, Ike?"

"I've just had word that Chris Taylor has been detained by hospital security, he went to see Ronnie, but was seen on camera going into Tommy Bowman's room and which as you know is under surveillance, he had a grand in his hand, looks like our drug-dealing friend is paying someone to be quiet. The police are on their way, quickly thinking of something that someone had said about Tommy."

Stone rang Bish, "Your lads are bringing in Chris Taylor, hospital security has him trying to pay Bowman to be quiet, I need your permission to try something. I want to take Angie with me to the hospital and see if we can get him to talk and one of your lads at his door guarding him if he does talk, this might be our best chance of getting something concrete on Greavsie."

"Nothing to lose by trying as long as Angie agrees."

"Bish, today we bought a house together, tomorrow, I get an engagement ring, today she was surrounded by four thugs, she wants Greavsie out of business as much as me."

"Ok, Stone, do it then ring me." Stone walked back into the living room. "Ang, we may have a way of getting to Greavsie," and explained what he wanted to do to her and Ike. "We'll go in my car," Ike said, "I have a private parking spot and hospital clearance he'd phoned to clear the way as it was well past visiting."

"You're letting us sit in baby, Ang, don't fart in his car please."

"It's a beautiful car, Justin, it's my retirement fund, Angie."

"Ang, it's a gas-guzzling monster that can't pass a petrol station without getting topped up and of course, the good doctor has to have his chocolate fix."

"Oh no, J T, I never eat in her."

"Ike, has the car ever gone past seventy?"

"Oh, yes, J T, I take it to the racetrack and give it a blast out with the roof off."

Stone stopped to speak to the security guards, same two as last Friday, "There'll be a police officer here within thirty minutes, check his or her credentials and escort him or her to Tommy Bowman's room please nobody else gets in here tonight."

"J T, I'll show you Tommy's room, I'll be in my office if you need me." Tommy Bowman's room was bare, no cards or fruit and his mother hadn't visited yet, and Tommy sat sullen. "Hello, Tommy."

"Hi, Ms Sanders, I'm sorry for what I did I don't like being on my own all the time so I end up getting high with my so-called friends who haven't even visited or phoned and I won't be back in class for a while."

"I know, Tommy, a punctured lung and inflamed kidney take a long time to heal. I also know you love history, particularly armed conflicts, and you're a very brave boy who's in a lot of pain after being beaten up by a thug three times your height and size, you are also scared stiff of Mr Greaves and his henchmen. I saw you, Barry Jackson, and Tony Greaves in the woods last Friday I was with my dog Bonzo he's the big black bull mastiff you saw. I overheard Greaves telling you how to deal the drugs in our school, he has now threatened me, and I have a bodyguard wherever I go, we will catch him.

"I will testify to what I heard, saw, and happened the next night and that means you're in trouble because I can put you with them in the woods receiving, Colonel Stone and his men then caught you dealing. Tommy, your life is over, you may be unhappy with no home life, living on happy meals and skunk, but you're 16 and very intelligent, you know you want to do something with your life, and it is not 18 months in a young offender prison. This is the man who caught you, Colonel Stone and who now controls your future he's the top army specialist hand-to-hand trainer, and as soon as we can get rid of Greaves, I'm going to marry him. I trust him with my life, and I want you to do the same."

Tommy sat up, showing no emotion, but listening. "I saw your demonstration when you downed the five men in less than ten seconds, can you teach me that then maybe I won't be afraid all the time."

Justin started speaking following Angie's lead, "Tommy, I personally or one of my friends will, one of my jobs is to teach new recruits hand-to-hand combat. Tommy, I want to tell you why I'm here, Chris Taylor," and Tommy shuddered, "was caught trying to come into your room, I take it by the shudder that you know he's the little brother of Ronnie the man who hit you too hard, causing all the damage and pain to your body. Chris Taylor had £1000 with him to give to you, to keep quiet about the beating up. My deal for you is none negotiable, I will get you enlisted into the army as soon as you are better, you will not go to jail, you will receive a decent wage every month, be trained in combat and should you get your grades move up in rank with a better pay packet.

"You will be part of my personal team, who are also my friends, I never let down my friends, you will become what you want to be, a decent caring human being. Drugs are not allowed, and you will be randomly drug tested the same as all my team; you will be protected from any harm. All I ask, and this may not even happen, but if we catch Greavsie, is you have the same amount of guts as Ms Sanders and tell the judge what happened on the Friday in the woods, you're dealing drugs in school will not be recorded, you go from this room on Monday straight to a hospital room at the barracks. What do you think Tommy?"

"Would I call you sir or colonel?"

"You answer me as sir and if I ask you something you address me as colonel."

"Well, sir, I would like to be an army cadet."

"Good choice, Tommy, now get better and I'll see you at the barracks on Monday."

"Yes, sir."

"Justin, can you do what you said in there, you don't think Greavsie is going to court do you?"

"No, I think Mr Greaves is heading for a more permanent ending."

"Justin, I can't marry you if you're in jail."

"Darling, it won't happen that way, now I'd like Ike to show us where Ronnie Taylor is."

Ike was in his room sorting paperwork, "Can you take us to Ronnie Taylor's room?"

Ike looked at Stone and saw the look, as they approached Taylor's door. "Ike, could you please wait around the corner, any cameras in his room?"

"They get switched off after visiting for privacy."

"Angie, stand behind the door do not let this man see you, close your eyes and listen to his voice," and leaving the door open with Angie behind out of view went into Ronnie Taylor's room.

"Well, well, well if it isn't the big ninja squaddie in the flesh?"

"Hi Ron, how's the collarbone?" Patting it hard and Ronnie yelped in pain. "Must be a bad break that, but you're on laughing gas, what's this say off/on switch and flipped the morphine drip off, oh, Ron, you're going to have some pain and sweating, oh dear, the call button is on the floor, you are clumsy, you'll have to wait until next nurse check at ooh one am wow three and a half hours with a broken collar bone and no morphine, must breed them hard in Manchester. Anyhow, I was nearby visiting young Tommy inflamed kidney badly bruised large hand mark, oh about the same size as your right hand, and a punctured lung from being hit so hard it collapsed, your younger brother visited him earlier tried to give him a grand to shut him up, he's in a not so comfy jail cell now. I brought another visitor, Ang, step in please."

Angie stepped into the room white as a sheet and shaking, Stone didn't even need to ask her the question one look was enough. "Ronnie, sit tight sunshine I'll be back in a jiffy then we can have a nice not so quiet talk," taking Angie out of the room and holding her close.

"That's him, Justin, he would have raped me if it hadn't been for Bonzo."

"I know Ang, but he can't hurt you anymore, his own boss did this to him that's the scum we are dealing with that's why the gloves are off."

"What are you going to do, Justin?"

"I'm going to hurt him, Angie."

"Good, make it hurt a lot."

"I intend to, you go and wait with Ike; I'll only be a couple of minutes."

Ronnie Taylor lay sweating, "I see the anticipation of what I'm going to do is making you sweat hard man. First, did you recognise that beautiful young lady, she recognised you by your voice, when you were stood behind her telling her what you were going to do to her, and walking over, looked at the x-ray, nasty break, Ronnie, baseball bat will do that but a human hand is much better at hitting the right nerve endings giving it a gentle squeeze causing him to shout in pain. Now that's no good, a Hardcase like you screaming like a little girl, here's the thing though, Ron, that girl you threatened to rape is the person I love most in this world so I'm a little angry, you can't say that Jimmy Greaves sorry, Tony, the dumb fuck, ordered you to, like young Tommy. No, you took this upon yourself, so this punishment is just for you," and he fastened his left hand in a vice-like grip on Taylor's mouth digging his right into the collar bone over stretching, turning, and twisting the nerve endings where they weren't meant to go until Ronnie passed out with the pain.

Stone removed the catheter, not only would he be in so much pain when he woke and he'd be lying in his own piss, then setting the room up to look like the catheter had been jarred loose and that the button had moved when Taylor was asleep he switched the drip back on dropping the flow to minimum which wouldn't control the pain when he woke, but it wouldn't be as obvious as if it was switched off and being on minimum could have just been an oversight. Ike drove back home, Stone cuddling Angie in all the way, "Ike, you say nothing, anyone asks his teacher visited Tommy out of regular hours."

"J T, did you leave him alive?"

"Yes, I did," and before she could ask, "Yes, Ang, he will be in tremendous pain when he wakes up, and his fighting days are over."

Stone sent Greavsie a text, 'Dumb fuck, trying to bribe a 16-year-old tut, tut, did you find big Ron got on your nerves too.' Ringing Bish, "HI, honey, we have a deal with young Bowman, when you get Greavsie, he will be in court. He's enlisted once he's better and, on my team, maybe I can make something of him, now we need to find Barry Jackson before Greavsie offers him a deal. Bish, my security here is top-notch, any breach and we're linked to the station plus we have a safe room. I think he'll send his A team next, but I'll have Chris and Tony, the girls have Jane and Julie plus support, and we all have comms, dad has Bonzo and he's down eleven men."

"Well, tomorrow the clubs open so he'll push hard there so I'll get extra men and women watching, the schools have all added extra security and are doing random stop-and-search checks, he's going to want revenge."

"I hope so, Bish, and I hope he comes for me he needs a lesson. Oh and Bish, Ronnie Taylor's out of the enforcement game."

"Do I need to know what you did to Taylor?"

"He was the one threatened to rape Angie, he'll need major surgery on the nerve endings around the collar bone and will have no feeling in his upper right side, I pulled his catheter out, set the morphine drip on low and put the call button on the floor. I was going to rupture him, but I couldn't work out how I could make it look like an accident."

"Stone, remind me never to piss you off."

"We're friends, I need a token nigger."

"This nigger is hung like an elephant."

"Yep and almost as big as one."

"Bish, we bought our house today, has a huge barn make a good-sized gym put in lots of machines, so when you're ready ring me, we'll get you a workout programme shift that fat, build some muscle things look bigger when you get ripped, even that tiny penis of yours," and hung up.

Twenty-One

"Enough for the night," Stone switched his phone off, "Greavsie wouldn't be able to reply till the morning.' Ike had gone home, Jane had got some relaxing bath salts from Angie and was enjoying a long soak, "Jo, its nearly bedtime."

"Let Bonzo into the garden and I'll make your cocoa, Dad. Ang, you want a cup?"

"Thanks, son, helps me sleep."

"And me, it'll calm my nerves."

"Angie, he's trained to be the best, he'll be getting a little tense he won't show it, you'll have to get him to relax, ease the tension, and can you do that energy sapper."

"George, you give me all the hard tasks," shocking him that she hadn't blushed and that she had an innuendo of her own. "Dad, before I go to bed, can I show you something in the cinema room?"

"Ok, set it up, I'll bring the cocoa, what are we watching?"

"When you and Jane were training, Granddad put on some Led Zeppelin while mam was cooking, this is what he shot," and they watched Bonzo head banging, Angie singing Black Dog, what a great voice she had hitting all the notes like a female plant and then drumming with the wooden spoons, Stone was struck like lightning the desire he felt when he saw Angie wiggling her backside, but then crying, when Thank You started playing giving him an idea that he'd definitely keep to himself. "The cocoa's kicking in, the alarms are all set, goodnight," and George high-fived everyone. "Jo, we'll come tuck you in."

"Dad, I'm thirteen,, not three," and grinning at his daughter and kissed her on the lips. Angie did the same, but added, "I love you, Josephine Roseanne Stone."

"I love you too, mam and dad," but this time Jo had the tears in her eyes, only her dad ever called her by her full name and only if he was extra emotional.

Stone and Angie lay in bed, her head on his chest, gently stroking his inner thigh feeling his erection growing, she placed her hand on it, as his stomach muscles rippled and she thought *look at that reaction from the man I love* and moved her hand up and down his expanding shaft as his stomach muscles contracted more fascinated with the movement, she also loved the feel of him in her hand pulsing growing harder hearing his heart rate starting to speed up and she knew what she wanted to do for the man she loved, not because he'd asked, but because she wanted to. She wanted to know what it felt like to have the man she loved cum in her mouth, wanted to know what it tasted like, and was it as bad as people said. The urge to do something she'd never considered was strong, so she moved the duvet cover out of the way and resisting no longer moved her head and took him gently in her mouth. Stone moaned loudly he knew somehow this was important to her, so he didn't stop her, eyes closed; he was warm, hard, and pulsing in her mouth as she tried to remember how he'd moved his mouth on her. He knew where to lick, put his mouth, how excited she was by the noise and all the body movements.

Taking him out of her mouth, she looked at his rock-hard penis wondering where to touch, the little hole where his sperm would come out knowing there would be a little clear liquid drip out before the hole enlarged as his shaft started pulsing and he ejected his sperm in a thunderous spray and found to her surprise that she wasn't frightened of the ending, she actually wanted him to feel her love for him in the most intimate manner possible. Feeling wetness between her legs her own breathing increased and a desire to please this wonderful man overrode any inexperience. Wanting to know what he liked, she moved her thumb around the head of his penis, listening to his sound and found he liked the back touched more than the front, then she used the tip of her tongue and moved up and down and side to side on his engorged shaft, his heart rate and breathing increased and stomach muscles started doing what hers had done and began contracting while his leg muscles stiffened.

Eyes wide open, very much enjoying all these new sensations, determined to bring Stone to the same mind-blowing orgasm that she'd had, she stuck the tip of her tongue in the little hole and heard Stone's breathing quicken, felt a little liquid seep out, licking around the head she felt his heart double tap as she caught just underneath the head at the back. Placing her right hand tightly on the bottom of his shaft she could feel his penis pulsing, knew he was getting near and still looking down seeing the clear liquid seeping out thinking 'this is the time,' she gently took the head of his penis in her mouth moving her bottom lip on the back between the head and shaft, nibbling gently where she thought he was most sensitive, her tongue licking round the head and the gentle pressure of her mouth sucking very gently, breathing through her nose to keep the pressure on she felt his body lock, toes curl, breathe held, stomach muscles contract loving the fact that she was capable of getting him to lose control completely. The noise started quietly and built up, up and up until with a huge ear-piercing roar he came in her mouth. Angie felt him cum first through the pulsing in her hand and then as the hot cum pulsed out filling her mouth, swallowing it all down, spitting it out was never an option, the consistency like a still-warm salty raw egg her throat took his seed into her stomach, the taste not unduly unpleasant increasing her suction getting every last drop into her mouth and kept on swallowing. Still taking huge breaths, stomach muscles still contracting with ferocious force his orgasm began to die down. Opening her eyes and looking at his rapidly declining erection she gently sucked on the hole making sure he was completely drained and kissing his shaking stomach muscles returned to his chest. "I think I just got my own back, Justin."

Stone's breathing was still far too erratic to speak, the orgasm had been the biggest and most prolonged of his life, the wonderful feeling of Angie's mouth on him and an ache that was simply gorgeous. "Your cum leaves a bit of an aftertaste, but not as bad as books make it out to be, I enjoyed doing that for you, it's made me so wet and so horny, can you make me cum now," and burying his head between her moist thighs licked her and she came hard and loud within a couple of minutes, both sated they lay in each other's arms. "Can we try a 69 sometime soon? I'd like to see which one of us comes first, I promise I won't bite you."

"Some women are multi-orgasmic, they can cum more than once."

"Really, I didn't know that, should we see if I'm lucky," and Angie opened her legs to Stone; this was the most erotic thing anyone had ever said or done if he had any ammunition left he'd have lost it there and then.

Lying with Angie's legs placed over his shoulders, he began licking her from the bottom right to the top aware that he'd catch several hot spots as his tongue travelled up her length which would be super sensitive so any contact would be amplified. "Justin," her voice deeper than normal, pushing herself against his tongue, "oh, oh, oh my," moaning continuously her breathing speeded up and her muscles began contacting. "Justin, Justin, I'm going to cum again," as she locked herself onto his mouth, moaned loudly and came for the second time in fifteen minutes. "Oh boy, oh boy, oh boy," Angie said, trying to get her heart rate under control.

"Ang, my darling, I said multi-orgasmic, multi, multiple we still have ten minutes, bend down," and putting his mouth on her already engorged now ultra-sensitive clitoris, began sucking and nibbling with his teeth feeling Angie's body respond yet again, his hands moved over her stomach feeling the muscles tensing continuing up to her breasts which he gently squeezed and flicked her nipples which he knew now she liked. With both hands on her breasts gently squeezing at the same time as he sucked on her clitoris feeling the pulse of the bud getting stronger and stronger, "Oh my God, I don't believe this," as the waves of yet another orgasm built when she came the third time it was so powerful her whole body shook and convulsed with the biggest orgasm she'd ever had and she'd had to grab Stone's pillow to scream into it, Angie lay breathing as she'd just run a marathon, she couldn't speak, she left teeth marks in Stone's pillow, her legs felt like jelly and stomach muscles were still doing somersaults, but the feeling she had, the total complete satisfaction of her third orgasm left her completely drained and unable to move.

Stone looked at the love of his life radiant in the afterglow, Angie still hadn't got her breath back she showed Stone his pillow with the teeth marks in it, "And you want to try a 69, Ang!" Stone pulling her on top of him pulled the duvet over them, Angie's legs were still shaking but her body hummed; she was the most content she'd ever been, kissing and holding her waiting for her to regain her strength. "Was it good for you, hon?" Angie just looked him in the eyes as her tears fell laid her head on his neck and cried gently, continuing to hold, and stroking her hair, in no rush to move, relishing being with the woman he loved.

Angie was still fast asleep in his arms, when he awoke just before the alarm went off, and not even a week had gone by. She was beautiful, funny, sexy as hell but natural with it and the way she came, he wanted to wake her up and see her cum again more than he wanted anything else. Gently he stroked her face, neck, breasts the nipples hardening even in her sleep, moving to her stomach, inside of her legs down to her knees and all the way back again, stopping to stroke her clitoris he felt the nub harden, he repeated only this time with his tongue and mouth. Angie woke feeling his mouth on her sex, placed one hand under the pillow to grab the bed rail and the other gently, stroking his short hair as she felt her orgasm building. Stone gently stroked her bum knowing she was extra sensitive on her pantie line; the other hand placed firmly on her left breast, the most sensitive of the two. slowing the movement of his mouth knowing she was very close by her breathing and her accelerated heart rate beating through her left breast, he cupped her bum with both hands and pulled her onto just the tip of his tongue very slowly licking her now throbbing bud, he could feel that her orgasm was going to be massive, she held her muscles tight and her heart rate was off the chart, but he didn't rush. The moan began deep in her throat, but he wouldn't go faster holding her bum so the only contact was the tip of his tongue on her erect clitoris, moaning louder her hips gyrating trying to get his mouth on her, needing the release from the unbelievable pleasure of his tongue, the bud pulsated on the end of his tongue, the orgasm was inevitable and placing his whole tongue over her swollen clitoris Angie began to scream and at the point of orgasm, he opened his mouth over her clitoris and sucked very gently moving his bottom lip on her as she came, finally pulling her hard onto his mouth as she bucked and screamed completely letting go. The pulsing orgasm of her body seemed to go on and on, so strong the waves afterwards continued for nearly a minute. Stone's mouth remained on her as the massive orgasm receded making sure she was completely drained and satisfied then kissed her mouth letting her taste her own cum, "Morning, my darling, I hope you like how I woke you up."

Still shaking and breathless from her orgasm, she held on to the man she loved unable to speak knowing her voice would crack and she would cry, sometimes saying you love someone is not enough, showing them, how much is totally unique to that person, and she felt totally loved. Deciding to save water, they showered together Stone's erection pressing into her lower back, "Oh dear, I've dropped the soap," bending over with a wiggle that drove him wild with desire, he pushed himself into her with a sharp intake of breath from them both, the feel of being inside her, the warmth, the tightness. Stone opened his eyes and watched himself slowly pushing into her, her bottom quivering with every push as she pushed back onto him and he thrust forward making sure she got every centimetre inside, knowing he was going to cum he increased his pace and as she kept pace he felt himself growing even harder causing her to gasp he stopped, "No keep going," bending over further putting her hands on her knees allowing him to push even harder crying out now in pleasure, he gripping her buttocks speeded up, his orgasm almost upon him, looking at himself entering Angie's warm damp sex as her beautiful backside bounced of his balls, her arched back and long hair dangling down in front and as her cries of pleasure echoed in the shower; he spurted his seed into her with a huge roar and pulled her tight against him as the waves and spurting continued, stroking her sides, back and hair and reluctantly pulling himself out turned her around and kissed her hard and deep, "I love you, Angela Sanders, I love you so much," and kissed her again, "look at you you're the most beautiful woman I have ever seen, I love you," and he kissed her again. "I didn't hurt you, did I?"

"No, I feel so much more making love with you behind me, your size caught me by surprise, do you like that way it can't be very flattering watching my bum and back."

"Next time, I'll find a mirror, you can watch what I see, God that was the biggest turn on ever watching myself go in and out of you, watching you push back, hearing you moan and it felt like a flood I'd come that hard."

"Can we do it this way again because I feel every inch of you, when you're really excited, you harden right up, when I bent over further and gripped my knees, I thought I'd gone to heaven and when you came it felt gorgeous. I'm going to throb all day and my voice is hoarse from screaming. I just hope the shower drowned out the noise or I'm going to be bright red over breakfast."

"The shower might have, but the bedroom is just normal insulation and Angie, you were a lot louder in the bedroom."

"Oh, shit, shit, shit."

"Darling, I'll insulate the bedroom at the new house and the walls are two feet thick, so we should be ok."

"Ang, don't feel self-conscious I love how you cum, and Ang."

"Yes, darling."

"I'll get you a throat spray for those special occasions."

"Oh, Mr Stone, that's why I love you so much you think of everything."

They were first into the kitchen, Stone switched on the coffee machine and put his arms around Angie and kissed her deeply, "I can't seem to get enough of you," and he kissed her again as one big hairy black dog thought he'd get in on the action and put his paws on Stone's shoulders, "See, Justin, even my dog loves you," and Stone got Bonzo between them and kissed Angie again. Bonzo, **thinking I love cuddles, almost as much as food and walks and master was super happy and smelling of that sex thing humans do.** "Dad, put that dog down he'll start humping pillows next to my legs, gross, and mam, haven't you had enough kissing this morning?" And Angie went bright red.

George walked into the kitchen, "Morning, anyone else hear the wind this morning howling and groaning."

Stone laughed Angie went even redder, "I see the stress thing works both ways, Angela," and Angie went the reddest she ever had as George looked at his son and winked, "Good night's sleep, son."

"The best, Dad, the best and the sleep was OK too."

"Dad, Granddad you're talking about sex again and I haven't even had my breakfast."

"How do you know we're talking about sex?" Jo pointed at Angie.

"I'm just having a flush, Jo."

"Mam, you said you'd never lie."

"Ok I won't, I made love twice with your father this morning and had the two biggest orgasms of my life," causing both Stone and George to spill their coffee.

"Now, son, that's an answer."

"Mam, what's an orgasm?" Stone and George both looked, "Son, that's one of the benefits of a wife, she gets to answer all those awkward questions, who's having what this morning and Angela, orgasms don't count."

"Jo, we'll find time today and I'll tell you what an orgasm is and anything else you want to know or are unsure about."

"Thanks, mam."

"Morning, everyone," Jane said as she entered the kitchen, "that's a lovely comfortable bed I slept like a log anyone else hear all that wind howling maybe I'll bring me ear plugs next time I stay. Jo, have you got your school project ready you know how stern that history teacher is."

"Jane, are you having breakfast?"

"Yes, Angie."

"Justin, make some of your gloop for our guest."

"Are you having some as well, Angie?" Jane said, "Or have you had enough gloop for a while," and she smiled.

"Oh, Jane, you can't have too much gloop one day you might just find out," and Angie smiled back at Jane.

Twenty-Two

Tony Greaves was not a happy bunny, the cryptic message left by Stone last night confirmed Ronnie wouldn't be back soon, his brother was locked up; schools had tightened security and were doing random checks. Tommy Bowman had cop protection outside his door, obviously some sort of deal had done meaning if they caught him, and he would have Angela Sanders and Tommy Bowman against him. He could put the frighteners on those two, but what hurt the most was his pride, no one had goaded him and got away with it. The fucking ninja squaddie and his mates had taken out eleven of his crew, which is why his sixteen-man goon squad, plus the Wheeler's and the Marshall Brothers sat in front of him.

"Tonight, we hit the clubs to make up a bit of ground, and Neil, Terry you need to recruit more kids, giving the ones we already supply these new tablets, selling at three for ten quid, every thirty they shift they keep £50 I make less, but they're fucking 100% addictive, they'll eat the fuckers like smarties then I'll be printing money. Jeff, Richard, each take eight men. Jeff, you get that fucking ninja squaddie out of the picture, knives, bats no guns we don't want the plod coming looking for us, he gets hurt badly make sure he's stuck in the hospital, take plenty of photos, do not fucking kill him just fuck him and his two buddies up. Richard, you bring me Angela Sanders and Tommy Bowman, Tommy we know will accept cash might cost more than a grand now maybe offer to re-locate him get him a flat somewhere, Sanders well we get pictures of her broken boyfriend and take it from there."

Breakfast done, they gathered in the living room, the full team had arrived and all had a cup of coffee and their game faces on Chris, Tony, Jane, Julie plus the five trainees Mach, Steve, Trevor, Andy, and John. Stone stood in the middle of the room, "Now that you lot have shared my wonderful coffee let's get to it, first Ang and I want to invite you and your families to Luconi's at 3 p.m. tomorrow, Mario and Gabrielle have kindly opened for us to celebrate our engagement officially. Chris, Tony, Mach, today we sort our little surprise, Mario's expecting you early tomorrow to set things up, Tony."

"Justin, are you planning something?"

"Oh, it will surprise you all right, Mrs Red Kryptonite," said Chris.

"It won't be something you'll be able to forget," said Mach. "Tony, are you going to tell me?"

"No, Angie, but it will blow your mind, you to Jo, big surprise, but if you think about what your Dad gets up to at home really it's just an extension of that."

"Now, let's sort this punk Mr Greaves and his scum suckers out, he will come after us today his ego will demand it, and Stone went through the events, anyone want to see the video maybe mark me out of ten."

"Boss, nobody here needs to see you perform, we still got the bruises from your little love taps," said Mach.

"Well, for me, it was an eight so going for a ten today then retire at the top getting married you know need to keep all my pinning moves for the missus, Justin, you don't need to pin me, maybe borrow Bish's handcuffs though," Chris roared with laughter, "Boy, Mrs Red Kryptonite has your number, boss."

"Yes, Chris that's one of the things she definitely has, now he's had time to get his goon squad together there may be twenty of them, four or five might even be good, now the gloves are off we inflict maximum damage, they all end up in the hospital, he'll want revenge and he may come out of hiding once his goonies are out of the picture. Bish will see how it's done by a supreme fighting team, then we all go back to training and I get married. We are the best of the best, they are just thugs at best, we take them all out and Greavsie is finished. The police find him, Angie, and young Tommy plus some of his crew convict him job done. He's going to be desperate to push his addictive pills, and he'll send a crew to get me out of the picture, plus he'll want Angie and Tommy unable to be in court.

"Plan is, Jane, you take Andy and John, you two keep in the background step in when something goes down. Julie take Trevor, I don't think Jo will be a target, but she has classes with Angie so if the threats there you are a double team. Mach, Steve, you stop any more drugs coming into the school, Chris, and Tony you stay back wait till they make a move on me."

"Justin, you are setting yourself up?"

"Yes, Ang, but I've done this before with much better-trained foes and these two have always had my back I trust them with my life, the difference this time will be that Greaves won't want to use guns too much publicity but his goon squad will have knives and bats and they will be used to using them, remember he's built his reputation on intimation. Bish is running the op at the pubs and clubs, but let's show them how it's done. Any questions, remember war footing tactics lads and lasses, we may cheese him off enough to crawl out of his hole. Everyone comms on always, now let's go and intimidate him," and they separated into their teams.

Angie and Jo both looked worried. "Girls, I need to get this sorted probably get an offer on this house and moving at the weekend, tomorrow, we're all going to Mario's, Saturday, we go for Lemmy. I need this put to bed today, and I'm supported by two of the best hand-to-hand soldiers I know, I'm not going to get hurt, keep your phone with you and stay safe, and do whatever Julie and Trevor tell you, I love you and kissed her on the lips."

And Jo went off to school with her minders. Turning to Ang, "We always knew once I started goading this scumbag that he would retaliate, making myself a target is the only way. He sees me as one man he doesn't understand what I, Chris and Tony can do even when he's seen the video, he'll see me alone and be overconfident, and we take him down. I'm not worried about me I can do this in my sleep, but I'm worried that when he comes for you, I can't be there to protect you, I've had to put Jane in charge of your care, yes, she's good, very good but she isn't me, so I can sort my end but I can't be there for you. I love you, Ang, nothing must happen to you be extra careful and do whatever Jane tells you."

"I will, Justin, I love you too," and they kissed and separated.

Angie's team heading to school, Jane driving his Discovery which had all the hidden extras, extra thick crash bars, side armour protection and run-flat tyres, Stone expected Angie to be attacked either going or coming from school, an attack inside the school was very risky with the number of teachers and kids, so it would happen soon or at three-thirty if it didn't happen straight away and he could push his attack then he might be able to protect her himself.

When there was just Stone, Chris, Tony, and George left, "We need to get in some practice boss somehow."

"Chris, you're a natural. Tony, once he's got over the initial nerves is rock solid as is Mach. I'm the weak link if I fuck up with nerves so maybe lack of practice works in our favour and you lot look up for it already, we need to have a quick go at the new stuff if time permits, but hell, it might be more fun warts and all after all I don't think anyone's going to complain."

"You really think, it's going to be easy, boss."

"We've been up against much worse, lads plus I have more drive to get the job done than just helping the army out of a hole let's get dumb fuck then we can have some fun, he wants me most of all you need to be close by, Tony, have your camera ready make sure you get it on film."

"Boss, you may get hurt."

"Chris, it's not going to happen; you and Tony are my support, we are the three amigos, seriously though we all need to practice our skills, to test ourselves. This is our chance to see how good we are in the real world not on a practice mat plus I'm never going back into combat I'd like to find out if I can still cut it, it's an ego thing. Dad, switch off the alarms but leave the cameras on and set to record, you and Bonzo can watch the action; do not let him out, Angie would kill me if I got him into attack mode or hurt. Dad, no matter what, you stay here, Greavsie wants me. Chris, Tony you keep out of sight on either side of me."

"But boss."

George stepped in, "Chris, give Justin his moment, he hasn't got anything to prove to us but I think he needs to do this for himself to finally be rid of the ghosts and be able to settle down. One last proper fight before the career ends and a new chapter starts with marriage and kids."

Stone looked at his dad with a raised eyebrow, "Well, I need to teach someone to fish, you and Jo were never that interested maybe I can teach my new grandchild while they're still in nappies."

"Chris, Tony, you take either side; Dad, you get a set of comms to, anything on the video let me know. I'm going to do some gardening, get rid of some weeds that way I have a shovel with me against knives and bats puts me on equal footing."

Jane drove the discovery Angie up front Andy and John in the back on the floor out of sight driving down the country lane, Angie smiled to herself remembering making love with Stone in the very seat she was sitting in. "Stone isn't messing about guys, the attack will come, orders are war footing, we protect his lady, take them down extra hard that way their boss gets the message. When the attack comes, I guard Angie, Andy, you take my right, John my left, Angie keeps behind me at all times, and this isn't going to be pretty."

Mach and Steve had taken up positions at school, Mach at the top gate Steve at the bottom in contact by comms. "Mach, have you ever seen the boss like this?"

"Yeah, Steve, I saw him lose it with Jane, made her look like an amateur and we both know she's world-class, if they touch Angie or Jo, god help them, the mood he's in they'll have to send a small army to get him, boy can he focus, being in love hasn't softened up the man one bit. He misses the action sometimes; he knows he'll never see combat again; Angie won't let him, but neither will Jo or George, and Greavsie has already threatened Angie twice there won't be a third time."

"Justin, you've got movement to your right, I count nine men closing in."

"Thanks, Dad, Chris, Tony, we are on," and just then Stone's phone rang, "Morning, Robert."

"Morning, Justin, I have three international buyers all wanting your house, can you do your video walk through the gardens and property and email it to me as soon as possible? I'll forward it on and you should get offers later today. I'll do it as my next job as soon as I can and get it over to you," and hung up.

"Chris, Tony, you in position?"

"Yes, boss."

"Yes, boss," crystal clear in his comms. "Dad, set the cameras recording."

"Ok son." George didn't say be careful or good luck, and Stone turning around faced the nine men, "You must be the goonies squad yeah some of you have the retarded look. Mistake one, you're on my property. Mistake two, you're all on camera pointing to the two cameras recording, and now the police can identify you. Mistake three, there's only nine of you, you should have brought more," and Chris and Tony appeared on either side. "Three each, boss."

"Now you have choices. Choice one, you all lie on the ground and we call the police, you get a comfy cell for a few hours and after they take your statements you go home, or choice two, involves getting really hurt, spending time in hospital, some of you will not recover completely, think of it as a reminder of the time you worked for dumb fuck. I'd go for number one every time, no, then he's either paying you stupid money or you are more frightened of him than me, gentlemen, I missed my morning workout waiting for you, so I need to get some practice. Chris, Tony, I've got this ok."

"Yes, boss," and taking off their jackets sat down on them, "boss, we didn't bring any popcorn," said Chris, "or crisps."

Tony chipped in, "I've got the video going, set it for slow motion don't want to miss any action."

"Forget popcorn, I fancy a bacon butty, beating goonies up always gives me an appetite, let's see nine men five seconds each, under a minute maybe I'll even have a fried egg with it slapping down some wannabes always give me the munchies."

Stone was using physiological tactics when faced with overwhelming odds, be confident about the outcome, it makes your opponent's wary and cautious which slows their reaction time. By appearing super confident and having Chris and Tony sit the fight out, they were wondering who they were facing. Stone removed his top leaving a training top on showing his physique which clearly showed how much work he put into getting into condition, making them even more wary, then a bit more show, you may have bats and knives, but I have this, and Stone twirled the shovel between his hands with speed and precision. "Boss, is the main event about to start? We've still no popcorn, coffee or bacon sarnies and I'm hungry and I didn't bring a cup of coffee," said Chris.

The nine men now had doubts, could one man be that good, should they find out. Stone now needed to take some of them out as quickly as possible and using their wariness against them he stepped forward raised the shovel and hit knees, elbows and shoulders breaking whatever he hit, stepping back five remained upright four remained on the floor. "I told dumb fuck not to send any more amateurs and what do we get the bottom of the barrel," which was more physiological tactics, Stone looked, three of the five needed taking out, the way they held themselves and balanced on their feet meant they could be dangerous, take them three the other two would lie down. The five standing men all rushed Stone at the same time, which sounded a good tactic, but they should have approached from different angles at different speeds and times, one mass moving forward gave Stone ample opportunity to balance himself and wait for their moves and counterattack.

Two swung their bats as they moved in, stupid against someone with Stone's speed and accuracy, as it left their bodies open to counterattack, first bat he took on the shovel handle using the flat of the shovel to break several ribs, second bat was headed for the side of his face as he dipped down allowing the arc of the bat to pass and pushed the end of the shovel into the chin of his opponent. Feeling the air from a knife headed for his stomach, he dropped to the floor into the splits the knife hit nothing but air, and flipping onto his feet hit the man on the front right knee and back left, the remaining two dropping their weapons and on the ground and lay down hands behind their backs.

Chris and Tony both clapped and whistled, "Encore, encore," said Tony as they went around the goons fastening their hands behind their backs and locking feet together, "boss, that knife got a bit close."

"Yeah I know, Chris, I felt the air move, perhaps I am getting old."

"Boss, who else do you know who would have dropped into the splits?"

Stone rang Bish, "Hi, hon, had a busy morning, could you send your biggest van to my house as soon as possible, we have nine goons for your collection straight to the hospital, only seven need hospital treatment for broken bones but I figure you keep them all in one spot, no we're all OK to be in later see you. Tony, get this lot on video and send it to dumb fuck's Facebook page."

Greavsie saw the Facebook message flash up clicked it on and saw his nine men including Jeff Marshall all trust up like chickens, 'should have sent the A team' Stone's message read to which he responded with, "I did, they're currently bringing your girlfriend back here where I'm going to fuck her in every hole and then I'm going to make her bleed from the same holes."

Stone phoned Angie, straight to answer phone, the same with Jane, Andy, and John. He then phoned Bish and told him, "They'll be travelling in the Discovery between here and the school; no one's answering phones, get some people on that road."

"Tony, you stay to wait for the van, Chris, you're with me," and ran to get his bike and two helmets. "Chris, keep ringing their phones to see if you can get an answer."

"Boss it'll be ok, Jane would die before letting anything happen to Angie."

Jane saw the two cars sit back from the bend, instinct and training took over as she slammed on the breaks pulled a three sixty and headed back followed by the two cars in pursuit, "You see, Angie, this is why we're the professionals," and turned onto the makeshift road, "I can't get through to Justin," said Angie surprising Jane with her calmness. "We're between masts going pretty deep into the woods, what's Stone got in this it drives nearly as fast as my bike," the trees blurring as she roared past.

"Andy, John, next turn get ready to jump out then come in behind us, I'm heading for the clearing. I don't want to explain to Stone that I've damaged his beloved Discovery, I'll stop there you sneak up on either side. Angie, you stay in the Discovery; the keys are in the ignition, if it all goes to shit, you drive away, no waiting, no excuses, no stopping or looking back, you GO. They wouldn't have seen Andy and John in the back cos of the distance and privacy glass, and they were lying on the floor, they'd just see two frightened girls." Jane braked hard, "Go."

Andy and John jumped clear and into the trees before the two cars rounded the bend, Jane hared into the bottom of the clearing pulling the handbrake to spin the Discovery round, got out and moved to the front having picked up the wheel brace, "Angie, its bullet and shatterproof glass just sit here, they can't get in."

The two pursuing cars fishtailed to a stop, four men got out of one, five out of the other, Jane locked at them she had the sun behind her tactic number one. "I thought the ninja squaddie loved his woman," said Richard Marshall, "he thinks this half pint can protect her," and pointed at Jane, tactic number two nobody who looked at her thought world-class martial arts. Jane surveyed the nine men looking for strengths, weaknesses, who looked capable, who was just there to boost the numbers. Putting on her best frightened little girl voice, "Why are you chasing us, what do you want?" Tactic number three give your support team time to get into position, Jane spied Andy and John moving silently behind the men.

"Greavsie never said anything about this little squirt, Rich," said one of the thugs. "Honey, I like them small makes them scream when they get this shoved up them," and he grabbed his dick.

"Rich, how about we take turns, we ALL fuck her, then the boss can fuck her on his own," pointing at Angie sat glaring at him in the Discovery. "It's no fun following him, they have no spirit left by the time he's fucked them," and then overconfidence took him and his two friends into Jane's area of expertise, hand-to-hand, Jane could beat most men, she moved like lighting clipping the skulls of his two friends just behind the ears where all the nerve endings were, doing maximum damage in a split second. The dick grabber didn't even have time to react to his two fallen friends as the hardest kick he'd ever received landed in his groin causing his balls to be driven upwards, "Hey lock, Andy, John, he looks a bit like Tony out of the Sopranos, now he'll be singing like one when he wakes up."

"Hardcase, just how hard did you hit him?"

"I think his balls are in his throat, Andy, I fucking hate rapists." Jane glared, "Who's next or are you going to do the right thing and lay on the ground, cos the next one gets severely damaged."

Richard said, "Lads, it's a fucking little girl," and they all moved forward, Andy and John moving into their space where Andy dispatched one with a precision head butt straight on the centre of the temple delivered with maximum thrust and John hit another one with a pinpoint accurate roundhouse kick delivered to the side of the head.

Moving forward to help Jane, but not needed, they stood and watched a grandmaster at work, Jane was nine stone wet through, but her hand and leg speed were amazing even against eighteen stone big boned men she wouldn't be beaten. Hearing the roar of a powerful bike behind them, they turned as Stone and Chris took off their helmets and watched Jane take apart the remaining large men. It was the first time Stone had seen Jane in proper combat, he was impressed, he saw himself in her stance and positioning he felt the hands and feet connect, the bones crack, saw two men stagger back up, one received a roundhouse kick with her left under the chin, the other got the right to the side of the head both out cold.

"Nice feet work, Hardcase, I always said you hit a lot harder than most men," said Stone. Angie leaving the discovery ran into his arms, "Hi, honey you leave any popcorn?"

"Chris, call Bish and tell him to send another van. Jane, how was it for you? Do you need a cigarette?"

"Stone, you can't beat proper action and I think mine should be a cigar I took out seven."

"I hate to break it to you, Jane, but the boss took out all nine, well seven actually because the remaining two had the sense to lie down, but the boss dispatched his seven quicker, and I and Tony didn't have any popcorn."

"I had to have one last go on the merry-go-round, Ang, I promise I'll now become a normal happily married man."

"Justin, there's nothing normal about you."

Twenty-Three

Tony phoned, "All collected, boss, I'm down at the station with Bish, did Hardcase do her thing too?"

"She did, Tony, good stuff in little bundles we're all good here, got nine more waiting on a van then we'll be down shortly." Next call was to Mach, "You need to catch Neil and Terry Wheeler, those are the last two of his main crew, let Steve know the good news. Chris, if I take a video with my phone, can you send it to dumb fuck's Facebook page?"

"Boss, you don't know how to do that?"

"No, Chris, I usually get Tony to do it for me I'm all fingers and thumbs with technology."

"Boss, can I record that Colonel Stone admits he can't do everything?"

"Oh, I don't know, Chris, some things your boss is exceptional at," and Angie kissed Stone.

The video was sent to Greavsie with the message 'A team all busted up by an old man and a little girl, time to fuck off back to Manchester dumb fuck.' "Chris, can you grab a lift to the station in the van? I need to get the house videoed and Angie's put on the market."

"Sir, it was a pleasure and a privilege seeing you work."

"Chris, that's the last live-action I'll be doing so I had to set the ball high." Stone rang his dad told him what had gone down, "I'm coming home with Angie on the bike be there in fifteen minutes stick the coffee machine on, what its already on, now why doesn't that surprise me."

"You've had a productive day, son, eighteen down three to go plus maybe some hangers-on like Barry Jackson, no one injured, Angie and Jo safe."

"Yeah, a good result, Dad, but I want him to be no longer a threat so yes today has gone well, but a rat cornered will react and we don't know what reaction he will have. I'm going to video the house then we're going to the estate agents."

Angie sat with George and Bonzo while Stone videoed the house and grounds, then he phoned Robert Charlton, "Robert, Justin Stone, I've videoed the house and grounds, do you mind if I drop the video into you now and can I get the keys for the Mill House, I'd like to show my dad and daughter. Angie will be with me so anything you need from her we can sort out today and get the ball rolling, OK thanks, Robert, see you soon."

"Dad, I've also got to go to the station, keep the cameras on and your phone and Bonzo with you. I'll take Ang with me on the bike and get Jane to drive the Discovery back, and then we go and pick up Jo and off to see the house."

Stone now rang Jane, "Can you take the Discovery to the police station after leaving Andy and John with Mach and Steve? Tell them to look out for Neil and Terry Wheeler, catch them on video on their phones, they'll approach the kids when school finishes unless Greavsie has told them what's gone down. Greavsie might do something stupid now, I'll meet you at the station in around half an hour, Ang and I must call the estate agents first."

Arriving at Charlton's, Robert was waiting for them in reception, shaking hands Stone handed over the video camera allowing Robert to download the footage to his laptop. "That's done, I'll just send this off to the three international buyers. I should get a concrete offer from all three within an hour and we could have a bidding war, I'll wait till they've finished bidding and I'll ring when I have a final offer on the table. I have the deeds drawn up ready, then it's a straightforward case of you coming into the office to sign and the money is transferred after the deduction of fees. Angie, if you can give me your house details, garden space, bedrooms, condition etc., I can draft particulars, do the same thing as Justin, and walk the house and garden with the video. We can process it by getting it valued and accepting an offer then you would have to come in, bring your current mortgage statements and fill out some forms then we pay off what is owed, remove the fee from what's left and the remainder goes into a bank account your choice. Justin, here are the keys for the Mill House, just bring them back tomorrow along with the video. Thanks for coming in Justin, Angie; I'll see you both sometime tomorrow."

"Ang, I don't believe in what's mine is mine and yours is yours everything goes into a joint account, then you have access to any funds you may need, in the meantime, I'll give you the cards and pin numbers we just stick to a budget plan that we agree to and keep a record of what we've spent on the house so we don't go too far above the budget."

"Justin, you are probably going to have at least 250k left, I might only have 50k."

"Your question is what, darling, we will be man and wife we share everything, not just fluids," and Stone leaned across and kissed her hard taking her breath away causing her to open her mouth and groan when Stone put his tongue in. "Justin, I'm leaking fluid," and she giggled.

"Ang, what am I going to do with you?"

"Oh, I don't know, maybe a repeat of this morning's performance."

"Now we go and see Bish, you come in with me, I don't want you sitting outside with Greavsie on the rampage."

Tony Greaves sat in his chair fuming that fucking ninja squaddie had just about single handed destroyed his business, all he had left were the Wheelers. His reputation was ruined, his status as the king of drugs finished, some of his own men would turn on him now they no longer feared him, one fucking man had taken everything from him, he would have to pull out of dealing here, find another crew and start again in another sleepy town all because of the fucking ninja squaddie. The trouble was his fear factor which he relied on to get the job done was no longer there, he was finished, what should he do now, how could he become feared again, if he took out the ninja squaddie, he'd recover his reputation, but he'd also be a wanted man. Stone's friends would move against him, perhaps he could destroy him another way, something personal to him, make sure that he felt pain every day for the rest of his life, take out someone he loved and couldn't replace, make it look like an accident, but make sure Stone knew it was him without having enough evidence to get caught, then he could point to the broken squaddie and say that's what happens when you fuck with Tony Greaves.

Arriving at the police station, Stone took Angie in his arms kissing her passionately totally unaware that Bish's office overlooked the car park, and all the team were watching. Walking into the office the first thing they heard was from Chris to Bish, "It's all in the technique, Bish, you have to get the correct lip pressure, tongue action just right."

"Don't look at me," said Jane, "I ain't been kissed in a while." Bish at six feet four inches touching three hundred pounds picked up Jane all five feet and ninety pounds and smacked his lips noisily on hers. Jane went rigid, but Bish didn't know her past. Chris jumped in and held Jane knowing she needed her friend's support and to let her know it was a joke, and Tony also stepped in, "See your technique is off, Bish."

Chris gave the OK sign, "You see, Bish, the boss gave a great demonstration of how to kiss a woman properly. Angie, was it good for you?"

"Chris, it's always good for me, why do you think we do it all the time, oh you mean the kissing part?"

"Boss, she's stopped getting embarrassed," Stone laughed.

"Ang, be good or I'll spank you."

"What again, Justin?" And he just shook his head.

Bish had sat back down, Jane was ok. "Stone, to bring you up to speed, we have his team either in the hospital or in our cells, we're missing Tony Greaves, Neil, and Terry Wheeler plus whatever goon squad he may have left if any. The man will be on edge and guess who his target is going to be, you've destroyed his reputation he must come after you or your family to regain his status."

"Yep, Bish, that's how I read it too."

"You have an idea, haven't you?"

"You are too laid back."

"I'm always laid back and you're not going to tell me, are you, Stone, you can't kill him."

"Ang said that too, plus I can't do anything that would endanger our future."

"Good advice, we like Angie, do you actually listen to her cos it would be a first."

"Bish, I got to go, you have the video and they've given you their statements, we'll see you at Mario's, bring your missus. Chris, Tony, and Jane we need to have a chat."

"Stone, you can use my office; I've got to go to the hospital and start doing interviews."

"Tony, sweep for bugs and we wait until Bish is at least a hundred feet away, ears that big miss nothing."

"You know I'm big all over," and Stone patted him on the belly.

"Yep built like a black polar bear."

"Yeah, but hung like a donkey."

"Well, bring your missus and we can find out the truth." When there was only Stone, Angie, Chris, Tony, and Jane left, "Jane, you ok, honey?" Angie asked.

"Yeah, I'm fine, Angie, Bish doesn't know me that well, but Chris and Tony were there."

"Ok, boss, what's your plan?" Tony said.

"Jane, I want you to dress up as Jo, you're about the same size and height, wear her school clothes and dye and cut your hair, he only knows what Jo looks like from a photo, he's never met her, then we put you in harm's way, but we have your back as always. He will go after Jo, he can't get me or Angie, there would be far too much heat now, he can't get Dad cos well, he's dad and he's trained plus Bonzo is always with him, he'll go for what he thinks is my weakest link. He understands who I love, if he got Jo, he knows it would finish me, therefore restoring his reputation, don't fuck with Greavsie cos he destroys you or your family. Jo would do it if I asked, but she's not as good as you, Hardcase, we catch him he's jail material."

"When do you want to do the switch?" Jane asked. "Right now, he has two men left, Mach, Steve, Andy, and John have them in sight at the school, my guess is Greaves will make a move as the school finishes, somehow make whatever he's going to do to Jo look like an accident. He may even try and kill her, then let only I know it was him, the man's never been caught, but he's never been under this much pressure and Jo is the softest target."

Stone rang Mike Foster, "Hi, Mike, it is Justin Stone, yes, thanks, it's been a good day for the good guys, but we still have the number one bad guy to catch. Thanks for allowing Angie to help today, now I need more help, can you pull Jo out of class now and Julie and Trevor, just get all three in your office, I'll be there in ten minutes to explain." He then rang Jo in class, she answered which got her a look from her teacher who in return got a look from Julie and he went back to the rest of the class.

"Dad, Mr Briggs is giving me daggers, what's up?"

"Mr Foster is coming to get you, Julie, and Trevor, we're on our way sit tight in his office for ten minutes, I'll explain when I get there."

Driving well above the speed limit, but with the blue light supplied by Bish on top of the Discovery and the siren going if anyone got in the way; they got to school in seven minutes and all bowled into Mike Foster's office, "Hi, Dad, hi, mam," which got a look from Mike Foster. Angie smiled, "Mike, me and you need to have a catch-up." Standing Jane stand next to Jo, Stone said, "Mike, can you get someone from your hairdressing class here?" And Mike rang the extension, five minutes later the teacher arrived and Stone asked, "Could you cut and colour Jane's hair to look like Jo's, in the next hour?"

"Stone, you going to owe me."

"Jane, you can have my bike I'll sign the docs once this is over, extra 50bhp faster 0-60 by over a second, all the bells and whistles, I'll be a happily married man I won't need the status symbol anymore."

"You're going to give me a 40k bike for a change of colour and a haircut, let's get this done."

"Generous, aren't I, and Jo before you say, 'I like the bike,' I'm thinking of getting you a quad, plenty of field space in the new home, cos I know you like bikes."

Stone's phone went; it was Robert Charlton, *god that man picks his moments* thought Stone. "Justin, I have a deal done on your house 1.25 million paid by bank transfer, our solicitor is transferring 750k to the Elliott Estate, the house is yours keep the key, paperwork for both properties will be complete by the end of today, you need to be out of your current home by Tuesday when the Sheik flies in. If you can call in tomorrow and complete your side of the paperwork, we'll conclude the fees then."

"Great news, Robert, I'll be down to sign and bring Angie's video tomorrow, thank you," going over to Angie and kissed her, "We have our house."

The hairdressing teacher did her magic, Jane and Jo looking like twins when she finished, apart from the cheek bones and eye colour. "Right, girls, clothes swap time."

"Jane, you need to lose the bra," said Angie.

"Mine will grow, mam, just not yet," causing Stone to laugh, "maybe get to the size of mams," causing Angie to blush and Stone to shake his head and point to the cleaning cupboard to change. Jane and Jo both had the giggles as they swapped and emerged from the cupboard; Jo looking beautiful and a lot older, Jane like a schoolgirl which was the whole point.

"Right, this is how we're going to set this up. Jane-Jo, you finish your lesson earlier than expected and all three of you rush out as if there's something big happening, Julie and Trevor, pick up your phones dash off towards the bottom gate as if there's an emergency. Jane, from a distance, you'll pass as Jo, so you wait a few minutes then walk out the top gate along the road. He may just try and run you down a hit and run in a built-up area would be a good plan especially with all the cars waiting for school to come out, but he may try abducting you;

do your best to sound scared. We'll all have you in sight, your phone will tell us exactly where you are from your GPS signal and its recording so we can hear everything that gets said if it doesn't get switched off, but Greavsie is a criminal not a mastermind, so he'll not be focused. Jane, try your best to be Jo, think how she would react, act scared keep in the shadows or your head down the longer he believes it Jo, the more he'll talk. He may threaten you with a knife and or fasten your hands you know what to do. Jane he may threaten to rape you, he may even attempt it. Jane, the code word if you feel threatened and unsafe is 'daddy' not dad, screw it if we haven't got enough evidence, you DO NOT risk yourself, understood, Jane."

"Yes, boss."

Stone looked Jane directly in the eyes, "Jane, you will not be abandoned, ever by me or any of my team, but what we need is for him to do his little bragging act, what a big man he is, what he's going to do with you. If you feel at risk, you think an attack in imminent or if he realises, you're not Jo, do your thing, war setting, maximum force he doesn't get back up, the main thing is he will have committed yet another crime and we have him. Jane-Jo, you pretend you're waiting for me, Julie, you point to the road as if giving her instructions, Jane, DO NOT use your phone, if he sees it, he'll take it off you we are banking that he wants, Jo, and phones are not allowed in the classrooms and you're out of class early for some reason and in a hurry to get away. The Discovery can't be seen from outside the gates he doesn't know we're here. Ang, Jo, you sit tight in Mike's office I'll ring as soon as we are done. Jane, Julie, Trevor give me, Chris, and Tony five minutes to get outside, lads, set your comms up."

"Lots of cars running, boss," said Chris, "can't get a good look in some of them, just listening for the engine roar."

"Plenty of foot traffic too, mainly women though," said Tony. Stone was talking with Mach and Andy who were watching Terry Wheeler letting them know what might go down, "Mach, let Steve and John know at the bottom gate, if any of you spot Greavsie, ring my mobile, but don't move in," and walked away; five minutes were up. Jane-Jo came out with Julie and Trevor, and taking out their phones, Julie pointed Jane-Jo to the road and they both ran off towards the bottom gate. Jane-Jo on her own waited two minutes and then kept her head down walked out of the top gate. Stone positioned himself behind her but in the crowd and couldn't be seen. Stone's phone went it was Mach, "Greaves is here, just gone past me, he's talking with Wheeler, now both moving towards Jane."

Jane-Jo walked past a long line of cars as Stone got caught in the middle of all the parents and had no view, Chris shouted into Stone's ear, "It's a snatch boss." Stone pushed past the parents barging them out of the way and watched helplessly as the Audi blocked Jane-Jo in and two people got out and grabbed her. Jane-Jo allowed herself to be grabbed, and the car sped off into the traffic with tyres screeching causing others to come to a halt. Chris said, "Whoever's in the Audi just took Jane."

"Tony, you get anything?"

"No, boss, whoever's driving has skills I didn't have time to get my phone out." Stone turned looking for Greaves and Wheeler; they were nowhere in sight. Jane had been abducted from under his guard. Stone's phone went, "Paybacks going to be a bitch, you meddling ninja cunt."

Twenty-Four

Well, thought Jane-Jo as she was bundled into the back of the Audi, Stone would be really pissed; the driver obviously had experience as he sped away causing cars to brake and mount the pavement, the two goons in the back that had grabbed her glared at her, Jane-Jo went for the actor of the year award, keeping her head down. "What do you want?" in a scared little girl voice.

The voice came from the passenger seat, "Your daddy's caused my boss lots of problems, so he wants to have a bit of time with you, teach you how to be a woman maybe film it and send it to your dad."

Jane-Jo pretended to cry and put her head down shaking her shoulders, "Oh, Greavsie going to like you, honey, he likes them young and frightened."

Stone stood and phoned Bish, explained what had happened; it all went down to fast there were too many people and too many cars, all they knew was that it was a new shape white Audi driven with skill and it's heading towards the old industrial estate. *Amateur hour again* thought Stone, no one had checked Jane-Jo for her phone which was switched on enabling Stone to listen and track her location. Setting off at a run back to his Discovery, where Chris and Tony were waiting and attaching the magnetic blue light (thanks to Bish) hitting the siren as they peeled out of the school gates towards the old industrial estate. Switching off the siren and removing the light, they pulled quietly onto the industrial estate, Tony tracking Jane-Jo's phone and recording everything that came through.

Tony said, "The car has stopped."

Stone pulled around the corner out of sight, "We don't know what car Greavsie is in or how many he has with him, if the phone gets taken, we need eyes inside."

"Chris, time to use the climbing skills you brag about, I need you on the roof, use that skylight to see if you can get a look at what's going on, we need Greavsie to incriminate himself, so we give Jane-Jo as much time as possible, but no risks we have enough anyway."

"Tony, you keep an eye on the front, I'll go round the back see if I can find a way in."

Jane-Jo allowed herself to be lifted out of the car, one of the goons purposely sticking his hand up her school skirt, "Oh, white panties, nice and virginal," Jane's worst fear and that of most women was being raped and the goon's hand left her in no doubt what his intentions were, Jane gritted her teeth she'd been in this position before.

Chris climbed the wall; it helped, it was old and cracked in places giving him a firm hand and foothold, peering through the skylight, he saw the big goon with his paw on Jane's backside. Chris knew Jane allowed very few people to touch her given her abusive upbringing, he knew she would be beyond pissed off now, "Boss, him and his goons are going to rape her."

Stone went cold, "Not going to happen."

Chris recognised the tone, "Boss, dial it back, please, its Jane not Jo."

"I hear you, Chris, but you don't know what Jane went through in her childhood, I do, I put her in that position, I'll get her out," and started to climb the back wall heading for the small office window.

Greavsie was feeling better; he had enough money to start again he'd leave the country, go somewhere warm with no extradition order, wait six months, and then start up again somewhere sleepy and quiet but first he would destroy the ninja squaddie's much-loved daughter. Neil Wheeler parked the red Audi next to the white one before getting out Greavsie sent Stone a text, 'I'm going to fuck your daughter in every hole, then I'm going to let my men do the same, and all coming to you live on the internet soon' and went into the building with Neil.

Stone made no noise as he entered through the window, his dormant skill set returning saying, "I'm inside," into the comms, "Greavsie and Neil Wheeler are entering the building, sir," said Tony also aware that his boss was getting close to another meltdown and once again Jane was the trigger.

"Boss, she'll be alright, she's brilliant at hand-to-hand."

"Tony, he thinks she's Jo! The fucking scum would hurt my thirteen-year-old daughter to get one up on me; the cunt isn't walking away, you fucking here me," Chris said.

"Boss, you aren't getting married if you step over the line, it is Jane in there not Jo and not Angie, plus you already made your last video. They're amateurs; remember, we're the professionals here. I'll guide you from up here," said Chris, "Boss, get your calm head on; we need Greavsie on tape still."

Jane sat on the chair in the middle of makeshift office, her hands tied behind her back, she'd used the little trick Stone had shown her, of pumping up her forearms by making fists with both hands, when you get tied up the blood flow recedes and the rope is no longer as tight, it also helped that Jane had super flexible wrists so as she sat there the rope no longer holding her arms together she felt better now she could fight.

Greavsie and Wheeler came up the stairs into the office, "Well done, Terry, Duncan, good grab, there'll be a big bonus for you. Donnie, your driving skills are still top-notch, here you are," and Greaves handed him two grand. "You can go; you don't need to be here for what happens next."

Jane-Jo in her best little girl voice aware of her three friends listening and keeping her head down, "Who are you? Why did you kidnap me? Are you going to hurt me? I'm only thirteen."

"Are you still a virgin, Jo? Has your dad brought you up to be a good girl, let's open your legs and get a look at the goodies." The huge goons put a hand on each of Jane-Jo's knees and standing to each side pulled her legs apart to reveal her white panties. "Mm, mm," said Greavsie white my favourite.

It had taken all of Jane's self-control not to attack the big goons, but she knew there wasn't enough evidence yet, "Why are you doing this? Who are you? What do you want with me? Why do you hate my dad so much?"

Greaves ignored Jane-Jo, "Terry, Neil, here, you go and handed them each a wad of cash, I'm moving abroad back in six months. I'll stay in touch, go and get yourselves an early tea. Time to leave my favourite ninja squaddie a good old-fashioned snuff movie that he can watch over and over again."

Before Stone moved into position and out of earshot, he said, "Tony, leave your phone recording try and get Greaves in view and then get outside, wait till you're out of earshot and take the Wheelers out. Chris, you climb down, stand outside the front door just in case the big goons decide to run."

Stone moved so he was behind the nearest pillar letting Jane know he was there, she saw him and relaxed, just button pushing now, and she was safe. "Duncan, set the video camera up, you know, Dunc, Terry, these snuff movies get great money, maybe we can combine the two," as Duncan angled the camera to get Jane in the centre and pressed record. "We'll see how this one sells, want to wait outside, I'll give you a shout. You both OK with sloppy seconds," Duncan and Terry nodded and headed out; Stone knew Chris wouldn't need telling to apprehend the big goons.

Jane kept her head down and her face turned away, "Please, mister, I'm only a girl, I'm only thirteen; I've done nothing to you." Greavsie was turned on by fear and intimidation, here he was alone with a pretty thirteen-year-old virgin, wearing a school skirt and white panties, he hadn't touched her yet and he was almost at bursting point. Greavsie couldn't resist, it was part of his DNA, "Your dad has cost me my business here, because of him I have to leave, but I want to leave him with a permanent reminder of my presence, you are going to be that reminder," and Greavsie took off his jacket, needing a bit more.

Jane-Jo said, "But what are you going to do to me?"

"I'm going take your virginity, then fuck you up the arse, then make you swallow my cum, maybe not in that order, but every time dear daddy looks at you for the rest of his life, he's going to see his once pretty daughter destroyed, raped so hard and often, that she'll never have kids."

"You really are a dumb fuck if you think I'd allow that to happen," said Stone stepping out from behind the pillow. Jane-Jo stood up, and had seen that look before, "Justin," using his first name for the first time ever. "Stand down, please, sir. Chris, get in here now, I need you," shouted Jane. "Justin, I'm OK I'm not hurt."

"Jane, he was going to rape my daughter, give her internal injuries, just because I stopped him from spreading his drugs because I destroyed his reputation and his ego. The man's going to die, 206 bones, you fucking motherfucker, and I'm going to do it with my bare hands, but first, I'm going to rip out your fucking tongue. I promised you if you EVER spoke or touched any of my family, I would break your body into pieces and cunt I'm a man of my word. Get out of the way, Jane."

"No, Justin, it wasn't Jo or Angie, it was me he threatened," turning like lightning to deliver a roundhouse kick to the side of Greavsie face knocking him out cold and standing over him. "He was going to try and rape me, not Jo, and then he was going to pass me to those big apes. Justin, sir, please think, Angie and Jo are waiting, this drug-dealing scum isn't worth what you would lose."

Chris walked into the warehouse, "Boss, we have the other four. Sir, we have enough evidence, just leave it, please leave it."

"Chris, he was going to rape and hurt my little girl," and switching the camera off, walked over to Greavsie, looked at Jane and Chris who were going to try and stop him, jumped up in the air landing with all his weight onto Greaves Achilles tendons audibly snapping both of them. "You both stay where you are.

I promised this man he wasn't walking away," and with his considerable strength, grabbed the kneecap of Greavsie right leg and twisted the cap clean of the muscle and tendon supporting it repeating the process to the left knee. "Thank you, Jane, and you, Chris, if anyone asks, he fell badly from his office down the stairs," and walked outside.

"That is the most scared I've ever been in my life, when I saw the boss's face change, fuck, Chris, we wouldn't have been able to stop him, thank God he loves Angie and Jo," and pointing at Greavsie. "That was going to rape me and pass me on to the big brutes like a piece of meat," and walking up kicked him with her full power in the ribs breaking several.

"Oh, Jane, don't feel bad, he ain't running anymore that's for sure, he'll be a bitch in prison which serves him right."

"I was just worried about the boss; I thought he might be heading for another meltdown, but this pointing at Greavsie, this I can live with."

"So can I," said Chris, "we should phone for an ambulance when he wakes up, he's going to be in tremendous pain."

"Chris, he'll go in the police van with the other three, no blue light."

"You're almost as bad as the boss, Jane."

Ringing Angie, "We got him, more importantly, we have on tape that he threatened to rape who he thought was Jo, he's going to be exactly what I told him someone's bitch in prison. He fell down some stairs trying to get away, I've busted both his Achilles tendons, they won't be able to repair them and both his kneecaps so he won't ever be able to run again, he'll limp from side to side and in the winter the pain from the cold will set into his joints. If it weren't for Jane and Chris, I'd have done a lot more damage, they both talked me down and reminded me about my future and their good friends. Jane knocked him out we were just waiting for the police van, we had the audio and the video, the job's done. I nearly went again Ang he was going to rape and hurt our little girl, I let him live, Ang, and I must live with that."

"Justin, you come home to me, our daughter, and your dad; we're your family, you protected us, you kept us safe, and you've ended the threat to me in a way that allows you to have a normal life. He has to wake up every day once he gets to prison knowing he's going to be butt fucked by some big hairy apes knowing he can't even run away, that's called justice Justin, I love you come home soon."

"Butt fucked. Ang, I think I'm having an effect on your vocabulary."

"Well, Justin, you affect me in every way humanly possible."

Stone rang Bish, "Hi, honey, we got Greavsie and the others can you send a van for five, Greavsie needs a stay in the hospital, no officially, Bish, he fell down the stairs. I've got stuff to do this afternoon so my statement will have to wait, Chris, Tony and Jane have all had a long day too, so we'll all come in tomorrow." Going back inside, he said to Jane and Chris, "I'm cool, just need a few words with dumb fuck."

Greavsie had started to come round and scream in pain as Stone put a hand over his mouth. "Dumb fuck, you fell down the stairs; I told you not to threaten my family, but you did it three times, the only reason you are still breathing is because my two best friends were here and they made me realise there's a better way than just killing you, and because I promised I wouldn't kill you. I've made sure you'll never run, but walk with a limp and in prison be fucked daily up the arse and pissing blood for the rest of your life, now shut the fuck up," and Stone lifted his head and crashed it down on to the concrete floor knocking him out again.

The police van arrived and loaded the four outside, "The main man is inside, he's had a fall so me and Chris will bring him out."

"Chris, you get the top, I'll get the bottom," and as they lifted Greavsie off the concrete floor, Stone worked his hands around Greavsie Achilles tendons making sure they were torn beyond repair and causing the man to scream in pain. "I thought they were tough from Manchester," as once again he passed out from the pain. Chris placed him in the van whereas Stone just dropped his lower body, "Oops slipped, looking at the big goons, see your boss, and guess who's next? I'll be paying you a visit you won't be having sex anymore not even with your own hands, you were going to rape my daughter."

"Boss, leave it."

"Chris, what if it was one of your kids?"

"I know, Boss, but a time and a place and we'll have your back covered."

Stone hugged Jane, "Thank you so much, I know what that cost you. Here's the key, a deal is a deal. I'm all right, you three, you don't need to worry anymore, and thank you for being there today. Right jump in, Jane, you can pick up the bike, and go easy at first it is super quick and heavier than yours so it'll handle a bit differently and you two can get your cars. We got the house today."

"We'll be moving this weekend, If anyone wants to give me a hand moving, I'll feed you well; Dad or Ang will plus you can drink as much coffee as possible."

"We'll be there, boss," they all said.

"I'll borrow three army trucks, start around eight and we'll start with a cooked breakfast, but tomorrow we have fun you two impress your wives and kids lots of reasons to celebrate now, lads."

Putting a heavy rug and his pillows in the boot, and telling him, "No chewing, big guy," told his dad what had gone down as they drove to school. Angie and Jo had sat patiently chatting with Mike Foster waiting for Stone to return who walked in kissing Jo and Angie on the lips and giving Mike Foster, the run down as to what had taken place. "We got the main man and all his cronies, hopefully, there should be no more drugs coming into school but the pills will still be circulating. It might be an idea to mention in assembly tomorrow how dangerous and addictive they are and maybe have some sort of amnesty where they can be handed in with no consequences."

"Good idea, Justin, also tomorrow, I am going to present Jo with her running trophy, if you'd like to be present."

"I'll be here, Mike, I'll bring my training team and they'll do phase two over the next two weeks, see who has potential and wants to take it further. Tommy Bowman won't be back to school; he's becoming an army cadet under my leadership we can maybe turn the young man's life around. Mike, thanks for letting us borrow your school; things will return to normal soon."

"Angie tells me you've just bought a house and getting married."

"Yes to both, house just confirmed today, we're on our way to it now and married hopefully before the end of the year."

"Angie, will you continue teaching?"

"Mike, Ang will do what she wants to do it's me that has to learn to be a normal husband and Dad."

"Yes, Mike, I will, Justin, you don't do normal."

"Ang, how about we video your place and then see the new one?"

"Yep, and I need to get some more clothes, I like wearing trackie bottoms and t-shirts they're comfortable, but I can't keep wearing your shirts."

"Ang, you look gorgeous in my shirt and sexy as hell."

"Dad, I'm in the car too."

"I know you are, Jo, you looked all grown up and very, very pretty dressed in Jane's clothes, you put make-up on you'd pass for seventeen, scary thought our little girl isn't little anymore."

"Then maybe you should make me a little brother or sister, mam can have some of them orgasm things."

Angie looked at Stone. George laughed so hard, "Son if I had false teeth, I'd have just spit them out."

"Dad, did you hurt him?"

"Yes darling, I did, and tomorrow me and your mam will answer whatever questions you have. There's going to be lots of changes, a new house, mam here all the time, granddad too, Bonzo and Lemmy, plus we need to talk to you about sex and love. The only time we may hold something from you is if we think it will hurt you."

"Like that nasty man, he was going to rape me. I looked it up; it meant he was going to force me to have sex with him without my consent."

"Yes, Jo, which is why I hurt him."

"Did you hurt him a lot, Dad?"

"Yes."

"Good."

"How do you feel now, son?"

"Pleased it's over and a bit flat because I left him alive."

"Son, you made the right choice, I'm proud of you. It would have been easy to snap his neck and say he fell but if you got past that, he'll wake up still alive, getting gang raped because he can no longer run or fight, you've made him easy prey in prison. If you killed him then his torment would have been over yours would have just begun, it was 100% the right decision. You're approaching forty, out of the field for nearly ten years, that's a young man's world you are leaving behind. Look at what you've achieved, a daughter who thinks the sun rises and falls with you, a woman you totally unconditionally love who feels the same about you, that's so rare son, a new house which you both picked.

"You were programmed to follow orders, no matter how insane; now you have love, happiness, money, and more children. Do what you want; you have nothing left to prove, you've done it all. What's bothering you, son, is that you haven't got any challenges left, have a child or two and bring them up from day one, not from four years, watch them grow every day, then have the satisfaction when you look back that's a good challenge to have, son."